THE
PLEDGE

THE
PLEDGE

KATHLEEN KENT

An Aries Book

First published in the US in 2021 by Mulholland Books,
an imprint of Little, Brown and Company,
a division of Hachette Book Group, Inc

First published in the UK in 2022 by Head of Zeus Ltd,
part of Bloomsbury Publishing Plc

9 7 5 3 1 2 4 6 8

A catalogue record for this book is available from the British Library.

ISBN (HB): 9781803284231
ISBN (XTPB): 9781803284248
ISBN (E): 9781803284217

Typeset by Divaddict Publishing Solutions

Printed and bound in Great Britain by
CPI Group (UK) Ltd, Croydon CR0 4YY

Head of Zeus Ltd
5–8 Hardwick Street
London EC1R 4RG

WWW.HEADOFZEUS.COM

For Jim

"Tell me, how does it feel with my teeth in your heart?"
—Euripides, *Medea*

1

Brooklyn, New York
Monday, September 10, 2001

Uncle Benny and the Homicide Squad from the 94th Precinct in Brooklyn had special code words they used to prepare later arriving officers for a murder scene: *round, sirloin, rib, and chuck. Round* meant there was no obvious external violence—little or no blood, perhaps a death by poison or overdose, or a discreet puncture wound to the back of the head by an ice pick. *Sirloin* was a single bullet wound, accompanied by a small amount of blood; *rib,* a knife wound with a bit more blood; *chuck,* multiple shot or stab wounds with lots of red.

But beyond that was *ground,* reserved for the most violent, rage-filled deaths, and with that designation, you knew to forget eating for the rest of the day.

When Benny asked me over the phone what the situation was in the fifth-floor walkup, I choked out the word: "Pureed."

"In the Janovicz apartment?" he asked, incredulous.

"It appears to be Stephan," I told him. "At least they think it's him."

"Jesus," Benny said. "Where's Mrs. Janovicz?"

"Out on the ledge," I said.

It would take twenty minutes for Benny to arrive at Kosciusko Street, which fronted the building, already blocked with local patrol cars, vehicles belonging to the homicide team from the 79th Precinct, as well as a fire truck and two ambulances. Just into my second year as a patrol officer, I had caught the radio call of a code 10-55, a coroner case, while driving up Bushwick Avenue, and recognized the address. The apartment of Stephan and Sophie Janovicz, the long-married Polish couple who owned two successful pastry shops, one in Williamsburg and one in Greenpoint, where I had grown up. Every birthday, anniversary, wedding, and retirement party my family ever celebrated was graced by a Janovicz cake. Their pierogi would have made the pope weep.

Homicide had beaten me to the location, as the station was literally three blocks from the building. I walked up the four flights of stairs but was stopped at the open door of the apartment by a no-neck uniformed sergeant named Lou Lozario, who told me I didn't want to see what was inside. When I explained that I knew the Janovicz family, he said, "Well, then, you *definitely* don't want to be here."

He looked strong enough to throw down a bull but was as pale as a bucket of milk and wore a small, crusted patch on his jacket, a result, very possibly, of upchucking what had remained of his breakfast. He was wide but short, and over his head I could see the lower half of a man's body, fully clothed, supine on the floor, his custom-made brogues neatly polished to a soft sheen. Where the head should have been was a pulpy mess; surrounding the body was enough blood to fill a bathtub. It was as though someone had upended a bucket of red paint all over the living room floor. There was no way for the detectives to explore the apartment without displacing the blood everywhere, and the sergeant's footprints had tracked like arrows to the doorway where we stood looking at each other in shared disbelief.

"We think it's the old man," he'd said.

"You think?" I'd asked.

A tic had started under his left eye. "Hard to tell at this point."

"Where's Mrs. Janovicz?" I'd whispered hoarsely, not really wanting to know the answer.

He'd jerked a thumb over his shoulder toward an open window where two detectives stood, talking to the air outside.

"She's out there, threatening to jump," he'd said, and by the tone of his voice, he believed it to be a foregone conclusion.

I met Benny on the sidewalk, and we exchanged a few tense greetings. But as soon as we approached the front of the apartment building, the stocky sergeant appeared in the entranceway like an oversize temple djinn.

"What are you doing in the seven-nine, Ben?" Lozario asked. He was using his bulk as a barrier, trying to look like he wasn't denying entry to a homicide cop from another precinct. "Things in the nine-four not hot enough?"

"How're you doing, Lou?" Benny asked, looking pointedly at the splash of vomit on the sergeant's jacket.

"Oh, peachy," Lou said. "I appreciate your stopping by, but we've got it pretty well covered."

Benny pointed upward. "The Janoviczes, huh?"

"Yeah, looks like."

Benny gestured to me. "Officer Rhyzyk here tells me Mrs. Janovicz is perched on the ledge, threatening to jump."

Sergeant Lou looked at me with a raised brow. There were only three Rhyzyk cops at that time in Brooklyn: Sergeant Bernard Rhyzyk, my uncle, who was standing before him, the notorious Phillip Rhyzyk, who happened to be my father, and me.

"She's been out there how long?" Benny asked.

Lou shrugged. "About half an hour."

"No luck talking her back in?"

"Nah, and she's too far away to grab. And honestly, I'm not sure we're getting her back into the apartment at this point."

Benny looped one arm through mine. "Oh, yeah? I got an idea that might help with that situation."

Lou crossed his arms and stared down at his size twelve double-wide shoes, frowning.

"Look," Benny said, "you gonna step aside, or do I have to use patrolwoman Rhyzyk here as a battering ram?"

The sergeant moved to the side, sweeping one arm out in a "be my guest" gesture.

I led the way up the stairs to the Janoviczes' apartment, then paused outside the door, letting Benny and Lou enter first.

I stared at Benny's back as he gazed at what was left of Stephan, still lying undisturbed on the floor. The forensics crew seemed uncertain how best to bag his mortal remains.

"The hammer's in the sink," Lou said. "Looks like she tried to wash it off. But the, uh, solid bits clogged the drain."

Benny pivoted on his heels, his face a careful mask of

professional detachment, and walked to the doorway, where I was standing.

"Did you see?" he asked, motioning with his head toward the body.

"Not really...yeah, some," I said.

He took one arm and steered me into the apartment toward the window where the homicide detectives were still standing. "Don't look," he ordered as we passed Stephan.

"What's happening with Mrs. Janovicz?" Benny asked the older of the two.

The detective shrugged. "She refuses to come in. She won't even talk to us."

"We got a net coming for the street, but I don't know if it'll be here in time," the younger detective said.

Benny turned to me. "Betty, see if she'll talk to you."

Suddenly I'd gone from being a spectator to being a participant. My heart began to thud in my chest. The most urgent coaxing I'd done thus far as a cop was to persuade a teenager to return a pilfered apple to an outdoor fruit stand.

The detectives moved away, and I ducked under the raised window, the wood frame cracked and warped, craning my head to the left. On the ledge, about a foot wide and covered with pigeon droppings and feathers, sat Mrs. Janovicz. Most of her skin and clothing below her neck were covered in blood, but her face, at seventy, still had the unstained porcelain appearance of a Dresden doll; her gray hair rolled and pinned neatly against her scalp, the pink beads draped around her throat mirroring her petal-pink lipstick.

She was staring off into the far distance, her lips moving slightly, as though talking to herself. Or in prayer.

"Mrs. Janovicz?" I said softly. When she didn't respond, I cleared my throat and called her name a little louder.

She turned her head to me, her brow wrinkled in confusion, or displeasure. "Who's that?"

"It's me. Betty Rhyzyk. Elizabeth, Phillip Rhyzyk's daughter."

"Elizabeth?" In trying to focus on my face, she leaned forward slightly, away from the building.

Instinctively, I held out a cautioning hand. "Be careful, Mrs. Janovicz. Don't lean away from the building like that."

"Elizabeth with the beautiful red hair?" she asked uncertainly. Fifty years in the States, and her Polish accent was still prominent.

I pointed to my hairline, turning my head so she could see the color of my hair; the hair my mother had laughingly called "hussy red." "Yes, that's me, Mrs. Janovicz."

"How are you? I haven't seen you in the shop for such a long time."

I felt a slight pressure on the small of my back—Uncle Benny, standing behind me, prompting me to talk her back into the apartment.

"I'm good, Mrs. Janovicz. Come back inside and we can visit some more."

She returned her gaze to the Brooklyn skyline, and took a breath. "No. I'm happy to sit here for a little while longer." She smiled and looked back at me. "Why don't you come out here and we can talk?" She patted the ledge like she was seated on the down-filled Victorian sofa in her living room. The sofa that was now spattered with her husband's brain matter.

Her lips began to quiver. "No one ever visits anymore." She covered her face with both hands and began to cry in earnest, her body rocking back and forth perilously toward the edge. "I've been so lonely—"

"Wait!" I said sharply. "I'm coming…I'll come out to you. Just, for God's sake, Mrs. Janovicz, stay still. Don't move, okay?"

Benny grabbed on to my belt with both hands, whispering hoarsely into my ear, "I've got you, but just sit right here. Don't go all Spider-Woman on me."

I carefully edged my way out, making sure the cheeks of my backside were perched safely over the bottom of the window frame, while my legs dangled into the void.

"Come closer," she said. "I can't see you so good. I left my glasses in my purse."

"That's okay, Mrs. Janovicz. I'm good right here."

Her crying jag over, she slumped against the building, one cheek pressed to the brick wall. "Septembers in New York are the best, don't you think?"

"Absolutely. The best," I said. "But, you know, it gets pretty chilly at night. Sunset is coming soon, and you don't have a sweater. You want to come back inside and get something a little warmer?"

"That's good, Betty," I heard Benny whisper behind me. "Keep talking to her just like that."

But she shook her head and raised one hand to her throat, her encrusted fingers stroking her necklace. I realized with a jolt that the rosy pink beads had, at some point earlier in the day, been white pearls.

"They're never going to believe me," she said sadly.

"What won't they believe, Mrs. Janovicz?" I asked.

"What Stephan's been doing."

"Are you talking about Mr. Janovicz? Whatever it is, you

can talk to me about it. Let's have some tea, and sit at the table—"

"No," she said sharply, shaking her head. "No. You'll take his side. Everybody always takes his side. 'Stephan' people say, 'Stephan is so good, so hardworking. He's a—'" She paused, and then said in Polish, "*Porządny facet*. You know what is this?"

"Upstanding guy," I said.

"Right. Upstanding guy." She laughed unpleasantly. "Standing up in filth, I say."

"Did he hurt you?" I ask.

She muttered something in Polish. "Yes. He hurt me. But not as much as he hurt my granddaughter."

I could feel Benny shifting his weight behind me. "Ask her about her granddaughter," he whispered.

"Your granddaughter," I say, desperately trying to remember the name of the little blond cherub whose photographs graced the wall behind the cash registers in the Janovicz bakeries. "You mean Anna?"

"Yes, my Anna," she said, and began crying again, her hands restless in her lap. "How could he do that to her?"

I carefully scooted a few inches toward her on the ledge and felt a second set of hands grab on to my belt. Reaching out, I said, "Mrs. Janovicz, please let me help you. If you were to fall, what would that do to Anna? How would we explain it to her?"

"Fall?" she said, her eyelids blinking rapidly, her gaze unfocused. "But I don't want to come in. I don't want to see him."

"The body's been removed from the apartment," Benny muttered behind me. "Tell her he's gone."

"You won't have to see him," I told Mrs. Janovicz. "He's not in the apartment."

Her dazed look was replaced by an expression of narrow-eyed suspicion. "He's always there. He never gives me any peace."

Her hand shot out and she grabbed my outstretched fingers with an iron grip, yanking me toward her. I heard Benny swear, and he slipped one tense arm around my waist.

"Don't you side with him! Don't you do it!" she said.

"No, I won't, Mrs. Janovicz. Look, I'm here with you, right? We're sitting here talking. Just the two of us."

She leaned closer to me, her grip causing my fingers to whiten, but she smiled knowingly. "But I understand you, Elizabeth. I know you don't fool with the men. You're smart that way."

She gave another tug on my fingers. "Come with me. We'll go together, okay?"

The tug on my hand became more insistent, and she looked away from me, out toward the expanse of rooftops that were beginning to darken into the shadows of the coming night.

"We'll need to hurry," she said, her chin lifting as though in preparation for flight.

Then Benny's voice harsh in my ear: "For Christ's sake, Betty, we're going to lose her. Say something...anything..."

"Okay, okay, okay," I managed, waving my free hand at her, like I was flagging down a bus. "But you can't go yet... I'm...I'm *hungry*."

"Hungry?" she repeated, turning to face me, her brow wrinkled with concern.

I had her attention again. "I didn't get a chance to eat anything this morning, and now I'm really starving. Do you think I could have just a little something to eat, Mrs. Janovicz? You know…before we go?"

She smiled at me. The grandmother whose greatest pleasure in life had been feeding people. "Of course, Elizabeth. Why didn't you say something earlier? We'll go into the kitchen, and I'll make you something nice."

Still holding my hand, she started scooting toward me as Uncle Benny slowly eased me backward through the open window. With surprising alacrity, Mrs. Janovicz followed, letting the two detectives help her climb back into the apartment.

She smiled graciously at the two men and asked, "Who's ready for some *Kołacz*?"

Later that night, I met Uncle Benny at Donovan's, his favorite Brooklyn bar, for a few shots of forgetfulness. It was the place where he worked his magic—what he called "Reaping the Grim." Reaping the Grim was always held within the revered walls of Donovan's: a collective, boisterous, secretive ritual meant only for the male officers to let off some steam, and distance themselves from the horrors of the job. But Benny had encouraged me to create my own ritual for expunging the terrible emotional hangover that comes from the aftermath of violence. And for me, that day, it had been running eight miles, the intense workout emptying my mind of everything but my body's response to the physical challenge.

We sat in a booth at the back, away from the steady flow of off-duty cops who perched noisily at the long oak bar worn smooth by a century of elbows levering pints of Guinness and shots of whiskey to pour down exhausted or relieved or embittered throats. Benny had ordered two shots each of Jameson for us and waited until I had downed the first before asking me how I was doing.

"Do you think she was right about Stephan?" I asked. "I mean, Jesus, it's hard to think of him that way. What she said about Anna, his granddaughter? He seemed like such a nice guy."

Benny wagged his head from side to side. "The world's full of nice guys who end up doing terrible things." He picked up the second shot and toasted me. "You did good today."

"I thought I was going to lose her there for a minute."

"Yeah, but you didn't. You instinctively knew to touch on the one thing that was at the core of who she was. Remember that. That's the best way to work your way out of a bad situation."

"What's going to happen to her?" I asked.

"Hard to say. The kindest thing would be for a long, relaxing, medicated stay in the hospital."

I shook my head. "Maybe the kindest thing would have been to let her jump."

"Except then, instead of me sitting here commiserating with you commiserating with her, I'd be trying to talk you out of your guilt that she jumped. You did what you were supposed to do. What you were born to do. Protect good people. Some people would say Mrs. Janovicz owes you for saving her life. But the truth is that the burden now rests squarely on your shoulders, Betty. You saved her life. That makes you her guardian angel forever."

He takes a sip of his Jameson. "You know, if I'm being honest, I never liked Stephan. Between you and me and this table, I don't care that Mrs. Janovicz aerated his brainpan. She was a good woman who was protecting her granddaughter. Anybody did that to you when you were a kid, I would have taken a chain saw to them, forget about the hammer."

"You always did look out for me," I said.

Sometimes more than my own mother, I thought. *And certainly more than my father.*

"And I'll always look after you," he said. "Listen, drink up and get some sleep tonight. Tomorrow will be a better day." He finished the last of his second shot of Jameson. "Here's to September eleventh. The sun will rise, the buildings will stand, and we, Officer Rhyzyk, will always have a job to do."

2

Dallas, Texas
Thursday, September 11, 2014

Crawling out of my deep sleep is like swimming against a strong ocean current, the lingering sensations of the dream bleeding through into consciousness: the sounds of distant sirens, the thick cloud of smoke to the west, the incomprehension on my father's face as he stands on the front stoop of our Brooklyn house, cradling a small transistor radio announcing the end of the world.

The feeling of Benny's hand gripping my arm, hard, telling me, *"Betty, I know you. Promise me you'll stay out of the city today."*

And finally, his whisper in my ear, following me into wakefulness.

"Betty, you can't help the dead....Save your strength for the survivors."

My eyes open to a brightly lit room. The clock on the bedside table reads six thirty-six. Jackie is already out of bed, her side of the mattress still capturing the warmth from her body. I can smell coffee percolating in the kitchen. Sitting up, I listen for any sounds coming from the guest bedroom, but there's only silence.

Inside my head I still hear the ghostly voice of Uncle Benny: *"Save your strength for the survivors."* He's been dead for several years now, but sometimes—when I run, when I dream, when I'm in distress—his voice speaks to me. Giving me advice, his homegrown Polish wisdom, his warnings. It comes from a place I don't quite understand—stronger than memory, deeper than mere sentiment, more profound than wishful thinking. Whatever it means, I'm grateful to still have him with me.

Running a hand through my hair, I walk barefoot down the hall and stand in front of the closed door, listening. Hearing nothing, I push the door open, and there's Elizabeth lying on her belly in her crib, fully awake, looking at me with wide, unblinking eyes and a somber expression.

"Hey, baby," I say softly.

She raises her head a little higher for a moment, her wet mouth open and slobbery, and then she lays her head back down on the mattress. She is exactly seven months old today.

I walk closer to the crib and sit cross-legged in front of her, so that our eyes are level. One tiny finger goes into her mouth, and she works it with her gums, her gaze never leaving mine.

The home birth back in February had gone smoothly. Mary Grace, the pregnant girl we had rescued from the streets, was in labor for only a few hours. The midwife had been happily surprised that someone so young, with such narrow hips—a girl who had been homeless for months, underfed, and exposed to the elements—could have given birth to a seven-pound baby with so few difficulties.

The only person attending the labor who had panicked, paced, fretted, chewed her cuticles raw, gotten faint, and thrown up, not once but twice, was me. I was finally banned from the birthing room by both Jackie, who is a pediatric radiologist, and the midwife after I'd asked one too many times, "Oh God, is it supposed to, you know, look like that?"

I was not invited back until the baby had been successfully delivered and cleaned up. The coppery tang of blood and mother sweat still permeated the air, but the baby no longer looked like a tiny perpetrator in a gruesome crime scene. I sat and stared at Mary Grace as she stared into her baby's eyes, her face swollen, limbs trembling from the hours of effort, smiling triumphantly, and I thought that I might live my whole life and not know what it was like to have someone gaze at me with such utter and complete infatuation.

Mary Grace smiled at me, and then asked the inconceivable.

"Do you want to hold her?"

A few years into my service with the NYPD, my patrol partner and I had come across a parked car in a snow-covered suburban shopping center parking lot. It was about five in the morning, the sky still dark, and the lot otherwise empty. But this car's engine was on, the exhaust billowing a dirty vapor into the wintry air, and the driver's side door was wide open. Approaching the car, we discovered that the driver, a male, and his passenger, a female, were passed out in what appeared to be a drug-induced stupor. With some effort we were able to rouse them toward consciousness, and we started searching for drugs. I found a small blue duffel bag on the back seat, but before I could unzip the bag, the man mumbled, "I wouldn't do that."

"Oh, and why is that?" I had asked, bouncing the bag casually in my arms. "What am I going to find inside? Heroin?"

"No," the man had said, his drug haze retreating rapidly with the frisson of fear. "A bomb."

For about ten seconds I'd been completely paralyzed. I couldn't move or speak or even form a cohesive thought. Even the fight-or-flight mechanism seemed to have frozen in the frigid predawn air.

"Do you want to hold her?" Mary Grace had asked. For all of my alarmed hesitation, she might as well have been handing me the bomb in the blue duffel bag.

I managed to get my arms under the little bundle and brought it to my chest without dropping it. Her. Without dropping her. I remembered to breathe, and Elizabeth looked at me with her large, liquid eyes, still vacant of any expectations or schemes or crushing disappointments...and then she began to wail.

Now sitting in front of her crib, I realize we've managed a truce of sorts in the past few months. She still regards me with as much skepticism as a baby can summon, but at least she no longer cries when I walk into her room. Well, mostly not.

Her head pops up again, her gaze shifting over my shoulder, and her mouth opens wide in a gummy grin. She waggles her arms and legs like a stranded starfish, and I know that Jackie has walked into the room. She sits down beside me, putting one arm around my waist, and sticks a finger through the bars in the crib, which Elizabeth grasps and tries to pull into her mouth.

"Poor baby," Jackie says. "Where's your mommy?"

It's been ten days since Mary Grace has disappeared.

For over six months, we—Jackie, Mary Grace, and I— had settled into a comfortable, amiable routine. I went to work at the North Central Dallas Police Department, Jackie went to work at the hospital, and Mary Grace stayed home with the baby, her every waking hour seemingly filled with all things Elizabeth. At the end of the workday, when Jackie and I returned home, Mary Grace was always ebullient, filled with energy, bursting with the joy of sharing every bit of developmental minutiae that the baby seemed to throw off hourly, like sparks from a runaway carnival bumper car.

There had been no indication that anything was wrong; that Mary Grace had been unhappy. But then, one day— September 1, to be precise—Jackie and I woke to find her gone, her bed empty and tidily made. We had said our usual good nights to her the previous evening, and I could hear her murmuring softly to the baby well past the time we turned out our lights. There were no signs that she had been taken forcefully; there was no note left and there have been no phone calls from her since that day. I put out a priority request to the Missing Persons Bureau, but there have, as yet, been no leads. The general consensus is that she has returned to the streets. But all of the patrol searches and investigative leads, and the countless hours that Jackie and I have spent driving up and down the roadways of Dallas, large and small, have been fruitless.

I'd contacted all my CIs, including Wayne, aka Flush, who had spent some time with her, living rough in Tent City, the gathering place of many of Dallas's homeless, but no one had seen her or heard from her since she had the baby. Wayne told me that he felt somehow responsible for her running away from a secure home. He said that if he'd spent more time with her, encouraging her to get a steady job, and her own place—goals he was working toward since he got clean and sober—she might have had more motivation to stay off the streets. And although he'd never said so, I suspected that he still had hopes for them to be more than friends.

He once asked me, his voice choked with worry, "If you can't find her, man, what chance do any of us have?"

Both Jackie and I had agreed it was time to hire private investigators to help find her.

What we don't talk about is what will happen if Mary Grace is not found. Or if she is found and has decided that motherhood, and all its demands and restrictions, is too much for her seventeen-year-old self.

The doorbell rings, and Jackie says, "There's Connie."

She kisses me, and stands up to let the nanny in. Connie had started working for us part-time shortly before Mary Grace disappeared; a way to give the young mother a few hours to shop or visit with friends. But I had a nagging feeling that those hours resurrected for Mary Grace the experience of being young, single, and free. Fortunately, Connie had been available to work for Jackie and me full-time.

From the living room I can hear the TV announcer solemnly revisiting the horrors of 9/11 from the site of the Memorial Museum, newly opened this past spring. I'm pulled back to the memory of my mother, a cup of coffee forgotten in her hand, staring at the family television set with uncomprehending terror. A look I hadn't seen on her face since my brother's suicide. The image of the first building falling was the final capstone to her living tomb. She died a year later from cancer.

A small, timorous squawk comes from inside the crib. Elizabeth's face is pulling together into a red-faced mask of discontent. We're a few seconds away from a serious crying jag.

I quickly stand and awkwardly pat the baby's bottom. "You hang in there, Elizabeth," I tell her. "We'll find your mama."

3

Oak Cliff, Dallas
Thursday, September 11, 2014

The neighborhood where the hostage standoff is taking place—just off Jefferson Avenue—is normally quiet and law-abiding. Small homes on small lots with detached garages are kept in good order, despite the cracking concrete on the driveways and the potholes that gouge the narrow streets, making them look like a lunar landscape. Most of the homes close to the avenue do not have bars on the windows, the barriers that come as standard issue on the buildings a few miles to the south. Local bicycle vendors pedal safely through the streets, selling fried chicharrón and real Coca-Cola, the kind sweetened with cane sugar, and kids sit on their front porches happily licking their way around melting *paletas*.

But the peaceful neighborhood has now been invaded by a herd of bustling law enforcement agents: patrol officers, DEA, and Dallas SWAT, complete with full robo-cop gear, and a hulking SRT van. Curious neighbors gather as close to the human barricade as they dare, but there is no jeering, and no press, which would not be the case if the standoff were taking place in the rich, and white, neighborhoods of Park Cities. The locals speak quietly in Spanish and cross themselves with dedicated frequency.

I park my car on the street and flash my badge to one of the patrolmen on the secured perimeter, and then again for the SWAT team leader, a senior corporal, so sleek and muscle-bound inside his black tactical gear that he looks like a lobster before boiling.

I finally spot Manny Ortega standing with a couple of DEA agents, his shaved head gleaming a dark amber, wearing his usual undercover garb: dirty jeans, ragged T-shirt, and worn cowboy boots. He's worked both Narcotics and Gangland, and there's not a jujitsu junkie or MMA fighter in Dallas who would happily cross his path in a dark alley at night. He's shorter than the DEA guys, but next to Manny they both look as menacing as TSA agents at the Lubbock airport.

"Hey, hey, *Detective Sergeant* Rhyzyk," he says. "Congrats on your promotion. How's it going?"

"Pretty good for a Thursday, except for all the paperwork I have to do now," I say. "How's Gangland?"

"Slangin' and bangin'. And your partner?"

"Riot's good. He's running with me almost every weekend now. Seven a.m."

Manny makes a face. "White people, man. I thought the whole point of being legal and paying taxes is so you don't *have* to run."

Manny knows that my partner, Seth Dutton, whose nickname is Riot, went through a health crisis six months ago and was off the job for several weeks. And I know that Manny suspects that Seth's health crisis was in fact a hellish withdrawal from a heroin addiction. An addiction grown from the pain pills he was prescribed after being shot on duty. Seth's now six months off narcotics, his sobriety bolstered by lots of running and gym time. He also meets with his NA sponsor several times a week.

Manny says, "Tell Riot I said to tell his mother to stop calling me."

I bite down on a laugh. "I think I'll let you tell him that yourself."

The DEA guys shift restlessly behind Manny. The SWAT team leader signals that they're ready to go into breaching mode.

"So, what's going on?" I ask Manny.

"Well, as you can see, the Boy Scouts are just about ready to tiptoe through the front door, but our guy inside's made an unusual request."

I look at the house where the hostages are being held. Manny was vague about the details over the phone, telling me only that I needed to come to the site ASAP for a full explanation.

"So, give me the rundown," I say.

"His name is Tomas Ezekiel Gomez, aka EZ. Honduran, twenty-five years old. He'll tell you, when he doesn't have a gun to his head, that he's a short-order cook. Got a hairnet and everything. But he's really here to set up a better heroin distribution channel from Honduras with the Sinaloa cartel."

"What's going on inside the house?"

"You ready for this? He's holding seven people hostage, four adults and three children. Two of the adults and the three kids are family, though. The other two adults are doctors. Doctors he kidnapped at gunpoint from a local clinic, along with some vaccination drugs."

"Vaccination drugs?"

"The house belongs to his uncle who's out of work. He and his wife have three little kids and no money to get them vaccinated. So Tomas kidnapped the two clinic doctors so that they could vaccinate the kids."

I give him bug eyes. "You're shitting me."

Manny shakes his head. "I shit you not. A modern-day Latino Robin Hood. He knew he was about to be arrested. So he figured the best way for us not to firebomb a house full of brown people, including himself, was to take some gringos hostage, thereby catching two birds with one stoner."

I glance over at the SWAT team corporal, who looks more than eager to commence a flash-bang order. "So, why did you need me? I don't get my place in all of this."

"He's told us that he'll give himself up peacefully, but only after talking to you. In private. Inside the house."

I rear back, studying his face. It doesn't look like he's pulling my leg. "And get my head blown off by somebody I may have arrested in the past, someone whose name I've forgotten? I don't think so."

He lowers his chin and speaks softly so that only I can hear. "He said he's got a message to pass along from your Mexican friend with the boots."

"El Cuchillo?" The Sinaloan enforcer who makes cowboy boots from the tattooed skin of dealers who invade his territory. Skin removed with a knife while the interloper is still alive. The wound he gave me at the base of my throat—a shallow cut made with his skinning knife—throbs as if the scar will open up again. "How do I know Tomas is not just going to finish off what the Knife was unable to do to me six months ago?"

"EZ said that he'd be facedown on the floor, hands behind his head. You agree to go in, and he'll send out the doctors and his family."

"What's to keep us from rushing him as soon as the people come out of the house?"

"He knows me. EZ said that if I give him my word that he won't be arrested until after he speaks to you, he'll let everyone go and allow himself to be taken into custody."

"Why's he doing this? He couldn't just tell me over the phone?"

"He was given instructions to talk to you in person by El Cuchillo."

"And what happens if I don't go in?"

"El Cuchillo kills EZ's entire family. All fourteen of them."

I look around at all the law enforcement ready to put their lives at risk—and very possibly the lives of the three children inside—to neutralize Gomez. It's a cool morning, but sweat is running down my spine and pooling at the small of my back.

"Look," Manny says. "EZ's a dealer, but he's as honor bound as these scumbags can be. He knows El Cuchillo will follow through with his threat."

The last time I'd been face-to-face with the Sinaloan enforcer, he'd shot and killed a police sergeant. The fact that said sergeant, Marshall Maclin, my predecessor, was close to being busted for illegal gambling and providing cover for the Sinaloa cartel did not merit his murder. I had no doubt El Cuchillo would make good on his promise to kill Gomez's family.

"Would you do this?" I ask Manny. "Walk in there alone?"

He rubs a hand over the top of his head, and finally nods.

"If EZ asked to see me with his solemn promise that afterward he'd give himself up? Yeah, I would."

"Does he speak English?"

"Better than me, Jefe."

I take a breath. "Okay, I'll do it. But Gomez has to first release the kids in the house, or no deal."

Manny pulls the SWAT corporal aside for a quick consult. While he's talking, the corporal looks over Manny's shoulder, giving me what Uncle Benny would have called the "stink eye." He's not happy about the change in plans, but he finally nods his assent. Manny walks toward the house, his hands up in the air. As he approaches, the front door opens a crack, and a frightened woman's face appears on the other side.

Twenty feet from the door Manny stops and yells, "Yo, EZ. Escuchame! Deja que los ninos se vayan primero y el sargento te hablara."

The door slams shut, and after a full minute of waiting, Manny turns to face me, and shrugs his shoulders. The door opens again. Three young children, two boys and a girl, come walking, blinking, out into the sunshine. They don't look scared as much as confused. Manny scoops up the little girl and hustles the two boys toward the far side of the SRT van. As soon as the kids see the robo-cops in full attack gear, the terrified sobbing begins.

A female police officer hands me her Kevlar vest, and I put it on. I check my service weapon for a live round in the chamber.

"Okay, then," I say, walking toward the house. "Viva la Raza."

The neighborhood crowd goes silent, watching the crazy redhead in the bulletproof vest approaching the house. I stand to one side of the door, my gun at the ready, and rap loudly on it with the back of my knuckles.

"Mr. Gomez, this is Detective Sergeant Rhyzyk of the Dallas Police Department. Detective Ortega says that if I come in to talk to you, you'll let all the hostages go. And then you'll surrender yourself to me. I'm coming in alone, but not before you open the door for me."

After a few beats, the door is opened by the same woman. She frantically beckons for me to come inside, and when I step over the threshold, she quickly closes the door behind me. The entry hallway opens onto a small living room. My heart hammers as though I've just completed a mile sprint, and I do a rapid sweep with my gun. In the living room I see three adults squeezed together on the couch, one Hispanic man and two Caucasian men still wearing their white doctor's coats. On the floor, facedown as promised, is a young Hispanic man, his hands clasped behind his head but with his gun close by.

I kick the gun away, and then pick it up. It's a Glock, one round in the chamber. The woman is trying to tell me something in Spanish, but the man lying on the floor tells her to shut up.

"You four leave the house. Now!" I give the woman a gentle push to get her motivated.

Keeping a close eye on Gomez, I make sure that the four adults make it to safety. From the front door I signal Manny, standing with the SWAT team leader, that I'm still breathing.

"I've got his gun, and he's on the floor," I yell. "I'm going to have my little chat with Gomez. But if I'm not out in five minutes, tell SWAT to make themselves at home."

I leave the door open and return to the living room. Gomez is still on the floor, his neck craned so he can look up at me.

"Can I get up now?" he asks.

"Get up...slowly." I make him lean spread-eagled against the wall so I can frisk him for hidden weapons.

"Move over to the couch and sit, your hands in your lap where I can see them."

He eases his way to the couch and sits down.

"It's about time, yo," he says. "My arms were going to sleep."

I stand facing him, my gun directed at his chest. He looks exactly like what he claims to be: a short-order cook. Skinny, bad skin, bad haircut, but he's wearing a watch that costs more than my car.

"What's this all about, Mr. Gomez?"

"El Cuchillo has a message for you."

"Okay, I'm listening."

"I'm going to stand up and turn around. In my back pocket is a phone. You only have to press the number one. It's programmed to call him. He wants to speak to you, and only you."

"Where is he now?" I ask.

He shrugs. "*No se.* Please, don't ask me any more questions. Just call him. My family—"

He stands and turns, and I pull a burner phone out of his pocket. I press "1" on the keypad and hear a ringing tone. I motion for Gomez to sit back down. A man answers the phone.

"Hello, Sergeant Rhyzyk." The voice is heavily accented, and relaxed-sounding. Almost friendly. But I know the words are passing through lips that rarely, if ever, smile.

"I hear you breathing," he says. "*Me recuerdas?*"

"Oh, yes, I remember you."

"It seems you've been able to provide your colleagues with information about me that they've never before had."

"You mean your prints lifted from the knife you left for me. I still have it, by the way. It's in my pocket now. I carry it with me always."

I had had two up close and personal encounters with El Cuchillo, the first at Delano's Gym, which he had torched, hoping to get rid of me—and Mary Grace, who had unfortunately gotten caught up in the case. El Cuchillo had left the pocketknife behind to offer us a quicker death than being burned alive.

"That's very touching," he says.

"What is it you want? I'm kind of in a hurry now. I have an arrest to make."

"I have some information for you. Something I think will be of great interest."

"You going to give me a heads-up on your next shipment of drugs into the States?"

"It's more about another one of your acquaintances. Evangeline Roy."

I grip the phone tighter, remembering to slow my breathing. The year prior I had been kidnapped, tortured, and held hostage for days by the cult-like, drug-dealing Roy family before being rescued by my team.

"I'm listening," I say.

"Her people have been interfering with our interests in Honduras."

"'Our' meaning the Sinaloa's?"

"I know that you have a special animosity for her. I'd like to offer some information."

"In exchange for what?"

"In good time. The Roy family has set up several religious missions north of Tegucigalpa, but they are not there to help the poor orphans left there following your country's CIA operations. They are a front, housing women and children but employing the men of the villages to shoot on sight anyone who is not with them, including the military, which is seriously inhibiting my business."

"Taking over your product delivery. Gee, that's a shame."

That's why there had been so few sightings of Evangeline in Texas, or anywhere else in the United States, immediately following the death of her sons. The remaining Roy clan had left for greener, more southerly pastures.

"I know where Evangeline Roy is," he says. "You want her out of business, and so do I."

"Why not just take care of her yourself, mano a mano?"

"Because it pleases me for you to do it."

"If she's in Honduras, I can't do anything about it. Other than wait for the two of you to cancel each other out."

"But she's not in Honduras, Sergeant. She's in Texas, where, unfortunately, it would be unsafe for me to be right now, thanks to you. She will be well protected but not inviolable. My people are working on finding her exact location. As soon as I know where she is, then you will know as well."

Evangeline Roy is back in Texas. Months ago she sent me a threatening note, promising revenge for the death of her two sons. Reflexively, I grab for the Saint Michael medallion around my neck. I've almost forgotten the man on the other end of the line. He's gone silent, but I can hear the sound of rain pounding against a metal roof. The kind of tropical rain that falls from the sky in heavy, relentless sheets.

"You went very quiet, Sergeant," he finally says. "I imagine this is not the best of news for you. But think of this. You bring down the Roy family, and perhaps they'll make you a lieutenant."

"If I could bring you down, I might make division major. Sounds like it's raining a lot in Culiacán today."

There are a few seconds of silence, followed by a long sigh, the kind of gratified exhalation that ends a satisfying meal.

"Very good, Sergeant. Once I give you the location of Evangeline Roy, you'll have two weeks to capture or kill her."

"Again," I say, "why don't you get one of your men to take care of it."

I hear his footsteps. He's walking across a wooden floor, his boot heels striking hard against the planks. The sound of rain is louder now, as though he's standing in front of an open window. "Do you remember me telling you of my fights in the boxing rings of Culiacán? Think of this, if you will, as a fond return to the blood sport of my youth. I happen to know that Evangeline is in Texas for two reasons. One, to set up operations. And two, to settle a score with you for the death of her sons. And she will want to make it as painful for you as possible."

He pauses a moment to let that sink in. "If I were betting, my money would be on you, Sergeant. I believe that you can win this battle. If you fail, yet manage to live, I will not kill you. But you will wish that you had died. Believe me. I need the Roy woman eradicated."

I hear him breathing raggedly into the phone. Almost as though he's amused. "I hear congratulations are in order. You are now the guardian of a new infant. A baby girl. *Felicitaciones.*"

There is another pause for me to metabolize the knowledge

that he knows about Elizabeth. "By the way, Sergeant, don't try tracing any of these calls. The phones will all be burners."

He disconnects, and I stare at the phone as I might a dosimeter after leaving a nuclear plant. He knows about the baby. He no doubt knows where I live. Which means he knows about Jackie, my colleagues, my schedule. A dark thought jabs painfully at my consciousness. The thought that El Cuchillo has had something to do with Mary Grace's disappearance.

I look at the young dealer sitting on the couch watching me intently. Gomez is going to jail, probably for a long time, and yet he's the one with the pitying look on his face.

"Now you the one wearing the clock, huh?" he says.

"You know what my clock is telling me?" I say, pulling Gomez off the couch and cuffing him. "It's telling me that you do not pass go, you do not collect two hundred dollars, and you do not have a get-out-of-jail card this time."

I lead him out the front door and across the lawn and hand him over to the DEA agents to make the official arrest. The bystanders break into polite applause and then disband, relieved that their neighborhood had not been decimated by gunfire. As the SWAT team packs up, I pull Manny Ortega aside, telling him of my conversation with the Sinaloan.

He sucks thoughtfully on his teeth. "Well, your job just got a lot more interesting. You gonna request a special task force to deal with this?"

"If Evangeline Roy is taking up shop again in Dallas, we're going to need federal assistance, DEA for sure. But we'll need more intel first. She may be operating out of Tyler, or Houston, for all I know. Can you let me know if there's been any uptick in activity from the ABT?"

"Man, the Aryan Brotherhood of Texas is toast. The ATF

just got seventy-three convictions across five federal districts. And another twenty-three arrests pending. If the Roys are using gang distributors, they'll have to choose another club. But I'll let you know if I hear anything hinky."

We say our goodbyes, and I watch EZ Gomez as he's being driven away by the DEA. The guy looks almost relieved to be under the protection of the federal government, even if it means incarceration. At least for today he knows his family's safe from El Cuchillo.

I call Jackie and tell her to make sure that the doors at the house are always locked and the security system armed, even when she's home.

"Why, what's happened?" she asks.

I don't want to alarm her. Yet. But with Evangeline back in Texas, and El Cuchillo's laser focus on me, I don't want to take any chances.

"Looks like I'll be starting a new case. Dirtbags to the factor of ten."

"Will do," she says. She says it lightly because she's been through this drill before. I don't tell her this is a whole other level of menace.

"Seriously, Jackie. All eyes."

4

Dallas Police Department, North Central Division
Thursday, September 11, 2014

I'm back in my office for no more than five minutes when my partner, Seth, knocks on the door, walks in, and sits in the chair facing the desk. He puts a half-empty bottle of Jameson on my desk.

"Manny Ortega called me," he says. "Thought you might need this."

I look at the clock. "Not at ten thirty in the morning."

"So, what did our Mexican friend have to say?"

I tell him about Evangeline Roy, her operations in Honduras, the conflict with the Sinaloans, and her alleged return to Texas.

"You think she's in Dallas again?" he asks.

My partner's nickname, Riot, comes from the old Texas saying "One Riot, One Ranger," and he's the bravest person I know. But sometimes recklessly so. The way a rescue cable glider in a hurricane is brave.

"Don't look so gleeful about it," I say. "I need another

shower and a new pair of underwear right about now. I'm giving an official update in the small incident room at two."

"You want me to start calling my CIs about any sightings of a maniacal redheaded harpy running around Big D?"

"Yeah, that would be helpful. Just make sure they know you're talking about Evangeline Roy and not me."

He grins and gives me a thumbs-up. "How's Elizabeth?"

"She's good. Growing like a baby shark."

"Any word on Mary Grace?"

I shake my head. The reminder of her absence grips me like the onset of a sudden fever. I had managed to forget about it for a full five minutes before Seth brought it up again. My partner has spent a lot of his own time poking into the dark corners of the city, looking for her.

"Nothing yet," I say. "We've decided to talk to some private investigators."

He gives me a questioning look.

"Peg Bartles and her partner."

"You mean Rocky Bentner?" He whistles. "Well, that ought to be fun."

"They're good."

"They're insane."

I make a shooing motion to Seth, signaling that it's time for him to stop the chatter and get back to work.

"They get results," I say. "And I really don't care how they get them."

Seth laughs and stands to go. "And here I thought you were working hard to get the crazy out of your life. See you at fourteen hundred hours for the update."

He walks out of the office and saunters back to his workstation, which is in a direct line of sight from my desk.

He swivels around in his chair so he's facing me, leans back, and upends an empty water bottle over his head, miming taking a shower.

I choke off a laugh, giving him a stern look, and then close the door. Seth and I first met the PI team of Bartles and Bentner while working a narcotics case involving the underage daughter of a wealthy tech inventor. The girl had become enamored of a dealer who sold heroin and cocaine to high school kids. My partner and I were chasing the dealer, and the PIs had been hired to track down the daughter. We traced the dealer to the home of his sister, a woman named JaeDee Ornell. She lived in a trailer in a run-down park not far from White Rock Lake. We were surprised to see Peg Bartles, all five feet four of her, answering the door instead of the dealer's sister.

Seth and I showed her our badges, and she invited us in. As she started to explain her and her partner's involvement in the case, two things became apparent immediately. The trailer had evidence of drug paraphernalia, and someone in another room was moaning loudly, as though in pain.

"That'd be JaeDee," Peg had said calmly, sitting on the lone couch and flipping through an old magazine. "She'll be back out in a minute."

"Is she all right?" Seth had asked, moving toward the muffled sounds.

"JaeDee's fine. She's just taking a shower."

The moaning had gotten louder, reaching an almost operatic crescendo. Now we could hear two voices, both in the throes of some animal abandon.

Seth and I traded incredulous looks. "You said you had a partner. Where is he?" I asked.

Peg casually brushed some bit of lint off her pants, stretched tight over her generous thighs, and said, "My partner's a she. And she's taking a shower too."

Seth pulled me aside and muttered, "What the actual fuck, Riz?"

"That about sums it up," Peg said, grinning, without looking up from her magazine.

A few minutes later, a diminutive Rocky Bentner joined us from the back room, fully clothed, her dark, shaggy hair still sopping wet. She looked to be no more than fifteen or sixteen years old, and was even shorter than Peg, but I found out later she was twenty-four.

Rocky looked at her partner. "JaeDee told me where the girl is." Then she looked at us and said, smirking, "She'll be out in a minute. She's just drying her hair."

Peg stood up laughing. "Okay, let's go bring the girl back to her mama. JaeDee's all yours now, Detectives. Good luck finding your dealer."

But JaeDee never would tell us where to find her brother, and despite all our efforts, including arresting her for manufacturing drugs, it took us another two weeks to track him down. I did some digging after our initial encounter and found out a few things about the PI team. Peg Bartles had served four years in the army, was twice married, and spent twenty years as a PI doing skip tracing and following marital cheaters. But her specialty became finding underage runaways once Rocky Bentner teamed up with her.

Rocky had worked two years with the Houston Police Department and one year as an undercover agent with Vice, because she could pass for a teenager. She left the force after she shot and killed a creep who had tried to rape her. There was no PI team in Texas that had a better find rate of missing kids than Bartles and Bentner. Their effectiveness lay in their ability to go places, often posing as a mother-and-daughter team, and do things that police officers were not able to do. Their unofficial motto seemed to be "We lie better than the liars, cheat better than the cheaters, and will happily steal the truth right out from under you."

I put a call through to Bartles's office and left a voice mail, giving them the general information about Mary Grace's disappearance and asking them to call me back.

I finish some incident reports, shift assignments, and a few personnel evaluation documents before calling my lieutenant to get the okay to contact the DEA about my conversation with El Cuchillo. Calling the DEA can sometimes feel like a "Who's on first" scenario. Special Agent Don Haslett was out in the field—his area covers all of North Texas and Oklahoma—and I was put on hold half a dozen times as his staff attempted to track him down. I was told that the guy has five cell phones. I first met Don face-to-face following my escape from the Delano Gym fire. I provided him with an artist's sketch of El Cuchillo, his fingerprints on the pocketknife, and the whereabouts of his hometown, the barrios of Culiacán. Information the Feds had never had before.

Haslett's voice finally comes on the line, and I give him a brief rundown.

"And you think he was calling you from Culiacán?" he asks.

"Can't be sure," I say, "but if you check your weather map,

you'll see it's peak rainy season in Sinaloa Land. No rain in Texas today."

"Thanks for the update. Let us know if he contacts you again."

"You can count on that," I say. "The next time I hear from the guy, my two-week countdown will have commenced."

After the call, I stand up a few times to ease the tension that's caused my right calf muscle to cramp. After my abduction by the Roy family, Evangeline had sought to immobilize me and render me compliant by having a cable surgically inserted behind my Achilles tendon. The cable was then attached to a length of chain, the far end of which was fastened to a heavy stone. The injury had been life-altering, and the doctors had told me they weren't sure I'd ever walk normally again. But the surgery to reattach the tendon was successful, and within six months I was running again.

I eat my lunch without really tasting it while putting in a requisition for more surveillance equipment. By the time I'm finished with my daily reports, I'm ready to bang my head against my desk, not to mention crack open the bottle of Jameson that Seth has left in my office. Being sergeant affords better pay, but I'd rather have a root canal without anesthesia than do these required daily reports.

One of my biggest concerns after being made sergeant was how my colleagues—Tom Craddock and his partner, Kevin Ryan—as well as Seth, would take to my elevated status. But everyone seemed genuinely pleased. The three of them had taken me out the first weekend after my promotion, and, with the exception of Seth, we got blind, stinking, joyfully drunk on tequila and really bad cop jokes.

But in the days that have followed, I've wondered if I'm up

for the job. I'd spent my whole career in the bullpen, taking pride in the relative freedom it offered when, often literally, running down suspects. And more than a little satisfaction in rubbing the powers that be the wrong way. Heavy is the head that wears the crown. And weary is the sergeant who's mentally got one foot still in the trenches and one foot on the ladder.

At two o'clock, I close my office door behind me and head for the incident room. A small wall-mounted television in the break room has been turned to a news broadcast revisiting the 9/11 memorial. A group of detectives, including Craddock and Ryan, are watching the solemn images—salvaged pieces of the Twin Towers, detritus from the civilians and rescuers who didn't make it out alive, photos of the dead.

Craddock's face sags with the weight of the moment. He crosses his arms over his large belly, drawing my attention to the crumbs on his tie. Infinitely sadder than the expression on his face are the minute remnants of his sack lunch, lovingly prepared by his wife, still mourning the death of their only daughter. A death caused by a drug overdose.

He senses my presence and turns to me. "You were in New York when it happened, right?"

"Yeah. I was on street patrol then in Brooklyn. You could see the smoke for days."

Ryan asks, "Did you know anyone who didn't make it?"

I remind myself that Ryan would have been only about fourteen when the Towers fell. Old enough to remember, but as he'd never been out of Texas, the visceral, all-consuming horror of it was probably missed. It's a cellular thing, this horror that, even a decade later, can reemerge like a malarial fever. The Twin Towers were a constant point of orientation for Manhattanites, a shrine to the best of New York's hustle. The reality that such lasting monuments could be destroyed changed the psyche of New Yorkers forever.

I catch Ryan studying me closely. "There wasn't a neighborhood that didn't have a somebody's somebody who was killed," I tell him.

The truth was, I had known at least a dozen police officers and firefighters who had been called to the World Trade Center. Almost four hundred firefighters and police personnel died when the Towers came down. But not all of them died instantaneously. Some of them died slowly and painfully from cancer or breathing-related illnesses. Others, like my mother, died by inches from a soul sickness, which soon manifested itself like a rancid parasite, poisoning her from the inside out.

"Let's just put it this way, Kevin," I say. "That was the day I stopped believing I was immortal."

I tap Craddock on the shoulder. "Okay, guys, it's after two. Meeting time."

They follow me into the incident room, where Seth and two other narcotics detectives—newly transferred to North Central—are waiting. The room had last been used as a strategy staging area for what turned out to be a successful bust in North Dallas. A raid at an auto repair shop had netted twenty-one packages containing a total of two million dollars in meth, discovered under the dashboard of a Volkswagen Jetta. The Jetta had been in the shop for "repairs." One of the two new detectives on my team, Joe Esparza, had helped make the arrest, earning him the nickname Jetta Joe.

His partner sitting next to him, Danny Philbo, is a transplant from Chicago. It's been a couple of years since he worked as a cop in the Windy City, but he narrows his eyes suspiciously at everything, as though he's squinting into a squall blowing off Lake Michigan. No one has yet given him a nickname. This is his first close encounter with me. He crosses his meaty arms and scowls, pinning his gaze to a place just over the top of my head.

"Good morning, Detectives," I say, clearing a space to sit on the edge of a table at the front of the room. "First of all, before we start, congratulations again to Detectives Esparza and Philbo for the auto-shop raid."

"Thank you, Sergeant," Esparza says. "Glad to be working with the North Central Division."

Philbo says nothing.

"This morning," I say, "I got a call from Detective Manny Ortega, currently with the Gangland Unit in South Central, asking me to come down to Oak Cliff, where a hostage standoff was taking place. The hostage taker, a dealer for the Sinaloa cartel, had demanded to speak to me. He gave me a phone with direct access to Alfonso Ruiz Zena, also known to law enforcement as El Cuchillo."

I happen to know that Philbo speaks fluent Spanish. But he looks quizzically at his partner, feigning ignorance, and Esparza translates by saying, "The Knife."

"Oh, right," Philbo says, nodding, returning his gaze to the wall behind me.

"El Cuchillo told me that Evangeline Roy and some of her people have returned to Texas from Honduras, where she's been operational for the past year and is evidently disrupting the transiting flow of drugs to the Sinaloans in Mexico."

Craddock and Ryan exchange looks of concern.

"Where was the Knife calling from?" Craddock asks.

"My guess, it was from his base in Culiacán," I say. "I spoke earlier to Don Haslett with DEA. As long as Zena is not in Texas, he's not our problem. But if the Roys are in Dallas, it is our problem. Zena said he's got feelers out. When he knows, we'll know."

"So, we're just going to wait until the cartel points us in the right direction?" Philbo asks. His mouth is all puckery, as though he's been sucking on a lemon.

"That's an *excellent* question, Detective Philbo," I say, getting up from the table and moving to stand behind his chair. "And the answer to that is no. We're not going to wait. We're going to start looking immediately. We're going to tap all our resources, all our colleagues in other divisions, and all our CIs to find out if Evangeline Roy is in our city. We're going to interface with DEA on this. And some of us, Detective Philbo, will be working the long, dark hours between midnight and eight in the morning to gather as much information as possible from our resident night-stalking citizens."

I know that Philbo is scowling, but he has too much invested in being the alpha male to turn around and lock eyes with me. Esparza—who will be partnering with him during the graveyard shift—gives him a dirty look.

"Detectives Dutton, Craddock, and Ryan are all too familiar with Evangeline Roy. Detectives Esparza and Philbo, I would like you to spend the next few hours memorizing every record of the Roy family we have on file. I want Evangeline's face to be as recognizable to you as your own mother's. We don't have any photos of her taken within the last decade, and she has aged significantly due to her past drug use. But there is an artist's sketch that's pretty close. Any leads, no matter how small, I want to know immediately."

I edge closer to the back of Philbo's chair. Close enough for him to feel my body heat. "Any questions? Detective Philbo?"

He sighs theatrically and says, "Not a one, Sergeant."

"Good," I say. "Meeting adjourned."

I walk back to my office but stop just outside the door. It's open. I know I closed it when I left for the meeting. Inside, sitting in my chair, craning her neck to read a report on my desk, is Peg Bartles. Her partner, Rocky Bentner, is sprawled across a visitor's chair, one leg hooked over the armrest, looking the part of a brooding, angry teenager: dark eyeliner, piercings, wearing more black than a stagehand at a Coachella concert.

"Man, your office is really boring," Peg says.

"Yeah, working undercover narco busts is really uneventful," I say.

I motion for Peg to get out of my seat, and she moves to sit in the other visitor's chair. She does not look embarrassed in the least about being caught snooping.

"You could have just called me back," I say. "But I'm thrilled you responded in person. Must not be very busy these days."

"On the contrary," Peg says. "We're extremely busy."

"Extremely," Rocky echoes.

"So, tell me more about this missing girl," Peg says.

"Her name is Mary Grace Miller, although I think Miller is just a name she's been using to cover her real identity."

Peg gives her partner a look. "What's her story?"

"She was living hard on the streets, pregnant and pretty hopeless. Whoever her family is, she made it clear that they didn't want anything to do with her. She's been staying with us since she gave birth seven months ago. Ten days ago she just disappeared. No note, and no word from her since."

Rocky has uncoiled herself from lazing in the chair and is now sitting alert, with both feet—encased in black Doc Martens—on the floor. "Have any idea where she might have gone?"

"No," I say. "We haven't a clue. We've been out looking for her. Filed a missing person's report after forty-eight hours, but so far we've got nothing. I've even had detectives looking off-hours for her. That's why I called you, hoping you'd be able to help us."

"Us?" Peg asks.

"Me and my wife, Jackie."

"Where's the baby now?" Rocky asks.

"At my house. We've hired a nanny while Jackie and I are at work."

Peg takes a piece of paper out of her pocket and hands it to me. It's a copy of an original photograph. The girl in the image looks to be about thirteen, with light blond hair and freckles. She's smiling crookedly, one eye shut against the direct sunlight. "It's Mary Grace. Where did you get the photo?"

Peg takes a breath. "From her father. Stepfather, as it happens."

I look from Peg to Rocky. "And he's just now looking for her?"

Peg shrugs.

"Who is he?" I ask.

"A potential client," Rocky says.

Peg takes the photocopy from me and puts it back in her pocket. "I think we've got a conflict of interest here. You ever hear of Alan P. Turner?"

"Turner as in Turner Properties?"

Rocky cracks her knuckles. "Turner as in owning every other fucking bit of commercial real estate downtown."

"I suspect your Mary Grace Miller is actually Mary Grace Turner," Peg says. "Her stepfather called us yesterday and offered us a shitload of money to find her."

"A *shitload* of money," Rocky says.

"You called him a 'potential' client. Turner's wealthy, connected, and related to Mary Grace," I say. "And yet you're here, talking to me."

"Yeah, well. We have some reservations about taking on Turner as a client," Peg says.

Rocky shifts restlessly in her chair. "Hence the conflict."

"There are some uncomfortable allegations surrounding Alan Turner," Peg says quietly.

I get up and close the office door. "Allegations such as—?"

"He likes young girls," Rocky says, frowning.

Peg lets that sink in. "He's had several cases settled out of court."

"The timing of this is very suspect," I say. "Why's he calling now?"

Peg shakes her head. "I don't know the answer to that. It's possible someone spotted her and, knowing her history, called him. Here's the thing: He didn't just know that Mary Grace was missing. He knew she'd had a baby."

The way she says it makes my throat constrict.

Rocky looks at me with as much sympathy as her Goth posturing will allow. "He showed a particular interest in finding the baby."

"The baby's name is Elizabeth. Does he know that she's with us?"

"Not yet," Peg says.

Rocky crosses her arms defiantly. "He's not going to hear it from us."

The tightness in my throat eases only slightly. "So, you're not going to take him on as a client?"

"My partner's right. The guy's a major perv," Peg says, standing. "We talked about it right after you called us. We'll take you on as our client, giving Turner a pass. I have to say, though, it's not going to be cheap." Peg grins. "But that shouldn't be a problem, you being bumped up to sergeant's pay and all."

"Oh, right, I'm just rolling in dough. Send me a contract with your rates, and I'll talk it over with Jackie. Have you got any ideas where you'll start looking?"

Rocky follows her partner to the door. "Where the wild things are."

Peg leaves the office door open as they leave, and I watch Rocky checking out Seth—sitting at his desk wearing a tight-fitting T-shirt—with the intensity of an X-ray technician. As she passes, she leers at him, sticks her thumb in her mouth, and starts sucking it enthusiastically. Seth almost falls out of his chair.

I call Jackie and tell her that the PI team will be sending us a contract.

"We can pretty much kiss this New Year's getaway goodbye."

"If they find her," Jackie says, "it'll be worth it. I love you for doing this, Betty."

"Yeah, well, don't go spreading it around. It'll ruin my rep."

After we hang up, I sit and look at the photos of Elizabeth that Mary Grace had texted me over the past few months. Her growth rate is startling, from a wiggly blob to a sturdy, chubby sentient being with the ability to capture and hold another's gaze. Smiling, laughing, beginning to make the nonsense noises that have the rhythm and cadence of proto-speech. She knows her name, though. Say her name, and you'll have her entire attention.

Craddock knocking at my door startles me. He's holding the remnants of a power bar in one hand.

"I may have something for you," he says.

He comes in, shoving the rest of the bar into his mouth, and sits down. Whatever it is he's sharing, it's not his afternoon snack. He chews thoughtfully for a moment, swallows, and says, "I figured I'd start looking at Evangeline's old stomping grounds. So I called over to Tyler and spoke to a detective in their combined Vice and Narcotics Department. He said no arrests of anyone with a Roy family connection have been made since the big bust at their compound last year. Their meth sales across the board are down, but heroin is on the rise, making people do strange things, stranger than usual. Full-moon weird shit, he tells me. He's a good ol' Piney Woods boy, likes to hunt and fish, so we shoot the breeze for a while, and then we hang up."

He leans forward in the chair. "Then I call over to the Harrison County Sheriff's Office. You know, the boys who found the headless body of El Gitano in Caddo Lake."

El Gitano was a cartel dealer who had the misfortune

of falling into competition with the Roy family. He'd been caught and killed, his severed head delivered to me in a box by Evangeline's son Tommy Roy. Tommy was shot and killed by Kevin Ryan during my rescue from captivity. Evangeline had lost her second son, Curtis, by my hand.

"Well, the sheriff tells me basically the same thing Tyler PD told me. No arrests with known Roy connections. But he did say that they've made some crazy arrests in the last few weeks in Marshall, Texas. Get this: his deputies arrested three people, small-time street dealers, all wearing red wigs."

"You mean red as in Bozo the Clown wigs?"

"I mean red as in ladies' fashion wigs. Two men and a woman were picked up selling their stuff while wearing the wigs. When questioned about it, all three said they'd been given free samples of H to wear them. They thought it was just some sick joke on the part of their supplier."

An unaccountable, woozy feeling like the hangover after a bad dream expands in my head.

"You say it was heroin?" I ask.

"Very pure, very strong."

"Who was the supplier?"

"New player on the block. A Honduran with the nickname 'Flaco.'"

"Any physical description other than skinny?"

Craddock shakes his head. "Not really. He just sort of disappeared after doing the exchange with the dealers."

El Cuchillo had told me that he'd been having problems in Honduras thanks to the Roy family setting up shop outside Tegucigalpa and interrupting the heroin trade with the Sinaloa cartel.

"And then I remembered what the Tyler detective had said

about unusual arrests made the last few weeks. Picked up the phone and called him back."

I sit back in my chair. I know what Craddock is going to tell me before he finishes his next sentence.

"He told me they'd arrested two heroin dealers wearing red wigs that they got from a supplier named Flaco."

We stare at each other, unblinking, for a moment.

Craddock says, "The heroin is stronger than anything they've seen before. They're selling it cheap too."

"Perfect way to guarantee return business," I say. "They have a bead on this guy Flaco?"

"Gone with the wind." Craddock stands and stretches. "I have calls into some old colleagues in Houston as well. We'll see if this is just an East Texas problem or something more ambitious."

He pauses at the door on his way out. "You know, it could just be a coincidence."

But he and I both know that that's not what's happening. Evangeline had believed that copper-haired people were special, chosen by God. She had taken great pride in recounting to me all of the supposed redheads from the Bible: King David, the Archangel Michael, even Adam and Eve. Both Evangeline and her two sons had hair the color of East Texas dirt. I believe the red wigs are a dark joke from the Roy family to my team—to me in particular. A fuck-you message from the matriarch: *"I'm baaaaaaaack!"*

Months ago, she had returned to me the Saint Michael medallion that she kept after I was taken prisoner. With the medallion was a note, written in her own handwriting: *"Vengeance is mine, thus sayeth the Lord. But I will help Him see it done, and soon."*

Ryan knocks at the open door.

"Can I talk to you for a minute?" he asks.

"Sure. Come on in. This is where the action seems to be."

He takes the seat that Craddock had just vacated.

"Everything okay?" As soon as I ask the question, I realize that everything appears to be more than okay. At the beginning of the year, he'd lost his brother-in-law to a drug overdose. Shortly afterward, his pregnant wife had had a miscarriage. Both the emotional strain at home and the grinding frustration that came from never seeming to make a measurable difference in stemming the tide of drugs coming into Texas had gotten to him. But now, sitting in front of me, he looks happy and healthy. No more pallid complexion, bruised-looking flesh under the eyes, or gnawed fingernails.

"Yeah," he says, smiling. "I'm good. I just wanted to thank you for hanging in with me while I was going through a rough patch."

The sentiment takes me by surprise. He's one of the best young officers I've ever worked with, and as I look at his hopeful, earnest face, his gratitude threatens to make me teary-eyed. I shuffle some papers around on my desk as a distraction. "You're a good cop, Kevin. This department would be the lesser for your absence."

His smile widens. He knows he got to me. "Had my resignation letter all written. I held on to it for months. Last night I tore it up."

The admission comes as a relief. "What changed?"

"It wasn't just one thing. I watched you come back from a life-threatening injury after being kidnapped and nearly burned to death by a major cartel player. And here you are, a sergeant." He looks around to make sure no one is in earshot and lowers his voice. "I know some of what Seth's gone through the last few months. Enough to understand that he made a Herculean effort to overcome an addiction to stay on the force. You stuck by your partner when a lot of people would have given up on him."

"Seth's also a stellar cop," I say.

He wags a finger at me. "Yeah, but that's not why you kept faith with him. A few days ago, my sponsee—you know, the kid I mentor through the Cops and Kids Foundation— completed ninety days of rehab. He's gotten his GED and was accepted to a community college. First one in his family to get past the tenth grade." He rests his arms on the desk, grinning with pride for his young charge.

The Cops and Kids Foundation was the brainchild of a former Dallas police chief who felt teens at risk, especially those without strong parental influences, could benefit from time spent with stable, mature law enforcement officers. Which should have excluded undercover narcotics detectives right out of the gate. But Ryan had lost his young brother-in-law to drugs, so it made sense that he would want to be involved.

He leans forward so I'll meet his gaze. "Kid says he wants to be a cop. There were so many times I thought he'd never make it. But I hung in there, and I actually made a difference in this kid's life."

"You probably *saved* his life, Kev."

"I realize there's not a damn thing I can do to stop the flow of drugs. Not really. But in the meantime, maybe I can help keep a few kids from checking out."

We grin at each other for a bit. "Feels good, doesn't it?" I ask.

He nods. "It'll feel even better getting Evangeline Roy behind bars."

At five o'clock, Craddock sticks his head back into my office and says, "Houston PD has picked up four dealers, all of 'em wearing wigs. It's a goddam epidemic."

5

Slugger Anne's Bar
Thursday, September 11, 2014

As soon as I sit down at the bar, the owner, Dottie, places the bottle of Jameson labeled PROPERTY OF THE POLISH CAVALRY in front of me with a glass. She watches as I pour a double and knock it back.

"That good a day, huh?" she says.

I pour another—a single this time—and let the whiskey work its magic. I don't tell her about my call with El Cuchillo, but I do tell her that word on the street is that Evangeline Roy is back in Texas. I relate Craddock's discovery of small-time dealers being bribed to wear red wigs, mimicking the Roy matriarch's scarlet tresses. As well, I tell her that Jackie and I will probably be hiring the PI team Bartles and Bentner to start looking for Mary Grace.

"If we can afford it," I say.

"Hey, I'll donate toward their fees if it'll help."

I know that Dottie, who has her ear to the streets, and who has given me vital information in the past, has put the word out to the sidewalk citizens to keep a sharp watch for Mary

Grace. She'd provided a home for Mary Grace for a few weeks before she moved in permanently with Jackie and me, and she'd bought enough baby stuff to furnish an orphanage.

Just the thought of an orphanage, and the baby's current motherless status, brings a sharp pain to my chest.

"Evidently," I say, "Mary Grace's stepfather is Alan Turner, the real-estate tycoon. He tried to hire Peg and Rocky to look for her, but they've given him a pass to help me find her first."

"He the bastard that threw her out of her home to begin with?"

"Very possibly."

"So why's he just looking for her now?"

Dottie quits talking and looks at me with growing alarm.

"Son of a bitch," she says. "The baby."

Dottie, a recovering addict and alcoholic, grew up on a cattle ranch in West Texas and is one of the toughest women I know. But in addition to building a successful, all-women club in a neighborhood that historically supported testosterone-fueled men's sports bars, she sponsors scores of fellow addicts through 12-step programs and volunteers almost all of her free time at food banks. Despite her sarcasm and rough exterior, her heart has all the resistance of a cream-filled Twinkie.

I raise my glass in a bitter recognition of her revelation. "Peg told me that he was aware that Mary Grace had given birth. He just didn't know where she is now."

"Not yet, he doesn't," Dottie says. "But they're not the only PIs in Dallas. He's got the money, he'll just hire someone else."

I drain the glass and think seriously about having another. But Jackie is waiting for me at home…with Elizabeth. I don't want to be staggering into the house like some drunken Auntie Mame.

"I just don't understand why Mary Grace hasn't contacted us."

I know what both of us are thinking in that moment. Maybe she can't contact any of us because the unthinkable has happened. The bar is filled with groups of women happily gathered together in a safe space after work or a workout, drinking and talking and going about their lives. I think of Mary Grace out in the world, possibly alone and frightened, and I shudder.

Dottie's gaze goes over my shoulder, and she says loudly, "Lock up your va-jay-jays, ladies. The fuzz is here."

From this, without even looking, I know that my partner, Seth, has arrived.

We settle into a booth at the back—my partner with his face pointed toward the wall to avoid the suspicious glares from the female patrons—and place our orders with the waitress: two cranberry juices. I'm over my limit, and Seth is not drinking these days.

When Dottie, still behind the bar, gets the order from the waitress, she yells at us, "Hey, I run a business here. I ain't making money off selling juice!"

Seth laughs. "Ah, Dottie, still as pleasant as ever."

"You know she loves you."

"I think I'd rather face a biker with a tire tool."

The waitress delivers our drinks, and we clink our glasses together in a toast.

"To my running partner," Seth says, "and DPD's newest sergeant, who daily kicks my butt in the best possible way."

It had taken months for us to repair the rift between us

caused by his narcotics addiction. And by his working secretly with the Feds to track our previous sergeant, Marshall Maclin. So far, his only negative response to my rise to sergeant status has been some gentle ribbing about my having to dress the part. I'd traded in my leathers for fitted jackets and slacks, and my Doc Martens for low-heeled boots in sensible colors.

"What do you think about the new guys, Esparza and Philbo?" I ask.

"Joe's a good guy, I think. Too soon to tell about Philbo. He's not what I'd call a team player."

"I hear he gets the job done," I say. "Although I don't think he's ever had to report to a woman sergeant before."

A wicked grin appears on Seth's face. "He better get used to it, or you'll have to go 'all Betty' on him."

I frown into my glass. I've worked with plenty of law enforcement officers who've had issues, not only reporting to female leadership but also simply working with women as partners and equals. Usually I'd found that the problem took care of itself by keeping my head down, going deaf to taunts and insults, and working hard at the task in front of me. The human animal, especially if it's male, can only take so much boredom before it goes on to torture something, or someone, else. Occasionally, I've had to liberally apply verbal pushback. And once, I was forced to give a concussion to an academy trainer—a guy who tried to choke me out during a defense tactics demonstration—when I was a cadet.

If Philbo was going to be a problem, there was plenty I could do as a sergeant to bring him to heel. Or force him out of the department. I could continue to assign him shit cases, the kind of cases that don't make the evening news but bring plenty of paperwork and midnight hours. Or, even worse, I could keep changing the schedule around so that his circadian rhythms had to go on life support, which for a cop means epic, near lethal amounts of caffeine, on top of too much booze.

But all of that will make for a restless, resentful, and angry cop. Useless to everyone, especially to me. The better tactic is often to kill the unsuspecting cop with kindness. Bludgeon him into cooperation by backing the officer up in a conflict with a suspect, as well as any admin complaints, if the complaints are without merit.

I take a deep breath, smile at Seth, and finish my drink.

"Yeah, well, if I do have to go 'all Betty' on him, I have you to back me up, right, partner?"

He winks at me. "Right you are, Riz. He won't know what hit him."

6

The House
Thursday, September 11, 2014

When I walk into the living room, Jackie is lying on the floor next to Elizabeth, wearing only workout pants and a sports bra. She's gazing rapturously into the baby's face. I'm gazing at Jackie's torso, having distinctly unmaternal thoughts. Immediately I feel guilty, and I wonder what my therapist, Dr. Theo, would have to say about these uncomfortable feelings. As if the baby senses my Rated M for Mature ideations, she looks up at me and sneezes.

I tear my eyes away from my wife's inviting form and go into the bathroom to brush my teeth. No need to breathe whiskey fumes over our little charge. Back to the living room, I lie down next to Jackie and kiss her neck.

"The agreement from Bartles and Bentner was just emailed to me," I tell her.

"What's it going to cost?"

I tell her the minimum fee for a guaranteed two weeks of searching, and her eyes widen.

"Yeah," I say. "But if they can't find her in two weeks, I don't think they're going to find her."

"What do you say, baby?" Jackie asks Elizabeth, who dips her head onto the blanket, rubbing her forehead sleepily against it.

"What does big baby say?" she asks me.

Clashing scenarios crowd my head: we find Mary Grace and she doesn't want to come back; we don't find Mary Grace right away but she shows up down the road, maybe years from now, after we've bonded even more strongly with Elizabeth; we find her and she wants to take the baby and then disappears again; we never find Mary Grace and her disappearance remains an agonizing mystery. And then, what to do about Elizabeth?

Uncle Benny always counseled me to find out the truth, to get to the bottom of things. He said the knowing was infinitely better than the not-knowing. He would say that a true Polish warrior would never utter the words *Wycofać sie*.

Retreat!

Although I do remember that strategically, and on occasion, he would utter the saying *Przesuń do tylu*.

Advance to the rear! And live to fight another day.

"How can we not?" I say. "She's family."

After dinner, my work phone rings. It's Tom Craddock.

"Well," he says, "you ready for this?"

He doesn't sound like he's going to impart good news, so I walk into my home office and close the door.

"I'm listening," I say.

"I just heard from Esparza. They got a tip on some unusual

drug activity on Greenville and went to check it out. Or better said, some unusual drug dealer accoutrements."

Despite the amusing way Craddock pronounces the word—*a-coo-der-mints*—the muscles in my lower back clench. "Tell me this doesn't have anything to do with red wigs."

"Bingo. He and Philbo picked up a dealer selling H on the street like he was a carney at the state fair. Almost as though he wanted to get busted."

"Where's he now?"

"County."

This means the dealer had already been processed and placed in Lew Sterrett Jail, the hulking brick compound next to the Trinity River.

"That was fast work," I say. Esparza and his partner didn't waste any time making an arrest that might give me a heads-up on the mysterious, and seemingly well-traveled, Flaco.

"The dealer wasn't able to make bail," Craddock says, "so he's sitting in a cell all by his lonesome."

"Why'd they put him in solitary?"

"It's for his own safety. He's evidently a suicide risk."

"I want to talk to him."

"He's not going anywhere anytime soon. I'll go with you if you want."

"Thanks, Tom, but I think I'll have Seth go downtown with me."

We say our goodbyes, and I disconnect the call. Tom is one of the most compassionate people I know, and a valorous cop, but to people who don't know him, he comes off as a redneck. An overweight, jowly, chicken-fried yahoo, as Uncle Benny would say.

Seth, on the other hand, is like a chameleon and can talk to just about anyone, from stone-cold bikers to the vulnerable and downtrodden. He's gentle with society's outliers. Little old ladies *love* him. A lot of women get breathless the moment he walks into a room. And for any females who are initially unimpressed, he can turn on the relentless just-a-farm-boy-from-West-Texas charm and bowl them over with kindness. When all else fails, he's got a warehouse full of dragon-slayer stories, enough to impress even hard-core gangbangers.

I hear Jackie calling to me. She's got Elizabeth ready for bed and wants me to help tuck her in. Because of the baby's reluctance to bond with me, Jackie thinks it's a good idea that I read to her every night. This works, only so long as my better half stays in the room with me. As soon as Jackie leaves, the baby gets fussy. Evidently, I'm scary to her even when I'm reading *Goodnight Moon*.

Walking into the guest room—which is now undeniably Elizabeth's—I'm bombarded by the sweet smell of baby products. Baby shampoo, baby lotion, diaper-rash cream, all combined to make even the hardest cynic weak in the knees with the sensory recall of early childhood.

Elizabeth is trying to pull herself upright, gripping the bars of the crib, happily blowing bubbles of spit from her motoring lips. As soon as she sees me, she lets go of the bars and falls onto her back. I wave. She scowls.

Jackie hands me a book, and we sit on the floor so Elizabeth can see us while I do my best impression of Story Time. As I read, a memory of my own mother sneaks into my mind. We'd had the same book, growing up, my older brother, Andrew, and I. *Goodnight Moon* was a bedtime ritual from my earliest recollection, and he would continue reading it to me even when I could decipher the words for myself.

In my mind's eye I'm about seven years old, and even though we sleep in separate rooms, I have crawled into bed with Andrew. Not because I'm terrified of some supernatural thing creeping around in the dark, but because I'm afraid of the living, breathing being downstairs. In those hours between dinner and midnight, I've not yet begun to be afraid for myself. My concern is for Andrew.

My father's drunken bullying has escalated into physical attacks. Like an infecting virus, his rage has jumped from my mother to my brother with sudden, forceful irregularity. He'd been all smiles at dinnertime. Telling jokes, recounting stories about the Rhyzyk family from the Old Country, about his day at the 94th Precinct in Brooklyn, the same precinct where Uncle Benny, my father's brother, works. The smoke from his cigarette unfurled in a gauzy scrim, softening his expression, fooling us into thinking that his lightened mood would last until he could pass out from drink.

As Andrew reads to me, my father's agitated voice gets louder, and my brother has pitched the volume of his voice louder as well, trying to obscure the escalating threat. There are footsteps stumbling up the stairs. Two pairs of feet, my father's and my mother's. The sound of her voice pleading, reasoning with her husband to stop, to come back to the kitchen.

Andrew keeps reading: "'Goodnight room, Goodnight moon...'"

The angry rumbling male voice gets louder. I can hear the

words from my father's outraged mouth. *"I've told him to stay the hell outta my office....That's my office, goddammit! I'll fuckin' whip the little bastard till he stops growing..."*

My brother continues to read: *"'Goodnight little house...'"*

I'm sounding out the words along with Andrew, our voices in the trembling, mindless cadence of a cathedral mass, one that is intoned through fear. Not of some invisible God, but of the god who stands now beating on the door, demanding that Andrew come out and face him.

The door slams open, and he stumbles in, my mother holding on to his arm, trying to restrain him. The light from the hallway is reflecting off two pairs of startled eyes. The unexpected sight of me in Andrew's room gives him pause. The whiskey has not yet completely eaten away at his ability to feel shame, or remorse, and he shakes his finger at my brother and threatens, *"Never again. You hear me? Or I will end you."*

My mother has edged her way backward, toward the threshold, her hand at her throat, her breathing quick and shallow. I can't see the expression on her face, I can only read her body language. The language of self-protection. And I have comprehended the fact that instead of moving toward us, covering us with her protective body, imploring her husband on our behalf, she has increased the distance between us.

I realize that I'm no longer reading to Elizabeth, the book lying forgotten in my lap. Jackie gently prods my leg and points to the baby, who's fallen asleep.

"Where did you disappear to?" she whispers.

I make a face and sigh. "To the land of past enchantments."

Jackie, who knows a lot about my childhood, intuits my meaning and gives me a hug. "You coming to bed now?"

Winking and leering, I say, "Only if you tell me a story, Mamacita."

We get up quietly, turn off the light, and close the door to the nursery.

7

Lew Sterrett Jail, Dallas
Friday, September 12, 2014

The Dallas County jail, affectionately known as Lew Lew to its frequent-flyer inmates, is composed of three towers—the North, South, and West Towers—and the county court. The seven thousand inmates are held for a variety of crimes, from Class C misdemeanors all the way up to capital murder. Regardless of their charges, the incarcerated fall into three categories: those who can't post bail; those who've had their court time and are awaiting transfer to state or federal prison; and those who are summoned from another prison by a judge and are awaiting their trial.

Our dealer with the red wig, Tony Diego, was a double loser—unable to post bail and considered too high a suicide risk to be put in the general population; hence the stint in isolation.

The West Tower is the facility with the mental health–care providers, and it houses some really dangerous, mentally unhinged prisoners. The total capacity is over fifteen hundred male and female inmates, which is a lot of hormone-driven crazy. Seth and I park in the open-air parking lot and cross over Commerce Street to the detention center.

After we've passed through Security, we're met by corrections officer Lucy Ganz, one of five hundred female officers at the jail, who comprise over half of the enforcement staff. She's been our liaison for numerous trips to the facility, and she smiles and waves as she comes limping toward us.

"Congrats on making sergeant," she says.

"Thanks. What happened to your leg?" I ask.

She makes a face. "Me and Tasha were escorting a big ol' hairy male prisoner to another floor. No surveillance in the elevators, so he thought he'd take advantage of the blind spot, and blew out my knee. Going to need surgery, looks like."

Seth shakes his head. "I can't believe they still don't have cameras in the lifts."

Lucy motions us past the large prisoner-intake room and starts leading us down a long labyrinthine hallway lined with dirty beige tiles. "Tell me about it. We've been petitioning for a dog's age. I'll be out of here before anything changes, though."

"You're leaving?" I ask. Lucy is a six-year veteran, and despite the danger, she liked the hazard pay and overtime that came with the job.

"Yeah, since I had the baby, it's getting hard to deal with the stress."

"You had a baby?" Seth asks.

Lucy is almost as tall as I am, and strong enough to take down most men.

She beams. "Yep, five months ago."

"Congratulations," I say. For a moment, I think of telling her, "I have a baby now, too!" just to see the look on her face.

A lot of the maximum-security cells in the West Tower are mostly glass for constant surveillance. And the isolation cells—forty square feet with a steel toilet, cement shower, and raised stone bed with a thin, plastic-coated mattress—are like fishbowls, affording no privacy and few creature comforts. As traumatic as it must be for the prisoners to be observed twenty-four seven, it's equally traumatic for the guards to be watching the inmates doing some of the things they do. Things that, in the outside world, would be done behind closed (and locked) doors.

Lucy stops in front of cell 22B and points to the figure sitting slumped over the mattress. She knocks on the glass to get Tony's attention and then holds up a finger, signaling "one minute." She then leads us to an interview room and tells us she'll bring Tony in right away.

There's a desk bolted to the floor, and we set up a chair on one side of the desk, and two chairs on the other. We take our seats and wait. A few minutes later, the door opens and Lucy leads in a handcuffed Tony.

Tony sits, and Lucy says to us, "You know the drill. Thirty minutes."

Before Lucy can close the door, Tony makes kissy noises at her and says, "Hey, Luce, I've been dreaming about you, girl."

Tony turns to us and tries crossing his arms before he remembers that his wrists are cuffed. He's short, maybe five foot four, and stocky, with round cheeks and a sparse growth of beard along his chin.

"You got a cigarette?" he asks.

"No, sorry," I say. "Your trial date set yet?"

"Nah," he says. "Haven't had no lawyer visit yet."

"Do you know why we're here?" Seth asks.

Tony does his best tough-guy bit and squints his eyes threateningly at my partner. "Arm wrestling?"

I can tell he's hurting, though, as he's glassy-eyed and sweating from withdrawal. "Hey, Tony," I say, knocking on the table to get his attention. "You really want to make friends with us. We're the only advocates you've got right now. You need a doctor? We'll make sure you get one. Looks like you're going to be needing some medical intervention, and soon."

"What do you want?" he asks.

"We're interested in who you made your last score from," Seth says.

"What do I get in return?"

"A good word with the District Attorney's Office for starters," I say.

He looks at me in a calculating way. I checked his arrest history before coming to the jail, and he's only had a few Penalty 2 arrests, and little prison time, for dealing small amounts of marijuana. But this time he's been bumped up to a Penalty 1 arrest, for selling heroin on the street. He'd gotten seriously addicted following a car accident, and was deeply in debt.

"I'd need guarantees," he says.

"Tony, you could be facing up to five years this time," I say. "The only guarantee you're going to get from us is word of your cooperation whispered in the DA's ear."

He rubs his hands over his face. "Man, I don't feel so good."

"The sooner you talk to us, the sooner we'll call for a doctor," Seth says.

I hand Tony a candy bar. Sometimes sugar takes the edge off the drug craving, so I always carry some sweets when I know I'm going to be talking to an addict. "You were arrested wearing a red wig. You want to tell me about that?"

Tony tears the wrapper off, and shrugs. "The guy I scored from told me to wear it." He takes a few bites, closing his eyes as the sugar floods his system.

"And you just put it on?" Seth asks.

"The guy was practically giving the H away. That was the deal. I got the product cheap, but I had to wear the wig."

"Who was the guy?" I ask.

Tony motions toward my pocket. "Gimme another one of those."

I hand him the second candy bar, and he eats half before answering.

"Don't remember."

"What'd he look like?" Seth asks.

"My memory's not so good when I'm craving." He looks at Seth meaningfully. "It'll be a lot better once I'm put right by the doc."

I take an irritated breath. "Come on, Tony, stop dickin' around."

Seth bumps his knee against mine, and taking the cue, I shut my mouth. He leans across the table. "Look, Tony, we promise. You answer just a few questions, and we'll get the doctor in here to take care of you. Okay?"

Tony pushes back from the table and turns his face toward the door, stonewalling us. He doesn't want to lose the chicken match, but he's shaking, and his eyes are pools of misery.

"Man, this is so unfair," Seth says. "You being in here after everything you've been through."

Tony sucks on his teeth. "What do you know about it, *pendejo*?"

"I know what Tango Blast did to you."

Tango Blast gang members had gotten their hooks deep into the south side of Dallas, recruiting young and violent prospective members. Male or female, you weren't usually considered for membership unless you'd already done prison time.

Tony gives Seth a hateful glare. "Fuck you."

"Instead of initiating you like a man, they sexed you in like a woman, didn't they?"

"Fuck you!" Tony yells. His breathing is rapid and shallow, and his complexion has taken on a waxy hue. He stands up, knocking over his chair. Being "sexed in" meant you were gang-raped, forever marked as every male gang member's punk.

"Freddie Morales. Remember him?" Seth stands up as well, tensed for a defensive move.

Freddie Morales was the head of the Dallas Tango Blast chapter, a gang member responsible for at least half a dozen deaths in the past few years. My eyes are ping-ponging back and forth between my partner and Tony, trying to get a handle on where this is going.

"You know he's dead, right?" Seth asks.

Tony's eyes go wide, and he backs up until his shoulders are against the wall. "What?"

"He got arrested and sent to Huntsville. Spent eight months in solitary and then got moved into the mainstream population. Within a week he was found strangled with a piece of wire stolen from the prison wood shop."

Tony's mouth is open, and he's hiccuping sounds that could be mistaken for hysterical laughter.

Seth perches at the end of the table. "You know how I

know? 'Cause I'm the one who arrested him. And I will tell you that he didn't go easy. The wire almost took his head off."

I had completely forgotten that while I was on desk duty back in January—thanks to my predecessor Marshall Maclin who tried to keep me distanced from his corrupt dealings with cartel members—Seth had made a few successful drug busts, Freddie Morales being one of them.

"The guy who shamed you is gone, as are two of his top lieutenants."

Tony stays pressed against the wall, but the expression on his face has turned triumphant. "You for real he's dead?" Tony asks.

"For real. I saw the body in the morgue. Naked as the day he was born, looking like a dashboard bobblehead." Seth rights Tony's chair and motions for him to sit down again.

Seth sits next to me and says, "Just a couple of questions, Tony, and we'll get the doctor to check you out. I promise."

After a moment's hesitation, Tony takes his seat across from us. He's trembling and sweating, but his defiant attitude is gone.

"Who sold you the drugs?" Seth asks.

"Just some guy," Tony says. "I'd never seen him on the streets before."

"Was he local?" I ask.

"No, Honduran."

"How do you know he was Honduran?"

"'Cause he was wearing a Buba López shirt."

"What does that mean?" I ask.

Seth leans toward me and mutters, "Soccer player."

Tony makes a face. "*Fútbol,* dude. Fuckin' gringos."

"Why'd he have you wear the red wig?" I ask.

"Fuck if I know. He just said it was to send a message. Said he'd be watching to make sure I kept it on."

Seth and I exchange looks.

"I thought he was just messin' with me. You know, a little more humiliation for the *maricón*. I'm used to it. But the guy set me up. Told me where to go to sell to some addicts ready to pay twenty a pop. Turned out they were UCs. They busted me, and now I'm here."

The undercovers were, of course, Esparza and Philbo.

"Almost as though he wanted to get you busted so someone in DPD would take notice," I say.

"I guess," Tony says. "Look, I told you everything I know. He disappeared after my bust, and that's the end of the story, man. Now, please...I need to see a doctor." He grimaces, holding his stomach, and lays his head on the table. "Please, I'm going to shit my pants."

"What does he look like?" Seth asks.

"Tall, skinny, long black hair, dark skin, dark eyes," Tony gasps. "Like every other Hondureño."

Seth gets up and pounds on the door.

Tony's hands creep across the table, and he grabs my wrist. I look down and see, on the inside of his arm, livid, vertical scars made by something very sharp and applied by a very determined hand.

"He had a Barrio 18 tattoo on his neck," he whispers. "Flaco. The guy's name is Flaco. He told me I'm dead if I give him up to the cops. That's why I gotta stay in solitary."

Lucy's evidently been watching us on the monitor, because she comes into the room with two medical support staff, who pry his fingers from my wrist and half drag him out of the room.

"They'll take him to the clinic," Lucy says. "Did you get what you needed from him?"

"As much as we could," I say.

"That guy's not going to last long in here," she says. "I've been doing this for a while, and my guess? Tony's going to be taking a long walk off a short pier. I just hope he waits until I'm out. The paperwork is epic."

We sit in Seth's car in the parking lot for a moment. I stare at the jail complex, thinking about the fear on Tony's face when he told me Flaco was serious gangland. Tango Blast was bad enough. They'd shoot you as soon as look at you. But Barrio 18 would find a way to compel you to kill your whole family, and then get you to eat your own gun afterward.

"You did your research, partner," I say. "I didn't know Morales was dead."

"Yeah. Took four prison inmates to hold him down while a fifth opened his windpipe."

"Tony told me the dealer's name is Flaco," I say. "A Barrio 18 gang member."

That gets a raised eyebrow from Seth. "Our man Flaco is probably the same guy selling heroin on the cheap in Tyler and Houston. He's marking a lot of territory, and if he's Barrio 18, he's going to be dangerous if cornered."

"He may still be in Dallas, watching to see if his message got through," I say. "Which means Evangeline will be close by."

That thought brings a sharp rush of anxiety. I instinctively pull out my phone and try calling Jackie. It goes to voice mail, but I do see a text she'd left me earlier. The message reads, Diapers please.

On the way back to the station, we stop at the closest megamarket. Seth waits in the car while I find my way haphazardly to the infant aisle. Having no idea about size, quantity, or brand, I stare hopelessly at a mountain of loin-swathing products with a dizzying array of packaging. I look for a picture of a baby closely resembling Elizabeth as a guide. My personal apocalypse might be right around the corner, but a baby has to eat, and sooner or later she's going to evacuate. While I scan the shelves, muttering obscenities, I take out my phone and try calling Jackie. Once again it goes to voice mail.

As I disconnect the call, I see out of the corner of my eye someone hovering at the end of the aisle. A woman with a red coat and a name tag.

"May I help you?" she asks.

Usually finding an employee to render assistance in the warehouse-size store is harder than tracking down a unicorn, but my confusion and indecision must have tipped some scales with customer support.

"I need diapers," I say. "But I'm not sure which ones to get."

"How old is the child?" she asks.

"She's seven months."

The woman beams, eager to help. "Oh, that's such a cute age. How much does she weigh?"

"I have no idea." I've placed my hand on my hip, displacing the jacket and exposing my gun.

She blinks a few times. "Is she your baby?"

"For the time being," I say.

"Ah, well, uh, okay," she stammers, backing away ever so slightly. "They come in sizes according to weight."

She gestures at the shelves like a game-show host. But I feel her will to help such a clueless, and potentially dangerous, customer ebbing away. I quickly scan the shelves, spying liquid detergent. I hoist one of the containers, a plastic tub containing 210 ounces, and hand it to her.

"She weighs about this much," I say.

She bounces it thoughtfully a few times, sets it back on the shelf, and picks up a package of diapers labeled "Number 2." "Twelve to eighteen pounds ought to be right." She thrusts the package at me, wishes me a good day, and walks briskly back to some safe place, probably a sheltered break room.

I pay for the diapers and walk back to the parking lot where Seth has parked. As I near the passenger-side door, Seth raises his phone, and I realize that he's taking a photo of me carrying a package of diapers the size of Montana. I throw the diapers in the back, slide into my seat, and face my partner.

"If you circulate that photo," I warn, "I will make your life a living hell."

He falls all over himself, laughing. "It'll be worth whatever torture you come up with to make this the screen saver on my computer."

I signal for him to start the engine. "Oh, it won't be me doing the torturing. I'll just get Dottie to do it."

8

Back in my office, I call Peg Bartles to let her know that Jackie and I have decided to retain them for a minimum of two weeks to start looking for Mary Grace.

"I have to tell you," Peg says, "we already gave Mr. Real Estate Mogul a hard pass. He did not take it well. He said he was going to sue for custody of the baby once he finds out where Elizabeth is."

"Can he do that?" I ask.

"Mary Grace is seventeen and still a minor. Her stepfather has sole custody of her. I think a solid case could be made by one of his diamond-drill lawyers that the baby belongs with the family. Such as it is."

There's a heavy silence on the phone while I ponder the situation.

"I can give you the name of a good lawyer," she says.

I hear someone talking in the background. It sounds like Rocky Bentner saying something about me taking out a second mortgage on my house.

"You still there?" Peg asks.

"Yeah," I sigh. "We'll cross that bridge when we come to it. If you find out anything, no matter the hour, call me."

"Will do," Peg says, and disconnects.

Turning to my computer, I do a quick search of Alan P. Turner. Noted as one of the wealthiest men in Dallas, he started out in banking and moved into real-estate development by buying up HUD properties and other "distressed assets." His main office is 1111 Commerce Street, hence the name of his parent company, Eleven Eleven Properties. There are quite a few photos of him attending philanthropic galas, on the golf course, and at the blackjack table. Evidently when he was not "distressing" people out of their homes, he was raking in the chips with other high rollers. He's fit and youthful for his sixty-odd years, but a suspicious lack of age-appropriate wrinkles and liver spots makes me think he has a plastic surgeon on speed dial. Peg referring to him as a "major perv" gives me a sour feeling in the pit of my stomach. I stare at Turner's cold blue eyes, so at odds with the confident smile, and my teeth grind together.

I check the time on my computer screen. With a jolt I see it's 11:11 a.m. My Polish grandmother would have said that it's a good-luck number, a sign of synchronicity, that things were harmoniously aligned in the universe. She also would have assured me that my guardian angel was, in that moment, watching over me. But I also know what Uncle Benny, my own personal guardian angel, would have told me. He would have said that the universe is writhing with random events and full of weird-ass coincidences. A lot of detectives, especially those in homicide, will insist that there are no coincidences. They'll work a case strictly from the head, trying to use mathematical precision, straight lines, right angles, and chemical swabs to untangle the mystery of brutal violence, both casual and furied.

But Benny, who was a homicide cop before state-of-the-art forensics, worked not only from his head but from his gut as well. He'd read the blood splatters and broken furniture of a crime scene as an ancient oracle would, feeling his way by instinct, room by room. Gliding like a planchette across a Ouija board, absorbing through all his senses the sum total of clues visible and invisible until the final, fatal message was spelled out: first came the heated argument, then the escalating struggle, then the frenzied attack, ending with blows to the head with an ax, the weapon then quickly hidden behind the cellar door.

I fervently hope my grandmother was right about the four ones being an auspicious sign.

My personal phone rings loudly, making me jump. It's a number I don't recognize, but I answer it anyway.

I hear El Cuchillo's voice over the airwaves like a lover's whisper. "She's in Dallas," he says. "Ticktock, Sergeant. You've got two weeks from today, which gives you until midnight on the twenty-fifth. I will not call you again, but if I feel you're lagging behind in your search, you'll know."

"Where exactly in Dallas are—?"

He's disconnected the call before I can finish. I have little doubt he knows her pinpoint location, but he's playing games, stretching out the fun to make me sweat. Maybe he'll run down the clock and tell me at the eleventh hour where she is. There's the number 11 again. A dark question blooms in my head. What if I find her, which could only be to his benefit, and then he eliminates me anyway? The longer I remain seated, unmoving, static, the greater my anxiety grows that this, in fact, is what's going to happen.

And then I hear Benny's familiar voice in my ear. *"Don't get stuck in the abyss of your own morass."*

"Get up!" he orders. *"Just do your job, and everything else will fall into place."*

I stand so forcefully that my wheeled office chair crashes against the wall behind me.

The small group has assembled in the incident room: Craddock, Ryan, Philbo, Esparza, and Seth.

"I've just received information that Evangeline Roy is in Dallas at this moment," I say. "The lieutenant has approved the six of us as a special task force to find her. Everything else is put on hold until we do."

"This information solid?" Esparza asks.

"El Cuchillo called me personally to give me the good news," I say. "Seth and I visited the jail this morning and spoke to Tony Diego. He told us that the dealer who sold him the heroin on the cheap is a Honduran national named Flaco, last name unknown. He's a member of Barrio 18. He gave Tony the red wig to wear."

"Sounds like our guy that's been selling heroin in East Texas and Houston," Craddock says.

"Sounds like," Seth says.

I look at Esparza. "You moved fast in picking up Diego. Good work."

"You're welcome," Philbo says, pleased with himself.

There's a patronizing tone to his response, and I take a breath before answering. "How'd you find him so fast?"

"We've got some good contacts in South Dallas," Esparza says. "All we had to do was put out the word to look for some idiot wearing a red wig and we got a hit within two hours."

"Hopefully those contacts will be put to good use in finding Evangeline Roy," I say, turning to a section map of Dallas that I've taped up on the whiteboard. The map outlined in red the seven police divisions: North Central, Northeast, Southeast, Southwest, Northwest, South Central, and Central.

"There are too few of us to cover every division, so I'm making the call to cover the areas that have the most drug activity. Detective Esparza, you and your partner will cover South Central, as that's the area you're most familiar with. Detective Craddock, you and Detective Ryan will liaise with Northwest Division in case the corridor between Dallas and Fort Worth sees an uptick in activity. Detective Dutton and I will take North Central and Northeast Divisions to monitor any traffic coming from East Texas. Lieutenant Bradford has already spoken to each division chief to let them know that we'll be coordinating to utilize whatever resources and manpower they can spare, and that we'll also have the backing of DEA on this, just to give some lift to any requests you all may have. Any questions?"

"Any prize for the first to apprehend?" Philbo asks.

"Yeah," I say, opening the door to signal the end of the briefing. "My undying gratitude."

As soon as I'm back at my desk, I call Special Agent Haslett at DEA.

"Our friend from Culiacán just contacted me," I say. "Evangeline Roy is in Dallas, according to him."

"I'll alert our two field agents in Dallas," he says. "You need anything—resources, surveillance—you let me know."

"Send me their names and contact information. That'll be a start. There are only six of us with DPD looking for her, and El Cuchillo has put a two-week clock on me personally."

"Do you want me to call Lieutenant Bradford about putting a watch on your family?"

"Probably. I'll let you know when."

We end the call, and I grab my jacket and close the office door. It's early afternoon already, the day half over. I walk to Seth's desk and see, lying next to his computer, his personal phone. The screen saver is the photo of me, looking sheepish and carrying the giant package of diapers.

I give him a dirty look. "I love you, partner, but you are *such* an asshole."

Seth and I check a car out of the motor pool and drive downtown to Commerce Street to the Double Wide Bar, or the DW as it's called by the regulars. On occasion, we used to go there after hours for their high-octane drinks and greasy, alcohol-buffering burgers. Seth once told me that as much as he loved the food and atmosphere, he never believed their slogan, which was "Drinks that hit harder than Dad." No one hit harder than his old man, according to Seth. And he had the scars to prove it. Something we had in common.

The bar is mostly empty, the usual lunch crowd already departed. We sit in a booth in the back, directly under a painting of a contorting latter-day Elvis. Dead fish on plaques and trophy heads of deer and elk cover every space on the wall. We're here to meet my CI Wayne and a street denizen named Johnny B. While I've known Wayne for a couple of years, he worked mainly with Seth before Seth's recent leave. I sort of inherited the informer while Seth was out.

Since moving in with Jackie's great-uncle, James Earle, who is a Vietnam vet, seven months before, right around when Jackie and I took in Mary Grace, Wayne has managed to stay clean and sober, attending 12-step meetings and working diligently at a local hardware store.

James Earle, a heavy lifelong drinker, has doggedly applied himself to the program as well. But he's had a few lapses and is growing an impressive collection of "desire chips," the little coins that begin the Day 1 count to sober living, given out as often as the participant is willing to keep coming back, again and again if need be.

After a few minutes, Wayne and Johnny B walk in. Seth waves to get Wayne's attention, and they make their way back to our booth and sit down opposite the two of us. Johnny's coppery skin and black hair, worn in a single long braid down his back, are in stark contrast to Wayne's Waspy appearance.

"You look good, Wayne," I say. And he does. Hair combed neatly and held back from his face by an abundance of James Earle's styling gel. He smiles, showing off his new teeth. James Earle had taken him to a dental college, where the students had had their work cut out for them. They'd pulled out what natural teeth Wayne had had, gray and rotting after the ravages of methamphetamines, and fitted him with an impressive set of dentures.

"Thanks," he says, grinning. "I feel good."

I look at Johnny B sitting next to Wayne, and the difference is startling. Johnny, according to Wayne, was working his way off narcotic pills by snorting heroin. And by the looks of him—thin, hollow-chested, and glassy-eyed—he's made a success of the transition. The fact that he hasn't yet graduated to shooting H makes him, in Wayne's estimation, still a reliable potential snitch. Wayne had met him the way he meets all his street contacts these days: trying to convince them to come to recovery meetings. No zealot like the newly reformed.

"Any word yet about Mary Grace?" Wayne asks, concern creasing his brow.

"I'm sorry, Wayne," I say, shaking my head. "Jackie and I have hired private detectives to continue searching. We're doing everything we can to find her."

Johnny leans over to Wayne and whispers something into his ear.

"Can we order something to eat?" Wayne asks. "Johnny here hasn't eaten in a few days."

We call over the waitress and order four hamburgers and three milkshakes. Johnny B orders a Yahoo Yoo-hoo by pointing to the drink menu, which is basically vodka with a splash of chocolate milk.

Johnny leans once more over Wayne's shoulder and whispers again.

Wayne nods and says, "Johnny wants to know if he's going to be paid for his information."

"Johnny," I say, forcing him to face me. "If you want to be a paid informant, you have to be registered with us first, and payment has to be approved by my lieutenant. And you also have to talk to me. Directly."

Johnny nods and clears his throat. "Uh, well, I was hoping to get some money, like, today."

His voice is grainy and hoarse, and peculiarly halting, as though he's not used to speaking above soft mutterings.

"Today, we can feed you and give you forty bucks for food," I say. "But this is strictly out of the goodness of our hearts."

His mouth twitches in disappointment, and he pulls himself up straighter in his seat. "How much will I be paid for information?"

Seth leans across the table until Johnny meets his gaze. "It depends on how good your information is."

"Wayne told us that you may know something about the Roy family," I say.

The waitress sets the drinks on the table, and Johnny drains half of his in a few gulps. He cups the glass in both hands, slowly rotating it between his palms as though he could coax it into a different shape.

"Johnny's from Arizona," Wayne says. "He's Native American."

"Tohono O'odham Nation," Johnny says defiantly, draining the rest of his glass.

"Why'd you leave?" I ask.

His eyes cut to my face, and there's nothing hazy about his distrust of me. "The reservation is on the border with Mexico," he says. "The Sinaloans have been using us as mules. I wouldn't, so they threatened to mess me up. But the Sinaloans aren't the only reason why I left."

"Tell her about the missionary group on the rez," Wayne prompts.

At that moment, the burgers are placed on the table, and we have to wait until Johnny is finished with his, which only takes a few minutes. When he's done, he leans back and signals the waitress that he wants another drink.

"Last spring a group of missionaries came," Johnny says.

"Church of the Flaming Sword, or some such shit like that. They were all young guys, some of them looked ex-military, except for one older, redheaded man who was their leader. Said he was a preacher. Remember those pictures of the Manson group? The people with the crazy eyes? They all looked like that. Spooked me the fuck out. A bunch of us wanted them off the land, but they'd been invited by one of the tribal elders. They stayed in his house and barn. The preacher went around telling people they'd been sent to liberate us from the Mexican cartels. Which was funny, because they started cooking up meth in the barn. Strong stuff. Started giving it away. People got hooked real fast."

The second drink arrives and he downs it like it's lemonade. He stares morosely into his glass, and I think I'm going to have to prompt him to speak again. But he shakes himself, as though he's just caught a sudden chill.

"Some Sinaloans came to chase them out. Four of the scariest fuckers you've ever seen. They show up in a big, expensive truck, all of them armed. They all walk into the barn. They don't walk out again."

His eyes meet mine, pupils pinned, and unblinking. "In the middle of the night, we heard screaming coming from a long way off. It went on for a good while, and then it just stopped. In the morning, nobody said anything to anybody about it. But there was a line at the barn. People waiting for their next handout of meth."

"What happened to the Sinaloans?" Seth asks.

Johnny turns his head to look at my partner. "Desert ate them."

"You said they were ex-military. What makes you think that?" I ask.

"I need another drink," Johnny says.

I signal the waitress and ask her for one more drink and the check. He waits silently until the drink is brought and, like the second one, downs it in a few swallows.

"What makes me think that?" Johnny asks. "Their weapons. They had military-grade firepower. Even had a grenade launcher in the hayloft. And they didn't just walk from here to there, they marched like they were in a fuckin' parade everywhere they went." He stares at Seth. "Self-important, puffed-up Anglos. Preacher said jump, they asked how high."

"What was this preacher's name?" I ask.

"I get my forty dollars now?" he asks.

Seth and I each pull out a twenty-dollar bill and hand them to him. He gives us his contact number, and he punches our numbers into his cell phone. Then he stuffs the forty dollars into his pocket and stands unsteadily. "Preacher's name was Martin. First or last name, I don't know."

"Why does Wayne think you know about Evangeline Roy?" I ask.

He places his hands, palms down, on the table and leans close enough for me to smell the alcohol on his breath. "'Cause I seen her. Martin'd been talking about 'Evangeline this' and 'Evangeline that,' like she was some kind of messiah. 'Evangeline's coming,' he would say. And one day, this car pulls up onto the rez, and this little woman gets out. Tiny, redheaded woman wearing ugly-ass shoes."

He swayed momentarily, as though he'd gone weak in the knees. "Looked like somebody's grandma. She even passed out candy to the kids. And then I saw her eyes. Looked right at me, and I almost shit myself. I left the next day. Packed a box of stuff, stole my uncle's car, and came here."

"So, you'd recognize her if you saw her again?" Seth asks.

Johnny staggers back a few steps, his head loose on his neck. "I'll never *not* see that old bitch, man." He taps his temple hard with his finger, as though trying to dislodge something from his brain, and then points at me. "You just make it worth my while to stick around long enough to be your scout."

"Where are you crashing these days?" Seth asks.

"Vickery Meadow in Five Points. Where the other brown people crash and burn."

He turns his back on us and walks away. He makes it to the exit door without falling and, thrusting it open with both hands, disappears into a blinding corona of sunlight.

"Didn't you bring him in your car?" Seth asks Wayne.

"Yeah," he says. "I guess he forgot." He scoots out of the booth and stands. "Hey, thanks for the grub. Let me know if you hear anything about Mary Grace."

We watch Wayne leave and sit for a moment more in silence.

Then Seth turns to me and asks, "You okay?"

Johnny B's burger basket is splattered with gobs of ketchup, the few remaining fries looking like fallen soldiers after a pitched battle. There's a vintage clock on the wall—the face of it a malevolent grinning cat—the large second hand counting down the passing of time in relentless jerking motions.

I consider ordering a Jameson, despite the fact that the workday is not over, but instead I wipe the grease off my hands and slide out of the booth. "Riot, ask me that question after my two weeks is up."

9

White Rock Lake
Saturday, September 13, 2014

Saturday dawns without a cloud in the sky and warm enough to wear shorts and a T-shirt. I decide to go running early—it'll be a perfect day to circumnavigate the lake and shed some of my anxieties in the process. I'm putting my sneakers on, going through a list of safety precautions in my head—make sure the alarm is set, keep all the doors locked—when Jackie comes out of the bedroom, yawning and holding her phone.

"The hospital just called," she says. "I've got to go in for the day."

"I didn't know you were on call this weekend," I say, lacing up my shoes.

She walks into the kitchen, and I hear the rattle of cups.

"We're really short-staffed," she says from the other room. "One radiologist out sick, and another had some kind of family emergency."

She walks back into the living room, holding a steaming mug of coffee.

"That's too bad, babe," I say, kissing her cheek. "I'll pick up dinner tonight."

Waving goodbye, I open the front door and breathe in the fresh air. The eight-plus miles will be just what I need. A nice long run to try and forget all the tensions of the last few days...

"Aren't you forgetting something?" Jackie asks.

I frown and nod. "Right. Your Glock has been cleaned and returned to the front console."

"No. The baby," she says.

Shit. The baby.

I'm only partially successful at hiding my irritation. "Can't we call Connie?"

"She works for us Monday through Friday. Saturdays and Sundays are her days off."

"What if I offer to pay her extra for a few hours?"

Jackie is walking away.

"Hey," I say. "Where are you going?"

"To the garage. To get the jogging stroller."

The jogging stroller. The large, egg-shaped baby carriage with three wheels that cost close to a grand, which Jackie gave me for my last birthday. I'd used it once. *Once,* and the baby wailed for the entire run. I was so wigged out by the time I returned to the house, cutting my run short, that I snuck one of Jackie's valium from the medicine cabinet. It's rare that I would take anything for anxiety—apart from a few shots of Jameson—but listening to a shrieking baby for close to forty-five minutes would shred anyone's nerves.

Jackie returns from the garage and wheels the jogger through the living room.

"Come on," I whine. Just like a baby. "She hated it the last time I took her out."

"Yes, but you've been spending more time with her. She's getting used to you."

As if on cue, we hear Elizabeth in her room, announcing that she's awake. Frowning and swearing under my breath, I sit in the living room, waiting impatiently for Jackie to dress and feed the baby. I consider, and then reject, the idea of wearing the SIG Sauer to the lake. Half an hour later, Jackie straps a gurgling infant into the stroller, stuffs some toys into the rear basket, kisses her goodbye, and walks into the bedroom to get dressed.

Elizabeth's head swivels, her distressed gaze following Jackie's passage out of sight. Her head whips back to face me, her eyes wide. She begins a frantic fidgeting, her lips puckering. But before she can work herself into a full meltdown, I grab the stroller, fling open the front door, and bounce it down the porch steps.

Whether from the initial jarring motion or the urgent running pace, the baby seems stunned into silence. After the first mile, I'm able to relax a little. I enter the park at the northern end and find that the trails are already busy with cyclists, runners, and walkers. I'm not alone in pushing a jogging stroller. Men and women huff away in various degrees of exertion while careening around the slower human obstacles in their path.

The lake is mostly calm, with only a slight chop, and several hundred yards from shore, I spot a rowing team, wearing matching colors, practicing the sweeping, coordinated movements to maintain rapid momentum. It's a women's group, their arms and legs toned and browned. I slow my pace to take in their graceful motions, but my tiny passenger begins making grunting noises—like an angry teacup piglet—and her legs begin to kick in consternation, relaxing only when I've picked up the pace again.

"Sheesh," I say. "First you hate the stroller. Now you can't go fast enough."

After a few moments, I check the top of Elizabeth's head and see that she's gazing at some ducks swimming in the shallows. Maybe she'll go to sleep. There is something hypnotic about watching sunlight reflecting off scores of little waves; the soft sparkling illumination works to calm the mind and relax the body. The thirty minutes of warmup has done what it always does for my well-being—all my limbs are working in concert together, and my thoughts are freed from the pull of the everyday.

I continue south past the White Rock Boat Club toward the bathhouse, the morning sun on my left cheek, bypassing solitary people walking their dogs. One of the dogs breaks free and makes a beeline for the water. He dives in with a mighty splash, the owner chasing after him, laughing and calling for the dog to come back onto dry land.

The splash triggers a memory from childhood. Being taken to the Prospect Park Zoo in Brooklyn by my mother. I'm ten years old, and it's just the two of us. We're sitting on benches at the outdoor Sea Lion Court, watching their enormous sleek bodies crash in and out of the water. They are performing the usual tricks: waving their flippers, taking bows, leaping from the pool through hoops. We had saved the aquatic show for last, having already visited the other exhibits: the aviary, the big-cat enclosures, the monkey cages. It's early spring, and the weather is the perfect mix of intense sunlight tempered by cool breezes. My mother is seated next to me, and she's wearing a simple black wool dress, her dark hair pulled loosely back, and she's sporting oversize sunglasses. She's smoking, holding the cigarette between long, elegant fingers, and I realize with a jolt, and probably for the first time, that my mother is beautiful. Not in the insipid manner of magazine models, or in the aggressively sensual manner of some celebrity actresses. Her facial features are too strong, too pointedly Slavic to be considered attractive in the classic sense. And she's too thin to be thought of as voluptuous.

But she carries herself with a certain grace and a tantalizing reticence that draw people to her. And she has a deep, throaty laugh that invites confidences. She loves music—especially jazz and classical. I can't remember a time as a child when the radio or the stereo was not on. At least when my father was out of the house.

It's a rare moment of complete, giddy joy. The sun reflecting almost painfully off the sea lion tank, the silly antics of the trainers, the applause and laughter of the audience, the lingering sugary film of cotton candy in my mouth, the oily, pungent smell of the fish treats for the performing animals— all combine in a heady blend that shouts, *This is a happy childhood.*

I'm only vaguely aware of the man sitting next to me. He's large, taking up a lot of space on the bench, his leg pressing against mine in an increasingly annoying way. He doesn't laugh so much as chuckle, a weird breathy stutter of exhalations in between inaudible mutterings. The biggest sea lion is dancing with one of the trainers—a young woman wearing a revealing sailor's outfit. Everyone is loudly singing along with the canned music: "Boogie Woogie Bugle Boy."

And then the man next to me puts his hand on my leg. I'm wearing shorts, and his palm is moist and clammy against my bare skin.

Surprised, I look up at his face, thinking that he's forgotten he doesn't know me. That perhaps he thinks he's sitting next to one of his own kids. The man is looking at me, his eyes narrowed, mouth open wetly as though in pain, his breath now coming in rapid pulses. His other hand is in his lap, rubbing at his pants as though trying to remove a stain.

Then another hand reaches across my lap from the other side—my mother's side, her fingers still grasping a burning cigarette. And in a hard, downward motion, she brings the glowing tip of the slender white cylinder onto the back of the man's hand. Even before he can react, I can smell the acrid odor of burning flesh. The man leaps up, yelling, holding his wounded hand protectively at his chest, and knocks over half a dozen people trying to get away.

Astonished, I look up at my mother. She pulls her sunglasses up onto her head so I can see her eyes, but her changing expression is hard to read—victorious...sad...resigned? After a long moment, she puts one arm around my shoulder and hugs me close. Pulling her glasses down again, she points her face back toward the dancing sea lions, and whispers, "I'm sorry."

In the same moment that I'm drawn back to White Rock Lake and the still-swimming dog and my steady progress along the jogging trail, I feel a rush of motion to my left. Instinctively, my mind goes into defensive mode...*Evangeline Roy*...A hulking, swiftly moving form is in my peripheral vision, and a loud voice close to my ear shouts rudely, "Get out of the way!"

I strike out with my left arm, my fist connecting with a human form. There's a loud crash as the cyclist is flung off the trail. It's a young man, dressed in fashionable cycling gear, lying sprawled next to his upended bike, the wheels still spinning wildly. The man had been going very fast within a hair's breadth of me, and if he had collided with the carriage, there would have been serious injury.

The man does a crab crawl on his back out from under the bike, and his face is bunched in furious outrage. In another few seconds, he'll be on his feet, yelling and threatening.

In four paces I'm standing over him, all five feet eleven of me, my hair on fire, my finger jabbed in his face. *"Hey, fucktard!"* I scream at the top of my lungs. "You blind? I've got a baby here! You could have killed her. You get up now and I swear to Christ I'll knock your jaw into your brainpan."

I'm breathing brimstone now, and my vision is tunneled, focused exclusively on the man's face, whose expression is now one of fear. He holds both hands up in a placating gesture. I kick some grass in his direction and walk away.

I begin my run again, refueled now with an excess of adrenaline, but not before checking on Elizabeth, who I'm certain will be crying. But she's fast asleep, and she stays that way for the rest of the run.

10

Sunday is typically one of my favorite days of the week. At least it was before I had to worry about Evangeline Roy and El Cuchillo returning to haunt me. It's the day I go running with Seth—usually at seven a.m., and a distance of seven to eight miles—followed by a huge breakfast at Norma's Café. Most of the time I go running by myself (yesterday being a notable exception), but I've found that the sessions with my partner have improved my endurance and my running times. Our natural competitiveness is the rocket fuel driving us beyond sore muscles, assorted blisters, shin splints, and on occasion in my case a hangover from Saturday-night festivities.

Seth says that the most potent weapon in his continuing recovery is the endorphins he gets from his daily extreme-workout routines—lifting weights and Thai boxing, Muay Thai being his new adrenaline fix, overtaking his fondness for tae kwon do—and the weekend runs with me. When we first started running together in the spring, he was out of shape, and more than a little irritated that I'd leave him in the dust. Lately, however, he's managed to find last-minute reserves of strength and blow past me. I do not take these losses lightly, and, in turn, they've caused me to increase my own time at the gym. At this rate, we should soon be ready for a national law enforcement strength-and-fitness championship.

After a quick shower and change at our respective houses, we're eating breakfast at Norma's Café, reviewing incoming intelligence from our department's CIs, when I get a call from deputy chief Ernest Darnell of the Terrell Police Department. He tells me that earlier that morning they picked up an "Unauthorized Discharge"—an escaped patient—from the Terrell psychiatric hospital, who was only a few miles from police headquarters. He said she had insisted on talking to me. That she had information as to the exact whereabouts of Evangeline Roy.

"Our chief got the BOLO from DPD that you were actively searching for her," Darnell says.

After a few beats, I ask, "And how would a mental patient even know who I am or that we're looking for Evangeline Roy?"

Darnell exhales. "She said the Roy woman visited her in the hospital. And told her to give you the message. The hospital staff wouldn't listen to her, so she took a hike, knowing she'd be picked up by us. She told one of the patrol officers, who in turn passed the message on to me. We checked with the hospital visitor registration after we returned her to care and, sure enough, found a signature dated two days ago: *E. Roy.* Designated as 'family friend.'"

My eyes must be bugging out of my head, because Seth mouths, "What's wrong?"

"Are there any security cameras at the front desk?"

"You kidding me?" Darnell asks. "They barely have a budget for the cameras in the violent offenders' ward."

"Can I talk to her over the phone?" I ask.

"She doesn't have phone privileges right now. So you'll either have to talk to the medical staff, who won't tell you anything, or you'll have to arrange a visit with her at the hospital through the weekend admin director, Mr. Rappaport. I can call him and let him know you're coming."

"That'd be great. What's the woman in for? I mean, is she even lucid?"

"Have no idea," Darnell says. "But I know she was returned to a minimum-security wing, so she's probably harmless."

"When are visiting hours?" I ask.

"Today from two to four p.m."

I thank Darnell for giving Rappaport a heads-up that I'll be visiting the hospital today with my partner and disconnect the call.

"What the hell was that all about?" Seth asks.

"Looks like we're driving to Terrell."

When we're in the car, I call Jackie and leave a message that I'll be with Seth for a few hours, following a lead. "And don't open the door for anybody," I warn.

The drive to Terrell takes about forty-five minutes, and I relate Darnell's call to my partner.

"Why did Evangeline pick this particular woman?" Seth asks.

"I don't know. Maybe Evangeline really is related to her. The fact that she's been committed to a mental asylum would be in keeping with the family MO."

"I hear that," Seth says. "You ever been to the hospital?"

I shake my head, and Seth gives a theatrical shudder.

"The stuff of nightmares," he says. "State hospital over a hundred years old. More than half the patients are considered a dangerous threat to society: rapists, murderers, serial pedophiles. The community keeps trying to revamp the place, but so far the state won't cough up the money. They even tried to privatize it but got no takers.

"I dated a nurse for a while who briefly worked in the geriatric ward there. She had to quit when her health took a dive. State inspectors found black mold behind most of the walls, free-floating asbestos fibers in air-quality samples, vermin in the air ducts. Awful place. It'd been two years since she'd left, and she was still having night sweats about it. I'll tell you one thing, Riz, I'd rather off myself than be committed to that place."

The rest of the drive to Terrell is uneventful, the weekend traffic light, the surrounding scenery as dull and flat as the surface of a brown paper bag. We drive through the middle of town—a collection of small, two-story businesses, some of them built before the Great Depression. A few blocks north and east of Main Street we arrive at the entrance to the sprawling hospital complex. We drive past the abandoned stone edifices typical of large asylums built in the late nineteenth century, overgrown with ivy runners, the windows crusted over with decades of dirt. The newer wings, at least those built after the Second World War, are set farther back from the road. It's a nice day, but I don't see anyone, patients or staff, outside taking the air.

We park in the visitor's lot and go in the front entrance. The receptionist is a large woman wearing street clothes, and she frowns when we show her our badges announcing who we are.

"I'd like to see Mr. Rappaport," I say.

She gives a labored sigh and picks up the phone. She murmurs something into the mouthpiece and then points to some chairs.

"Have a seat," she says. "He'll be out when he can."

She gives us a dark look for good measure and then goes back to reading her magazine.

I stage-whisper to Seth, "Where's your charm now, cowboy?"

After twenty minutes or so, a man in a rumpled doctor's coat, tinged gray from too many cycles in an industrial dryer, approaches us on squeaking shoes and holds out his hand for us to shake.

"I'm so sorry I've made you wait," Rappaport says. "We've had a difficult day."

He looks like he's had a difficult year: bloodshot eyes surrounded by droopy, bruised-looking flesh, a day-old beard, and bedhead hair.

He leads us down a hallway to his office and moves some files off the visitor's chairs so we can sit down. He could build a substantial fortress out of the stacks of paperwork and patient folders covering every flat surface.

"Deputy Darnell called me and said you'd be coming in," Rappaport says.

I nod. "He told me that one of your patients went walkabout today—"

"Yes," he interjects. "Mrs. Carmody. Elaine Carmody."

"He also said that Mrs. Carmody told the patrolman who picked her up that she needed to get a message to me. In person."

Rappaport smiles and ducks his head, almost as though he's embarrassed. "Mrs. Carmody is a sweet lady but completely delusional. She often has lengthy conversations with people who aren't there."

"And yet she knew my name. She also said she was visited two days ago by a woman who wrote her name in the visitor's log: E. Roy. I think that woman may have been Evangeline Roy, someone we are eager to apprehend."

"Yes, well…I wasn't here on that day. If I had been, I would have taken note. Mrs. Carmody has been with us for over a year, and she's never had a visitor before this past Friday."

"Do you have any family on record for her?" I ask.

"No. As far as the hospital records show, she has no next of kin."

I look at Seth, and he shrugs.

"Could we speak with her?" I ask.

Rappaport begins to shake his head. "She's had quite the adventure today. I'm not sure—"

"Could you just ask her?" Seth asks, leaning forward and giving the admin his best earnest look. "We'd only take a few moments. And, who knows, a second visit might be good for her. You can sit in if you think she'll be more comfortable."

Rappaport still looks uncertain. "I'd have to okay it with her doctor. I tell you what, I'll try contacting him. If he okays it, I'll have her brought to the common area."

He directs us back to the front waiting room, where we sit down again. This time the receptionist doesn't even deign to look up from her reading material. I stare at the dilapidated and water-stained ceiling—missing tiles exposing decaying air ducts, electrical wiring hanging down in dangerous-looking clusters—and a memory surfaces of my mother taking me to visit one of her aging aunts who'd been hospitalized at Bellevue psychiatric. I was thirteen at the time. Old enough to have heard plenty of taunts and threats from my father that he'd commit me to Bellevue for acting crazy. The crazy in my case was typical teenage angst, infused with a good dose of stubborn defiance.

The first thing I remember about the hospital, where we'd been escorted by a burly attendant through several locked, cagelike doors, was the smell: human excrement, with an underlying stench of something—milk, food, human body parts—rotting. And the sounds. The shouting, shrieking, and calling out of agonized or fearful or enraged displacement. A combined symphony of hopelessness.

The second thing is my poor demented aunt screaming in Polish, *"Zatrzymaj to, zatrzymaj to, zatrzymaj to…"*

Make it stop.

Mention Bellevue to a lot of older New Yorkers, and they'll shake their head or shudder the way Seth did about this facility. Compared to the old Bellevue, Terrell seems like a summer camp.

Rappaport approaches us and says, "The doctor has given his permission. Follow me, please."

We trail Rappaport's squeaky progress down a maze of hallways to an elevator, which takes us to the third floor, then through a series of locked doors to a large common room painted a chalky blue color. The odor of decrepitude is less toxic than I remember from Bellevue, but it's definitely present. The admin directs us to sit anywhere and says he'll return shortly with Mrs. Carmody.

There are several worn and musty sofas placed around the room, but Seth and I pick two straight-back chairs to perch on. There is absolute silence. It's after two o'clock, but we are seemingly the only visitors on-site. There are drawings done by the hospital's patients tacked up on the walls, some more sophisticated than others. A few of them look like toddlers executed them. One drawing re-creates in great detail the outside of one of the older sanatorium buildings. At each Gothic window the faces of women appear, pale and sickly, all depicted with their mouths open, singing. Or screaming.

"Well, this is a comforting space," Seth mutters to me.

Less than five minutes later, Rappaport reappears with a woman. She's dressed in street clothes—sweatshirt and drawstring pants, sneakers—and is fiftyish, her light brown hair pulled back into a ponytail, and completely unremarkable. Other than having a slightly myopic air, with watery blue eyes wide and unfocused, she doesn't present as someone who's been locked up in a psych ward for over a year.

Rappaport tells her to sit on the sofa closest to us, and then he leans against the wall behind her to give some semblance of privacy. She looks at us with open curiosity, a slight expectant smile on her face.

"Mrs. Carmody, do you know who I am?" I ask.

She blinks a few times and doesn't answer. I look at Rappaport, and he shakes his head discouragingly.

I lean in a bit closer. "I'm Detective Betty Rhyzyk from the Dallas Police Department."

More vapid blinks, but she smiles more broadly.

"I heard you left the hospital earlier today. You told the policeman who picked you up that you needed to talk to me. That you'd been directed by someone to contact me. Perhaps the visitor you had on Friday, who signed the guest register as E. Roy?"

She presses her fingers against her lips, which have begun to twitch wildly. Her throat is convulsing, as though she's trying to swallow something that wants to escape her mouth. I realize that she's silently laughing.

"I knew she'd come," Mrs. Carmody says finally. "She told me to wait patiently, that she'd find me. And she did. She came to me."

"Who came to you, Mrs. Carmody?"

"She took me in when no one else would have me. Gave me succor. Fed me, clothed me. Got me off drugs. Folded me into her family. Gave me the *word*," she whispers hoarsely.

I already know who she's talking about, but I ask the question anyway. "Could you give us a name, please?"

She's not laughing now, and her mild manner has retreated behind an increasing ferocity of tone. She leans in closer, her face contorted not so much with anger as with a feral certainty. The certainty of a religious convert. A martyr not afraid of the pyre.

"Evangeline Roy," she trumpets.

Rappaport has taken a few steps toward us, but I hold up a hand to stay him.

I keep my breathing calm, and I resist the impulse to pull back. Her face is six inches from mine, her two eyes blue beacons of fierce resolve. I remember the fire-and-brimstone-laced language of the Roy family cult. The cult that caused otherwise reasonable people to do unreasonable things. I can only imagine the obsessive commitment if a follower was full-blown crazy to begin with.

"What words are we talking about, Elaine?" I ask, deciding our unique status of being up close and personal with Evangeline puts us on a first-name basis.

"She wanted me to give you a message today," she whispers, her eyes alive with a malicious mirth.

I lean in even closer. "And what message is that?"

Her fevered breath in my ear.

"That Evangeline is in your house."

I rear back, every nerve firing. "What are you—"

"You're here. And she's there. Right now!" She's giggling again, and I stand up, fumbling for my phone.

Seth jumps to his feet as well. Moving in, Rappaport pulls a convulsing Elaine Carmody to her feet. She shrieks with hysterical laughter even as Rappaport drags her from the room and down the hall.

"You can't hide from her," she yells. "She'll find you. She will find you—"

Jackie's phone is ringing, but there's no answer. I disconnect and try again. Still no answer. Looking at Seth, I yell, "Call Craddock or Ryan...call somebody, anybody, and tell them to get to my house...*now*! Evangeline Roy is there."

We're twenty minutes west of Terrell, Seth driving a steady ninety miles an hour, when my phone finally rings. It's Jackie's number, and I answer it fearfully. I'd called every few minutes with no answer.

"Betty, what the fuck is going on?" It's Jackie's voice. "I've got four patrol cars here, and a hundred messages from you."

My heart is pounding so hard I think I'll pass out. "Where've you been?"

"I was taking a nap with the baby."

Elizabeth is crying in the background, and Jackie's voice sounds raw, scared, and more than a little pissed off.

"Have they checked the house?" I demand.

"They've checked every square inch, inside and out. Will you please tell me what's going on?"

I collapse against the car door with relief. "Just have the patrol officers stay with you until we get back. Seth and I are fine. I'll tell you about it when I get home, which should be in about thirty minutes."

We make it to my house in twenty, and I hold on to Jackie—who's holding the baby—like I'm never going to let go.

11

Dallas Police Department, North Central Division
Monday, September 15, 2014

Holy cannoli," Craddock says after I've filled the team in on Sunday's events in Terrell. "Sorry I couldn't respond yesterday. I was dove hunting with some buddies. We don't even get phone reception out on the lease."

"Which is why you picked it in the first place," Seth says, and Craddock laughs.

"So, you think it was just an elaborate hoax?" Ryan asks me. "A way to get under your skin?"

"I honestly don't know," I say. "I've got surveillance on my house for the week just to be sure. One thing I'm certain of is that Evangeline Roy is going to keep making her presence known until she's caught."

"Or manages a way to confront you personally," Seth says.

"That'll singe her short and curlies," Philbo mutters to his partner, Esparza.

There is a moment of silence, all eyes looking everywhere but at me. It was said just loud enough to make certain I heard.

I look sharply at Philbo. "Are you referring to me or to Evangeline Roy?"

Philbo doesn't answer, so I turn to Craddock and Ryan.

"You want to fill us in on the progress, if any, you made over the weekend with your CIs or law enforcement contacts?"

"We mostly made a lot of phone calls," Craddock says. "We split up the area west of here. I called Denton and Tarrant County Sheriff's Offices. Kevin called Johnson County Sheriff's Office in Cleburne, and also Granbury PD, but it's been pretty quiet all over. No big uptick in drug traffic to signal a new source. Also, zilch from my CI in Arlington."

"No more red wigs sighted?" I ask.

"Nada," Ryan says. "We did make the drive down to the DEA Dallas office Saturday afternoon."

The office where special agent in charge Don Haslett parks his briefcase on the rare times he's not out in the field. A large glass-and-stone building surrounded by a sturdy iron fence, a stone's throw from the Trinity River, DEA Dallas covers the area as far west as Lubbock and as far east as Tyler.

"We met with Fred Dunlap, one of Haslett's subagents," Craddock says. "Don had told him of your conversation with El Cuchillo, so they've been made aware of the possible presence of Evangeline Roy in Texas again."

"Probable presence," Seth corrects.

"We managed to contact the receptionist on duty at the hospital on Friday," I say. "She gave us a description of the E. Roy who visited Elaine Carmody. It was a match to Evangeline.

"Detectives Esparza, Philbo, anything to report?"

"Saturday we trolled the streets around Deep Ellum and Tent City but came up with nothing," Philbo says. "Jetta Joe here had to go home to the wife and kids at dinnertime, but I stayed and talked to a couple of my regular night-stalkers. No reports of any rogue redheads."

Esparza says, "Ditto from me."

"Anything about this guy Flaco?" I ask.

A chorus of noes.

"All right," I say, disappointed. "Let's keep looking. Keep me informed."

I sit in my office, feeling deflated. I'd managed to go an entire hour without worrying about Mary Grace, that concern crowded out of my head by my greater anxiety for the safety of Jackie and Elizabeth. It seems that the red wigs popping up all over Texas, as well as the message from Elaine Carmody, did what they were intended to do. Made me aware that the Roy matriarch was in my backyard again. And turned that awareness into a constant, waking fearfulness.

My phone rings. It's Peg Bartles.

"Give me some good news."

"Sorry," she says. "No can do. We've pretty much exhausted downtown. I did talk to your CI Wayne and got some names of people to contact. We're moving farther south of I-30 and east of 45 for a couple of days. Rocky's doing most of the street pounding. I just sit in the van and hover, like the good den mother I am."

"Okay, thanks for calling. Tell Rocky to be careful. We just had a drug-related gang shooting in that quadrant a few days ago."

Peg expels a breath. "Don't I know it. I'll check in tomorrow or the next day."

We disconnect, and Craddock, holding a half-eaten MoonPie still in its wrapper, walks into the office.

"May have a lead on this Flaco guy," he says.

I motion for him to sit down. He puts the MoonPie on the desk and pats it absentmindedly, as though fearing it'll grow legs and wander off. "Remember when Ryan worked that high school drug party bust with you last year? Well, he ended up mentoring one of the arrested teenagers through Cops and Kids."

"Yeah, Ryan told me about his sponsee."

"Anyway," Craddock continues, "after our meeting this morning, Ryan calls this kid on the off chance he may have heard about our dealer through some of his druggie friends. Sure enough, the kid has heard there's a new dealer in town. Someone named Flaco."

"Could be a coincidence. Lot of skinny Hispanic guys nicknamed Flaco. Ryan find out where he's slinging his wares?" I ask.

Craddock grins and picks up his MoonPie. "You're going to love this." He takes a bite and mumbles, "J's Food Mart."

I walk briskly to Seth's desk and ask him, "Want to unchain yourself for a few hours?"

He grabs his jacket from the back of his chair. "You don't have to ask me twice. Where're we going?"

"Whitehurst Avenue," I say.

My partner looks at me incredulously for a moment. "Ah, hell no."

★ ★ ★

Several years ago, Seth and I worked a buy-and-bust in front of a tiny, nondescript convenience store named J's Food Mart. That area in Northeast Dallas, over a twenty-year period, had come to resemble a poisonous jelly donut—the outer rim of run-down apartments occupied mostly with hardworking and underserved families. The toxic center, represented by the convenience store and surrounding strip mall and parking lots, was filled at all times with prostitutes, high-dollar crapshooters, and gangbangers. And, of course, drug dealers. Lots and lots of dealers. The DEA and ATF had been working to help clean things up, but most of the busts were still left to Dallas police.

A spate of shootings fueled by competition between gangs had caused the death of twin toddlers—the bullets piercing the thin walls of their bedroom—as well as a father of eight children. The gunfight involved at least two dozen rival gangbangers and was commenced in broad daylight on the stretch of Whitehurst Avenue in front of the food mart. The shoot-out was the tipping point. The chief did a major sweep and then set up a special task force to remove the remaining dealers with buy-and-busts.

Perversely, it wasn't just the poor and desperate buying the drugs. It had become a mecca, and a rite of passage, for thrill-seeking rich teenagers. The high was as much about walking away from the strip mall alive as it was from the drugs. Ironically, because the dealers didn't want to destroy the darling little cash cows, the kids were probably safer on Whitehurst than in other disreputable neighborhoods.

The dealer we had set up was a guy with a long record and, according to the pavement princesses whom he pimped, a very short fuse. He was also a speed freak and as a result extremely nervous and paranoid. His street name was Jizzy. His favorite turn of phrase being "That's right. Jizzy all over you now." *Har-har-har.*

I had made several small buys from him, posing as a onetime rich Highland Park resident brought low through an addiction to Oxy. My hair unwashed, my clothes torn and dirty, I made a pitiful spectacle, though it didn't stop Jizzy from trying to talk me into working for him. We had set him up to do one last larger buy in front of J's Food Mart—several hundred Oxy for ten bucks each. When I leaned over to check the number of pills in the plastic bag, he slid his hand down my shirt. Reflexively, I pushed his arm away, knocking the bag and most of the pills onto the sidewalk.

He freaked, pulled his pistol, and, screaming profanities at me, pressed the barrel against my head. The world shrank to a narrow beam directed at the convenience store sign, and I wondered if my last irrational thought would be *Does the 'J' stand for Jizzy?*

I took a ragged breath and said, "How about fifteen dollars a pill? And I do all the picking up."

And Jizzy, without missing a beat, tucked his gun back into his pants and said enthusiastically, "Yeah, baby, I'm all over you now."

In a gesture of renewed goodwill, he actually helped me pick up some of the pills. I completed the buy, and a rattled group of nearby undercovers, including Seth, made the arrest.

Seth said to me later, "I really thought for a moment I was going to have to get me a new partner."

I was sitting in his car, still shaking from nerves. "Yeah, well, you may still want to. I think I shit my pants back there."

★★★

Now we exit I-635 at Skillman and drive the short distance past sprawling apartment buildings to the Whitehurst Avenue strip center that accommodates a *lavandería,* a dollar store, a bail bondsman's office, and a pet supply store. J's Food Mart is closed, boards covering the windows. A piece of graffiti over one of the planks reads, IF YOU CAN READ THIS YOU PROBLY DON'T LIVE HERE.

We park and sit on the far side of the nearly abandoned lot, observing the comings and goings of people shopping, and hope not to get made as cops. At least not right away. Before we left the station, I had borrowed one of Seth's extra T-shirts that he always keeps in his desk. Nothing shouts plainclothes detective louder than a blue blazer, slacks with a wide belt substantial enough to support a badge and holster, and sensible shoes.

To fill the time, I tell him about my worries for Mary Grace, and about Elizabeth's slow progress in warming up to me. Seth tells me about his new girlfriend, Patty. They've been dating three months, which is quite a record for my partner. He usually goes through women like a shark through a school of mackerel, but maybe he's met "the one."

"Only problem is," he says, his eyes scanning the storefronts, "she's got cats."

"Maybe they'll grow on you, partner."

"I'll tell you what's grown on me. Cat hair, and lots of it."

I pull one long strand of blond hair from his black T-shirt and hold it up to the light. "This belongs to Tabby, does it?"

Seth laughs. "She's fine with my not drinking. Works out

a lot, eats healthy. I think she's good for me." He catches me giving him a look. "What?"

"Imagine that," I say. "Bad boy turned good. Just don't start taking yoga classes. We'll have to stage a second intervention."

Seth is looking at something intently through the windshield.

"What is it?" I ask.

He points to the *lavandería* in the middle of the strip. Earlier we'd watched a woman with two small kids load up a washer with dirty clothes and then leave again. She'd been the only one in the place. But now there are three men inside, and they're not doing laundry. They're standing at the large plate-glass window, their arms crossed over their chests, looking at us.

"They must have come in the back entrance," Seth says. He pulls a pair of binoculars out of the center console and focuses on the men. He then passes them to me. "Take a look at the middle guy."

The man in the middle is taller than the other two and quite slender. He's wearing a V-neck T-shirt. On one side of his neck is tattooed a large *X;* on the other side, the number 8. Barrio 18.

A sudden hard rap on the passenger-side window startles us both. It's a kid about ten or eleven years old. He makes a motion for me to roll down my window. When I do, he hands me a piece of paper and then bolts away.

The handwritten text on the paper reads *I'm watching you.* I've seen the handwriting before. It's the same as on the note that Evangeline sent me last January when she returned my Saint Michael medallion. The one she'd taken after kidnapping me.

I snatch the binoculars up again and focus on the tall man inside the laundry. He makes a gun with his fingers, his thumb as the trigger. He directs his hand at me, as though taking aim, and fires.

"*Hola* Flaco," I whisper.

Seth calls for backup, but by the time the patrol cars arrive, the three men have gone, having retreated quietly through some rear exit.

I notify the rest of the team, as well as Special Agent Don Haslett's office, that we'll be first concentrating on the area in and around the Whitehurst strip mall. Flaco's territory will be wider than this section of Dallas, but he's in my backyard. The strip mall is only six miles from my house.

Seth and I do a walk-through of the *lavandería*. We don't find anything other than some discarded cigarette butts, empty detergent packets, and unclaimed articles of clothing.

Something shiny on the floor catches my eye: a crumpled cigar band. I scoop it up with a tissue and show it to Seth. It's a Baccarat Gordo, a popular Honduran cigar brand.

"Well, well," I say, pocketing the band. "Our skinny friend likes to smoke fat cigars. Let's see if we can pull any prints off this."

"Now, wasn't this more fun than doing paperwork?" Seth asks.

I resist the urge to do a jig. "You have no idea."

12

The House
Monday, September 15, 2014

I pull into the driveway, taking note of the manned unmarked police car a few houses down. Before going home, I'd first circled our block and was relieved to spot a second patrol car with two officers watching the entrance to the alleyway. Our front-to-back surveillance protection, in addition to our internal home-security system. The lieutenant hadn't wasted any time notifying the deputy chief of the North Central Division of the threat made to me and mine by Evangeline Roy. Cops don't like it when other cops are threatened. It's only for seven days, but I'm grateful for the extra eyes, nonetheless. I give the undercover in the front a subtle wave and walk into the house.

James Earle is on the floor in the living room, belly down, making faces at Elizabeth, who is strapped into a rocking seat, laughing unreservedly as only a chubby seven-month-old infant can. She'd also, at some point, gotten a good grasp of his well-greased hair, because it's standing up as though he'd stuck his finger in an electrical outlet. Her hands are still glistening with aromatic styling gel. He grins at me sheepishly and sits up, smoothing back his hair.

"Hey, Red," he rasps. "How's it going? Any word about Mary Grace?"

I sit down next to him. The baby has stopped laughing, and she gives me her best side-eye.

"Not yet," I say. "The PI called me earlier today. They're trying."

"You see our cop friends outside?" he asks. "I thought I was going to get my head blown off when I pulled up in front of the house. Fortunately they talked to Connie and got it straightened out. Those detectives weren't fooling around."

"Good to know. We've also got two patrolmen by the alleyway in back."

"Well, that should make you feel a little safer. I volunteered to sleep on the couch for a few nights. Help keep Connie company during the day."

I try to hide a smile. Connie's an attractive single woman, and at least thirty years younger than James. "That a new shirt you're wearing?" I ask him, teasingly.

At that moment Connie walks in from the kitchen, drying her hands on a dish towel. "Hey, you're home," she says. "Jackie said she'd be a little late at the hospital."

She sits next to Elizabeth, who looks at her with wide-eyed adoration. I should be overjoyed that the baby has bonded so strongly with her caregiver. But I feel the sharp jab of jealousy. Or maybe, if I'm being entirely honest, it's closer to the sting of resentment. It was love at first sight between child and nanny. At this rate, I may need to be satisfied with a reluctant hug.

James Earle is now looking at Connie with frank appreciation as well, his leathered face softened by the renewed flame of hopefulness. I feel guilty for allowing such petty thoughts. He's always been there for Jackie and me with hardly a thought for himself.

Standing up, I say, "I'm going to change. James, you know you're welcome to stay with us as long as you like. But I think we'll be okay for the night."

I look for a moment at the two of them seated on either side of Elizabeth, laughing and talking, completely at ease with each other. A long-repressed memory of Uncle Benny strikes me. Benny, at our house in Brooklyn, sitting at the table with my mother, laughing and talking. Tea and poppy-seed cake on the table between them. The smoke from my mother's cigarette curling through the air like a welcome banner. I stand at the entry to the kitchen, staring at my handsome uncle still in his police uniform, and for the millionth time I wish that he were my father, not the angry drunk married to my mother.

I'm fourteen years old, tall and gangly, with unruly red hair, pale skin that refuses to tan, and already a complete awareness of my lack of romantic interest in boys. But there are no adequate words to describe my devotion to Detective Sergeant Bernard Rhyzyk. He faces me briefly and winks, and then turns back to my mother.

I listen to them talking for a while longer, relishing the convivial wash of welcomed, familiar company, watching my mother's finger gently tracing the rim of her teacup. It's unsettling, this sensual circling of fragile porcelain, saved only for special occasions. I look at my mother's slanting eyes, her smiling mouth, and the realization, like a pole

slammed into my head, comes to me: she's in love with him...
and he with her.

My first emotions toward this understanding are soaring,
jubilant, victorious—and more than a little vengeful. This
would deservedly hurt my father. And then, hard on the
heels of those first thoughts, is the terrible knowledge that,
in retaliation, Phillip Rhyzyk would do more than hurt his
brother and wife. He would kill them.

I wanted to call to them, to warn them of this danger. Tell
them that if I could see it, then certainly my father could too.
I stood in an agony of silence until Uncle Benny thanked his
sister-in-law for the tea, gave me a quick hug, and walked out
the front door.

James Earle is saying something to me.

"You all right?" he asks. "You look like you just saw a
ghost."

"I'm fine. Just remembered something I'd forgotten."

When Jackie returns from the hospital, I tell her of this
memory. We're eating a late supper together in the kitchen, the
baby sleeping in her crib. James Earle left soon after Connie,
but not before pulling me aside and asking my opinion about
dying his gray hair dark again. I assured him he was a silver
fox, and he left with a smile on his lips.

Jackie, ever the romantic, has dimmed the kitchen lights so
she can light a few candles. She's changed into a loose shirt
that falls off one shoulder, exposing her rose tattoo at the
collarbone. Her hair is still damp from the shower and falls
in waves around her neck. No matter how badly my day has

gone, looking at Jackie by candlelight smooths out all the rough edges.

"Why do you think I buried that memory for so many years?" I ask. "It seems a revelation like that would have stuck with me."

"Well," Jackie says, toying with her fork, "you said that your father finding out about it would have gone badly for your mother, and for Benny." She reaches over and squeezes my hand. "You were being protective of them. Your father was a dangerous man, and you made sure he wouldn't find out from you by burying that knowledge."

"I think remembering it might have given me solace that my mom had at least found a little joy in her life."

Jackie pours more wine into my glass. "Was Benny ever married?"

"For ten years," I say. "Aunt Mary. I was pretty young when she died of a stroke, but I remember her being a really nice lady."

"And he never remarried?"

I shake my head. "He kept a photo of Mary on his desk always. It was on his bedside table in the hospital when he died." For a moment I stare into the candle flame, wondering whatever happened to the picture of his wife. His few remaining personal items had been mailed to me after his death, but I don't recall ever receiving the photograph.

Jackie stands behind me and wraps her arms around my neck. "You're sad," she whispers in my ear and kisses my cheek. "Leave the dishes. Come to bed with me."

★ ★ ★

Later, I watch Jackie sleeping, curled on her side, her eyelids fluttering in dream mode. I can't imagine my life without her. Without her love, her understanding, her passion. And I wonder what it must have been like for my mother to have had so little joy in her life, apart from whatever happiness she gleaned from her two children—one of whom, my brother, committed suicide in his twenties. And the other one destroying any hope of grandchildren. I can only think she would have delighted in holding Elizabeth. And she would have been more than a little amused by my ward's unenthusiastic responses to me, Helen Nowak's wild, risk-taking, won't-back-down daughter.

It's not that I disliked the idea of having my own children so much as I didn't like the idea of *anyone's* children. I was always the asshole who sighed loudly whenever anyone boarded a plane with a whimpering child, or scowled at the kid having a temper tantrum in a store. Who glared fiercely at parents who couldn't control their screaming brats in a restaurant. No wonder Elizabeth recoiled from me. Babies are canny. Closer to beasts than to human beings. They can smell disapproval from a hundred yards away.

My mother, on the other hand, adored babies, and never passed up an opportunity to coo over one. A melody begins to play in my head; a lullaby sung to us when we were little. I whisper the words, *"Oj lulaj, lulaj, Siwe, oczka stulaj...."*

Go to sleep, go to sleep, close your blue eyes...

The very act of humming the song begins to make me drowsy. I snuggle closer to Jackie, and, breathing in her scent, fall into a restless sleep.

13

I've directed the team—Craddock, Ryan, Philbo, Esparza, and Seth—to meet collectively at the station every morning before dispersing out onto the streets, at least until we get a fix on either Flaco's location or Evangeline Roy's.

I point to the large map detailing the division districts in the greater Dallas area. "DPD Patrol Units, sector two-forty, will handle the on-the-street canvassing in and around Whitehurst Avenue, where we were yesterday. I want this team to spot-focus on some individual areas closer to us. And I'd like all of you to check in personally, face-to-face, with any CI you've got. No more phone calls, unless it's them calling you with any sightings or updates."

I pass around a printout of some hot spots. "You're all aware of DPD's most recent TAAG posting."

Started in 2008, the Targeted Action Area Grid is a statistical data-gathering program directed by the chief of police to highlight neighborhoods in Dallas where conditions are favorable for crimes to occur. Released daily, it compiles relevant information such as arrests, calls for service, specific crimes committed, and known-offender locations as indicators for marshaling maximum resources to probable high-crime areas. This year there are thirty such areas in Dallas.

"Because of where Flaco was sighted," I say, "I've narrowed the TAAG locations down to this general triangle: 635 to the east; US 75 to the west; and to the south, I-30. The three areas I've targeted are the Five Points, in particular Vickery Meadow, the Forest and Audelia area, and the Baylor University Hospital area, focusing along Gaston Avenue. The lieutenant has already requested up the chain for more money for our CIs. We want to let as many contacts as possible know that there's monetary reward for productive leads.

"Detectives Esparza and Philbo, I'd like you to canvass the Gaston Area. Craddock, you and Detective Ryan will take the Forest and Audelia area. Detective Dutton and I will take the Five Points area."

"Oh, man," Philbo says. "Dutton, you get all the fun. Must be teacher's pet."

Seth slowly swivels his head in the direction of Philbo's bulky form. "Tell you what. I'll let you carry my books to class for a while."

Philbo snorts unpleasantly and gives my partner a withering look. I disperse the group and walk back to my office with a smile on my face.

I'm in my office for a few minutes when I get a call from the duty desk that I have a visitor. A private investigator named Howard Decker is here to see me.

"Hold him off for ten minutes, then bring him back," I say.

I call Peg Bartles, who picks up on the second ring.

"Still no news to—" she says.

"Do you know a Howard Decker?" I ask, interrupting her.

There's a pause. "Yeah, I know Howard."

"He's here, asking to see me."

"I'd bet the farm that Turner has retained him. The minute we told him no, he probably called Howard. And if he is working for Turner, he's already been shadowing you for days."

I breathe deeply to quell a rising sense of anxiety. And a sudden hot flush of anger. "I'll call you back after he leaves."

Disconnecting the call, I sit and brood over the presence of the PI. I'd had no awareness of being followed. If he has been hired to track down Mary Grace, I should be happy that another set of eyes and ears are out looking for her. But all I feel is a sense of dread, remembering that Peg had called Turner a major perv.

Decker is escorted to my office by a duty officer. I'm not sure what I'd been expecting, but it certainly wasn't the average-looking citizen standing before me. Dressed in a collared golf shirt and khaki pants, he is of middling height and has a slightly receding hairline and nondescript facial features. Pure vanilla. He shakes my hand and presents his card, and I gesture for him to take a seat.

"Detective Sergeant," he says, looking at me with frank appraisal.

"How can I help you, Mr. Decker?" I ask.

"I've been retained by Alan Turner to find his granddaughter."

This catches me off guard. "His granddaughter? What about his daughter?"

"Stepdaughter," he says. "And finding her is not my job."

His curt, clipped speech is belying the first, mild impression he made. He gives a half smile. It's not warm and fuzzy. "Besides," he says, "you've already got that angle covered. Bartles and Bentner, I believe?"

"And why would I know anything about Mr. Turner's granddaughter, assuming Mary Grace had a child?" I say.

Decker pulls out his phone, enlarges a photo on the screen, and shows it to me. It's a photo of me, taken from behind, carrying a gigantic package of diapers.

"Let's cut the shit, Sergeant," he says, his voice low, all pretense of Mr. Nice Guy gone now. "Mary Grace Turner's infant is in your care, which Mr. Turner is very grateful for. But he still has full parental custody of Mary Grace, as she's still a minor. And, by extension, it's not going to be hard to convince a judge to grant custody of her child to him as well."

My initial anger over being followed is fanning a deeper outrage at this creep inserting himself into our lives, threatening to take away Mary Grace's baby without any consideration of her wishes.

I think about closing the door, but I'm not eager to be walled off from the rest of my team. Seth has gotten up from his desk and stands facing me. He's trying to read my expression.

"Your employer didn't seem to have any interest in finding his stepdaughter when she was living on the streets, hungry and afraid," I say. "And you think that's going to bode well for his attempt to take custody of her baby?"

Decker's put his phone on the desk. The screen is blank, but in that moment I'm certain he's taping our conversation. It's what a good PI would do. It's what I would do if I were in his shoes.

"Again," he says, "that's not my decision to make. We know that the baby is in your care. Mr. Turner has asked only that you save yourself the expense, and embarrassment, of a custody trial."

"Embarrassment?"

He gives the half smile again. "Sergeant, personally I don't give a damn what your private life is like. And frankly, neither does Mr. Turner. But this is Texas."

"Meaning?"

"Meaning it will matter to some judges."

I sit back, forcing myself to unclench my fists. There are tiny, erratic motes of light in the periphery of my vision. Decker continues to stare at me like an IRS auditor: dispassionate, persistent, and with the full weight and influence of a big institution backing him up. I want to reach across the desk and slap the complacency right off his face, but instead I reach out and pick up his phone. I bring it to my lips and say, "Mr. Turner, we'll see you in court."

I toss the phone at Decker, who barely manages to catch it. "Goodbye, Mr. Decker. And if I catch you following me in the future, I'll have you arrested before you can say Harry Bosch."

"On what charge?"

"On being an invasive asshole."

He follows me to the open doorway. He leans in so I can't miss the sincere menace in his eyes. "Don't *you* be an asshole, Detective. You have no idea what you're messing with."

Motioning to Seth that I'm okay, I close the door on the retreating Decker and spend the next ten minutes harnessing vengeful fantasies involving a finger vise and a ball-peen hammer. When I feel in control of my emotions again, I walk to Seth's desk and ask him for his phone. Entering his security code—1996, the last year the Cowboys won a Super Bowl—I enlarge the screen-saver image, the photo of me carrying the package of diapers, and focus on the parking lot surrounding us. And there, a few yards behind me, is a man in a golf shirt and khaki pants holding up his phone, obviously taking a picture of me. I tell Seth about the PI's visit and about Turner's desire to take custody of Elizabeth.

"What are you going to do?" Seth asks.

"Talk to Jackie about finding a good family lawyer."

He tugs at his chin. "That's going to cost big bucks, partner."

"Don't I know it."

I walk back into my office and call Peg Bartles. "Decker was here," I tell her, "and he verified that he's working for Turner."

"I just hate it when I'm right," she says.

From Peg's phone I hear the sounds of the streets of South Dallas in the background. Rough avenues populated by rougher inhabitants. The shrill call-and-response of the dispossessed and the marginalized punctuated by profanities, and by the intermittent, frantic entreaties for money, for cigarettes, for drugs. I think about Mary Grace possibly lost and wandering in their midst.

"Any advice for me on dealing with either Decker or his boss?" I ask.

Peg lets out a heady sigh. "We don't find Mary Grace in two weeks, you should turn the baby over to Turner. You're probably not going to win this fight. Not in Texas. And not on your salary, which is now coming to us."

"Okay, thanks, Peg."

I disconnect and stare at the wall. If we can just find Mary Grace, she can be the one to say to a court, to a judge, what her wishes are. If she wants her stepfather to take custody, then so be it. But if she's in any shape to take care of the baby, we'll do our best to be the firewall between her and the rest of the world. On the other hand, if she wants Jackie and me to continue caring for Elizabeth…

I veer away from that thought. Being "Ciocia (Auntie) Betty" for a few weeks, or months, is one thing. But caring for an infant full-time is scary on a whole other level. If I'm being totally honest with myself, I have to recognize the sentiment that raised its hopeful little head when Peg talked about returning Elizabeth to her extended family. It was relief. And hard on the heels of *that* feeling was the sting of guilt.

My phone rings. It's Johnny B telling me he's got some information, and to meet him in Five Points.

14

Five Points, Dallas
Tuesday, September 16, 2014

When I first heard there was a Five Points in Dallas, I had to laugh. Being from New York, I knew about the notorious nineteenth-century neighborhood huddled on the mean streets of lower Manhattan: a tightly packed collection of disease-ridden slums contained within Centre Street to the west, the Bowery to the east, Canal Street to the north, and Park Row to the south. It was ruled by local gangs, mostly ethnic Irish, with names such as the Bowery Boys and the Dead Rabbits. It was so dangerous that even the police wouldn't dare to enter during the day, much less at nighttime.

But for several years running, Five Points in Big D had been ranked as one of the most dangerous neighborhoods in the metroplex, even though it was sandwiched between the upscale NorthPark Mall and the expensive homes in Lake Highlands. Our targeted area is Vickery Meadow, composed mainly of run-down, decades-old apartment complexes housing a diverse population besieged by violent drug dealers. It's where Johnny B said he was currently living.

As Seth and I drive south toward Vickery Meadow, I try calling Johnny. I have to call him three times before he finally answers.

"Yeah," he says, sounding like he's deep into a narco high.

"Hey, it's me," I say. "Where do you want to meet?"

There is a long silence on the other end, and I think that maybe he's nodded off. "Johnny!" I snap. "Wake up. We'll give you half an hour to get it together. Either you tell us a safe place to make contact, or we're coming to your squat."

"You don't know where I live," he says.

"How about we just bang on every apartment door until we find you."

"Okay," he says. "You got money for me?"

"You got information for us or not?" I ask.

"I said so, didn't I?"

"Then I've got money for you."

He sighs raggedly. "There's a greenbelt behind the Wildflower Apartments on Pinehurst. A few yards in, there's a trail. Follow it toward the park. Give me forty-five minutes."

He disconnects the call, and I tell Seth where we'll meet Johnny.

"Didn't a couple of guys just get shot there?" he asks. "Where the fuck do they come up with these names? Wildflower, my ass."

Forty-five minutes later we park next to the apartment complex, closest to the greenbelt. The day is overcast and still, with the bleak appearance of a coming rainstorm. Only a few people are out walking their dogs, beefy, pit bull–looking specimens wearing thick collars. Half a dozen kids are in the parking lot, kicking a flaccid ball around. The minute we get out of the car, they scatter. Several of the dog walkers pull out their phones, no doubt calling their neighbors, giving them a heads-up that two cops have arrived.

"We might as well be in uniform," Seth says. He gives a friendly wave to a very large man holding at bay a pony-size dog with silvery fur the color of gunmetal. The dog shows his fangs and growls.

We find a small footpath through the greenbelt and within a short distance come across the trail to the park. There are trees on either side, perfect hiding places for muggers and drug dealers.

Seth makes a disapproving noise. "All eyes, Riz."

I ease my jacket behind the holster of my gun. "I hear that."

There is a rustling behind us, and I turn. The large man is walking along the path in our direction, his impressive biceps bulging with the effort of keeping his dog controlled. The dog's snout, nostrils flaring, points like an arrow at us, his muscles quivering with the effort. Or in anticipation.

"Yeah, I see him," Seth mutters, and we pick up our pace.

So does the man behind us. We hear his accelerating footsteps crunching along the trail, as well as the labored breathing of his pit bull. I look over my shoulder. The man is closing the distance. He's wearing dark shades, so I can't see his eyes, but there's no doubt that he's not walking just to give his pet some fresh air.

We travel another ten paces, and then Seth abruptly pivots and walks back toward our follower. The man stops dead in his tracks, but the dog goes crazy, pulling at the chain lead and snarling. Seth stops within a few feet of the lunging pit bull, one hand resting on top of his gun.

"You need something?" Seth asks.

"Not a good place to be walking," the man drawls. His voice is a bass rumble, and he smiles unpleasantly. "A hundred feet up the trail, and you're going to be introduced to some members of a Honduran drug gang."

He gives a one-word command and the snarling dog goes silent and sits as pretty as a poodle. I move to stand next to Seth. The man pulls up his shades to rest on top of his head, his eyes searching the trees surrounding us.

"I'm going to take five seconds to say this," he says quietly, "so you need to listen. Go back the way you came. Whatever you're here for, you need to do it somewhere else."

Seth leans in. "We're cops."

"No shit, Sherlock," the man says. Then he points to his chest. "DPD Gangland. Leave. Now."

He turns and walks away, the dog obediently trotting alongside him, and disappears off the trail into the greenbelt.

"Some undercovers have all the fun," Seth says.

I call Johnny B and tell him that plans have changed. He needs to meet us behind the 7-Eleven a block away from the Wildflower Apartments.

"We'll wait for you, but don't take too long," I tell him, and disconnect.

Seth and I keep eyes in the backs of our heads as we make our way to the car, but if we're being followed, our pursuers are utterly silent. And there's no sign of Pit Bull Man in the parking lot.

I drive the short distance to the convenience store, pull around to the side, and park the car next to a large dumpster, the engine idling. As soon as we're in position, the sky opens up, the rain falling hard. The day has turned ten degrees cooler. We have a view of the street, but the watery curtain makes distant objects appear fogged and insubstantial.

"Hondurans in the 'hood," Seth says loudly over the drumming of rain on the car. "They moved fast."

"Yes, they did. I can reach out to Manny Ortega to ID the undercover with the dog. He might be able to tell us if Flaco's one of them."

We sit without talking for a few minutes. Seth shifts restlessly in his seat, rapping the backs of his fingers on the passenger window. If I know nothing else about my often-surprising partner, I've learned to trust his gut instincts about when things might go sideways.

I study his body language and ask, "You nervous about this meet?"

He shakes his head and gives me a hangdog look. "It's Patty. I'm going to have to make a decision soon."

"About?"

"About whether we take it to the next step."

He puts air quotes around the last two words.

"Ruh-roh," I say. "She talking about moving in, marriage, sharing T-shirts…what?"

He sighs heavily.

"It's only been three months," I remind him. "And there is the issue of the cats."

"When were you sure about Jackie?" he asks.

I smile at the memory of seeing Jackie for the first time, her hair, worn long at the time, swept back in a disheveled ponytail, her skin still dewed from a run through Central Park. She looked at me and smiled and it was like biting down on an electrified wire. "It took me all of a minute and thirty-eight seconds to know for sure."

"Never had any doubts?"

"Not once. Can't swear she'd say the same about me."

Seth grins. "Yeah, well, I'd never ask her to."

"Thanks for that vote of confidence, *partner,*" I say, punching him in the arm.

He laughs and rubs at his triceps where I connected. "All I know right now is that I'm crazy about her. But I'd be less scared walking into Huntsville in high heels than committing myself to monogamy for the rest of my life."

"Sounds to me like you have your answer."

"I just don't want to lose her."

"Yeah, well. There is that," I say. "Ask me something easy, like do we, or do we not, wait for backup to breach a trap house filled with Sinaloans."

Seth points through the windshield at an approaching figure, running hunched through the downpour.

"Looks like our CI," he says.

The figure runs up to the car, opens the rear passenger door, and flops inside, a wash of rainwater following in his wake. Johnny B couldn't be any wetter if he'd jumped into a swimming pool.

I hand him some napkins to dry off his face. He squeezes water out of his braid, and it runs in rivulets onto the seat.

"What have you got for us, Johnny?" I ask.

He holds out his hand. "I need money."

"You know the drill," I say. "You'll get it once you give us something useful."

"A new jefe in town," he says reluctantly. "Honduran.

Name's Flaco. Taken up shop in Vickery Meadow along with half a dozen enforcers, and more showing up every day."

I steal a look at Seth, who asks, "Have you seen him?"

Johnny smirks. "Yeah, I've seen him. Talked to him too."

"What do you mean you 'talked to him'?" Seth asks.

Johnny holds out his hand again, and I slip him sixty dollars.

He looks at the bills as if I've handed him a dirty tissue. "That's it? Man, I got to live."

"If this guy Flaco's got his crew here, you wouldn't have gotten within twenty feet of him," Seth says.

Johnny's eyes cut to me and linger. I'm the one doling out the money. He's angry, but he's also desperate.

"I did talk to him. I told him I'd sell for him if he'd, you know—"

"If he'd give you product," I finish for him.

"Yeah," Johnny says.

I hold up another sixty dollars. "Anything else you'd like to tell us? Anything overheard, gossip, rumors, threats on rival gangs?"

Johnny stares at the money for a long time. I realize that what I thought was rain on his face are tears. He slumps back in the seat. "I didn't used to be this way," he mumbles.

His inhalations come faster now. "I'm Tohono O'odham Nation!" He slams his fist, hard, into his chest. "We've *never* signed a treaty with the Feds. We still speak our language. We resisted your religion. We made the desert bloom when *your* ancestors were painting their bodies blue and eating each other, man!" He glares at us fiercely, and it's hard to meet his gaze.

He turns to look out the window, shaking his head. "More

than half of us have diabetes. We're fat. We're sick, if not with drink, then with drugs." He takes in a ragged breath. "My sister sells herself on the side of the road."

The last is said in a near whisper.

"He's going to come for you."

I don't think I've heard him correctly. "What did you say?"

He looks at me, his lips stretched taut. "Flaco said that a female cop would be sniffing around for information about him. He called you by name. He said that Evangeline Roy had something special in mind for you."

The collision of thoughts—Mary Grace disappearing, my worries over Jackie and the baby, the pressures of my elevated status at work—congeal around one image: Evangeline waiting patiently to avenge the deaths of her two sons. She surgically skewered my leg with a metal cable, chaining me to a stone, and that was when she wanted me as a brood mare. I can't imagine what she has planned for me now. My chest constricts, and my vision begins to blur.

"Why would he tell you all that?" Seth asks.

Johnny's head turns from me to my partner. He chuffs out a humorless laugh. "Because he knows I'm a snitch."

Before we can react, he grabs the sixty dollars from my hand, opens the door, and walks rapidly toward the street.

Seth reaches for the door handle, but I put a restraining hand on his arm. "Let him go," I say.

I feel gutted, my anxiety singing at foghorn levels. I look through the windshield, watching Johnny's retreating figure staggering through the storm. His jacket is too big for his gaunt frame, his pant legs drag through the puddles, and his braid clings like a wounded animal to his back.

His hands are in his pockets and his head is down when he

steps into the street. There is a massive blur of motion to his left. He turns and faces the oncoming object. His arms sweep wide as though in acceptance. A large black SUV slams into him, runs him down, and passes over his bulk effortlessly. The sound his head makes when it connects with the pavement is of disintegrating bone and flesh.

The SUV doesn't stop; it doesn't even slow down. It continues fast to the end of the street and takes a hard, sliding turn onto another road. Through the wash of rainwater, the flattened figure on the ground looks like a discarded suit bag.

I'm too stunned to react; my hands grip the steering wheel. I've become aware that Seth is yelling something.

Fumbling for the handle to open my door, I fall out of the car and begin running toward Johnny. My feet slip, but I manage to stay upright until I'm standing over him. The rain has reached monsoon proportions, and I have to shield my eyes with both hands to see. He's not moving, and blood from his broken head is streaming with the rain into the gutters. There are no other cars on the street and no pedestrians; no one who could serve as a witness.

I kneel down, putting my fingers on Johnny's throat, but there is no rhythmic thrumming beneath the skin to signal life. I'm vaguely aware of Seth behind me, making a call to emergency services.

"He alive, Riz?" he asks.

I shake my head and continue holding on to Johnny's lifeless hand until the ambulance techs pry his body away on a stretcher.

15

The House
Tuesday, September 16, 2014

After a twenty-minute shower and a double shot of Jameson, I sit in my office with the door closed, head in hands, trying to shake the sights, and sounds, of Johnny B being ground into roadkill by a thousand pounds of steel. There was no doubt in my mind when I talked to the homicide detectives, who showed up on the scene following the patrol officers, that the hit-and-run had been no accident. There was also little doubt in my mind that Flaco had been in the vehicle, if not as the driver, then as a passenger. Unfortunately, I was not able to give a description of the SUV, other than that it was large and black and moving at a high speed.

I'd remained standing in the street, pummeled by the rain—and by the memory of Johnny telling us that he'd been made as a snitch—even after his body was removed. Seth finally led me back to the car, placing me in the passenger's seat. He wanted to take me home, but I made him drive me to the station to make an incident report.

At another time, the sight of Sergeant Rhyzyk dragging

herself into her office, soaked from head to feet and leaking like a sinking ship, would have been comical, and grist for "remember when" stories that would have lasted from now until Doomsday. But my team was out working the streets, the department blessedly quiet.

I called DEA special agent Haslett to bring him up to date on Flaco's sightings in East Dallas. Then I called Manny Ortega to pass a message on to his fellow Gangland undercover, the muscled man with the large pit bull, to keep us in the loop on Flaco's whereabouts. I was fairly certain that he would move on to another neighborhood after getting rid of Johnny B, but it would be good to have a set of watchful eyes in Five Points.

Upon returning home, I found out that Jackie had been held late at the hospital, and I was glad that Connie was happy to stay until she returned, giving Elizabeth her dinner and a bath. I was in no fit state to be cheerfully playful with the baby, and I wondered at the parents who were, day after day, resilient enough to push aside their own tragedies and appear smiling at their children's demands. Yet one more reason that I was unfit to be the guardian of a helpless infant.

I hold the two Saint Michael medallions, worn on separate chains around my neck, in both hands, squeezing them until the metal discs cut grooves into my palms. One was given to me by Jackie; the other was a fifty-year-old medallion brought by my grandmother from Poland. She had worn it for decades, as had my mother. And when I was fifteen, my mother gave it to me. The tradition was to wait until I'd turned sixteen, and, on the eve of my birthday, it was to be placed around my neck and solemnified by a Polish prayer: "*Święty Michale, broń nas w bitwie.*" Saint Michael, defend us in battle. But life in the Rhyzyk household had turned dire, and that night, she must have felt that I needed the protection more than she did.

Before she'd given me the medallion, the evening had started like so many nights at home. My father stoking himself into a rage by downing half a bottle of whiskey and muttering rancorous, self-pitying musings about how poorly his life had turned out. There were only the three of us at dinner, as Andrew had left earlier to be with friends. My mother and I sat at the table, hardly daring to breathe, fearful of doing or saying anything that would escalate my father's black mood. As the silence stretched on, I became aware of his gaze burning into the side of my face.

I looked up and locked eyes with him, and I knew something unpleasant was about to happen.

His top lip curled away from his teeth. "There it is," he said, smoke billowing out of his nostrils in humorless laughter.

"There's what?" I asked, sweat beading along my upper lip.

"Don't be fuckin' coy," he said, pointing his cigarette at me. "You know what I'm talking about."

I looked back down at my plate, pretending to resume my meal. But I did know what he was talking about. He'd caught the disgust and dislike...no, not dislike...cold, unfiltered hatred, in my expression.

My mother's placating voice. "Phillip—"

"Shut up!" he snapped, without taking his eyes off me. "You think I don't know what's going on with you, don't you? Well, I do know. I know what you get up to when you go out with your friends."

"Don't you think—?" Her voice again at the other end of the table, tremulous and strained.

"One more word out of you, and you'll wish you hadn't opened your mouth." He said it quietly, which was more terrifying than if he'd been shouting. "Look at me."

I dragged my eyes from my plate, doing as he asked.

"You putting out?"

My face burned with embarrassment. "What?"

He leaned in closer to me. "You stopped wearing boy's undershirts and started wearing a bra all of a sudden."

The thought of my father rifling through the laundry basket filled me with an undefinable shame.

"You're putting out for the boys, aren't you? Getting nasty in the back of somebody's car, hmm?"

The bark of derisive laughter coming from my mouth surprised him more than if I'd slapped him. His insinuating, lascivious tone was pitched to bring me to maximum humiliation. But he really didn't know. He didn't know the first fucking thing about what I'd been up to. In that moment, I wanted to tell him. I wanted to tell him why I'd started wearing silk underwear and a bra. I wanted to shock him down to his socks by telling him it was because a girl, a girl I'd been having marathon make-out sessions with for weeks, had bought them for me. I wanted to see the look on his face when I told him what a turn-on it was for me fantasizing about her slowly removing the new underwear from my body using only her teeth...

He made a grab for me and missed, knocking his glass onto the floor. I pushed back frantically from the table, dodging his swinging fists. My mother had quickly moved to his side, pleading with him to stop. He shoved her back and lunged at me. He was blind drunk now, and I easily sidestepped him. He turned to my cowering mother and started hurling obscenities about her slut daughter. And she just stood, head down, hands clenched, and let him.

I shoved him away, screaming at him to leave her alone. At fifteen, I was nearly as tall as he was. He raised his fist to me, but something in my expression, my unflinching posture, made him stagger uncertainly.

"Do you see what you've raised?" he yelled at my mother. "Do you see what a goddam whore she's become?"

I looked at my mother's pale face, the fear in her eyes, her quivering form. In that moment I was angrier than I could ever remember being.

"Why don't you fight back!" I shrieked at her.

I screamed once more for good measure—the veins standing out like bridge cables in my neck—grabbed my coat, and fled the house, trying to outrun the guilt I felt, worried that my father, left to his own devices, might seriously injure my mother.

I didn't know where I was going. It didn't matter as long as I ran. It was a chilly night in Brooklyn, the streets slicked with a light fall rain, but I had a coat, and my sneakers, and I could stay out all night if necessary.

The sidewalks were dark in between the widely spaced streetlights but still busy with pedestrians returning home from work, or shopping at the corner grocers, or fleeing the rain inside a neighborhood tavern. I stopped at a pay phone and called my brother at his girlfriend's house, but it went to voice mail.

"Andrew," I pleaded, "you need to get home. It's Dad.... He's—"

My voice began to wobble, and I disconnected the call before breaking down completely. Someone swore at me loudly to move out of the phone booth. I ran some more, until I came to a liquor store and stood outside, begging several customers to buy me some Jameson, the whiskey Uncle Benny always drank. A man, already inebriated, took my twenty dollars and returned with a bottle of cheaper whiskey, and laughed at me when I complained.

Taking the bottle, I soon found a recessed doorway in a warehouse building and sat in the shadows, where I proceeded with grim determination to get as drunk as I could, as fast as I could. The whiskey was vile, abrading the tender flesh of my throat like turpentine stripping off paint. After half a dozen swigs, the taste became merely medicinal and I stopped gagging after every swallow.

I tried calling Andrew once more, but again the call went straight to voice mail. Within twenty minutes, the world had softened to a gossamer glow. My fear and anger had diminished to a vague anxiety; the bite of the cold and damp had been reduced to a mild discomfort. In fact, the liquor had warmed my body like a heater, and I unbuttoned my coat. The cool air was bracing, and I felt, in that moment, that I could run for miles. I slid up the wall with surprising ease and took a few steps toward the street. The sidewalk tilted like a deck on a sailing ship, and I would have fallen had I not grabbed on to a tree and held on. I tried closing my eyes, but the rocking motion intensified.

I must have groaned, because an older man stopped to ask if I was okay. He patted my shoulder in a grandfatherly way.

"Here," he said, "come with me. You need to sit down. You don't look well."

The sound of a kind voice, and a concerned touch, made it easy to let go of the tree and lean against his solid bulk, and I let him start to lead me back into the shadows. When I paused, his arm folded more forcefully around my waist, and the leading became a persistent tugging.

Somewhere in the back of my reptilian brain a self-preserving alarm was raised, and I stopped and tried to pull away from him.

He breathed hotly into my ear, "You need to come with me."

I started flailing, and when he grabbed a handful of my hair, all of the rage against my father found a new target: the man who was trying to pull me into a lightless, vacated warehouse.

I became a wild thing, twisting, biting, spitting. I kicked his shins with my sneakers and tried to knee him in the groin. He deflected my knee with his leg, but I could tell the connection would leave a bruise. I was able to shove him hard to the ground, where he lay for a moment, the wind knocked out of him. I kicked him a few times for good measure before the contents of my stomach found their way up into my throat, and I turned away and vomited violently onto the pavement.

Stumbling and retching, I moved back toward the street and into the light, and then I ran. I ran for the better part of an hour and found myself in front of Benny's house. But in the end I didn't ring his doorbell. It's not that I didn't think he would help me. It's that I wanted, needed, to have something in my life that was good and safe and uncomplicated, set apart from the wash of violence that had threatened to swallow my family. And by extension, the mayhem on the street that seemed to have followed me out of my house that night like a rabid dog. I sat on Benny's stoop, miserable and cold, feeling I had only myself to blame for the attack.

Benny's favorite saying had always been *"Don't get stuck in the abyss of your own morass."* A silly yet constant aphorism that had become a private joke between the two of us. One that made total sense given the absurdities of day-to-day life among so many flawed and broken people, and the ease with which a person could fall into the miseries of their own making. And yet here I was at Benny's front door, doing the very thing he had always counseled me against: feeling sorry for myself.

When I finally returned home, sometime after two o'clock in the morning, my mother was waiting for me. She'd been crying, but there were no marks or bruises on her that I could detect. She could see from my disheveled hair and the scratches on my neck that something bad had happened during the few hours that I'd been gone.

"There was a man," I said. "But I got away."

She hugged me fiercely and took the Saint Michael medallion from her neck and placed it around mine. "Saint Michael, defend us in battle," she intoned.

She then whispered to me that from now on, things would be different. That she'd been a coward to let her children take the brunt of her husband's anger. She'd made a pledge to God and all the saints that, if I returned safely, she'd make sure Andrew and I would never again be assaulted in our own home. Taking her wooden sewing box from the cupboard, she selected a large needle and a spool of coarse thread and headed for the bedroom she shared with my father.

When I asked her what she was doing, she looked at me with a settled defiance and answered, "I have some sewing to do," and then closed the bedroom door.

I didn't see my father the next morning and assumed that

he was still sleeping off his drunken evening. I found out later that, after I had left for school, my mother—who had patiently sewn my father tightly into his blankets up to his neck—had taken a broom handle and beaten him methodically about the torso with it; telling him that if he ever laid a hand on any of us again, she would poison him and gladly spend the rest of her life in prison.

He sustained two broken ribs and a swollen liver, which rendered physical retaliation too painful. He was off duty for a week, and everyone figured that he had gotten a well-deserved pounding from another cop. He took my mother's threat seriously, though, because even though the drinking and verbal abuse continued, he never again struck any of us. My suspicion was that he actually respected my mother for giving him such a righteous beatdown.

Nie trać więcej słów na temat zrobienia czegoś.

Let the stick do the talking.

There's a soft knock against the office door. It's Connie saying that Elizabeth is asleep and asking if she can leave for the night. I thank her and tell her to go home. But I wait until I hear the front door close before tiptoeing into Elizabeth's room.

I stare at the baby sleeping peacefully in her crib and think back to the fire in Delano's Gym. The conflagration started by El Cuchillo that almost ended Mary Grace's and my life. We had saved each other that night. And by extension we both saved Mary Grace's yet unborn baby. Some people believe that the rescued person forever owes a debt of gratitude to her rescuer. But I believe what Uncle Benny believed. That once you've saved someone's life, you are forever linked to them, forever responsible for protecting their well-being.

Now, looking at Elizabeth breathing softly into her fitted sheet decorated with pastel baby animals, I think there's not a chance in hell I'm going to let anyone take her away. At least not without a fight.

16

Dallas Police Department, North Central Division
Wednesday, September 17, 2014

U h-oh," Seth says to me as I stride past his desk. "You're wearing your leather jacket again."

"Sharpened my canines, too," I say, walking into my office. "Let the team know I'll see them in the incident room in twenty minutes?"

He gives me an exaggerated salute. "Do I need to pass out the Kevlar vests?"

"Let's see what Philbo throws at me first."

I close the door and make a call to Peg Bartles. She answers after a few rings, and it sounds like I've roused her from a deep sleep.

"Did I wake you?" I ask.

"Rocky and I had a late night trawling some clubs. We still got zilch to report, though."

"I need the name of a good family-court lawyer."

She yawns loudly into her phone. "How good? Like J.Lo good, or Uncle Billy Bob good?"

"Like Alan Turner good."

There's an intake of breath. "He's made contact?"

"No," I say. "Not yet. But I want to be prepared. I want to know what my realistic options will be if and when he comes calling. I'm not just going to fold and let him walk all over us."

"You go, girl," she says. "But you know it's going to cost *mucho mula,* right?"

There are some rustling noises for a few seconds before her voice sounds in my ear again. "Okay, her name is Keri McCall. I'll text you her number. Give her a ring, tell her I sent you. She'll be straight with you about your chances."

I thank her and disconnect. I haven't even discussed hiring a lawyer with Jackie yet. She came home from the hospital last night exhausted. So I ran her a bath and let her go right to sleep. If nothing else, we can have a consultation with the lawyer and take it from there.

I'm just leaving my office when my personal cell phone rings.

"Detective Sergeant, this is Howard Decker."

Shit. Alan Turner's PI.

"I'm busy right now, Decker," I say impatiently. "What do you want?"

"Mr. Turner would like to meet with you in person."

"About?"

"Oh, I think you know. He's well aware that you've been taking care of his stepdaughter's baby. And he'd like to talk to you about future arrangements."

I'm tempted to tell him that I've engaged a lawyer and that we should let independent parties decide what's best.

"Look, just so you know," Decker says, "Mr. Turner is a very determined man. But he's also reasonable. Maybe if you just talk to him first. See what he has to say. He'll meet you on neutral ground. What do you have to lose?"

I recall the photo of a smiling, handsome Turner. A self-assured man with a winning smile and cold blue eyes.

"I'm sure Mr. Turner is *very* persuasive. Let me talk to my significant other and I'll let you know."

"I'd be happy to pick you and your partner up at your house and drive you to wherever you—"

Of course, being a thorough investigator, he's already found out where I live.

"I don't think that will be necessary," I say. "I've got to go now. I'll let you know what we decide."

Disconnecting the call, I close the office door behind me and make my way to where the team is assembled. I try taking deep breaths to steady my emotions, but I'm agitated and more than a little angry. Leaning against the wall just outside the incident room, I listen to the voices of the men inside. The words are unclear, but their tone is not. They're frustrated. I need to tear my thoughts away from worrying about Mary Grace's whereabouts and focus, as a team leader, on the problems at hand. Flaco and Evangeline. They need to be found and apprehended. But so far, we've been left holding our asses while they evade us and thumb their noses in the process. What I've been doing up to now has not worked. We keep stumbling over Flaco, but it's only because he's been setting the stage, dropping the clues, managing to be several steps in front of us. And now his cat-and-mouse games have most likely caused the death of Johnny B.

It's been purely calculated guesswork on my part, setting the search zone for Flaco in East Dallas. But it's not a physical barrier like a net. Flaco could be anywhere in Texas right now. I certainly don't need any reminders that I'm the bait, drawing Evangeline ever closer. What I do need is a lure, something I can control, that will entice either of them to come to me at a prescribed time and place. Some hounds to drive the fox.

From the men's expressions when I enter the room, I can tell that they see all too clearly that I've got nothing new to give them.

Craddock is the first to speak.

"Sorry to hear about your CI being run down. Man, that's a hard way to go."

I think of Johnny standing in the road, his arms wide, facing his death head-on.

"*I'm Tohono O'odham Nation...We made the desert bloom...*"

A sudden swell of emotion tightens my throat. "He didn't deserve to die like that. Detective Ryan, I'd like you to see if we can get any hits on traffic cameras in that area. Maybe we can trace the SUV's license plate."

"So, what's next?" Esparza asks.

Philbo, sitting next to him, crosses his arms over his chest. The sarcastic expression on his face reads *Oh, boy, this is going to be fun.*

"We've got patrol doubled now in Five Points," I say. "And we have a gangland UC contact in Vickery Meadow who'll keep his eyes open for Flaco. Speaking of—Tom, did we get any hits off the prints on the cigar band?"

Craddock grins and hands me a printout of a mug shot. "FBI came back with a hit. Flaco's real name is Roberto Flores. He was arrested once in 2008 for conspiracy to deal large amounts of cocaine. He made bail, which had been set at ten thousand dollars, and skipped the country. Since then, he's been absent. Most likely working in Honduras. I'm hoping DEA can give us some more intel on the guy."

I study the mug shot. It's the same man I saw in the *lavandería*.

Turning to Kevin Ryan, I ask, "Have you spoken to Don Haslett's guy at DEA in the last twenty-four hours?"

He nods. "I called Fred Dunlap first thing this morning. Do we want to make it official and bring him in for increased surveillance?"

"I think we need to," I say. "We've got to find a way to start listening in on the Hondurans who're taking up shop in Vickery Meadow. DEA can expedite wiretaps when we need them. We have to assume that Flores may be using an alias. If so, we need that name."

There is a pause; everyone stares down at their notes or off into space, reassessing, reordering priorities. Philbo sighs and stifles a yawn.

"Detective Philbo," I say. He looks up and squints at me, as though I've disturbed his nap time. "You were with Narcotics in Chicago, right?"

He sighs and shifts in his seat. "That's right."

"How many drug-related arrests has the DPD made so far this year?"

"I don't know," he answers, shrugging. "All sectors? Maybe a thousand. Maybe more."

"And how many arrests involving drugs were made in Chicago the year you left?"

"In 2012? CPD made over twenty thousand arrests."

There are some low whistles in the room, and everyone swivels to look at Philbo. "But, uh, Chicago's got over two and a half million people compared with Dallas with, what, a million or so?"

"Still," I say, "that's an epic amount of law enforcement action. How many arrests did you make that year?"

His chin comes up and he sits a little straighter in his chair. "Me and my partner made four hundred and thirty-three."

"That's an amazing record, Detective. Tell me, how many gangs are there in Chicago?"

He looks at me cautiously. He's not sure where all this questioning is leading. "Almost seventy currently active. Vice Lords, Black P Stones, Latin Kings, and on and on." He looks almost proud of those staggering statistics.

I stand and start pacing. "And how many of those arrested for drugs were gang-related?"

"Most of them. Our drug arrests were almost always made in cooperation with Gangland."

"DPD's current policy is to separate engagement and execution into different divisions with occasional overlap," I say. "Gangland goes after gangs, and when they're caught with drugs, that possession charge, or charge of intent to sell, is just added on top of the robbery, weapons, or assault charges. Right?"

Now I have Philbo's attention. He cocks his head to one side—he's listening.

"I've been going at this the wrong way. We've been focusing on the drugs, when we need to be targeting the Honduran gangs for something else, anything, that will take them off the streets and lead us to Flaco.

"Detective Esparza, I'd like you to work with Detectives Craddock and Ryan on the DEA angle. Search their databases. See if they can provide any further information about Flores, his activities, his habits, or his intentions. Detective Philbo, you're going to be working with me and Detective Dutton on some targeted operations with Gangland. I think your experience could be very valuable."

I have to turn away so as not to smile at the contorted expression on Philbo's face. He's puffed up about his Windy City stats. But I've managed to remove him from the comfort of his current partner, sandwiching him between the two cops he's already worked hard to alienate.

I dismiss the team and walk back to my office. Seth pokes his head in, grinning.

"Man, you're good," he stage-whispers. "Philbo's going to get a hernia trying to figure out why that little attaboy you gave him just now feels like a reaming."

"Divide and conquer, partner. Let's just hope killing him with kindness was the right move."

17

Stan's Blue Note
Wednesday, September 17, 2014

I call Manny Ortega from my office to set up a meeting about cooperating with the gang squad to find Flaco. I also give him a heads-up that I'll be bringing along a new, potentially prickly team member by the name of Detective Dan Philbo.

"Yeah, okay, that's cool," Manny says. "I'm sure his experience with gangs in Chicago will be of use. But, uh, we already got a lot of swinging dicks in our squad. We don't need another hotshot pissing all over everyone to make his mark."

"I hear you, Manny. But I need him to feel like he's part of a team. Otherwise he'll continue to make my life difficult. Can you just stay cool for the hour it's going to take us to talk strategy and eat our cheese fries?"

"*Claro que sí, Sargento.* Just call me frosty."

The three of us drive downtown for our meeting on Lower Greenville in near silence—Seth and I seated up front and

Philbo uncomfortably perched in the back seat. I check his disposition in the rearview mirror several times. He sits, unmoving, arms crossed, staring out the window. Seth gives up trying to make small talk with our petulant colleague after getting only a few monosyllabic grunts in response to his questions.

We park in front of Stan's, next to a line of about a dozen gleaming, tricked-out motorcycles. It's almost five o'clock, and everyone is there for the happy hour and beer-battered mystery meat. A long-standing staple on Greenville, the bar was opened by the blues player E.E. Stanley in the fifties and is an egalitarian mix of college students, football fans, and off-duty cops who, when not glued to the thirty big-screen TVs, can play pool, throw darts, or listen to live music.

The three of us make our way to the outdoor patio in the back. Manny is already holding a table, and we join him. He's wearing a Harley-Davidson T-shirt, a leather vest, and shades, his scarred, bald head as shiny as a bowling ball. The other customers on the patio have given him a wide berth, no doubt wondering when the rest of his Old Guard Motorcycle Club is going to show up.

He flashes his teeth and gestures for us to sit down.

"Hey, Riot," he says to my partner, "you grow any prettier, and you'll have to get the sergeant here to assign bodyguards."

Seth throws him air kisses, and Manny laughs. He holds out his hand for Philbo to shake. "Welcome to Texas, *ese.*"

I know that Manny's got a killer grip, and despite whitening knuckles and popping arm tendons, the two men squeeze hands for the count of five, like two pythons mating in a mud slide.

They finally break contact, and we all order drinks. Philbo

almost sprains his optic nerves rolling his eyes at the three of us ordering sodas. He orders a beer and says to the waitress, "Lucky me. I'm not driving."

While we wait for the drinks, Philbo takes in his surroundings, surreptitiously studying our Gangland friend. He points to Manny's T-shirt. "You ride?"

Manny smiles good-naturedly. "Does the Pope shit in the woods?"

"Your bike out front with the other ladies?" Philbo asks.

Manny nods, puts his elbows on the table, and leans in. "2012 Street Glide."

"The pearl-blue one?"

Manny's chest swells ever so slightly. "You know it."

Philbo leans in as well, motioning with a "come on" gesture. "Bring it."

Manny counts off the attributes of his prized possession on his fingers: "One-oh-three Twin Cam, six-speed cruise-drive transmission, IDS, and a Brembo four-piston caliper, front and rear."

"Dual-front-rotor brake system?" Philbo asks.

Manny looks at me, grinning and nodding with approval. "Okay, Detective from Chiraq, what you got?"

"H-D Fat Bob."

Manny throws his head back and laughs loudly. "Oh, man, that's sweet. What year?"

For the first time since I've met him, Philbo grins with pure pleasure. "Just picked it up, brand-new off the lot. Had to wait for the custom seat to come in."

"You want to check out the Glide?" Manny asks Philbo.

They exit out of the patio, talking engine parts and speed ratios, and I look at Seth.

He asks, "Did we just get dumped?"

"First time for everything, partner," I say.

Seth throws his sunglasses onto the table. "You know, I think I could really grow to dislike that prick."

I pat Seth on the back. "Easy there. You're supposed to be the calming voice of reason pulling *me* back from the edge."

"I tell you one thing right now, Riz. Philbo either gets with the program, or I'm going to make his life very unpleasant."

Seth's idea of making someone's life unpleasant, especially an obstreperous cop's, has historically involved a dead rodent in a locker as well as a live serpent in a desk drawer.

As though reading my mind, my partner says, "You think our city boy might scream like a toddler at finding a hairy tarantula in his coffee cup?"

Before I can urge reasonable restraint, the waitress brings everybody's drinks. Seth and I sip our sodas and wait impatiently for the newly enamored detectives to return. Ten minutes later, they come back to sit at the table again, and I resist the urge to make smart-aleck comments about their dewy complexions.

"Manny," I say, "you know we've not had much luck yet in pinning down this guy Flaco. I've been focusing on the drug connection. So far, it's not been working. Detective Philbo here has had a lot of experience coordinating undercovers and resources with Gangland. I asked to meet with you because I want us all to hear what he has to say about how the cooperation in Chicago is organized and implemented." I look at Philbo. "The floor's all yours."

He takes a long drink of his beer, relishing the attention. "Last few years, I worked O Block on the South Side, sixty-four-hundred block of South Martin Luther King Jr., otherwise known as 'Murder Drive.' Lots of low-income housing and ground zero for gangs, particularly the Black Disciples. There were more shootings on that stretch of road in 2011 than in many other parts of the city combined.

"We had our sights on an upstream heroin provider, a Black Disciples leader named Derrell Wayans, nicknamed 'Young D.' But the organization was too tight to set up any undercover activity. Every UC we sent in got zilch. His dealers were too afraid of reprisals if they got sloppy. Derrell had only one vice that we knew of. Not drugs, not gambling. The man was a fool for a beautiful woman. He had a constant stream of girls, some of them pros, in and out of one of the apartments he held in Parkway Garden on O Block."

"Sounds like Vickery Garden in Five Points," Seth says.

Philbo makes a dismissive noise. "You could make that comparison. If you want to compare a nurse shark to a mako."

Seth goes very still, which is never a good thing. I quickly say, "Yeah, yeah, we get it, Detective Philbo. Let's not get sidetracked by 'mine is bigger than yours.' How'd you circumvent the bottleneck?"

"We put eyes in the henhouse," he says.

I recall my thought at the station earlier. *Some hounds to drive the fox.* "We're all ears," I say.

"The problem was getting inside one of Derrell's controlled units. So we went to the mayor and, with the help of the FBI and some fast-tracked surveillance warrants, got an order to shut down the electricity on the whole block." He laughs with the memory. "It was winter, and you could hear the outraged shouts all the way to Wrigley Field. We let them freeze for a few hours and then sent in a couple of undercover Feds dressed as utility technicians to set up cameras and listening devices right under their noses. We turned the lights and the heat back on, and then just sat back and listened to the dumbasses talk about the who, what, when, and where of every drug deal that Derrell was involved with. We greased the wheels by sending in one of our snitches, who happened to be the most gorgeous piece of ass you've ever seen." He winks at Manny and takes another few swallows of his beer. He turns to me and leers. "You'd be surprised what a guy will give up when he's getting his knob polished."

"Actually, Detective Philbo," I say, deadpanning, "that's the least surprising thing you could tell me. Did you get a conviction on him?"

Philbo nods. "Him and six of his crew."

I turn to Manny. "Flaco will need a base of operations if he doesn't already have one. If Gangland could find out where he's looking to set up operations, we could locate an abandoned house or apartment that we could use as a staging area. Maybe provide one of your CIs as a front to drive him toward what Flaco would think was a safe space. If he's already settled somewhere, maybe we can come up with a distraction to get inside."

"We'd need federal assistance with this," Manny says.

"I've already talked several times with Don Haslett at DEA, and he assures me he can help with warrants and surveillance technology."

Manny stands to leave. "Sounds good. Now comes the fun part. Finding Flaco." He claps Philbo on the back, hard, making him wince. "Welcome to the club. Nice to have another rider on the force."

He walks away, the long key chain clipped to his belt rattling. A minute later, Manny texts me. I wait until Philbo gets up to go to the bathroom to show it to Seth, who snorts out loud. The text reads P's nickname should be Squid. Check it...He ends the message with a devilish smiley face. When I ask Seth what it means, he tells me it's biker slang for a poseur, an inexperienced rider who usually sports a brand-new bike, and who, often as not, uses it for window dressing rather than a serious riding machine.

Before Philbo gets into the back seat of our car again, Seth mutters to me gleefully, "I can't wait to tell Craddock and Ryan about Philbo's new nickname."

At that moment, I decide I'm going to ask Jackie if we can have calamari for dinner. Chopped into little tiny pieces.

18

Austin Street Shelter
Thursday, September 18, 2014

In my dream I hear someone crying. It must be Elizabeth, awake and distressed, alone in the dark in her crib. I need to get up and go to her, but I'm so heavy-limbed with sleep that I can only move my legs weakly. I stretch my fingers out to wake Jackie, but my hands won't obey the thoughts. Jackie's breathing is deep and steady, which is troubling because she's usually up to comfort the baby before I can even perch on the side of the bed.

The crying has become more urgent, more insistent. And now I realize that it's not the baby crying, but Mary Grace. The weeping is raw and hitched and so filled with despair that I feel my own tears welling underneath my eyelids. It's a sound worse than the reckoning over loss. It's the sound of hopeless abandonment.

Overwhelmingly, the pleasant, smoky scent of aftershave, cigarettes, and whiskey blankets the air around my face. And I feel the warm breath of someone bending down next to me, leaning close to my ear. I know, without seeing, who it is. The comfortable aura of love and acceptance embraces me as surely as a hug. It's a presence that has come to me, unfailingly, when I needed it the most. The man who should have been my father. My father's late brother, Uncle Benny.

His voice now whispers urgently to me from the void, *"Wake up, Betty. Time to go to work."*

I open my eyes and hear the phone ringing and see that it's Peg Bartles. I listen for any sounds coming from the baby's room before taking the call, but I've left the crying behind in my dream.

"Did I wake you?" she asks.

I answer the way James Earle would. "That's okay. I had to get up to answer the phone anyway."

The clock reads twelve thirty and the sound of a hard rain lashes the windows. Fortunately the call has not wakened Jackie.

"Where are you?" I ask.

"We're at a shelter downtown. There's someone you need to talk to."

I'm immediately alert. "Did you find Mary Grace?"

"No. But we talked to someone who saw her the day before she disappeared."

I cradle the phone in my neck and start dressing. Pulling on jeans and boots.

"It's a girl Mary Grace met while living on the street," Peg continues. "The girl has been staying at the Austin Street Shelter, and Mary Grace stopped by to give her some money."

"Does she know where Mary Grace was going...where she is now?"

"No, but, uh, we're not the only ones who've been looking for your girl."

"Shit," I say, tugging on a sweater and walking out of the bedroom and toward the coat closet. "Is it the stepfather... or his PI?" The thought of Howard Decker snooping around the same territory makes me want to throttle the little bastard.

"No...someone else." There's a pause, and the caution in her voice brings me up short.

"What do you mean 'someone else'?"

"A woman fitting the description of Evangeline Roy was at the shelter."

The skin on my scalp shrinks like plastic under heat, and I race down the hall and open the door to the nursery. Elizabeth is on her back, sleeping peacefully, her mouth making little sucking noises, as though seeking the comfort of the bottle. There is no one else in the room, but the glass on the windows, through which blue ambient light filters, appears as fragile as a thin coating of ice. A flimsy barrier keeping the wolves at bay.

Leaving a note for Jackie, I finish dressing and, after a brief moment of consideration, clip my badge and gun to my belt. I drive to the end of the block, alerting the night patrol officer watching the house that I'll be gone for at least an hour.

"No one but no one is to enter the house except me," I tell him.

The traffic on US 75 south toward downtown is light, and I arrive within twenty minutes. The shelter, south of Deep Ellum and less than a mile from the city marshal's headquarters, is a collection of large, warehouse-size buildings housing at least four hundred men and women nightly. The first time I met Mary Grace was when she was living rough in Tent City with Wayne, my CI. It was a frigid, rainy night, much like tonight, and I took both of them to the shelter for a brief period before Jackie and I took Mary Grace into our home.

Rocky Bentner is to meet me at the corner of Hickory and Cedar, and when I park on the street, I can see her silhouetted under a streetlight, leaning against the barrier fence surrounding the shelter. Before I can get out of the car, a man appears out of the shadows and approaches her. Rocky's small frame—dressed in ratty dark jeans and a hooded raincoat—is dwarfed by his superior size. He stops and leans over her in an intimidating way. I can't hear what he's saying, but he wraps both hands around the metal bars, pinning her between his arms. As I open the car door to rush to her aid, her face comes up, her pale skin made pearlescent under the streetlight, and she stares into the man's face. She spits out a few words, her mouth twisted into a feral grin. The man immediately drops his arms to his sides and, turning, walks rapidly away.

"What was all that about?" I ask her, stepping onto the sidewalk.

"He told me I had to give him a blow job or he'd mess me up," she says, pushing off the fence. "I told him fine but that as soon as he put it in my mouth, I'd bite it off and swallow it." She gives a derisive snort. "I guess he believed me."

"Where's Peg?"

Rocky points down the street to a van parked thirty yards away. Peg's hand comes out of the open driver's-side window and gives us a leisurely wave.

"She didn't seem in a big hurry to come help you," I say.

Rocky lifts up her raincoat. Nestled inside a holster clipped to her belt is a tidy taser gun. "Peg knows I can handle myself."

"I can see that. So, what's the story with the girl?"

"Name's Tina—"

"Tina what?" I ask.

"Tina P. That's all she'd tell us. She got to know Mary Grace when she was staying at the shelter. Your girl disappeared on September first, right? About four o'clock the day before, Mary Grace showed up here and gave Tina fifty bucks. Two days ago, a woman came to the shelter, bringing warm clothing and a bunch of brochures for some mission she's running. She was asked to leave the premises for trying to tag converts and did so, but not before she asked if anybody knew Mary Grace. This woman talked to Tina."

"What did the woman look like?" I realize that I'm leaning in, towering over her like the asshole that just walked away.

Rocky blinks a few times at the intensity of my tone, and I back up a few steps. "Older, dumpy, bad skin, red hair," she says.

I can barely hear Rocky's words for the roaring in my ears. Two days ago was the sixteenth of September. Evangeline was in the heart of Dallas, boldly hawking her rabid ideology the very same day that Johnny B was being run down by one of her dealers.

Rocky's expression is usually a careful mask of millennial disdain. But I catch her concerned look. She says, "When Tina found out that we were looking for Mary Grace on your behalf, she asked to speak with you."

"Can I talk to her now?" I ask.

"I left after lights-out, which means I can't get back in. But you can if you've got your badge."

While Rocky waits in the van with Peg, I flash my badge to the surveillance cameras and am buzzed in through the main gate. I'm met just inside by Billy Sands, the night security manager. An ex-cop, Billy's been a lifesaver whenever I've brought in a floundering CI needing shelter for a night or two. I'm tall at almost six feet, but Billy's got a good seven inches on me, and he must put in two hours a day at the gym. He's got a heart of gold but a face that would scare the bejeezus out of anyone looking to start trouble.

"Hey, Detective, how're you doin'?" he rumbles. His dark, pitted skin looks like a lunar landscape under the harsh overhead lights.

"Pretty good, Billy. Listen, I need to talk to one of the women here. A Tina P. She asked a private investigator I retained if she could meet with me."

He looks at his watch. "Now? We just got some of the antsier ones settled for the night. There're some newcomers and they unsettle the regulars."

"It's important, Billy, or I wouldn't ask. It's part of a case I'm working."

"Okay. Anything for the DPD. Follow me," he says.

He leads me into the women's sleeping section, where most of the overhead lights are turned off but it's still noisy with coughing, groaning, and creaking cots. He points out the night proctor—a former homeless veteran named Kiko, a middle-aged woman with thousand-year-old eyes. Billy pulls Kiko aside and confers quietly with her for a minute. While they're talking, I watch the women sleeping restlessly on their cots made of rigid, unforgiving mesh and built low to the ground. Most of the women are bundled head-to-toe under whatever blankets and bedrolls they've been given by the shelter or whatever they've managed to scrounge on their own.

A motion against the far side of the room catches my eye, and I see in the deeper shadows the outline of a woman pressed against the wall. She's not slouching in the usual weary, exhausted stance. She's standing upright, rigid and alert, her hands in both pockets of her camo-colored pants. And though it's too dark to be certain, I feel her watching me with more than a wary curiosity.

Billy brings Kiko over and makes an introduction.

"I'll be in my office if you need me," he says, and walks away.

Kiko takes me down a side hallway and unlocks a storage room with cleaning supplies and a few folding chairs.

"We use this room for counseling sometimes," she says, lisping through broken teeth. "No one will disturb you here, baby."

Kiko soon returns with a young woman, who stands in the doorway, blinking, gnawing at the cuticle on one finger. She's wearing baggy pants, an oversize Dallas Cowboys sweatshirt, and ill-fitting high-top sneakers. It's hard to guess her age, but she appears to still be a teenager. And frightened.

"Go ahead, baby," Kiko says to Tina, giving her a gentle push toward the empty chair. Kiko looks at me, nodding sympathetically. "Y'all take as much time as you need. I'll just be in the big room close by."

Kiko closes the door partway and shuffles off. Tina's head is down, her bangs a curtain partially obscuring her face. Her eyes, however, are focused intently on me.

"Tina, I'm Detective Sergeant Rhyzyk—"

"I know who you are," she says, her voice soft and hard to hear. "Mary Grace told me all about you. How you and your girlfriend took her in. That you've been taking care of her and her baby. That Rocky person, she works for you, right? Rocky says Mary Grace has gone missing."

"Rocky works for me, and, yes, Mary Grace disappeared the day after she saw you two and a half weeks ago. Did you and she talk?"

Tina nods, her chin still tucked into her neck. "She only stayed for a little while. But she gave me some money."

"Did she give you any indication that she would be leaving? Was she going to meet somebody?"

Tina shakes her head, her finger going back into her mouth. I rest my arms over my thighs and lean in closer. But not too close. I don't want to scare her.

"Tina, it's really important that you tell me if you know where Mary Grace is."

"Honestly, I'd tell you if I knew," Tina says. "She didn't say anything about going away and leaving her baby. It's Elizabeth, right...the baby's name?"

"That's right—"

She looks up at me hopefully, her hair falling away from her face, her hands clasped tightly between her knees. A large strawberry-colored birthmark covers most of her left cheek. "The baby's still with you, right? I wish I could see her. At your house, I mean."

I can see where this is going. She's grasping at straws, at any life raft that floats in front of her, needing to be rescued. She rubs unconsciously at the birthmark on her cheek, inflaming the skin to a bright scarlet.

"Maybe you can, when we've found Mary Grace," I say.

The light of desperate hope fades from her eyes, and her chin comes down again. I want to put my arms around her and assure her that things will get better. But I know they won't, not anytime soon.

"I heard that a woman came to the shelter a few days ago," I say. "A kind of missionary."

Tina reaches into the back pocket of her jeans and pulls out a crumpled brochure and hands it to me. On the front of it is a stock photo of a smiling girl about Tina's age, sunlight surrounding her head like a halo. A Bible verse is quoted in a banner at the top. Below the banner is a familiar illustration: upswept wings transected by a sword. The emblem of the Roy family. A pregnant Mary Grace had been given a similar brochure by Evangeline months ago. Not knowing how dangerous the Roy matriarch was, Mary Grace unfortunately told Evangeline her name.

"The woman who gave you this, what did she say to you?" I ask.

"The usual 'you're going to hell if you don't listen to me' rap. But she told me that if I joined her mission, she'd give me everything I needed—clothes, food, medicine. Salvation. The only hitch was I'd have to go with her to Honduras, wherever that is. It sounded too good to be true…"

She looks at me, her expression open and vulnerable, and I know exactly what she's been thinking: *It may be too good to be true, but I don't have any other options.*

"Might take her up on the offer. I've got nothing else." Tina hunches her shoulders, her arms tight around her waist.

"Tina," I said, "I know things are rough right now, but the woman is dangerous. I'd stay away from her. Did anything else happen?"

"She passed out a lot of those brochures before security told her to leave."

I reach out and gently touch her on the knee. She flinches as though I've struck her. "Did she ask you about Mary Grace?"

"She asked a lot of people here. She said Mary Grace had been interested in the mission. And I..."

"And you told this woman that you knew her."

"Yes, I told her we were friends. I told her about how good you and your girlfriend were, taking care of Mary Grace and the baby and—"

I rear back in my seat, trying to control my alarm. And my anger. "Did you tell her the baby was still with us?"

"I didn't know Mary Grace was missing. I thought they were both still living with you." Her eyes get glassy with tears. "Is Mary Grace in trouble? Does this woman have something to do with it?"

I take a few steadying breaths. "I don't know."

Tina blinks a few times, then buries her face in both hands and begins to cry in earnest. Finding a roll of paper towels on one of the shelves, I tear off a sheet and hand it to the sobbing girl. She blows her nose, and after she's calmed some, I ask her, as gently as I can, "Tina, do you know who the baby's father is?"

She shakes her head, but when she peeks up at me through her bangs, I sense she's not telling me the truth.

A slight noise outside the partially open door distracts me. I hold a finger to my lips to signal Tina to stay quiet. We sit in silence for a brief moment, and the noise comes again—the slightest squeak of a rubber sole against the worn linoleum. There's the beginning of a shadow in the hallway, someone lurking and blocking the light. Billy had mentioned that there were people new to the shelter—people who, I realize now, might be there to continue spying for Evangeline.

I stand quickly, walk to the door, and yank it open. Poised within earshot of us is the woman I'd seen standing against the wall. After the initial surprise of being discovered, she spends exactly four seconds trying to look lost. Gazing around, looking confused while furrowing her brow.

"Is the bathroom—?" she starts to ask.

When she sees the stony expression on my face, her eyes go dead. The kind of vacancy that signals either the beginning of a grand mal seizure or a mass-shooting spree. Her gaze shifts over my shoulder, and I know Tina has come to stand behind me. The woman's eyes find me again.

"Evangeline says hi," she whispers.

She turns and with a burst of speed sprints toward the big room.

"Stay here," I order Tina, and follow the woman down the hallway.

There's a fire alarm just inside the sleeping area, and the woman activates it, setting off a deafening siren. She vaults over cots, scattering personal belongings as the residents begin trying to untangle themselves from their blankets. The woman's fast. As soon as my eyes adjust to the dark, I see that she's already made it to the front exit. Kiko is struggling to extricate herself from her guardian post in a lounging recliner close to the door, but she's moving too sluggishly to offer assistance.

The woman slams through the door at the exact moment Billy barges from his office, his eyes wide, his breathing agitated. Unable to stop my forward momentum, I slam into his bulk and am knocked back, almost to the floor.

"What the hell?" he roars as I regain my footing.

"There's no fire, Billy," I yell over the shrieking alarm and pointing to the front exit. "Criminal suspect pulled it. Look after Tina—"

I bang through the door in time to see the woman vaulting over the security fence with the skill of a gymnast. It takes me longer to boost my greater weight over, but I'm yelling to Peg and Rocky, still waiting in their van, to give chase. I drop down to the sidewalk, gesturing wildly to get the PIs' attention and signaling them to follow the woman as she runs north on Hickory.

I know that given enough time with my longer stride, I can outpace the suspect, but I have no idea if she has a car waiting close by. Peg's fortunately kept the engine running, and I can hear the van's tires squeal as she jams it into gear and rockets up the street just behind me. As I approach the T-intersection of Chestnut, pumping my legs as hard and as fast as I can, the woman, now about thirty yards away, is fumbling at the door lock of a small green sedan. She throws herself into the driver's seat, starts the engine, and steps on the accelerator. As the woman pulls away, Peg races past me in the van, turns right onto Chestnut, and gives chase.

Winded, I slow to a stop, hands on both knees, and watch. Because of the late hour, there are no other drivers on the road, and it's a straight shot to Santa Fe Avenue. With dogged accuracy, Peg aligns her vehicle just behind and to the left of the fleeing car, and performs a beautiful, and effective, classic pursuit maneuver with her front bumper. The sedan is knocked into a sideways spin and jolts up onto the sidewalk and into a chain-link fence. Peg then glides into position just behind the sedan, blocking any escape.

Peg and Rocky are out of the van and able to grab the woman as she scrambles from the passenger-side door. Rocky easily trips her and flips her onto her back, allowing Peg to use her superior weight to pin the woman down. It's a practiced, almost balletic coordination, and I realize as I jog up to them that it's probably been used many times.

"Nice tactical execution, Peg," I say, panting. "But you know that's illegal in Dallas, right?"

Peg just shrugs and doesn't even try looking guilty.

"You learn that in the army?" I ask.

"Nah," Peg says. "The Kroger parking lot at Christmas."

The woman on the ground is struggling wildly, but Peg—at five feet four inches and 180 pounds—plants her knees firmly on the suspect's arms and, calmly reaching down, pinches the edge of one of the woman's nostrils between the two fingernails of her thumb and forefinger.

When the woman starts screaming in pain, Peg tells her, "Well, stop struggling and I'll stop pinching. You don't, and you'll be able to wear a chain through your nose."

Rocky asks her, "What's your name?"

The woman tries spitting at her, and Rocky takes a few steps back. "Try that again and I will tase the *shit* out of you."

The woman renews her flailing and screams again when Peg applies more pressure.

"Hey," Rocky tells the woman, "you don't start cooperating with us, you'll be able to fit a chandelier through the hole in your nostril, forget about the chain."

I squat down next to the woman. "Come on. You might as well tell us. What's your name?"

She looks at me with venom, but answers, "None."

"Nun? Nun what?"

"None-Of-Your-Business."

Peg squeezes the woman's nose just enough to get a

reaction, and she looks at me, outraged. "You're a cop. You going to let them do this to me?"

"Absolutely not," I say. "We're going to wait right here for a patrol officer, Ms. 'None-Of-Your-Business.' I'm arresting you for disorderly conduct, disturbing the peace, and pulling a false alarm."

"No!" she yells.

"You can get your car out of impound once you've made bail." I stand and smile down at her. "Maybe your cult leader will pay it for you."

The woman goes very still, her eyes two glittering orbs of malice. "Evangeline is going to take your life apart, piece by piece. And then she's going to take you apart, piece by piece."

"Jesus," Peg says, looking up at me and shaking her head. "And I thought Rocky was dark."

A patrol officer handcuffs and takes the woman into custody. The identification found in her car names her as Donna Parcell of Wylie, Texas. As the officer drives away, we can see her busy at work in the back seat, trying to kick out the windows with her sneakered feet.

"Huh," Peg says, waving at the departing vehicle like a prom queen. "She doesn't act like a Donna."

"Thanks for your help. The both of you," I say.

Rocky fiddles with one wicked-looking spiked earring. "We still haven't found your girl, though. You want us to hang out in front of the shelter some more?"

I shake my head. "Go home and get some sleep. I'll ask Billy to keep an eye on Tina. I think Evangeline is done with this place. She'll move on, just to keep me on my toes."

We say our good nights, and when I get home, Jackie and Elizabeth are still sleeping, oblivious to Aunt Betty's midnight escapades. I take a pillow and blanket and bed down on the floor in the baby's room, next to the crib. But it's a long time before I can fall asleep.

19

Dallas Police Department, North Central Division
Friday, September 19, 2014

After downing three cups of coffee strong enough to strip paint off a wall, I gather the team in the incident room to review yesterday's events, and to strategize about future surveillance for Flaco. The bulk of Thursday was spent marshaling intel and surveillance support from the DEA, and giving Philbo time to work with Manny Ortega and his Gangland UC to plot out how to approach Barrio 18. Craddock has brought kolaches and more coffee, and I wait for the men to inhale their share of fat, sugar, and caffeine, which I hope will energize them for the morning's meeting. Only Seth is missing; I got a text saying he'd be a few minutes late.

"Donna Parcell was processed into Central Division on Hall Street about two a.m. Thursday morning," I say. "She was issued a citation, with a stated date and time to appear at the county courthouse, and then released. I had asked to have her detained until I could speak with her, as I suspected that she'd try to contact Evangeline, but she had no priors, and they had no probable cause to hold her. And despite trying to kick out the windows in the patrol car, she was cooperative, even cheerful, after making her phone call. Yesterday a young redheaded woman picked her up, and they left together. But not before offering some missionary brochures to the desk sergeant, along with a hearty 'The righteous shall be spared from the sword,' or some such nonsense."

"So, we can assume the redheaded woman was sent by Evangeline Roy?" Esparza asks.

"I'd say that was a good guess," I tell him.

"So, what now?" Craddock asks, reaching for the last kolach.

"Now we go to work finding her." I turn to Ryan. "What commitment do we have from DEA?"

"I spoke to Fred Dunlap about our plan to coordinate with DPD Gangland, and he agreed to give us quick turnaround on any surveillance we'll need."

Craddock swipes the powdered sugar off his lips. "All we had to do was mention that Barrio 18 was trying to set up shop within Dallas city limits, and he was all in."

"Excellent. Detective Philbo, do you want to give us—"

At that moment Seth saunters in, wearing a brightly colored T-shirt. This one with a whimsical cartoon image that he usually sports only on the weekends. It's a picture of Squidward, the whiny character from SpongeBob SquarePants. A fucking squid...

Craddock guffaws, spitting out the last of the kolach in his mouth, Ryan chokes on his coffee, and Esparza palms a grin. Seth had evidently let even Philbo's partner in on the joke. Everyone except the wannabe tough-guy biker.

Philbo looks around, confused, but Seth wears a mask of innocence.

"What'd I miss?" Seth asks.

I turn my back to Philbo and give my partner a stern look. "We've got DEA surveillance backing, and Detective Philbo was just about to tell us his ideas for corralling Flaco," I say. "Right, Detective?"

"Yeah," Philbo says, glancing around as the team stuffs down their laughter. He suspects the joke's on him, but he doesn't yet know the punch line.

"I spent the day with Manny Ortega and his undercover from Five Points. The UC confirms that Barrio 18 is a growing presence with half a dozen gang members already there, and word that more will be coming."

Philbo opens his laptop and pulls up a satellite map of the area surrounding the Wildflower Apartments. He points to an area a few blocks north—a sprawling grouping of apartment units with a now-abandoned retail-car lot on one side, liquor and convenience stores on the other.

"This three-block area of loveliness is named the Ivy Apartments. Ortega's UC thinks this is where the Barrio 18 is looking to take up shop. Twelve hundred units, filled with West African, Asian, and Hispanic families mainly from Central America. Tons of kids, the usual prisoner-in-training teenagers and gangbanger hopefuls, but little police presence within the resident courtyard areas. It's like a warren with back alleyways, not only between the units but also leading into the car lot and through back entrances to stores. Poor lighting, multiple escape routes, and lack of police presence, and you have a perfect setup for selling drugs. Ortega's UC, whose street name is Hunk, by the way, is going to keep eyes and ears open on which unit, or units, they occupy. As soon as they know, I'll know."

"And then I'm assuming I'll be the next to know," I say.

"Oh, of course, Detective," Philbo says. His patronizing tone works like a nail through the head. "After all, you're the sergeant, Sergeant."

"Any more sightings of Flaco in Five Points?" I ask.

Philbo shakes his head. "But if his crew is there, he'll have to contact them one way or another. If he doesn't show up in person, which he probably won't, we'll get his conversations on a wire. We should have more intel by Monday."

I end the meeting, and as I'm walking out the door, Ryan beckons me into the break room. He looks positively giddy.

"There's something I wanted to share with you," he says, and gives a dramatic pause. "Karen's pregnant again."

His happiness is a force field of pure electric energy. "Holy cannoli, as Craddock would say. Congratulations. I'd give you a hug, but it might cramp my Wicked Witch of the West vibe."

"Hey," he says, "we'll be setting up playdates for the kids before you know it."

He laughs at the look on my face and points at me as if to say, *Gotcha, didn't I?* He's still laughing as he walks back to his desk.

I have to admit that it's refreshing to see optimism on the face of a narcotics detective. The attrition rate of most law enforcement involved in the war on illegal substances is high. They either care too much about the staggering human toll—the unimaginable violence and continued suffering of addiction—and end up burning out, or they care too little and end up being singed by the seductive pull of untraceable cash and a quick high.

My cell phone rings, jolting me back to the present. I answer, steeling myself for the possibility of hearing El Cuchillo's voice again. Every bit of relief from this morning's teasing and the good news from Ryan evaporates within heartbeats.

"Sergeant Rhyzyk?" a man's voice asks.

"Yes, speaking."

"This is Alan P. Turner."

I pull the phone away from my ear as though it's on fire. Alan P. Fucking Turner. I'll want to take notes, so, instinctively, I mark the time on my computer. 11:11 a.m. The coincidence, for a second time, gives me a jolt of adrenaline.

"Do you know who I am?" he asks into the silence.

"I know who you are," I say, grabbing for a pen and paper.

"I was wondering if you could speak to me for a few minutes?"

"I'm listening."

"I'd like to meet with you. And your partner, of course."

There was the slightest pause before he said the word *partner*, and I want to hang up before he says another word. "What about?" I ask through gritted teeth.

"I understand that you've been taking care of my grandchild, for which I'm very grateful—"

"And?" I say, cutting him off.

There's an intake of breath on his end. Mr. Turner is evidently not accustomed to being spoken to like one of the little people.

"And…I'd like to discuss arrangements going forward. But I really don't want to talk on the phone. Can you meet with me in person?"

"I'm not sure that's a good idea."

"Please, I'm having a reception tomorrow. Just give me ten minutes of your time."

"I'm going to be busy tomorrow." I look at the name of the family-court lawyer Peg Bartles had given me, Keri McCall, and seriously consider giving Turner the standard "Talk to my lawyer" line.

"Too busy to talk about the fate of Mary Grace's baby?" he asks.

"*Fate*'s an ominous word, Mr. Turner. And the baby has a name, by the way. It's Elizabeth."

"Look," he says, "I understand that you've been taking care of Elizabeth for months now. And I'm very grateful for that—"

"We also took care of your stepdaughter," I say. "Funny, you haven't asked after her well-being."

He sighs. "I tried for years to help Mary Grace. She came from a rough background, and I worked to give her every advantage. But she chose another path. I'd like to try and make a difference in my granddaughter's life. Before it's too late."

I have to hand it to the guy. He sounds sincere, but there's a little too much of the game-show-host sparkle to his delivery.

"I'll send you the address and time of the event tomorrow. It's a charity gala. You'll be able to see for yourself what kind of life Elizabeth could have. I don't want to shut you out of her life completely. But we have to think about what's best for her going forward. Please."

I take a deep breath. That hopeful, troublesome impulse has lifted its thorny little head. *You could have your life back as it was before. Just you and Jackie...Lingering over coffee in the mornings. Drinking wine by candlelight late at night. Making love undisturbed on the living room floor...It's Jackie's birthday today and, instead of a short dinner at home with one eye on the baby, we could be staying out all hours celebrating.*

"Hello?" Turner says.

"I'll think about it," I say, and disconnect the call.

A few minutes later, a text comes through with the address of the gala. I snort out loud. The event will take place at Southfork Ranch, about a half-hour drive from Dallas. The real-life ranch where the fictional TV soap opera *Dallas* was filmed. The invitation reads WESTERN ATTIRE A MUST.

I know two things for sure. If I do decide to go, it won't be in a cowboy hat; and I won't be going with Jackie. I need to look Turner in the eye and ask some hard questions, like "Do you know where Mary Grace is?" and "Why did she leave home in the first place?" It always makes Jackie a little uneasy when I go full-on cop in a social situation. But I've learned to trust my instincts about people, observing their reactions under the hot spotlight of intense scrutiny. Maybe the reason he isn't asking about Mary Grace's whereabouts, or her condition, is because he knows *exactly* where she is.

It might be useful to observe Alan P. Turner in his natural habitat. He'll be on his turf, imagining he holds all the cards. It might also be to my advantage to let him see that I can't be easily intimidated or bullied. The reasonable part of me is whispering that if I go, I should show up in full professional mode. Sensible clothes, sensible shoes, sensible attitude. The kind of attitude that makes for a safe bet as a guardian of an infant. Or, barring that, a reputable babysitter.

But another part of me—the larger part, which is not so reasonable, the part that's enthusiastically chosen undercover narcotics work—wants to show up in black leather and the kind of boots that kick down doors.

I know what Uncle Benny would advise. He'd tell me to be myself. Even if that self has teeth and claws and breathes fire.

20

Southfork Ranch
Saturday, September 20, 2014

Anyone who watched prime-time network TV during the eighties can hum the theme song to *Dallas* as well as answer the question "Who shot J.R.?" I was young at the time, but I do remember my mother sitting in our dark living room in Greenpoint, Brooklyn, a cigarette in one hand and a gin and tonic in the other. It was one of the few shows she watched faithfully, bringing endless taunts from my father, who quipped she couldn't find Texas on the map if her life depended on it. Nor could she tell one end of a horse from the other.

To which she'd mutter, once he'd left the room, *"Znam tyłek konia kiedy go widzę."* I know a horse's ass when I see one.

Accessing the three-hundred-acre ranch by its long entranceway is like taxiing down a very exclusive private airstrip. One that, despite the gala-in-progress, is still pastorally quiet. Peaceful, that is, until we roar down the driveway on Manny Ortega's Harley-Davidson Street Glide.

There's valet parking for all the Mercedes-Benzes, Beemers, and Jaguars already in the parking lot. And the look on the valets' faces when Manny and I pull up is worth the hair-raising half hour spent weaving through Dallas traffic. Once I had decided that I would go "all Betty" on Alan P. Turner, it was only fitting that my ride should be someone who was edgy, dangerous, and, most important, brown.

Manny parks his Harley a few feet from the parking kiosk, and as we're climbing off, one of the valets comes running, his hands waving defensively.

"Sorry, folks. The ranch is closed today for a private function."

Manny throws him the keys to the bike. Getting right in the kid's face he growls, "I find a scratch on it, and I'm gonna blame you personally. You feel me?"

The valet is young, maybe eighteen, and he looks at the undercover—dressed in full biker leathers, hobnail boots, and wraparound shades—and blanches.

I flash my badge at him. "That's okay. We've been invited by Mr. Turner."

Taking Manny's arm, as though he's my date, we saunter off toward the enormous tent that's been set up on the lawn where the fictional Ewings often held their barbecues. The tent, just a few yards from the iconic house, is enclosed on four sides by nearly opaque plastic, so the guests—maybe two hundred of them by the volume of the conversational buzz—don't get an eyeful of us until we pass through the main entrance. There is an official greeter, a young, attractive woman of maybe twenty-five, ticking names off a guest list. When she turns to face us, she startles and drops her pen—which lands next to Manny's hard-worn boot—and has to scramble clumsily to retrieve it. When she's upright again, I announce us.

"Detectives Rhyzyk and Ortega," I say.

"Uh..." she says, frantically searching her list. "I don't see...What are your names again?"

"That's okay, Amanda," a man's voice says. It's Alan P. Turner himself. He's dressed in starched jeans, a pristine white cowboy shirt with pearl snap buttons, and boots of some exotic leather. Probably harvested from an endangered baby rhino, stitched together by blind, underage nuns from Guatemala. He's holding a glass of champagne in one well-manicured hand, and the other hand is holding an unlit cigar.

He's tall, silver-haired, and tanned, as though he's just returned from a month in the Riviera, or the Maldives, or wherever billionaires spend their summer vacations.

"They're my personal invites," he tells Amanda. He turns a brilliant smile to her and then beams it in our direction. He deftly pockets the cigar and holds a hand out for me to shake, which I do, reluctantly.

"Detective Sergeant, welcome to Southfork." His voice is deeply masculine with just a trace of a Texas accent.

"Thank you, Mr. Turner. This is Detective Manny Ortega. I didn't think you'd mind my bringing a guest."

Turner holds out his hand for Manny to shake, but my colleague has caught his host's raking glance of disapproval. Manny holds both his hands up apologetically and says, *"Perdóname, pero no habla inglés, señor."*

He gives me a wink and then strolls toward the buffet table, his boot heels striking hard on the dance floor, scattering expensively dressed invitees in alarmed waves as though he were Moses parting the Red Sea.

"One of your fellow undercovers?" Turner asks, his mouth downturned at the slight.

"One of the best officers in the DPD. He earned his scars the hard way."

"No doubt." Turner gestures for me to follow, leading me toward the back of the tent. Along the way, he greets half a dozen florid-faced men and their tightly tucked wives (or girlfriends) but doesn't stay to talk at length. He also doesn't introduce me to anyone, seemingly impervious to the whispered speculations about the tall redheaded Amazon swathed in black leather being seated next to him at a small private table.

"Would you like something?" he asks, beckoning to a uniformed waiter hovering nearby. "Hector, I'll have a Macallan neat. And make sure it's from the rare cask bottle."

"Absolutely, Mr. Turner," Hector says, practically genuflecting in front of his boss. "And for you, ma'am?"

"Just water for me. Light on the glass," I tell the waiter, who pauses for a moment, confused. He then scurries away to get the drinks.

When I look back at Turner, his eyes are on me in a calculating way, the way a boxer just entering the ring assesses his opponent, but he seems amused by my order.

"'Light on the glass.' Spoken like a true whiskey connoisseur," he says. "Let me guess. You're a Jameson drinker, right? The preferred drink of the men, and the women, in blue."

His use of "and the women" sounds like an add-on for my benefit. And his familiarity with cops drinking Jameson is bullshit. I'm sure that's just one more bit of information he's gleaned about me from his PI. The Macallan rare cask whiskey is several hundred dollars a bottle, no doubt. He's letting me know up front that he's got money to burn. I give him a tight smile.

He leans closer over the table, as though settling in for a cozy chat. He gives me his most sincere look. "Thank you for meeting me. And thank you for taking care of my granddaughter."

A country-and-western band has begun to play, forcing me to lean in closer as well.

"You've thanked me already for that," I say. "Jackie and I care very deeply for both Mary Grace and Elizabeth. Mary Grace chose to give birth in our home. And when she left, she chose to leave the baby with us."

Turner takes the cigar out of his pocket, and another waiter appears immediately to light it. He takes a few strong puffs, exhaling the smoke with a satisfied sigh. Hector returns with Turner's whiskey and my water.

"Any word on where Mary Grace is now?" He asks the question lightly, as though the answer is of little importance.

"I would ask you the same question."

He shakes his head. "I have no idea where my stepdaughter is."

We stare hard at each other for a few beats.

He taps some ash into a crystal ashtray, takes a few sips of his whiskey. "As I mentioned on the phone, Mary Grace has had a long, troubled history. Drugs, drinking, boys. Lots and lots of boys."

"Funny, I never knew her to do drugs. And I never saw her drink."

"She's lived with me since she was twelve. I think I'd know about her habits."

"What about her mother?" Mary Grace had never spoken of her parents.

"She's out of the picture completely," Turner says. "I married the mother, in part, because I felt sorry for her. I was trying to rescue her, I suppose. Very attractive but, as they say in the south, a hot mess." He taps the cigar into the ashtray a little harder than is necessary. "We divorced less than a year later."

"You don't appear to be the kind of man to marry a woman just because you felt sorry for her."

He clutches his chest theatrically as though I've wounded him.

"I do have a heart, Sergeant. I continued to care for Mary Grace when it became apparent that her mother wasn't capable. Unfortunately, the daughter turned out just like her mother."

A few more ashes are flicked unnecessarily into the ashtray.

"What's the mother's name?" I ask.

"Renée."

"Renée what?"

He studies me. "And this is important because?"

"Because maybe she knows where Mary Grace is."

"I can assure you, my ex-wife won't know what day it is, let alone where her daughter is."

I don't break eye contact for the count of five. Finally he sighs and says, "Broussard. Renée Broussard. But I don't know what name she's using now."

"How did you know Mary Grace had given birth?" I ask.

Turner smiles. "There's very little that goes on in this city that I don't know about."

"Do you know who the father of the baby is?"

He puffs thoughtfully on the cigar, his gaze flicking restlessly across the room. "I have no idea," he says, tap-tapping the tip of the cigar against the patterned crystal again.

The nervous fiddling is a tell. He's not revealing the whole truth. Just like Tina at the shelter. How many more people know who Elizabeth's father is but can't, or won't, say?

Something across the room has caught Turner's attention. It's a gorgeous girl, rail thin, with long, glossy blond hair and breasts the size of cantaloupes on steroids who looks almost too young to be holding a glass of champagne. She throws Turner a dazzling smile.

He catches me watching him. He takes another sip of his whiskey, savoring the aromatic liquid. "You know the best thing about whiskey?" he asks. "Besides its taste, I mean. The liquor can stay inside the bottle for a hundred years without an appreciable change in its flavor. So, its value appreciates as well. In some ways it's a better investment than property."

He smiles, and I wait for him to make his point.

"But do you know how whiskey begins its life?" he asks, pointing his gaze toward the girl again. "Water, yeast, and malts. Same as beer. Simple, unsophisticated, unrefined. But once it's stored in aged oak barrels, left alone in the dark to absorb all the wisdom of the wood, it becomes something it could never be if left to its own devices. It would never fully mature."

The girl is smiling at him again.

"You see," he says, turning back to face me, "whiskey will only ever gain its flavor inside the cask."

His expression is unmistakable. I've seen the same lustful look a thousand times on guys in a dark peep-show theater.

I have to bite my tongue on a sharp remark about young, unsophisticated mash rubbing up against aged wood.

"Can we talk about Elizabeth, please," I say.

"She should be with her family," he says.

"Are you married?" I ask, knowing full well that he's not.

He exhales a long stream of cigar smoke. "No. But then neither are you."

"Not for lack of trying," I say. "I've been in a stable relationship with a woman I consider my wife for ten years."

Turner cocks his head. "Stable? I'm not sure an objective third party would call this past year of your life stable."

His mouth is smiling, but his eyes are not. He scoots his chair closer, puts both elbows on the table, and thrusts his face close to mine. Anyone watching the move might think it was a play for intimacy. But there is no warmth in his eyes.

"I know all about you," he snaps. "Your injuries, your commendations, your many successful busts. And I also know about your breakdowns and your associations with junkies, queers, and street urchins. You're a hot mess as well, Detective Sergeant. You've got a violent streak a mile long. Right now, for instance. You'd like to put your fist in my face."

"Actually," I say, "right now, I'm thinking of a place much lower."

"Look around," he says, gesturing with his cigar. "Every person in this place is rich and in a position of influence. Just from where I'm sitting I can see a county commissioner, two criminal district judges, and one family court judge. All here because of me."

Out of the corner of my eye, I see a concerned Manny Ortega making his way toward us. He's holding a plate of food in one hand and a drink in the other. He drops the refreshments carelessly on two different tables as he passes, causing the seated guests to stare after him, openmouthed.

"Why do you think I invited you here?" Turner continues. "Did you think it was for us to have a friendly chat, to get to know each other better? I brought you here for you to see, and *understand,* that I want custody of my granddaughter. And there's no amount of money or persuasion I'm not willing to use to fight you and your *girlfriend* in this."

Manny stands utterly still behind Turner. But it's not a passive stillness. It's a stillness ready for defensive action.

"I know about you as well, Mr. Turner," I say. "Enough to know that the blond smiling at you from across the room is probably already too old to keep your interest for long. Despite the age of your wood."

There is a moment when I know I've hit the mark. Turner goes rigid and blinks a few times. But, recovering, he grins, showing a lot of perfect teeth. "Very good, Detective. I like a challenger with some fight in them. But don't *ever* mistake my civility for weakness. Not only will I delight in taking you apart in family court, but, just for laughs, I may lodge a complaint of harassment with your division chief, whom I happen to know quite well."

As Turner is talking, two burly men in dark suits appear on either side of Manny. Turner's bodyguards, who are both taller than Manny, stand glowering down on the undercover's head. Without looking at either of them, Manny slips the lanyard with his detective's shield from under his T-shirt and lets it dangle over his chest. The reveal takes some of the starch out of their intimidation tactics.

I stand but lean down close to Turner, making sure he can hear me over the increasing volume of the band. "You know, it's fitting that you'd throw a party here at the Ewing ranch. If I recall the TV show correctly, the plot involved a few wealthy Texans doing their best to destroy their own family. The original series ending is especially memorable. J.R. lost everything and ended up pointing a pistol at his own head."

Turner makes a show of ignoring me, gazing at the light playing across his crystal cocktail glass. "Should I read that as a threat, Detective?"

I dump my glass of water on top of his remaining, very expensive whiskey. "Read it more as a warning sign, Mr. Turner. Just don't ever mistake *my* civility for weakness."

Manny and I walk toward the exit with all eyes on us. As I pass the blond girl, I say, loudly, "He just told me he's being treated for an STD."

We leave the tent with the two bodyguards trailing us.

"You want to really freak them out?" Manny mutters as we cross the lawn toward the parking kiosk. "Let's go jump in the pool."

I laugh out loud. "Thanks for backing me up in there."

"No problem. It was kinda fun. Homie here was making some serious points with a couple of the Highland Park matrons. Seriously, though, there were a lot of young, *young* girls at that party. I got a twelve-year-old daughter at home, and it wigged me the fuck out."

"Yeah, tell me about it. I want to take a shower now."

As we approach the valet, the bodyguards turn around and walk back to the party tent. Manny slips a big tip to the young man watching his motorcycle, and as we put on our helmets, he asks me, "He gonna go for the kid?"

"Looks like," I say.

He holds up his fists in a mock boxer stance. "You gonna

fight it, though, right? I can see it in your face." He emits a low whistle. "But you better start racking up the overtime, Sargento. It's going to cost you."

I perch behind him as he kick-starts his bike and revs the engine loudly and repeatedly, causing the valets to cover their ears.

"Yeah, that's what everyone keeps telling me," I say, but my voice is drowned out by the motorcycle burning rubber down the long driveway.

21

The House
Saturday, September 20, 2014

I walk into the house, feeling like a hundred miles of thunderstorm. All I want is a double shot of Jameson and some quiet time in my office to cool down. My encounter with Alan Turner has made me angry. And, if I'm being honest, guilty. It's an opportunity for me to back out of pursuing custody of Elizabeth. Turner has very deep pockets, and we do not. As well, he seems absolutely dedicated to winning a battle in family court, and I'm still unsure of committing to a responsibility I feel neither ready for nor completely willing to undertake. The conflict twists in my gut like a nest of vipers, pitting my own best interests against the guilt I feel for abandoning Elizabeth to someone who, at best, is a ruthless opportunist. The resulting anxiety feeds my anger even more.

I knew that Jackie was on call at the hospital for most of the day, but I can hear familiar voices, a man and woman, talking in the kitchen. When I peek in, I see James Earle keeping company with Connie. Something bubbling on the stove fills the entire house with an inviting aroma. James Earle stands at attention, brandishing a wooden stirring spoon to emphasize a story he's telling, and wearing one of Jackie's mom's aprons. His longish hair is gelled and meticulously combed, and he's wearing another new starched shirt. He's recounting one of his many outrageous Vietnam tales (one without a high body count), and Connie is leaning one hip against the counter, laughing. By the way his eyes are lit up, I can tell he's totally fallen for her.

Connie sees me standing in the doorway and waves. James turns to me, and knowing me as well as he does, his smile fades and his brows come down with concern.

"Where's the baby?" I ask.

Now Connie's smile has lost some vigor as well. "She's down for a nap."

"Everything okay, Red?" James asks, handing the spoon over to Connie.

I walk to the far side of the kitchen and pull the bottle of Jameson and a glass out of a cabinet. Pouring a stiff measure I say, "Peachy."

James follows me out of the kitchen and into my office.

I've drained half the glass before I'm even settled in my chair. James rests against the doorframe and waits.

"I went out to see Alan Turner today," I say.

"Mary Grace's stepdad?"

"That's the one." I take another sip. I don't offer him a drink, as I know he's trying to stay sober.

"Let me guess," he says, scratching at his chin. "He's going full-on Tet Offensive."

"Looks that way."

He walks into the room, pulls up another chair, and sits. "What are you going to do?"

"I think Jackie really wants to pursue custody." I can't look James in the eye. "If we don't find Mary Grace soon."

He rests a hand on my arm, and when I finally look up at him, it's all there in my face: the doubt, the uncertainty, the misery.

"It's a big decision. You've got to be certain."

But that's just it, I want to tell him. *I'm not certain. I want to make Jackie happy. I want to keep Elizabeth safe with us, at least until we find out what happened to Mary Grace. I want to do what's best for everybody. But that may mean turning the baby over to her family, such as it is.*

"One thing I know about you, Red, is that you'll do what's right." He squeezes my arm for emphasis. "Jackie's the most important thing in your life, but this won't work unless you're a hundred percent sure that you're ready to be a full-time parent. 'Cause that's what this is." He looks down at his hands clasped in his lap. "I don't think Mary Grace is coming back. Do you?"

"I wish I knew, James."

"I know that Elizabeth is a helpless baby. And there's nothing you like more than charging into the breach to rescue something helpless. But the truth is, Mary Grace abandoned her post. And now a member of her family has stepped in."

"So, you're saying that I should just step back and let a man of dubious moral character take custody?"

"No, that's not what I'm saying. There's not another human being I know on this earth who fights harder than you when your mind is made up. And if you decide to go all in with this guy Turner, he's sure as hell going to learn what it's like to tangle with the Shield Maiden of Greenpoint, Brooklyn. To paraphrase my old boss General Westmoreland, a fight is often won not just by capabilities but by sheer bullheaded, iron-willed intention."

I chuff out a laugh. "I will certainly own 'bullheaded.'"

"But at the end of the day, you have to be honest about whether you're ready and willing to take on this responsibility." He begins to raise himself out of the chair by pressing both palms against the armrests. I have to remind myself that he's seventy-one. He smokes and until recently drank heavily and consumed enough cholesterol to choke a horse. Vices at age seventy ravage the body far more than they do at forty, or even sixty. He's already in advanced middle age, looking straight ahead to the fragility of old age. The realization makes my throat close up with an unbearable sadness.

"You need to talk honestly to Jackie about this," he tells me. He pats my shoulder so I'll meet his gaze. "And talk to Connie. She really loves that baby. She may have some wisdom to impart."

I stand and give him a quick, fierce hug. "You really like her, don't you?"

He winks at me and gives me a wistful smile. "No fool like an old fool."

He rejoins Connie in the kitchen, and after a period of quiet conversation, he has her laughing again.

A half hour later, I hear the front door close, and soon Connie is standing in the doorway. Motioning her into the office and telling her to take a seat, I thank her for coming in on a Saturday and give her a rundown of my conversation with Alan Turner.

Connie listens in silence, her forehead creased with worry, eyes focused intently on me. Her hands are tightly clenched in her lap. It's the first time we've been in the same room together for longer than it takes to say "Good morning" or "Good night." In reality, I've given her very little attention or thought until this moment. I let Mary Grace and Jackie handle the initial nanny interviews and hiring details. My only input had been "If you're happy with her, then I am too."

I realize that the woman sitting in front of me is younger than I had first thought, even though the corners of Connie's eyes and mouth are crinkled with tiny age lines. Her tawny shoulder-length hair is often worn swept back into a ponytail, but I notice that it's highlighted with subtle blond streaks that are most likely applied in a good salon. Her makeup is subdued, her neatly trimmed fingernails glow with discreet polish, and her street clothes are simple but of good quality. I can see why James Earle would be attracted to her. She's not the typical dowdy, sensible-shoes-wearing child caregiver featured in a Hallmark movie of the week.

"What are you going to do?" she asks.

"I'm not sure," I say, toying with my now-empty whiskey glass. "Turner's got a fortune to spend. And he's Mary Grace's stepfather. I don't know if there's much we can do."

"You can't let Turner have Elizabeth."

Her forceful tone brings my head up. Connie's more than concerned. She's distressed to the point of tears.

"I know you've grown very attached to the baby—"

She's shaking her head. "It's not just that."

Connie takes a few breaths to calm herself. "I'm sorry. I mean, yes, I've grown to care deeply for Elizabeth. I really do. But it's more than a simple attachment. As soon as I heard you and Jackie talking about Turner, I became worried." She twists one of her rings around on her finger. "He's not a nice man."

I wait for her to continue.

"I've heard things. He's done bad things, to a lot of people."

The way she says it—quietly but with conviction—makes it sound like she has some inside information. The nanny network is fast and furious, and because of the vulnerable nature of the caregivers, as necessary as a paycheck. Nannies are privy to the most cloistered aspects of people's lives and see, up close and unfiltered, the worst of human nature. And, all too often, the wealthier the patrons, the more odious the behavior.

"Anything you'd like to tell me about Turner now?" I ask.

"I just—" she starts to say.

The sound of a window breaking in another room jerks us both to our feet. The relentless anxiety that either Evangeline, or the Knife, would invade my home surges like a tidal wave.

"What's that?" Connie whispers.

"Stay here," I tell her, moving quickly.

Elizabeth has started a fearful wailing from the nursery. I run down the hallway and fling open the door to the darkened room, hearing the sound of crunching glass under my foot. The window has been smashed. A block of concrete sits in the middle of the room. It had been thrown so hard that it's ripped the window shade off its track. Elizabeth looks impossibly small and helpless in her crib.

Connie is right behind me, and she scoops up the crying baby and runs from the room. It's late afternoon but still light outside, so I have a clear view of the backyard. There's no one there. Whoever threw the concrete was fast on their feet. Painted in red on it is *E 5:21*.

It refers to Ephesians verse 5, chapter 21, and, in the warped ideation of Evangeline Roy, it means to submit to the will of a vengeful, fearsome, Stone-Age God. It was painted on the stone I was chained to after I'd been kidnapped by the matriarch's sons.

I speed-dial the plainclothes detective parked out front. Two minutes later I hear sirens, and he tells me the two patrol officers stationed behind our house have apprehended someone running from the alley.

Their patrol car pulls up in front of the house so I can get a look at the perpetrator. Seated in back, her hands cuffed behind her, is Donna Parcell.

An officer opens the door, and Donna leers at me.

"Good afternoon, Detective," she says.

I get right in her face. "That hunk of concrete landed three feet from an infant's crib, you piece of shit."

She meets my gaze defiantly, and then her eyes shift behind me. I turn to see Connie standing on the porch, holding the baby, who is still hiccuping from her crying jag.

"Is that Elizabeth?" Donna asks. "I see you!" she yells at Connie. "You can't protect that baby forever."

My head whips back around, and her tigerlike expression fills me with dread.

"An eye for an eye, Detective," she murmurs, her lips twitching gleefully. "A child for a child."

I take three steps back to keep from slamming her in the jaw. The officer quickly closes the door.

Making sure I have the officer's full attention, I say, "I want to press child-endangerment charges against this woman, as well as home invasion and threatening a police officer. And I want to be apprised of exactly when the arraignment hearing is set. Is that clear?"

"Crystal, Sergeant," the officer says.

He climbs into the driver's seat to join his partner just as Jackie pulls into the driveway. She gets out of her car and, in a glance, takes in the plainclothes detective standing on the lawn, the patrol car with lights flashing parked in front of the house, the curious neighbors gathering out on their front yards, and Connie still holding a red-faced, whimpering Elizabeth.

She looks at me exasperated. "Jesus Christ, Betty. I've only been gone for a few hours!"

After dinner, and after the baby's been put to bed—we've moved the crib into our room for the night and taped a plastic tarp over the broken window—Jackie and I sit on the couch in the living room. Jackie holds a glass of wine, doing her best to contain her anger, while I clutch a double Jameson like a diabetic holding on to her last piece of candy. I've told her about my meeting with Turner and the events leading up to Donna Parcell's second arrest. I give her a moment to process my deception in meeting with Turner without telling her.

Earlier, Connie had been almost inconsolable with worry, begging us to let her stay the night. But I had finally convinced her that we'd keep an eagle eye on Elizabeth, assuring her that we'd have extra squad cars on patrol in the neighborhood.

This gentle, caring nanny had even pulled me aside, asking me if I'd keep my gun close at hand.

"Shoot them if you have to," she had whispered fiercely. The anger in her voice stayed with me.

Jackie finally looks up at me. "I can't believe you didn't tell me about going to see Turner," she says, her voice carefully modulated. But there are bright red blotches on each cheek to signal her displeasure. She hardly ever yells, or even raises her voice to me. And therein lies the problem. It makes it difficult for me to maintain my self-righteous posturing.

"I'm sorry, Jackie. I just thought it would be to our advantage to get the lay of the land."

"And you didn't think I'd be able to make a reasonable judgment about the situation?"

"The man's a nasty piece of work. I just wanted to spare you the—"

"The what—the inconvenience? Or did you think my attachment to Elizabeth would make me too emotional? Did it occur to you that if we do decide to file for custody, you've given him ammunition to build a case against us? And you took Manny Ortega out there with you?" She shakes her head and drains her glass of wine.

I reach for her hand and squeeze it. "What do you want to do?"

She looks at me for a long moment and then asks, "Where is the number for the attorney that Peg Bartles gave you?"

I hand her the piece of paper. When Jackie reads the name, she nods and says, "I know Keri McCall. I've testified for her in court during a few custody cases. She's a good lawyer."

She grabs her phone from her bag and dials, putting the phone on speaker mode.

While it's ringing, she says to me, "All of this is pointless if we don't even know what our chances are of gaining custody."

With a flash of guilt, I wonder if I should be more forthcoming with Jackie about my conflicted feelings where Elizabeth is concerned.

A woman finally answers.

"Hi, Keri," Jackie says. "This is Dr. Jackie Nesbitt."

"Hey, Jackie," Keri answers. "It's been a while. Everything okay?"

"Actually, I really need your help. It's kind of urgent. Is there any way my partner and I could see you tomorrow? It's about a child that may be in danger."

"For you, absolutely. I'll put you to work in the greenhouse. Come by around one o'clock. Oh," she says, laughing, "and be sure and wear your rubbers."

22

New Hope Greenhouse
Sunday, September 21, 2014

Keri McCall, Jackie reminds me, is an attorney who's practiced for over twenty years in the Dallas family-court system. More important, she's a fierce child advocate who has used Jackie's official testimony as a pediatric radiologist to prove abuse and injury. Keri's been married to the same man for decades, has three near-grown children, and spends every Sunday tending the New Hope Greenhouse, which provides fresh produce for homeless shelters in the city.

She's one of the rare people who have slogged their way through the maddeningly inconsistent, and often inequitable, hallways of family justice while maintaining a minimally jaded view of humanity as a whole. Apart from being a lawyer, she has an engineering degree from Southern Methodist University, and is a black belt in jujitsu. So, not only can she kick some serious ass in the courtroom, she can kick some serious ass in general.

Jackie insists she's almost always the smartest person in

any room, and coming from Dr. Nesbitt, that's saying quite a lot. Jackie says she trusts Keri to give us a straight, clear-eyed estimation of our chances if we decide to seek custody of Elizabeth.

It had rained the night before, so we took Keri's advice to wear our rubber boots. The greenhouse is on an acre lot behind a church, and we pick our way carefully over the muddy ground toward the enclosed structure, which must be twenty feet wide and at least forty feet long.

Typical for a Texas fall, the weather is pleasant, and the greenhouse is left open to the elements. A petite woman with gray streaks through her dark hair walks toward us.

She gives Jackie a hug and then takes my outstretched hand in both of hers. Normally this kind of greeting puts me on guard. It's the kind of affectation that politicians use to ingratiate themselves with their constituents. But I realize immediately that Keri has used it as a "capture" move to immobilize me long enough to look deep into my eyes and do a probing exam of my intentions. Her eyes are intensely blue—almost violet—and she gives me an unblinking stare for the count of five.

When she finally smiles at me, I realize I've been holding my breath.

"Okay, let's put you to work, and you can tell me what's so urgent." Keri turns, motioning for us to follow her back into the greenhouse.

There are half a dozen volunteers moving through the rows of pots and planters, some transplanting seedlings for the autumn crop, some culling the last of the withered summer plants. Keri hands Jackie and me a couple of trowels and instructs us to make indentations in the soil of a long planter so she can transplant several small lettuce plants that are growing in a container.

Jackie tells Keri about Mary Grace, her giving birth to Elizabeth seven months ago, and her subsequent disappearance. I fill Keri in on the discovery of Mary Grace's past and my meeting with Alan Turner. Contrary to full disclosure, neither of us says anything about Evangeline. At the mention of Turner's name, Keri stops abruptly.

"What was Turner's ex-wife's name?" she asks me.

"Renée Broussard," I answer.

"She contacted our office several years ago."

Jackie and I look at each other.

"I know it sounds like an unusual coincidence," Keri says, "but evidently she had been contacting a few of the top child-custody lawyers in town. I didn't talk to her, but she spoke at length to one of my colleagues. I remember it because Alan Turner's such a big deal in Dallas. Broussard had previously agreed to give Turner custody of her only child, who I can now assume is Mary Grace, and she wanted to know what her chances would be to change the order. She made an appointment with our office but never showed up."

"What were her concerns?" Jackie asks.

Keri shakes her head. "Hmmm, I can't really talk about the specifics. Client confidentiality and all. But I do know what's been reported in the news about him."

She hands me a hose and tells me to start watering the new plants. She takes off her gardening gloves and smooths her hair back from her face.

"Okay, so, assuming Mary Grace can't, or won't, be taking back custody of Elizabeth, you want to know what your chances are against Alan Turner, who sounds determined to battle this out in court. Let's put the subject of how much this is going to cost aside until the end of the discussion. My first question to you both is, how committed are you to becoming legal guardians of this infant?"

She's addressed the question to both of us, but she's looking pointedly at me.

"I just want Elizabeth to be in a safe, nurturing environment," I say.

Keri gives me a sad smile. "To 'serve and protect,' right, Sergeant?"

She turns the water off and takes the hose from my hands.

"Let's look at this in the cold light of day," Keri says. "Pluses and minuses as far as the law is concerned. One:"—she holds up a finger as she begins to count off—"Mary Grace chose your home to give birth in. She wouldn't have stayed for so long if she felt unsafe. Two: although the circumstances of her disappearance are still unknown, she evidently chose to leave the baby in your care. Three: you two have been together for ten years as a committed couple. Four: you both have exemplary, steady-paying jobs. And, five: Elizabeth has been living, and thriving, in your home consistently for more than six months. That holds a lot of weight where guardianship is concerned."

"What about the rumors of Turner being a sexual predator?" Jackie asks.

"Irrelevant in this case, as all his accusers have settled out of court," Keri says. "Any judge worth her salt will understand this on an emotional level and take it into consideration. But again, Turner doesn't have any felonious sexual misconduct on his record.

"Now, let's look at the minuses. One:"—she lowers a finger—"he has sole custody of Mary Grace, who is still a minor. And even though she apparently left of her own accord, that point can be argued. It can even be argued that you had something to do with her disappearance."

Jackie and I both startle. It had never occurred to either of us that anyone would accuse us of being involved.

"That's crazy," I say.

Keri shrugs. "A good lawyer will look at every possibility." She lowers a second finger. "Two: he has a track record of already being a custodial parent of his stepdaughter. Three:"-—another finger down—"he has tremendous standing in the community and can call on all kinds of character witnesses. Four: this is Texas, and although there's no statute forbidding lesbian or gay couples from adopting, there is still a hearty bias in this state. Just look at the sentiments of the current governor. Depending on the judge you get, opinion could sway in Turner's favor. And five—and I said I'd hold this to the end of the conversation: Turner has a vast fortune, and he can drag this on until doomsday."

All of her fingers have been lowered and bunched together to make a fist. She holds the fist up in front of my face. "This hammer will come down hard on you. It will drain your finances and expose you to the kind of scrutiny and press that, believe me, you don't want. Trust me when I say that Turner will have the media on you like white on rice. It will be relentless, and it will not be kind."

The three of us stand silent for a moment. I sneak a look at Jackie, and it kills me to see her looking so deflated.

Keri puts a hand on Jackie's arm. "Look, I'd be willing to help you all I could. I'd even be happy to minimize my own fee, but being realistic, at bare bones the court costs are going to run you at least fifty thousand dollars."

Rocky Bentner was right about taking out a second mortgage.

"Go home," Keri says. "Talk it over for a few days. Then let me know what you decide. I know it's a heavy rock in your path, but I wouldn't be a good friend, or an ethical lawyer, if I didn't give it to you straight."

Jackie nods and walks away, toward the car. I hang back, giving her some minutes alone. Knowing Jackie the way I do, she'll need some time to think through everything.

"Between you, me, and the tomato plants," Keri says to me, "Turner's a pig. But I know his legal team. They are prosecutorial assassins, and they will crucify you. If I were you, I'd try and talk Jackie out of it."

I thank her and walk to the car. We drive back to the house in utter silence.

Connie had come in for a few hours to watch over Elizabeth while we met with Keri. We don't have to tell her how the meeting went. She can tell by our downcast expressions. She gathers up her things and leaves quickly so we won't see her crying.

23

**Ivy Apartments, Five Points
Monday, September 22, 2014**

It's early morning, and there are five of us crammed into a large surveillance van in an alley a few blocks from the Ivy Apartments. With me are Seth, Philbo, Manny Ortega, and a surveillance specialist from the DEA, on loan from Agent Fred Dunlap. The specialist, a twenty-seven-year-old tech wiz named Dave Moreno, gives us a thumbs-up that he's receiving a strong sound signal from inside apartment 302. On a monitor is a clear image of a man and a woman arguing in rapid-fire Spanish standing in the living room, where packing boxes and a few pieces of furniture are scattered about.

"They're talking about a washing machine delivery," Moreno tells us.

Philbo had worked all weekend with Manny's muscle-bound UC Hunk (after a line from the animated version of Hercules: "Hercules? Honey, you mean *Hunk-ules*!") to pinpoint exactly where Flaco and his boys from Barrio 18 were setting up operations, as well as to attain a warrant for the surveillance. Hunk already has a reputation at the nearby

Wildflower Apartments as a consistent buyer of cocaine and heroin. Unbeknownst to the gangs, he always purchases with marked bills and gives the product over to Dallas narcotics. The gang with the biggest presence in the Five Points area has been the Young Crips, an all-black group with half of their members under the age of twenty, which has been in perpetual conflict with rival Hispanic gangs. Manny assures us that with Barrio 18 moving in, things left as they are could get bloody, and soon.

Philbo gives the signal that Hunk, as arranged, is nearing our vehicle, marked as a commercial moving van, on foot and without his giant pit bull. We open the back doors quickly, and Hunk squeezes his massive form into the crowded space, perching at the end of a bench bolted to the floor.

"Hey, big man," Manny nods. "*¿Qué pasó?*"

"As you can see, they got their front already moved into three-oh-two," Hunk says.

The "front," Manny has explained to us, is a single mom from Honduras with a toddler. They will use the apartment to move product in and out—heroin hidden in packages of diapers—with the woman working as the mule. She'll carry the diapers into the apartment, unload and sort the drugs into garbage bags. Then her male partner will carry them to a dumpster close by. A dumpster where there are no cameras, and poor lighting. A classic MO for Honduran gangs. As soon as the woman took the lease, paying cash for the first three months in advance, we knew where Barrio 18 would set up.

"That was fast," I say.

"You're telling me," Philbo says. "She signed the lease on Sunday, we got the paper from the judge at eight that night, and we had our guys putting in the cameras at two a.m. this morning."

"How'd you find out about the woman?" I ask Hunk.

"I've got four apartment supers on a bonus system. They tell me who's moving in and who's moving out. They think it's 'cause I'm looking for new customers."

"Image looks good," Seth says, looking at the monitor. "Who's the guy?"

"Barrio 18," Manny says. "Probably posing as her boyfriend. He'll be there when she brings the product in to make sure she's not skimming."

The toddler, looking less than two years old, comes into the room, crying. The two adults continue to argue, ignoring the kid.

"Any word from Flaco?" Seth asks.

"Not yet," Philbo answers.

Hunk massages his left biceps. "He'll be staying off-site for sure. Minimize his chances of being swept up in case the woman gets busted."

"Flaco's already been busted once, and he's a fugitive," Manny says. "He'll want to see the apartment. But my guess, he'll have the boyfriend doing FaceTime on a cell phone." He turns to Hunk. "You want to tell Sergeant Rhyzyk here the good news?"

Hunk grins, rubbing his palms together. "DPD Gangland is moving in on the Young Crips tomorrow. We'll be busting five of their finest. I'll be arrested with the rest. And then"— he pauses, making a sweeping motion with his hand—"I'm outta here and back on desk for a while."

"That way," Manny says, "we spare the good citizens of Five Points a gang turf war. *And* we give Barrio the sense that the streets of Five Points are all theirs. At least for a while. Christmas come early, right, Sergeant?"

"Good work," I tell Hunk. "Stay safe."

Hunk nods, bumps fists with Manny, and exits the way he came in, his heft rocking the van.

Manny says, "I've got to bounce too. You got everything you need?"

"You really came through this weekend, Manny," I say, winking at him. "In more ways than one."

Manny taps me on the arm, motioning me to follow him outside. He closes the doors to the van and I follow him to his Harley.

"Squid did good this weekend," he tells me. "I don't think he slept more than two hours since Friday night. Kept things tight. Let our boy Hunk take the lead. Mostly."

"So," I say, "you're suggesting Philbo's still an asshole, but he's our asshole now?"

Manny straddles the bike. "I'm saying the guy wants to be part of a team. He's just old school. Never worked with a woman before."

"Yeah, I get that."

"You know anything about his past?" he asks.

"Some," I say. "Only what's in his performance evals."

He eases his helmet over his head. "The guy's been shot. Twice. Wife took the kids and left. Youngest son died in some stupid accident. That's why he left Chicago. The guy's broken. That hard shell, man? It's about as thick as the nightie my old lady wears every Valentine's Day."

He kicks the engine to life. "He's a good cop. He's just gotta get used to Detective Betty, is all."

Grinning, he leans into the bike and roars away. My phone rings and I answer it.

"Detective," the familiar voice of El Cuchillo says. "You're not moving fast enough. I think some motivation is in order."

A stabbing pain, like a drill through the bone, flares in one temple.

He's already disconnected the call.

Four more days before El Cuchillo follows through on his promise. Rubbing hard at my temples, I try to slow my breathing and focus on the task in front of me, which is finding Flaco, who will, hopefully, lead me to Evangeline.

I call Jackie and tell her to be extra careful, to stay alert, and to call 911 at any sign of being followed or of strangers in the neighborhood. "And give Connie the same message!"

When I climb back into the van, I can see on the monitor that the couple in room 302 are still arguing. I send Philbo home to get some much-needed sleep, and spend the next few hours watching the screen with Seth and Dave Moreno.

24

The House
Monday, September 22, 2014

Driving back to the station, the sun not quite at its zenith, I get a call. It's Lucy Ganz, the corrections officer from the Lew Sterrett Jail.

"Hey, Betty," she says, "I just thought you ought to know that Tony Diego was found bleeding in his cell this morning. He'd cut his wrists. He bled out so quick that by the time we got him to the infirmary he was gone."

Tony Diego. The red-wigged dealer who'd been picked up by Esparza and Philbo. I pull off the road into a parking lot and turn off the engine.

"I thought he was under close observation," I say.

"He was. Evidently not close enough. He found a sharp edge on his cot and gouged both arms so deeply, they looked like shredded beef."

I think of the determination that must have taken.

"I hate to say I called it," she says. "Poor guy was a pool of misery. I just thought you ought to know."

We end the conversation, and I sit in the parking lot, staring out the window. The news sits heavy on my chest. Tony will be just one casualty in a storm sure to follow Evangeline's toxic presence. Turning on the ignition again, I look at the clock; it's 11:11 a.m. A prickling at the base of my skull says someone is watching me. I scan the parking lot to see if anyone is nearby. A man is sitting in a truck with his engine idling. A woman is struggling to pull her dry cleaning out of the trunk of her car.

Seemingly nothing out of the ordinary. No Roy spies, no obvious gang members. And yet the feeling of being observed closely is swelling like a balloon inside my head. Suddenly I'm so tired I can hardly keep my chin from dropping to my chest. Leaning my head back, I close my eyes. The days and hours are slipping by at a frightening clip. Thursday midnight, my deadline with the Knife, will be here soon.

I try to slow my breathing, calm my thoughts. I'm so tired, I could easily drift off to sleep...

A warm breath on my forehead, and the sharp, peaty smell of whiskey and Old Spice fills the car. Uncle Benny's voice in my ear, the tone commanding, urgent.

"Betty, go home!"

My eyes snap back open. Now my feeling has ratcheted up to a deep, unfocused anxiety. I try calling Jackie, but the call goes to voice mail. Connie's phone goes unanswered as well. An immediate terror blooms in my head—El Cuchillo has taken action in trying to motivate me in finding Evangeline. I'm ten minutes from my house. I put the car in drive and try not to speed as I race for home.

I pass the plainclothes detective on our block and give a distracted wave. He's slumped down in his seat, sunglasses on, his cap pulled low, but he raises a finger to let me know all is well.

Connie's car is not in the driveway but, entering the front hallway, I call out to her anyway. There's no answer. The house is very quiet. She's probably out somewhere with the baby. But why isn't she answering her phone? Living room, kitchen, hallway, all empty.

Jackie's and my bedroom is quiet, the bed neatly made, the only disorder some of my dirty clothing tossed into one corner.

A dark premonition sits heavy in my chest. I open the nursery door and step inside. The crib is empty.

Behind me a woman's voice says, "Hello, Elizabeth."

Evangeline Roy stands primly against the far wall, holding a gun in one hand, which is pointed at me. Somehow she's gotten past two patrol cars and my home security alarm, almost as though she passed through brick and mortar like a specter. Her eyes, two burnt holes in a pale blanket. She smiles, showing as much warmth as a plague mask.

She holds out her other hand and points to the floor. "I'll take your gun and both of your phones, please. Just toss them down, easy."

I hesitate and she raises her gun. "Now," she says.

The spit has dried up in my mouth, and my heart is racing. I ease my gun and my two cell phones onto the floor, glancing over at the empty crib again. She picks them up with surprising agility, and places them in her voluminous skirt pockets.

"Where's the baby?" I ask.

She cocks her head playfully and studies me. "That is the question, isn't it?"

Following hard on the realization that Connie may also

have been taken hostage, I have a dark, irrational thought that our trusted nanny voluntarily kidnapped Elizabeth. That she had been planted in our home by the Roy matriarch. That she is even now putting Elizabeth in danger....The desire to rush at the woman holding the gun is almost overwhelming.

Evangeline calmly walks to the rocker—the chair where first Mary Grace and then Jackie and then Connie have spent countless hours rocking Elizabeth to sleep—and sits, spreading her skirt out like a debutante's ball gown, and demurely crosses her ankles. "I think you'll want to listen very carefully to what I have to say. The lives of your loved ones will depend upon it."

Loved ones. Plural. Jackie hadn't answered her phone, and she still hasn't called me back. Fear restricts my vision, tunneling it into a long, narrow tube where nothing exists except the redheaded menace seated in front of me.

"How did you get past the detective out front?" I croak.

She grins, showing yellowing teeth. "It was surprisingly easy. Once he was rendered unconscious. The gentleman you saw in the car is one of mine."

Her East Texas accent lends every word an air of church parlor civility.

"Where's Connie?"

Evangeline shrugs and looks coy. Her maddening game-playing could mean that both Elizabeth and Connie have been kidnapped. I struggle to hold on to the belief that Connie is who she portrayed herself to be—a caring nanny. But with this evil bitch, nothing is as it appears.

I try to still the trembling in my legs. "What do you want?"

"Right now? What I want—" She loses the smile, her eyes now circles of hate. Her mouth quivers with emotion, but the hand holding the gun is steady. The sunlight through the window harshly picks out the meth-etched pockmarks in her skin that no amount of makeup can hide.

"What I want," she says, her voice hard and flat, "is for you to wake up in the middle of each and every night, knowing your child is gone. I want you to imagine, over and over, the possible agony of her last few moments. The pain, the hopelessness. I want you to understand what I've had to endure after you killed my two sons."

"You're talking about a baby," I whisper.

She leans forward in the chair, rocking it gently, the crazy pouring out of her like a poisoned fog. "Have you ever drowned puppies? No? They whimper when they're taken from their momma. A kind of mewly pitched yelping. But even when they're only a few days old, after the first one is chucked into the river, they know what's coming. Their cries get higher, more desperate. Mercifully, they drown real fast."

She stands abruptly from the rocker, the gun pointed at my chest. "Now, drop an infant into a pool of water, and they can stay under much longer than an adult can. It's a survival instinct all babies have. The heart slows, the brain too. Some can last for five minutes, or more, if the water's cold enough. Of course, that instinct fades after they're about six months old. How old is Elizabeth now? Seven months?"

Paralysis. Like when I'd been handed the blue duffel bag holding the bomb. Or when Mary Grace had offered to let me hold Elizabeth for the first time. My breathing sounds loud in my ears. Sweat pours from my hairline, stinging both my eyes, but I can only blink.

I hear someone behind me, but I'm slow in turning—too slow—and a hard blow to the back of my head brings me to my knees. Another blow to my temple and I'm on the floor, staring at the threads in the carpet, staring at Evangeline's feet. Her shoes, ugly orthopedic grandmother shoes, walk toward me. Evangeline stops and, kneeling down, brings her face closer, her cheek resting on the carpet, her eyes boring into mine.

"I'm not going to kill you, Elizabeth. I want you very much alive. I want you to look for me, although you won't find me. And you won't find the baby. Ever." She pats my shoulder.

Moving a little closer, she whispers into my ear, "Welcome to hell."

I reach for her, but she pulls away, grinning. Evangeline and her accomplice—a man wearing black sneakers—leave the room, gently closing the nursery door behind them.

I falter getting to my knees and have to pull myself up using the slats in the crib. Inside, resting on top of the soft bunny-patterned sheets, are my phones and gun.

Crushing nausea surges, and I wheel away from the crib and lurch desperately toward the bathroom.

But the vomiting, acidic and crippling, overtakes me before I can make it to the sink.

25

Dallas Police Department, North Central Division
Monday, September 22, 2014

Where was the plainclothes who was posted out front?"
Craddock asks.

Our team of six, along with Fred Dunlap from DEA, is crowded into the incident room. All of them, to a man, look shaken. I'm holding a bag of ice to the back of my head, which has numbed the throbbing. But the four headache tablets I took still haven't calmed the pounding inside my skull. I'd refused an ambulance ride to the hospital by telling the EMT that if he didn't want his family jewels kicked up into his tonsils, he'd help me off the stretcher and into Seth's car.

"Patrol found the detective unconscious in the back seat of his car. He'd been jabbed in the shoulder with some kind of sedative," I say.

"He's still woozy," Seth says, "but he'll recover."

Seth was the second person I called as soon as I'd recovered enough to speak in full sentences. My first call, repeated every ten minutes, had been to Connie. Every call went to message.

"Where's Jackie?" Ryan asks.

Jackie was the third call. I'd been desperate to know that she was safe, so I had Seth contact her immediately. I didn't have it in me to tell her that the baby was gone until I had the house on lockdown and a forensics team looking at our security footage for clues to who took Elizabeth from the house.

"Jackie's great-uncle James Earle has taken Jackie to stay with her mom," I answer. The bag of ice has in that moment become too heavy for my arm to support, and I drop it into my lap. "She's—"

She's devastated, I mean to say. And I didn't even tell her the entirety of Evangeline's threats. All Jackie knows was that the baby and Connie are missing. I've seen Jackie in stressful situations (many of them caused by me), but I've never seen the level of terror she wore when she arrived home to pummel me again with her questions. Questions I had no answers for. The intermittent nausea I experienced at the house rears its ugly head. I close my eyes and remember to breathe through my mouth.

"What exactly did the Roy woman say?" Esparza asks.

I tell them as much as I can remember. When I get to the drowning puppies part, my voice gives out. A loud bang startles all of us. Philbo has brought one clenched fist down onto the table, hard enough to scatter papers over the floor. He'd only gotten a few hours' sleep before being called to the station. White as a sheet, his face looking murderous, he stands abruptly and rushes out the door.

I look at Esparza, who tells me, "Just give him a moment. He'll be okay."

Philbo's reaction fires two conflicting emotions through my brain. Relief that he's still empathetic enough to be moved by a child in danger. And wariness that he reacted in such a volatile way.

"What do you want us to do?" Craddock asks.

"I'll first let Agent Dunlap tell us what DEA is initiating."

Fred Dunlap takes center floor. "I met earlier with Lieutenant Bradford to start officially establishing a federal task force made up of Dallas police and DEA agents that will focus exclusively on finding Evangeline Roy and associates. Sergeant Rhyzyk will be the coordinator within the DPD. This operation will include an interdiction squad canvassing flights in and out of Love Field and bus and train stations. We've contacted the DFW airport police and put out a BOLO statewide to Highway Patrol, forwarding stills of Evangeline Roy taken from Sergeant Rhyzyk's home security video. We've also circulated photos of the child. Lieutenant Bradford has issued a child abduction bulletin—"

Dunlap's phone rings, and he answers. After a brief exchange, he ends the call. "We got a tentative ID off the security footage for the man who was with Evangeline in your home. We compared his face to mug shots in our data system and got a hit."

"Wild guess. Flaco?" I say.

Dunlap nods. "That's right. Roberto Flores."

"And what about Connie?" I brace myself.

"Looks like Connie left the house, with Elizabeth, at exactly ten o'clock. She had dressed the baby and, apparently, packed an overnight bag. Evangeline Roy is seen entering the house a little after eleven o'clock, using a small handheld jamming device to disable the wireless security alarm. She picked the lock and was recorded walking in alone, looking in every room, and then entering the nursery. She was seen taking something out of the crib—a piece of paper—which she folded and pocketed. The Roy woman was in the house only a short while before you arrived. Roberto Flores entered the house after you and was the one who hit you from behind."

Dunlap gives me a questioning look. "Why did you go home? Is that your usual routine?"

Every good detective loves questioning questionable behavior. What could I say? That my dead uncle Benny had whispered urgently in my ear? I'm pausing too long, and the room has gotten very quiet.

"I had an urge to check in on the baby." My tone sounds overly defensive even to my own ears.

Dunlap studies me for a beat. He then says his goodbyes, telling me he'll be in constant communication. As soon as Dunlap has left, every cell phone in the room blasts a siren alert in unison.

Ryan holds his phone up. "Amber alert for Elizabeth is out."

"For the rest of us in this room," I say, "we're going back to the streets. Esparza, I'd like you and Detective Philbo to make sure that one of you is in that surveillance van at Five Points twenty-four seven. Flaco's going to be contacting his dealers at the Ivy Apartments. And I want a close watch on the young Hispanic male in apartment three-oh-two. He'll be the one making the drops. Hopefully he'll be able to lead us to Flaco if we don't get a hit on a location from Flaco's phone first.

"Detectives Craddock and Ryan, I'd like for you both—"

The vocal exertion has made me dizzy and I grab on to the table in front of me to steady myself.

"You need to take five?" Seth asks.

"No," I mutter through gritted teeth. "What I need is to finish the meeting so we can get to work. Detective Craddock, I'd like you and Detective Ryan to go to Connie's house immediately. I've texted you the address and forwarded a copy of her résumé. If you can't find her at home, then check every reference."

Ryan asks, "You checked out everything before she started working for you, though, right?"

"Mary Grace and Jackie did all the follow-up."

Craddock gives me a funny look. "You didn't do a background check yourself?"

I yank the phone out of my pocket and call Jackie again. When she answers, her voice sounds panicked. "Hey, it's me," I say. "No, nothing yet. Listen, I'm just confirming you and Mary Grace checked Connie's references before she started work for us?"

Her response feels like how I would imagine biting through a thermometer would; I feel a cold, viscous pearl of mercury sliding irreparably down my throat. "Mary Grace told me that you'd done all the checking! That you'd cleared her."

I mumble something in closing and disconnect the call. When I meet Craddock's gaze, his eyes widen in alarm. "We're on our way to Connie's now," he says.

He and Ryan leave the room, Esparza following behind. I collapse into a chair, and I rub both hands hard at my temples.

"Didn't you and Jackie discuss this before you hired Connie?" Seth asks.

We're alone in the room, but a hot flash of anger and embarrassment fills my chest. I shoot him a dark look, but the painful truth is that Jackie and I hadn't talked about Connie's past. Not really. We'd been so busy with our respective jobs, and Connie had been so thoroughly capable and reliable. From the beginning, Mary Grace seemed to bond strongly with her, as did Elizabeth. There was no indication that we should doubt either Mary Grace or our own instincts. And we were relieved when our nanny moved so seamlessly from part-time to full-time.

But why would Mary Grace actively lie about who was checking Connie's references? It didn't make sense. Unless Connie was not who she said she was, and Mary Grace needed for some reason to hide her true identity.

There was a darker truth chipping away at my skull like a bone saw. I didn't follow through on checking Connie's references myself because I didn't care enough to know. I was happy to let everyone else take responsibility for the baby. To my mind she had been a temporary inconvenience.

Who else had lied or hidden things from Jackie and me?

The throbbing in my head is making reasonable thought almost impossible, but I do remember the vehemence with which Connie had spoken about Alan Turner's character. I stand up, motioning to Seth to follow. As with any criminal investigation, we had to eliminate the possible from the probable.

"What are we doing?" he asks.

"*You're* going to request an evidentiary search warrant for Alan Turner's house based on his threats to take Elizabeth. It's got to come from you so the judge won't ban me from the search. I want Turner to see my face when we tear his house apart."

"Riz," he says, and pauses. "Turner saying he's going to fight you in court is pretty thin probable cause of abduction, even if he was being a dick."

"Please, Seth, these are extraordinary circumstances. There was a reason his stepdaughter, who he had full custody of, ran to the streets in the first place. The worst that can happen is the judge turns us away with a laundry list of what more she needs to sign the warrant." I grab his arm. "Please."

"Okay," he nods. "I'll do my best. What do we do while we're waiting for the signature?"

"We're going to pay a little visit to the county courthouse. Donna Parcell is being arraigned at three o'clock."

"She's not being arraigned at the Sterrett?"

"Like I said, extraordinary circumstances. I made sure the prosecutor's office jumped all over this. I want the bail set high and the bitch returned to jail until sentencing."

26

**Frank Crowley Courts Building
Monday, September 22, 2014**

The County Criminal Courthouse on Riverfront Boulevard is a few blocks from the Sixth Floor Museum at Dealey Plaza, where the two Xs marking the approximate locations on Elm Street where JFK was shot were removed only last year. The prosecutor from the DA's Office had texted me that the arraignment would be heard in one of the third-floor courtrooms. And though the victim—me in this particular case—does not typically attend, all we had to do was flash our badges to the bailiff to take a seat on a bench at the back.

The courtrooms in the building are generally utilitarian and spectacularly ugly chambers, devoid of any aesthetic charm. No deeply oiled and aged wooden panels or stately judges' podiums at the Crowley. The hallways and waiting areas have all the warmth of a Soviet-era municipal center.

I answer an incoming call from Peg Bartles.

"It's all over the news," she said. "What can we do to help?"

"I don't have time to explain everything right now. But

hang tight. I'll call you later. In the meantime, I'm sending you a photo of Connie. Keep an eye out."

There are several people, men and women, waiting for arraignment in the courtroom, and I spot Donna Parcell right away. She's wearing county-issued coveralls and handcuffs, but she still looks defiant, and smug. If I could shoot flames from my eyes, she'd be smoking from both ears. Sitting next to her is her attorney, who is not wearing the threadbare suit of a public defender. His tie alone probably cost him more than a patrolman's weekly pay, making me think Evangeline is paying the legal fees.

Scanning the spectator area, my breath catches, and I grip the bench in front of me, hard. Near the bar are two young women, sitting shoulder to shoulder, whispering to each other and trading encouraging smiles and waves with Donna Parcell. They are exact copies of one another, with pale, translucent skin, and brilliant red hair. I don't recognize them, and yet I know with a certainty that they're here at Evangeline's bidding. More of her chosen few: the copper-haired children beloved by her angry, vengeful God. The acolytes who would gladly throw themselves in front of a moving car if the Roy matriarch willed it. One of the women looks behind her and catches me staring, and she nudges her twin. They both turn to me and return my stare, their blue eyes empty and unblinking.

"You know who they are?" Seth whispers.

"No, but I can pretty well guess *what* they are," I say, refusing to look away.

The bailiff announces the judge, who briskly enters the chamber. Everyone stands briefly and, like two mechanized dolls, the twins swivel in unison to face forward again. The plaque on the bench reads JUDGE LETITIA ANDERSON, and she settles herself in her chair and proceeds to call the first accused to stand and enter his plea.

Within fifteen minutes, two defendants have been arraigned, and the judge calls Donna Parcell, along with her lawyer, Barry Adams, to stand. She also motions to the prosecutor—a young harried-looking woman named Grace Muñoz—to come forward.

"Ms. Parcell, you are accused as follows," Judge Anderson says. "Child endangerment, attempted battery of a police officer, stalking, and vandalism. How do you plead?"

"Not guilty," Parcell responds.

Adams holds his hand up. "Your Honor, we'd also like to request that the charges of child endangerment, battery, and stalking be dismissed. Certainly, we will gladly entertain the charges of vandalism before the court, but my client has no criminal history—"

Muñoz motions impatiently. "Your Honor, Ms. Parcell was arrested only a few days ago on criminal trespassing and resisting arrest. Two days ago, the defendant hurled a large piece of concrete through a window into an infant's nursery. If it had struck the infant, who was sleeping in her crib at the time, it would have killed her, and it could have seriously injured any adult in the room."

One of the redheaded women grins and grabs at her sister's hand.

Judge Anderson frowns. "Was the infant injured?"

"Thankfully, no," Muñoz says. "But there is a further complication. The infant in question is missing as of today, possibly abducted. Law enforcement has strong reason to believe that Donna Parcell was involved in the—"

"Your Honor," Adams snaps, "my client has been in jail for two days."

"Donna Parcell has admitted to being part of a group of dangerous individuals that we believe is responsible for the infant's disappearance," Muñoz says. "The State asks that a high bail be set and that she be remanded to jail until her trial date, as she has proven herself to show callous disregard for the lives of others."

Judge Anderson sighs. The bench never likes haggling this late in the day. "What does the State request in bail?"

"We would ask that bail be set at one hundred fifty thousand dollars," Muñoz says.

Adams makes a dismissive noise and shakes his head. "Even if nothing is discounted from the charge sheet, your Honor, the maximum fine is not even twenty-five thousand dollars."

Anderson purses her lips and takes a hard look at Parcell, the previously smirking woman now adopting an attitude of pious submission. She gestures to the two attorneys. "Approach the bench."

While the murmuring at the bench continues, the twins bow their heads and clasp their hands together, appearing to pray. Their monotonous whispers are like the slow drip of waste from a septic tank.

"You doing okay?" Seth asks me.

I turn my gaze to my partner, and he flinches. "Ask me again after the judge's ruling."

The bickering in front of the judge breaks off, and the lawyers return to their desks. Muñoz does not look happy.

Anderson looks pointedly at Parcell. "The charges remain as they are. Bail is set at fifty thousand dollars, with a pretrial requirement of home confinement, with a few exceptions augmented by electronic monitoring. Your lawyer will explain everything to you."

"'A few exceptions,'" I mutter to Seth. "What the hell does that mean? She's not going back to jail?"

Anderson bangs her gavel and announces a fifteen-minute break. As she leaves the courtroom, Donna Parcell is removed by an officer to begin processing for her bond and release.

I try catching Muñoz's eye as she rushes out of the courtroom. "Call me at the office," she tells me, clutching her briefcase to her chest like a shield.

"Well, at least she'll be monitored," Seth says. "Riz?"

I've closed my eyes against a surging tide of nausea. The throbbing at the back of my skull has spread, turning my dull headache into the beginnings of a true migraine, fracturing my vision, making even the shallowest of breaths painful.

"I'm okay," I gasp. "I just need some air."

Seth helps me to my feet and leads me out the door. The hallway is nearly empty, the courthouse quiet. It's after four o'clock, and almost everyone has left for the day. My partner props me against a wall and cribs a bottle of water from a sympathetic bailiff. I take a few sips, the cold water settling my stomach.

I let my partner direct me toward the elevators, our footsteps loud on the marble, my head lowered to shield my eyes from the light. When I look up again, I see the twins standing together, smiling vacuously, watching us. They move to the side to let us pass.

Quietly, one begins to sing. *Rock-a-bye, Baby, in the treetop...when the bough breaks...*She laughs.

And I lose it.

"What did you say, you fucking sock puppet?" I scream,

pushing my face against hers, forcing her backward into the wall. *"What did you just say?"*

Now both of the twins are giggling hysterically.

"That's right," the other twin says. "Hit her. See what happens."

I feel my partner's presence, his arm and then his shoulder coming between me and the insane woman. He's using his body as a wedge, a shield, not so much to protect the taunting woman as to protect me from myself.

"Riz, she's fucking with you," he says urgently into my ear. "She wants you to be physical with her. Stop. Just stop."

Gently at first, and then roughly, he drags me away with both hands. Then he pushes me back several feet, wrestling with my thrashing arms like a martial arts defender.

"Quit it!" he yells to me. He turns to the twins. "Get the hell away or I'll arrest the both of you. *Now!"*

The sisters join hands and disappear through a stairwell exit.

I want to tell my partner that we have to follow them. That they could take us to Evangeline, but I've lost the power of speech. Seth takes one arm and shepherds me into the elevator, through the lobby, and into the parking lot. He props me up in the passenger side of his car and gets into the driver's seat. We both sit, waiting for the draining ebb of adrenaline. I fumble in my pocket for two more headache pills. I chew them to a bitter pulp and choke them down.

"I almost hit you," I say, looking at his face in profile, still flushed from anger.

"Yeah, well," Seth says, gripping tightly at the steering wheel.

"Thank you for being a good partner."

He takes a steadying breath. "I think you need to see a doctor, Riz."

"I don't have time."

He turns to me. "It is not your fault this happened."

I look away from his well-meaning expressions of sympathy. But I know the truth. This happened in part because of my selfishness. I underestimated Evangeline Roy's hatred of me. And like always, it's the people who care for me who take the punishment. The welling of tears threatens to spill onto my face. I can't let myself break down, get stuck in the abyss of my own morass, as Uncle Benny would have said.

"There's no time," I say again, digging my nails into my palms to finish tamping down the self-pity. "We're going to park outside Turner's house while we wait for the judge to sign the search warrant."

27

Alan Turner's Mansion
Monday, September 22, 2014

Turner's French country-style home—all eleven thousand square feet of it—is situated in Highland Park alongside other equally grandiose houses that sell in the tens of millions, keeping the upper-tier real-estate ladies in plenty of Botox. It's surrounded by an ornate metal fence and guarded by a locked electronic gate. I tell Seth to park in front, blocking the driveway, and he kills the engine.

"How do we know he's even home?" Seth asks.

"We don't. But if he is, I want him to see us. Besides, if the judge signs the search warrant, I don't want to waste time kicking down the door."

He looks at his watch. "If we don't get the call from the clerk soon, it's not going to happen till tomorrow."

My personal cell rings with Jackie's number displayed. She asks if there've been any new developments. I tell her about the arraignment and promise to call her in an hour. While I'm on the phone, Seth calls Philbo for any updates.

"Squid says Gangland is all set to arrest the Crips

tomorrow," he tells me after disconnecting the call. "And the mules in apartment three-oh-two are bagging some dope for delivery. Hopefully we'll hear something from Flaco soon."

A patrol cruiser pulls up behind us. There's no siren, but the lights are flashing.

Seth gives me a look. "Well, that didn't take long."

"Rich white people, partner," I say.

Highland Park police are not a part of DPD. They serve only the "island city" of Highland Park, a two-square-mile residential neighborhood surrounded on all sides by the greater Dallas County. Their annual budget for safety personnel and equipment is five million. Average response time is under two minutes.

The patrolman, wearing a crisp black uniform, approaches Seth's car cautiously. Seth shows him his badge and says, "We're waiting on a warrant."

The officer makes a show of taking in the magnificence that is Turner's mansion and then leans down to look at me in the passenger seat. "You'll need to wait for it on the street. Can't block a private driveway."

He gives me a patronizing smirk. Any other day, I'd let it pass.

I show him my badge. "That's 'Can't block a private driveway, *Detective Sergeant*.'"

The officer loses his grin at my tone.

Seth starts the engine. "Don't you have some rogue landscapers to harass?"

The officer pushes away from Seth's car and returns to his

cruiser but doesn't drive away. Seth parks on the curb across from Turner's house.

After fifteen minutes, the gate begins to open, and Seth nudges me. A black Mercedes sports model glides into the driveway, and before the gate can close again, Seth trails the car to the front of the house, the Highland Park cruiser following behind. Turner gets out of his car but doesn't look surprised when Seth and I follow suit. The patrolman doesn't get out of his cruiser, but he's rolled down the window so he can hear any words exchanged.

"Sergeant Rhyzyk, good to see you again," Turner says. "You've brought a different partner this time. Good choice, considering the neighborhood." He waves to the patrolman. "It's all right, Officer. I'm pretty sure I'll be safe with two of Dallas's finest."

The cruiser backs up and drives away. Turner unlocks the front door and says, "Come on in, Detectives. I have nothing to hide."

We follow Turner into the cavernous entry hall, our footsteps muffled by the intricate parquet floor and expensive Persian carpets. He leads us to a large sitting room, its three walls lined with custom-made cabinetry filled with leather-bound books.

He takes a seat in one of the plush wingback chairs and motions us to sit on the couch.

"We prefer to stand," I say. "You know who I am. This is Detective Dutton."

He steeples his fingers under his chin and asks, pleasantly, "What can I do for you, Sergeant?"

"You can tell me where Elizabeth is," I say.

He gives me a puzzled look, but the pleasant smile doesn't falter. "I don't understand."

"She's been taken from my home."

Puzzlement turns to what looks like genuine surprise. "What do you mean 'taken'?"

"Do you know a Connie Winslow?"

He shakes his head, looks hard at me for a moment, and then stands. "Who's Connie Winslow? What's going on?"

The doorbell chimes, and Turner strides from the room. A minute later, he returns with a man dressed casually and with a shock of perfectly coiffed silver hair and the self-important air of legal counsel on retainer.

"My personal lawyer, Frank Adair. I called him as soon as your car entered my driveway. Are you telling me that Elizabeth, an infant who was in your care, and under your protection, has been abducted?" Turner demands.

"I have a lot of Dallas law enforcement looking for her now," I say. "We need to eliminate you from the suspect list."

"Wait a minute," Adair says. "Not without a search war—"

Turner holds up a hand to silence the lawyer. "You think that I would kidnap my own grandchild? You're out of your mind."

He takes a few steps toward me, the thin layer of sociability evaporating from his face like fog off a burning lake. "I didn't need to kidnap her, I'm going to use the courts. And when we find her, if we find her, I'm not only going to get custody of Elizabeth, but I'm going to make it my personal quest to see you busted back to writing parking tickets. Now get out of my house."

I turn to go, but a sound coming from the second floor

makes me pause. Walking into the hallway, I look up the grand, curving staircase.

"Who's in the house with you?" I ask.

"None of your fucking business," Turner snaps. He turns to Seth. "Either the two of you leave right now, or I'm calling your precinct captain."

The sound comes again. Footsteps and a soft murmuring voice. Two voices. One is birdlike and high-pitched like a child.

I start moving up the stairway, Seth right behind me, hissing, "Riz, what are you doing?"

Turner is down below, yelling angrily to his attorney, "Get on the phone, *now!*"

Another few steps, and a woman appears at the top of the stairway—Hispanic, young, wearing a loosely fitting dress, her hair in a long dark braid over one shoulder. Behind her, peeking around her legs, stands a girl of about three years of age. Her eyes wide and dark. One finger stuck in her mouth. My first thought is that she is frightened. My second thought is that she is frightened because a determined, almost frantic Amazon is rising up from the dark hallway and racing toward her.

The woman looks at me with alarm. "*¿Qué pasó?*"

"Detective!" Turner roars. "That's my housekeeper. I'm not telling you again to leave."

The woman pushes the child farther away—protecting her. From me.

"*Perdóname, señora.*" I turn and walk rapidly down the stairs, almost knocking into Seth in my haste to leave. Without saying another word to Turner or his attorney, I exit the front door without closing it behind me.

Seth gets into the driver's seat, barely waiting for me to close the passenger-side door, and backs out of the driveway, tires squealing.

"What in the actual holy hell did you think you were doing?" Seth asks without looking at me. "We'll be lucky to escape this with a warning."

"The guy's a total scumbag!"

I've barely finished speaking when Seth jerks the car to a halt, making my head knock hard against the seat. He studies me the way a forensics tech scrutinizes a crime scene. Searching for clues, not only of past violence but of future ones as well.

"Do I need to be worrying about your mental health?" he asks. "Again?"

I know what he's imagining. The Betty Rhyzyk of eight months ago. Forced into therapy. Anxious, sleepless, almost jobless, tied to a desk. Chasing down echoes of Evangeline Roy. Stepping over the bodies of CIs murdered in the street. Suspecting my partner guilty of those same murders.

"That was a mistake," I say, not sure whether I'm referring to Turner or to my partner.

"No shit."

"I'm sorry." I exhale loudly and look out the window, anywhere to avoid Seth's probing gaze. "But if something happens to that baby—"

I thrust away desperate, dire imaginings. Turner may somehow be involved in her disappearance, but my gut instincts tell me Elizabeth was not in the house.

Seth's phone rings. He answers and listens. "That was Philbo," he said. "Flaco made contact with the mule."

I'm immediately impatient for Seth to put the car in gear

again, but he turns to me and says, "I'll ask you again. Am I going to have to run interference with you from here on out... *Sergeant?*"

And there it is. A white-hot glimmer of resentment; perhaps a growing lack of confidence in my advancement. And the first glimpse of the gulf that could finally separate me from the man who's had my back for years. Who saved my life. Who wrestled demons, real and imagined, with me. Weathered a brutal addiction and returned clear-eyed, seemingly without any lingering anger.

I place my hand on his arm. "Right now, it's just me and you, Riot. That's not going to change."

"Uh-huh," he mutters, putting the car into drive. "It already has."

28

Ivy Apartments, Five Points
Monday, September 22, 2014

We've just pulled up next to the surveillance van when Craddock calls.

"Kevin and I went to Connie's house," he says. "It was locked up tight, and no one was home. No car in the driveway. The neighbors either don't know her or don't know where she is now. I don't think there's an alarm system, so if we can get a warrant, we should be able to get into the house within twenty-four hours with no problem."

"And the references?" I ask.

"You're not going to like it. As far as we can tell, they're all bogus. What now?"

"Check in with Fred Dunlap and see if DEA's got anything new. Then I want you to set up a watch at Alan Turner's house. Don't park too close, but I want to know who's coming and going. Anyone at all, diaper truck, food delivery. And if you spot Connie's car, I want her taken into custody."

The call ends, and the full measure of my carelessness

regarding Connie squeezes my head like a vise. I follow Seth into the van, and I'm surprised to see both Esparza and Philbo huddled next to Dave Moreno, the DEA specialist.

"Thought you'd be getting some rest," I say to Philbo.

"And miss all the fun?" he answers, deadpanning.

His skin looks gray from lack of sleep, and even Esparza has dark circles the color of coffee under both eyes. The only one who looks fresh-faced, as though just up from a nap, is the young surveillance tech.

"What have you got?" Seth asks.

"The mule in the apartment?" Moreno says. "The woman calls him Junior."

Esparza shakes his head. "He's not a mule. He's a *soldado,* a soldier. Big difference. In the hierarchy of Barrio 18, he answers only to his boss, his homie, which in this case is Flaco."

"How do you know he's a soldier?" I ask.

"His shoes. He's wearing Nike Cortez. And by the way he wears his belt."

"You been studying up on Barrio 18."

"In a way," Esparza says, his lips stretched into a mirthless smile. "My mother's Honduran, so it goes with the territory."

"He doesn't have any obvious tattoos."

"The young ones don't anymore. Makes it harder to identify them on the street."

"Go on," I prompt Moreno.

"Flaco contacted Junior at about five o'clock. They both used burners with no Wi-Fi. They were only on for a short period of time, and then both phones were switched off. Junior was trained well. After he greeted Flaco, he just listened, and he didn't repeat anything his boss said. But we did hear Junior say that he'd be turning the phone on again tomorrow at ten in the morning."

"Can we get a location on Flaco?" I ask.

Moreno shakes his head. "Difficult. The Stingray can pick up signals from a smart phone in seconds. Dumb phones are harder to catch. No geotracking. Given enough time to track down his phone tracking number, we can ping Junior's phone like a regular cell tower would and capture his number that way. But I have no idea how often they'll be ditching their burners and breaking in new ones."

"So, what do we do?" Seth asks.

The tech looks from my partner to me and shrugs. "Honestly, the fastest way is to get ahold of Junior's phone somehow and pull Flaco's number off it. Once we have the number, assuming Flaco hasn't ditched it, we can track him pretty easily. Barring that," he pauses, "you can always arrest Junior and hopefully grab the burner before he can warn his boss."

My personal cell rings. It's Jackie. I'd told her I'd call her in an hour's time, but in this moment, I'm too agitated and let the call go to messaging.

"What's been happening in the apartment?" I ask.

"The woman has spent most of the day repackaging the heroin. At nine o'clock tonight, Junior's going to make a drop in the dumpster for pickup."

Seth folds a stick of gum into his mouth, which he does when he's nervous and expecting action. "We know who's picking up?"

"Barrio 18 boys, for sure," Moreno says. "Which means they'll be loaded for bear."

I stare at the screen recording the woman feeding her toddler in real time as though she hadn't spent hours bagging enough heroin to poison every resident of the apartment complex. Junior sits at the table, playing games on his smartphone and watching what looks to be porn. After a moment I realize it's gotten very quiet in the van.

"Some decisions are going to have to be made, Sergeant," Moreno says. "Do we make an arrest at the pickup tonight? Or do we follow the Barrio boys, hoping they'll lead us to Flaco?"

We have until ten o'clock tomorrow morning before Flaco gets in touch with Junior again. Whatever is going to be done has to be done within that time period.

"I need a few minutes to think," I say. "Seth, I'll be in the car."

The afternoon is devolving into lengthening shadows and cooling air. Sunset won't be for another hour and a half, but by nine o'clock, pickup time, it will be fully dark. I sit in the driver's seat out of habit, pulling two more headache tablets from my pocket. I swallow them with the last of the bottled water and rub at my temples. Sitting in the quiet of the car, I realize that my vision is blurry. Seth is most likely right. I should have gone to the hospital because I probably do have a concussion.

I close my eyes for a moment and am startled by a rap on the window. It's Philbo, holding a large Styrofoam cup in his hand. Unlocking the doors, I motion for him to get into the passenger seat. When he's seated, he hands me the steaming cup.

"Coffee," he says. "Black and bitter. Just like my ex-wife."

I take a few sips, letting the caffeine hit my empty stomach like a shot of pure adrenaline.

"Thanks." The offering should make me grateful. Instead, it's made me wary.

Philbo exhales, rubbing both hands over his face. "You know, Chicago'll be getting cold at night already."

"Tell me about it. Thirty years of dealing with New York winters."

He stares straight ahead, as though studying something on the horizon. "Ortega's a good guy. A good cop."

"Yes, he is that."

He lets me take a few more sips without glancing in my direction.

"I know what it's like—" He clears his throat abruptly to cover the quaver in his voice. And, in my head, I finish his thought: I know what it's like to lose a child. I nod into the silence, my chest constricting, making it difficult to keep the emotion out of my breathing.

He clears his throat again. "I dealt with some of the worst gangbangers you could imagine when I was with CPD. I mean straight-up psychopaths. And Barrio 18 is right up there with the first-rate killers. You know what their motto is? 'Pocos pero loco.' Smaller but crazier."

I wait for him to make his point.

"You've got to know that if we try and arrest Junior while he's in the apartment, he's gonna try and take everyone with him. Including possibly the woman and the kid."

"Yeah, I'm aware of that. The best time would be right after he makes the drop in the alley, before he gets back to the apartment."

Philbo nods. "Agreed. Let's say you do get him in cuffs and take him in for booking. It's going to be almost impossible to get him to talk. Unless he's given a strong enough incentive."

I picture Philbo with his bullish shoulders, Marine-style buzz cut, and zirconium stare, going Raging Bull on a suspect. "He'll lawyer up right away."

"It won't matter," Philbo says.

"I don't follow."

"You know what Barrio 18 does to snitches?"

"I can imagine."

"No, I don't think you can. Not in your worst nightmare. Give me and Esparza some time with him. I'll go through the motions, playing the nice guy. I'll shake his hand, wish him luck, Esparza'll pat him on the back. Then we'll tell him he can wait for his lawyer in his cozy little cell. But not before we lift a few stills from the surveillance video and circulate the buddy-buddy photos anonymously to his Barrio *hermanos*."

Making Junior out to be a snitch. We're riding a fine line of some bad practices. But I know what Uncle Benny would probably say. *"Nosił wilk razy kilka ponieśli i wilka."*

The wolf will take many victims but is himself eventually taken too. Live by the sword, die by the sword.

I catch and hold Philbo's gaze. His eyes appear a little too glittery, a little too wildly expectant. Rasputin selling his snake oil to the empress. "You've done this before."

He gives me a wide grin. "At the very least we'll have Junior's phone with Flaco's number, so we can trace his homie's location, assuming he hasn't ditched the burner. Anything else Junior reveals to us will be gravy. If we're not satisfied, he goes to jail with a target on his back."

Now I'm the one staring out through the windshield, playing the different scenarios in my head. I need Philbo's cooperation on the team, but his outlaw tactics are giving me pause. One thing is for sure, I want Junior to look into my face and believe that I'd be willing to set him up in order to get to Flaco. That I will move heaven and earth to get to Evangeline and find Elizabeth. And maybe Mary Grace.

"I need Seth following the pickup crew," I say. "And I want Esparza to go with him. He got a lot of shadowing practice on your bust with Jetta. I want to be the one in the room with you and Junior."

Expecting some pushback, I'm surprised when Philbo says, "Sounds like a plan."

I send Philbo to the surveillance van, telling him I have to make a few calls first. Peg Bartles answers on the first ring, and I tell her to relieve Craddock and Ryan in a few hours at Turner's house. And to stay there until she hears from me.

Then I call Jackie, burdening her with the reality that I have no good news yet to share.

29

Lew Sterrett Jail, North Tower
Monday, September 22, 2014

Junior is sitting handcuffed in a holding cell, one side of his face scraped and oozing like raw hamburger meat.

He did not go down easy. The team had watched as he made the drop—placing a large black trash bag with repackaged heroin into the dumpster in the dark alley. He then waited for a low-slung sports car with four passengers to pull up. Without any words exchanged, a man got out of the passenger side, scooped up the bag, and quickly got back into the car. The driver made a leisurely departure, no engine revs or squealing tires to call attention to the maneuver. Seth and Esparza followed the sports car in Esparza's truck, lights off, easy does it.

Then Philbo, waiting in the deeper shadows of the alley, rammed into Junior with the force and speed of an offensive tackle. He knocked him to the ground and twisted his arms hard enough to break bones. I got the cuffs on him but managed to get kicked in the thigh for my efforts. Smaller and leaner than Philbo, Junior proved to be surprisingly strong. It took

Philbo grinding Junior's face into the pavement to get him to stop struggling. Two patrol cars on standby helped with the arrest and transported him to the county jail, where four uniformed guards forcibly dragged him through processing.

As we've been waiting, Junior's Live Scan fingerprints and mug shot were being run by the DEA for background. Moreno has Junior's phone, and we hope to have Flaco's location as soon as he turns his burner on.

It's taken little more than an hour to process him, which is fast for Lew Lew. A call from Fred Dunlap to the warden greased the wheels, giving us the all-clear to do the custodial interrogation. Seth calls to let me know he and Esparza followed the pickup car to a neighborhood in far East Dallas and a modest house with an attached garage. The sports car drove in, the garage door closed, and soon after, lights in the house came on. He'll sit tight and check in with me in another hour.

Philbo and I watch Junior on a video screen sitting motionless, glaring menacingly into the security camera near the ceiling. I've had another two cups of coffee, and my body feels strung together with barbed wire, every tight nerve on fire. I cross my arms with my hands tucked up under my arms to control the shaking.

"He's not the usual twitchy player," I say.

Philbo crosses his arms, studying the prisoner. "He didn't get to be a *soldado* by rolling over."

My phone pings with a text from Dunlap.

"We got a positive ID," I say, showing Philbo the screen. I enlarge it and summarize aloud: "Ernesto Martinez, born in California, age twenty-six, graduated juvie, served eighteen months in San Quentin for narcotics sale at nineteen, three years in Huntsville on an illegal weapons charge and attempted kidnapping."

"That's it?" Philbo asks. "Wow, very slick. There's no way this guy doesn't have some bodies in the basement."

"The home address he uses is in his mother's name. She lives in Dallas."

"Huh, interesting. That's going to come in handy. *Vatos* just *love* their mamas."

The look on Philbo's face raises a big red flag. "Dunlap reminded us that if Junior demands a lawyer, we have to stop the interrogation," I say. "No more questions."

"Right, but we're not going to question him. I'm going to talk. He's going to listen. Trust me on this. Follow my lead." He meets my gaze without blinking, "And just be yourself."

"Oh, yeah? What's that?"

"A scowling, relentless hard-ass."

When we enter the interrogation room, Junior shifts his gaze from the camera to us. If he's surprised to see a woman, he doesn't show it. His face is a mask of dead certainty. Philbo instructs the guard to remove his cuffs. As soon as the guard has closed the door, Philbo leans in, grabs one of Junior's hands in both his own, and, smiling broadly, brings it up as though he's giving it a friendly shake. It takes only a few seconds, but the move startles Junior, who had prepared for every kind of physical confrontation but this. He hesitated for only an instant before throwing off Philbo's grasp, but the camera had already captured what looked like friendly cooperation.

Junior wipes his fingers on his jeans. "What the fuck, man."

Still smiling, Philbo takes the seat across from Junior, and I stand against the wall. A staring match commences between the two men. It's several minutes before Philbo breaks the silence.

Pulling the Miranda warning out of his coat pocket, he says, "'You have the right to remain silent. Anything—'"

Junior makes a sucking sound through his lips and looks away. "I ain't talking to you."

"'Anything you say can and will be used against you in a court of—'"

"I want my attorney." Junior cranes his head around to give me a venomous look.

"'In a court of law. You have the right to an attorney. If you cannot afford an attorney, one will be provided for you.' Do you understand the rights I've just read to you?"

Junior swivels back to Philbo. "I want my phone call, *puto*."

"With these rights in mind, do you wish to speak to me?"

Junior makes a cutting motion across his throat.

Philbo sits back in his chair, holding up both hands. "Okay. No questions. I'll just tell you a little bedtime story."

"Guard!" Junior yells.

Philbo laughs like he's heard a good joke and slaps the table with his palms open. "Dead man talking."

Junior stands and leans over the table. "Oh, yeah, you threatening to fuck me up?"

For a moment I think we'll have to tackle Junior for a second time, but Philbo looks relaxed in his chair. He laughs again and says, "I don't have to, asshole. Your homies are going to do it for me. That little handshake you gave me is going to get you a *luz verde, puto*."

Having a green light on your head gets you assassinated.

"I didn't give you nothing," Junior says, but I can see the replay button being pushed inside his skull.

The guard opens the door. "We got a problem?"

Philbo points to Junior's chair. "Sit the fuck down, or by midnight everybody in Dallas, in or out of jail, is going to see you shaking my hand." Junior sits and Philbo waves to the guard. "We're all good."

As soon as the guard has closed the door again, I take the seat next to Philbo. I want to see Junior's face up close. The raw skin of his cheek offers a tempting target.

Junior crosses his arms, his eyes ping-ponging from Philbo to me. "Nobody gonna believe it."

Philbo smiles unpleasantly. "The camera never lies, my man."

Junior skewers me with a hate-filled glance. "What you lookin' at, bitch?"

Pointing to his face, I say, "That's going to sting when your head goes into the jail toilet."

Philbo raps on the table to get Junior's attention. "I know you think you're a tough guy and all, but I'm going to spend five minutes talking to you, and then Sergeant Rhyzyk and I are going to leave you to the system. Which, I think you know, will not go lightly on you this time, what with your record and all the heroin you dropped into the trash bin tonight.

"Now, it's no never mind to me if you talk to us or not. Because even if you don't, we're going to leave here and have a nice dinner somewhere and go sleep in our own beds tonight. But if you don't talk to us, I think you know what's going to happen. My bet is, you won't last two weeks."

Junior turns his head and spits on the floor.

"Go fuck your mother."

"Funny you should mention 'mother,'" Philbo says. "'Cause that's exactly the theme of the story I'm going to tell you. Once upon a time in a land far, far away, the enchanted land of Chicago, there lived a really bad guy. A soldier, not unlike yourself, for a very big drug lord. Now this drug lord controlled the east side of Chicago, and I don't have to tell you that he got that way by killing a shitload of people. Now, our soldier, by the name of T-Bone, had the very bad luck of getting arrested. By me, as it so happens.

"We brought him into a room, very much like this one. And he was caught on surveillance shaking my hand. Kind of like you did tonight. And like you, he was a hard case and wouldn't talk. So, somehow, a still photo from that tape got circulated and made it all the way to the big bad, and very paranoid, drug lord.

"Now, this soldier, who didn't blink at killing just about anyone else, had a mama that he loved. I mean he *really* loved his mama. Sweet little lady, about yea tall—"

Philbo holds his hand out about five feet off the floor.

"She was so small, she fit quite nicely into the fifty-five-gallon metal drum that the big bad drug lord kept handy for burning the relatives of snitches alive."

The transformation in Junior is immediate. It's like watching a balloon being filled with too much helium, the skin stretching right up to the point of exploding. Junior's eyes flick in my direction, and I give him a few slow nods.

Philbo breathes a sympathetic sigh. "I think T-Bone was almost happy to have his throat slit after that."

Junior clenches and unclenches his hands, his breathing shallow. Philbo stands.

"Sweet dreams, asshole. You've got less than twelve hours to tell us where we can find Flaco. I need some concrete info by nine thirty tomorrow morning. And that's not a question, by the way, it's a—" He turns to me. "What would you call that, Sergeant Rhyzyk?"

"A declarative sentence," I say.

"Right, a declarative sentence. You can call your lawyer now."

I rap on the door, and the guard lets us out of the interrogation room. Another guard takes us back through processing. The temperature outside is cooler, the air cleaner. Breathing deeply, I roll my shoulders to try and ease the tension. The interrogation tears at my gut like a hernia. Anyone looking at that security video, especially a defense attorney, can make a very compelling case for police intimidation and violating Miranda, unless Junior waives his right to silence or convinces his lawyer that he'll give information for a plea deal. If he takes a plea, he'll be signaling to the world that he is indeed a snitch. Our best hope is that he calls us back in to talk without a guarantee of a reduced sentence in order to save his family. At any rate, a whole bunch of somebodies may lose their lives long before a trial will be scheduled.

"What do you think?" I ask.

Philbo shrugs. "We'll see. But I don't think Junior's getting any sleep tonight."

I study Philbo's face in profile; his hard demeanor is a marked contrast to the man of a few hours ago, still gutted by the loss of his son. But I also remember his look of manic cunning when he talked about setting Junior up. "Kind of convenient that T-Bone had a beloved mother who got executed by a ruthless drug lord," I say.

Philbo turns to me, his eyes two slits of nothingness. "It wasn't his mother. It was T-Bone's little sister. But we work with what we're handed, right, Sergeant?"

We're in Philbo's car when my phone rings. Billy Sands's deep voice erupts in my ear.

"Hey, Betty, I think you need to get down to the Austin Street Shelter." There is a pause. "We've had an incident."

Billy is one of the most laid-back people I know, but he sounds distressed.

"What's happened?"

"Remember that girl, Tina P., that you talked to? Well, she hanged herself from the roof tonight. She jumped off the building with a noose around her neck. Right out in front of the shelter. The rope she used broke her neck like a twig."

The news tightens my chest painfully, and I motion for Philbo to pull over into a parking lot. "Oh God, Billy, I'm really sorry to hear that."

"Homicide's here. But I think you need to come down and talk to them."

"They want a statement from me?"

He clears his throat nervously. "It's not so much they want to talk to you as they think you need to see what was found on the body."

Philbo hits the siren, and we make it to the shelter in twenty minutes. It's evening and we can see the lights of the gathered patrol cars for several blocks. Uniformed officers struggle to keep a crowd of people, most of them shelter regulars, away from the front of the building. A form is lying motionless on the ground, covered by a tarp. A pair of forensics techs are just packing up their gear.

Billy greets us at the gate. "Man, we're gonna have our hands full tonight. This has freaked these folks the fuck out."

He takes us to the lead homicide detective, who introduces himself as Detective Butler. Butler squats down next to the form and pulls a corner of the tarp away, revealing the pale and quiet face of Tina P., the birthmark on her cheek still vivid, a circlet of red gouged into the skin around her neck. The rope had already been removed by forensics. She looks very young and very broken.

"Billy said you talked to her on the eighteenth."

"That's right," I say. "I was hoping she could help me with a missing persons case. But it didn't pan out."

Butler stands, his hands in both pants pockets. "So, you didn't talk to her after that?"

"No. That was the last I'd spoken to her. Why?"

Butler gestures to his partner, who's holding a large piece of cardboard. Butler takes it and shows it to me. About a foot square, it's covered in black Magic Marker printed in almost childlike block letters. It takes me a moment to absorb the meaning of the words.

Offer your bodies as a living sacrifice
This is on you Det. Rhyzyk
D 32:41

"This was found hanging around her neck," Butler says. "Have any idea what this means?"

"It's a Bible verse," I say. "Deuteronomy. 'When I sharpen my flashing sword I will take vengeance on my adversaries and repay those who hate me.' I know who sent the message. Evangeline Roy."

I briefly fill Butler in on our search.

Billy taps me on the arm. "Tina'd left the shelter for about a week, and no one seemed to know where'd she'd gone. She came back earlier tonight, saying she'd been staying with a missionary group. I think it was the redheaded wack jobs we chased out previously. Tina was ranting to the regulars here about how she finally had a purpose in her life. How when you're a 'true believer,' death is only the beginning. It was like she'd taken a crazy pill. I think she threw herself off that roof to prove a point."

I have a vision of the Roy matriarch whispering her cultish poison into Tina's vulnerable, desperate ears, minute by minute, hour by hour, day by day. "And Evangeline Roy talked her into it."

Out of the corner of my eye, I see Philbo staring down at Tina's lifeless face. His expression is hard to read. Some of the manic glint has returned to his eyes, but his mouth is pulled into a grim line. He clenches and unclenches his fists and then scrapes one palm over his lips.

Some of the shelter regulars have edged their way closer, their voices getting louder with worry, with panic, and, some, with excitement. A tragic, but welcome, distraction.

One man says, loudly, "A little more height and her head would have popped right off."

There is raucous laughter, and then I see Philbo charge. The man is dressed in dirty clothes, and he guffaws with the staccato gurgling of the clearly insane, but Philbo grabs him by his jacket and practically lifts him off his feet. Billy and I rush to intervene, but Philbo lets go of the man so abruptly that he stumbles and falls to the pavement.

I grab Philbo's arm and order him to wait in his car. For

a moment he looks at me, and I think that something really dangerous is about to happen. His jaw works back and forth, and I can almost hear his teeth grinding.

"*Detective,*" I say sharply. "Pull it together."

He blinks a few times and walks away. I return to finish up with Butler, and we watch as Tina's body is lifted onto a gurney and wheeled away to the ME's van.

Billy walks me toward Philbo's car. "Man, what a shame," he says. "I don't know if she has any family. Hell, I don't even know her last name." He pauses for a moment. "You know, back when I was on the force, we had a name for guys like Philbo. We called them blow jobs. It wasn't a question of *if* they'd explode, it was just a matter of *when*. You gonna be okay with him?"

I nod and thank him and get into the car with Philbo. We don't say a word the entire drive back to my house.

30

Connie's House
Tuesday, September 23, 2014

When I open my eyes, there's a moment of complete confusion. I'm in my car, on a dark street, but I don't know where I am or how I got here. I tug uselessly at the seat belt, finally unbuckle it, and fling it away as though it's a snake wrapping itself around my torso. I'm hyperventilating, ready to throw myself out of the car, when I remember why I'm on this street in front of this particular house.

Earlier, after Philbo dropped me off, I stood outside my front door, the house dark and silent, thinking of all that had transpired in less than twenty-four hours. Connie and Elizabeth going missing, my coming face-to-face with Evangeline, Tony Diego's suicide, the arrest and interrogation of Junior, and now Tina's suicide.

Standing in my driveway, the hours sat crushingly on my shoulders, the pain in my head almost unbearable, and yet the thought of giving in to sleep while Elizabeth was still missing felt like a betrayal. *Another* betrayal. Jackie had begged me to stay with her at her mother's house, believing our home too unsafe to occupy. I had told her I would but not to wait up.

But instead, I had gotten into my car and driven directly to Connie's house. I recall that during the drive I'd called Peg Bartles, still watching and waiting with Rocky Bentner at Alan Turner's house, and had given her Connie's address, asking her to meet me there as soon as possible. I must have fallen into a deep sleep as soon as I'd parked.

I didn't dream so much as drown in a thick soup of black mud, which burned my eyes, nose, and ears like boiling tar. When I finally crawled to consciousness, I was gasping for air. My fingers clawed at something just out of my reach.

I see it's after midnight and hope everyone on my team is getting some rest before we gather at the station at eight o'clock. Seth and Esparza had watched the drug house until they were relieved by a surveillance team from DEA.

Peg's van pulls up behind me, and both Peg and Rocky quietly slip into my car. Peg is in the front passenger seat, and Rocky in the back.

"You look like shit, Rhyzyk," Peg says.

I tell her about Tina, and there's a quick intake of air from Rocky. "Oh, man," she says. "What a fucking waste."

"And you think she took a dive off the roof because Evangeline told her to?" Peg asks.

"Evangeline Roy is a master of manipulation. She's indoctrinated hardened adults. Someone that young and vulnerable didn't stand a chance." I force the image of Tina's dead face from my mind. "What happened at Turner's house?"

"For the few hours we were at Turner's," Peg says, "the only car that entered or exited the property was his black

BMW." She looks at the small house across the street. "So, this is Connie's place?"

The three of us study the modest brick home, with no lights glowing from the inside and no porch lights on.

"Craddock tried the doors. They were all locked," I say. "He didn't see any indication of a security system, but of course that doesn't mean there isn't one."

I give Peg a meaningful glance. "I need to get into that house, but I don't want to involve anyone from the DPD."

"Which, I suppose, means you don't have a warrant," Peg says.

"And no key."

Peg studies me. "Desperate times call for desperate measures, right?" She cranes her neck to look at Rocky. "You got your lock kit in the van?"

Rocky gives her the thumbs-up, gets out of my car, and disappears behind the van. A few seconds later she reappears, carrying a small backpack, and gestures for us to follow while jogging stealthily toward the backyard fence.

"It can't look like anyone's broken in," I say to Peg.

Peg just gives me a dry laugh. "Rocky's got this covered."

Rocky vaults the six-foot fence like a gymnast and unlatches it from the inside. Peg hands me a pair of latex gloves and puts on her own pair. I follow her into the backyard. I tense for a moment, waiting for the barking of nearby neighborhood dogs, but everything is silent.

Rocky walks to the back porch and crouches down to study the back door. In front of it is a screen door that looks twenty years old. Rocky lifts a small can of WD-40 out of the backpack and sprays the hinges until they are soaked. She eases the screen open and secures it with a small potted plant.

KATHLEEN KENT

Rustling around, Rocky pulls out a lockpick set. She has the door unlocked by the count of ten.

She whispers, "I just love these old locks, don't you?"

The three of us enter and pause in the kitchen, listening for the beeping sounds of a security system.

Peg says, "I think we're good."

Rocky eases the door shut, and we let our eyes adjust to the dark.

"What are we looking for?" Rocky asks.

"Any clue as to where Connie's gone," I say. "A digital camera with photos, a journal, a datebook, home computer—"

We split up and start looking through closets and drawers, using the lights on our cell phones in bursts to orient ourselves. It's a small house, with two bedrooms, one bathroom, and a combined living and dining room. The furniture is sparse, but everything looks clean and neat. I start in what looks to be Connie's room. Her folded clothes are stacked in an orderly fashion, the hanging clothes evenly spaced, her shoes placed tidily on racks. There are a few empty hangers, and there's an open space on a shelf next to a suitcase. The bed is neatly made with no signs of a struggle.

I move into the bathroom and look through the medicine cabinet. There I find the usual array of aspirin and Tylenol, bandages, and disinfectant cream, but no prescription medications. On a hanging rack in the shower is a bottle each of shampoo and conditioner. The grout between the shower tiles is dry.

Rocky comes out of the guest bedroom, shaking her head.

"The bed's made. But there's nothing in the drawers or the closet," she says.

We join Peg in the living room. "You know, it's kind of odd

that there are no framed pictures anywhere," she says. "Like she doesn't have a family, or life beyond her work."

"Or at least not one she wants known," I say.

There are no computers or electronic devices on or in the desk tucked into a recess next to the kitchen. In a desk organizer, I find a few utility and credit-card bills addressed to a Connie Winslow at this address. There are no unusual or exorbitant charges. Tucked behind the bills is a colorful brochure. I pull it out, my phone light reflecting brightly off its shiny surface.

As I unfold it, my body grows rigid, and the pain in my head, which had receded, comes roaring back to life. I've seen the brochure before; on the cover is an enraptured young woman, a celestial light ringing her head, and, emblazoned across the top, is a Bible verse in a colorful banner. Also on the cover is an emblem—upswept wings transected by a sword. The Roy family emblem.

Connie, the woman who had spent months in our home, who had cared for Mary Grace and Elizabeth, is connected to a woman who talked about drowning a baby with as much indifference as sinking a plank of wood. A lunatic who talked a young girl into hanging herself just to prove a point.

Something's gone wrong with the walls. They've grown spongy, wavering as though nearing collapse. Threatening to bury me under the weight of the falling roof.

A firm hand on my elbow, and I realize that Peg has been calling my name.

"What is it?" she asks.

The room tilts crazily, and she steers me to the nearest chair. Rocky takes the brochure from my fingers and shows it to her partner. Peg forces my head down between my knees.

"Breathe," she says, patting me awkwardly on the back. "You'll be okay."

Rocky hands me a bottle of water, but my hands are shaking too badly to grasp it. Peg sits down next to me and waits patiently for my attack to pass.

"You know, I had a kid," she says quietly. I look at her in surprise. "It's true. I gave him up for adoption 'cause I was too young and stupid to take care of an infant. I even got to help pick out the parents. An Episcopal minister and his wife. I was told they were good people, a nice house, big yard, yada, yada, yada. But I never got over it. And I *chose* it. That's why I joined the army. It was a kind of punishment. So I can't imagine how bad you must feel having Elizabeth stolen right out from under you."

"I let Connie into our—"

A hard rap at the front door makes us freeze. The rapping comes again.

A male voice says, "Dallas Police. Anyone home?"

Panic swells in my chest, but Rocky looks calmly at Peg and signals for us to slip into the main bedroom, which is shielded by blackout curtains. Flashlight beams shine in broken shafts through the living room blinds. The beams progress around the house. Someone tries the back door, and for an alarmed instant I wonder if Rocky has locked it behind us. The twin beams continue until we hear footsteps on the front porch again. The doorknob is tested, and then the footsteps retreat.

Rocky moves soundlessly to the street-facing windows and peeks out.

"DPD patrol," she says. "They've left."

Peg says, "I think now's the time for us to leave as well."

★ ★ ★

After reassuring Peg and Rocky that I'm okay, I drive to my partner's house and stagger to his front porch. Seth comes to the door in his underwear, scratching at his hair in irritated swipes. "What the fuck, Riz?"

I lean against the doorframe so I won't collapse. "Can I crash here? I don't want to disturb Jackie or her mom."

He takes in my wavering, zombie-like presence, and his irritation turns to concern. He opens the door wider for me to come in. I immediately sink onto his couch, the couch where we've spent countless hours talking and drinking beer, and, in my case, pretending to be interested in football. He scrounges up a pillow and a blanket and perches on the coffee table.

"Patty here?" I ask.

"Nah, she left a while ago."

"Thanks for this, Riot," I murmur.

"You need anything? Water, something to eat?"

I shake my head, my eyes two open pits of despair. "We good?"

He throws me a weak smile and gives my leg a squeeze. "I gave you my favorite blanket, didn't I?" He stands and shuffles off to bed with a backward wave.

I pull the blanket up under my chin. It's the well-worn crocheted monstrosity his grandmother made for him for his eighteenth birthday, with the Cowboys logo hot-glued onto one corner. With everything that's happened in the past eighteen hours, I'm not sure I can fall asleep. But I begin to lose consciousness almost immediately, the weight of the blanket settling over me like a temporary reprieve from all my transgressions.

31

Dallas Police Department, North Central Division
Tuesday, September 23, 2014

I open my eyes to a dark form looming over me and jerk upright, thrashing against the blanket twisted around my legs. It's Seth, holding a mug of steaming coffee, and he jumps backward to keep the scalding liquid away from my skin.

"Hey, hey, hey," he cautions. "It's friend, not foe."

In the space of a few rattling heartbeats I orient myself. I'm on my partner's couch, still fully dressed, my personal cell phone on the coffee table buzzing with an incoming call.

Seth hands me the coffee and says, "It's Jackie again. She's probably left five messages in the last fifteen minutes. I'm leaving in twenty if you want me to drive."

I realize I should call Jackie, apologize for not sleeping with her at her mother's, and for not calling enough yesterday with updates. But I have to hope she knows me well enough by now to understand that I've crawled into a space of tunnel vision dedicated to one end.

So, instead of doing the decent thing, I text her: I'm fine, with Seth, and will call you when I have positive news. Love you.

I lock myself in the bathroom, splash frigid water over my face, and run damp fingers through my hair. I briefly consider using Seth's toothbrush, but instead smear some toothpaste on one finger and do my best to scrape the acrid fog from my mouth. The expression that greets me in the mirror would not only turn a man to stone but melt his eyeballs inside their sockets.

I fold myself into the passenger seat of Seth's car, letting my partner drive so I can check messages and make calls confirming that the team will be at the station early. Ten o'clock is the critical time when Flaco will be turning on his phone and dialing Junior's number, the number to the burner now in the custody of the DEA.

Seth steals a few glances in my direction. "When was the last time you ate?"

I shrug and mumble, "Not hungry yet."

He calls Craddock and tells him to pick up a dozen anything as long as it has a lot of fat and sugar in it.

My work phone rings, and I see Lieutenant Bradford's name light up the screen. Taking a deep breath, I answer, and spend the next five minutes being tongue-lashed for "terrorizing Alan Turner's domestic help" and "initiating an unauthorized house search."

No sooner do I disconnect the call when my partner's phone rings. He answers, listens, and ends the call. "That was Judge Whittaker's clerk. We didn't get the evidentiary search warrant for Turner's house."

We drive for a few more minutes in silence. "I did something last night," I say, turning to face my partner. "Actually, I did several things last night that were bad."

I tell him about allowing Philbo to pressure Junior in the

interrogation after he'd been Mirandized, and about Tina's suicide. And then I confess to breaking into Connie's house.

"How'd you do that?" he asks.

I give him a look, and he says, "Ah, our friends Bartles and Bentner."

"I found a brochure from the Roy ministry in her desk."

He exhales a soft whistle. "Tying Connie to Evangeline. So, you're thinking she was a plant?"

"Looks that way."

We've arrived at the station, and Seth pulls into his parking space. He turns to face me. "Just so you know, I'd have done exactly the same thing if my kid was missing. Hell, I'd do the same thing if you were missing. And probably much, much worse."

I nod gratefully and begin to pull at the door handle. Seth reaches for my arm to hold me in place. "Riz, why'd you go home yesterday in the middle of the day?"

"I had a hunch."

"No bullshit, Riz. Why'd you go home?"

I've just admitted to my partner two things that could get me demoted, suspended, or even fired. He knows more about me than any other human being except Jackie—and there've been some things over the years that Seth and I experienced together that I haven't felt comfortable revealing even to my life partner. Not because she'd judge me, or wouldn't understand, but because I didn't want her to worry about my safety.

But convincing Seth that my dead uncle speaks to me is not something I can do. It was only a few months ago that I was on the verge of a breakdown. How do I explain rationally, and reasonably, in the cold light of day, *"Oh, yeah, well, my uncle Benny comes to me while I'm running, or sleeping, and whispers warnings in my ear...in real time...from beyond the grave."*

"Seth, I promise you that someday I'll tell you. But today is not that day." I pin him with my gaze, trying to telegraph the importance of his trusting me.

"I'm going to hold you to that promise," he says. "In the meantime, you might want to consider running any future crazy maneuvers past your partner first."

I wait for the team to settle into their chairs in the incident room. Craddock made good on his breakfast delivery, bringing several dozen kolaches and an industrial-size thermos of strong coffee. The sugar and caffeine have hit my system like jet fuel, and for the first time since waking, I feel as though all the gray matter inside my head is firing in unison. I glance at the clock, which reads eight fifteen. Less than two hours before Flaco makes his call to Junior.

"Here's what we've got," I say. "I just got off the phone with Fred Dunlap, and they've identified the burner service carrier through the mobile ID number inside Junior's phone. There was only ever one incoming number, which we know is Flaco's. We're going to assume that both dumb phones were purchased at the same time, most likely for cash, so we probably can't track down the seller, at least not quickly. And if there was a cash buy, there will be no record of who bought the phones anyway.

"Detective Ryan informed me before our meeting that he retrieved, through a reader on a traffic signal, the license plate from the SUV that ran down Johnny B." I gesture for Ryan to continue.

"The SUV is registered to a woman named Estella Cruz."

"Honduran?" Esparza asks.

Ryan nods. "I was able to trace her address to an apartment building in downtown Dallas."

"Very expensive apartments," I add. "Tell them what else you found out."

"Flaco, Roberto Flores, has been out of the country for a long time, so it got me thinking he'd need a safe place to reestablish his network. Maybe reconnect with some old contacts. I did a little digging and discovered who posted bail for Flaco when he was busted a few years ago." He waits a beat and then says, "Estella Cruz."

Philbo groans appreciatively. "Now, that's a smart fucking cop, right there."

"A smart fuckin' cop who just happens to be my partner," Craddock says, grinning and reaching for the last pastry.

"We think Cruz was also a girlfriend," I say. "Maybe still is."

I look at the way the guys are sitting. They're all tense muscles and gnashing jaws. Like mastiffs alert and ready, waiting for me to blow the whistle.

"Okay, so what's the plan?" Seth asks.

"The DEA surveillance van will be parked in the vicinity of Cruz's building at nine thirty. Dunlap is with a judge now, getting a search-and-seizure warrant signed for Cruz's apartment. Esparza, you're going to be in the van as well to take the call from Flaco at ten o'clock. You're going to use the exact same greeting Junior used yesterday."

"'What's happening?'" Esparza says. "Only using the local slang, '¿Qué pajó?'"

"The Stingray will capture the call, and if we're very lucky, like yesterday, Flaco will do most of the talking. Junior did little more than say yes or no."

Esparza looks doubtful. "You think Flaco's not going to notice he's not talking to Junior?"

"Hey," Philbo says, looking pointedly at me. "We work with what we're handed, right, Sergeant?"

His remark feels like he's working me. I wanted him to be part of the team, but this could be a dangerous pattern.

"The worst that can happen," I say, breaking eye contact, "is that Flaco ends the call and ditches the phone. The rest of us will be stationed around the building, waiting to execute the warrant. And maybe make a couple of arrests.

"So, do what you have to do at your desks, and we'll leave in teams for downtown in half an hour."

As everyone leaves the incident room, I pull Ryan aside. "That was good work on the Estella Cruz connection."

He smiles, pleased, and ducks his head. Kevin Ryan is one of those guys who will retain his boyish good looks well into middle age and will probably be blushing when he's eighty.

"When we execute the warrant, though, I want you to stay in the DEA van with Esparza," I say.

He stares up at me, puzzled and surprised.

"Look, call me superstitious, but I'm thinking of your wife right now. We'll have plenty of backup. With everything on my mind right now I'd just feel better if you hung back on this one."

He's disappointed, but he says, "Sure, no problem."

Returning to my office, I see Craddock talking quietly with the station manager. The manager hands him some bills, which Craddock quickly stuffs into his pants pocket. He turns and startles to see me walking toward him.

"It's a little early to be starting the playoff betting pool," I say.

"Ah, yeah," he mutters, and tries to slink around me.

"Tom, what's going on? You look guilty."

I've said it teasingly, but he doesn't look happy.

"I've, uh...I've started a collection. For Kevin. You know, to get a baby gift from all of us. I just thought, with everything you're dealing with these days...With, Elizabeth being, uh, missing and all..."

He stammers into silence.

"And you thought it would upset me." I reach into my pocket and pull out all the money I've got. "Tom, there is a Polish proverb *Łakomy wszystkim zły, sobie najgorszy*. It means that it's a blight to bemoan the good fortune of others."

I reach out and give Craddock's arm a squeeze. "Buy them something nice. And by the way, I'm keeping Kevin in the van. You'll be partnered with Philbo this morning."

"You're a good egg, Detective Sergeant Rhyzyk," he says.

"Yeah, yeah," I say, turning away, my eyes misting. "Don't be such a suckass."

32

Main Street, Downtown Dallas
Tuesday, September 23, 2014

Across the street from the Joule—a small boutique hotel that caters to high-flying businesspeople and wealthy out-of-towners recovering from cosmetic surgeries—there is a small fenced-in park that borders Stone Place Crosswalk. At the far north end of the park is a favorite tourist attraction: a gargantuan, intensely blue and red-veined fiberglass eyeball thirty feet tall that stares unblinkingly at the Joule, either in judgment or apathy.

The surveillance van is parked on Main just to the east of the park, in close proximity to the Wilson Apartment building, where Estella Cruz resides. It's nine forty-five, and Fred Dunlap and I are inside with Moreno, the DEA tech, Ryan, and Esparza. Esparza's on a headset, ready to answer Junior's burner when the call from Flaco comes in. Craddock, Philbo, and Seth are waiting next to the park. Dunlap's DEA agents, six of them, are gathered in the hotel's parking lot. They've already done a search for Cruz's black SUV and located it in one of the resident parking spaces. The front bumper is dented like it's hit something dense.

A discreet questioning of the doorman reveals that, as far as he knows, Cruz is currently in her apartment with a male visitor. Dunlap gives a radio signal, directing his guys to gather in the lobby; as soon as Dunlap and I join them, they'll accompany us up to the apartment on the eighth floor.

Esparza's face is impassive, but there's a narrow band of sweat glistening along his hairline.

Just after nine thirty, Philbo had called to tell me that Junior had not met his deadline to share any information regarding Flaco. And that he was refusing to speak to us further.

At nine fifty-five, I call Seth and tell him to take Craddock and Philbo to the lobby, joining the DEA team.

At exactly ten o'clock, Junior's phone rings, and Esparza accepts the call immediately.

"*¿Qué pajó?*" he says. He's studied Junior's voice; raising his own deep baritone to sound younger.

There is a pause, and then the voice on the other end says, "Nice try, Detectives. Evangeline sends her regards."

We wait for the sound of the phone disconnecting, but for some reason Flaco keeps the line engaged. Faint street noises continue in the background. Confused, Esparza shakes his head. The Stingray continues to collect data from the burner.

"He forget to disconnect?" Moreno asks, disbelieving.

Dunlap and I bolt out of the van and run the half block to the apartment building, joining our combined teams in the lobby. There are a few residents waiting for the elevators, staring curiously at the law enforcement signifiers emblazoned across our Kevlar vests and at our weapons and Blackhawk tactical battering ram. One of the agents, with arms like two live oaks, is carrying an active-shooter response shield, weighing close to forty pounds. We move the residents aside and step into the large freight elevator, joined by a maintenance man, who keys the panel into express mode. Dunlap quickly explains to me the apartment layout: entryway, kitchen to the right, dining area to the left. Two bedrooms on either side, right and left.

When the doors open, the maintenance man points us in the right direction, and we move quickly to the end of the hall, to number 517, Cruz's apartment. The carpet muffles our footsteps, and there's no talking. We split into two groups, hugging the walls, but as we approach the door, I see a piece of paper taped at eye level. There's a rushing sound in my ears, and the wavy lines have returned to the periphery of my vision.

On the piece of paper is a crude drawing of a large eyeball—red-veined and intensely blue, like the one in the park—below which is written, "We're watching you."

My tongue feels stuck to the roof of my mouth. I stand to one side of the door and bang loudly on it. "Dallas Police officers with a search warrant. Open up, please."

There's no sound from inside, and I wait thirty seconds to pound on the door again. "Open up, Ms. Cruz. Dallas Police Department with a warrant to search your apartment."

A door down the hall opens, and a man pokes his head out. One of the DEA agents gives him a cautioning wave, and he quickly ducks back inside.

"Estella Cruz, this is the last time I'm going to ask you to open the door. If you do not let us in to execute this search warrant, we'll have to breach the door forcefully, and I don't think you want us to do that."

I count to thirty and look at Dunlap. "This does not feel good."

Dunlap motions me to step back and brings two of his agents forward—the one with the battering ram, and the other with the shield.

To a third officer he says, "As soon as the door is breached, toss in the flash grenade."

There are clicking sounds coming from inside the apartment; someone is unlocking the door. It swings open, and two DEA agents rush inside, sweep back, and secure a petite woman wearing a filmy robe and fuzzy slippers. She yelps in surprised outrage. Kitchen and living areas are clear. A small bedroom to the left is empty. In the master bedroom, though, a naked man cowers and tries to cover himself with the sheet. He's dragged roughly from the bed, handcuffed, jerked upright, and thrust onto the couch next to the woman.

"Are you Estella Cruz?" I ask.

She spits out something in Spanish and stares at me defiantly. Fred Dunlap holds up a photo on his phone and says, "It's her."

I turn my attention to the naked man. He's Hispanic, but he's not Flaco. "Who are you?"

"Check my dick for my ID," he says. The words are meant to sound tough, but he's clearly terrified.

I turn back to Cruz, holding up the piece of paper I snatched from the door. "Did you leave this on the door?"

She chuffs air out through her nostrils and gives me a half smile. Dunlap instructs his men to start searching the apartment. The items to be seized are phones, computers, relevant paper files, and any illegal substances. Seth brings a towel from the bathroom and throws it over the naked man's lap.

"Where's Flaco?" I ask Cruz.

"You think he'd be stupid enough to be here? I haven't seen him in years."

"Oh, really, then why was he driving your SUV in Five Points a few days ago? An SUV that was involved in a fatal hit-and-run accident?"

I still couldn't confirm for sure that Flaco had been in the vehicle when it struck Johnny B. But Cruz's head jerks up, and her eyes widen, telling me that she didn't know her SUV had been involved in a man's killing.

Craddock walks out of the main bedroom, holding up a wallet. "Found this in this gentleman's pants pocket. We're running the name on the driver's license now to see if he's got any outstanding warrants. But he's definitely not Flaco."

Moreno radios me from the van. "Stingray's still pulling data on the open line that indicates our guy's in the area. But it can't pinpoint a radius of more than a few hundred yards in any direction."

"Flaco's not in the apartment. Where's the epicenter of the signal?" I ask.

"The gated park."

The park across from the Joule Hotel, with the giant eyeball. *We're watching you.*

Estella Cruz is now fully aware that she's in trouble, and her attitude has gone from defiant to anxious. She looks at me with large, startled doe eyes.

"Flaco called you, didn't he?" I say. "To let you know we were coming. That *I* was coming."

Her eyes flick nervously to the paper, and in that moment I know what the note means.

I shout for Seth to follow me and, without checking to see if he's heard the command, run for the elevator. I punch frantically at the buttons and then race for the stairwell. I'm already down two flights before I hear Seth clattering after me.

"Riz," he calls. "What's going on?"

"The park," I yell over my shoulder.

At the bottom, I bang through the exit door and sprint west down Main Street toward the Stone Place Crosswalk. There is a metal railing around the park to keep out pedestrians, but it's only a few feet high, and I vault over it easily. There's no one else inside, but there are thick bushes on the back side of the eyeball, thick enough to hide a grown adult. The mammoth orb which earlier had appeared merely creepy, now seems menacing. I pull my gun and crouch down, waiting for Seth to join me. A small dark object has been placed at the base of the sculpture.

"That look like a phone to you?" Seth asks.

Our acrobatics have attracted attention, and a small crowd is gathering. Standing, we cautiously approach the looming eye, our guns still drawn. There on the grass is a cell phone. I pick it up and put it to my ear. It's still connected.

"Moreno," I say.

His voice comes in, loud and clear. "Sergeant Rhyzyk?"

"I found the burner. Detective Dutton and I are in the park. Flaco was here."

I turn off the phone, and my head snaps around. A quick search of the bushes behind the enormous sculpture reveals no one hiding and no further clues. Seth follows me onto Elm Street, on the northern side of the park. We scan the street, busy with morning traffic but few pedestrians.

"He is one slippery son of a bitch," Seth says.

Dunlap radios me: "What's going on?"

"We found Flaco's burner in the park," I say. "But no sign of the man."

"Both Cruz and the naked guy have no outstanding

warrants," Dunlap says. "There's very little here that will be helpful to us. We have their two cell phones but no computers or tablets, and there are no drugs in the apartment. We'll have the SUV towed and see what forensics can find. If we can lift any of Flaco's fingerprints, or evidence of Johnny B's DNA on the bumper, we can arrest Cruz on obstruction, maybe even manslaughter. But as of now, we don't have enough to arrest her."

The crippling frustration over missing Flaco is so overwhelming that, for a moment, I think my legs may give out. Angered, I disconnect the call. As I turn to Seth, I catch a flash of copper out of the corner of my eye. A glimpse of long red hair on a young woman who's holding up a cell phone. She's grinning at us and appears to be taking video footage. Of me.

She's less than half a block away, and when she sees that I've spotted her, she turns and runs. Everything in my line of sight except Evangeline's acolyte—she's one of the twins who taunted me in the courthouse, I'm sure of it—is excluded, and I put all my energy into chasing her. I get within twenty feet and she throws herself into the passenger seat of a car idling at the curb, which quickly joins the westward flow of traffic on Elm Street.

Seth has followed after me, and we both stand, panting for air, watching the car receding into the distance. On the strength of my anguished yell alone, every window in every high-rise building on Elm Street should implode, alongside my hope.

33

White Rock Lake
Tuesday, September 23, 2014

I run.

Passing the grand houses in Lakewood, their windows frosted with golden light and gauzy curtains, passing the old-growth trees on half-acre lots that have withstood the strain of their own weighty limbs for nearly a century.

I extend the length of my stride as I near the lake, the streets gently rising and falling over what was once an ancient seabed. "It's layers of Austin Chalk," Jackie had informed me when I first described my delight at finding a part of Dallas that wasn't as flat as a pane of glass.

"Like the White Cliffs of Dover," she had added, astonishing me once again with her seemingly endless knowledge of the natural world.

The night she talked about the chalky hills was one of the first we'd spent in our new home. Entangled in the sheets of our bed, our bodies molded into a landscape of momentary quiet, Jackie had whispered, "Did you know that rocks come from a source called a Mother Rock? But chalk is made up of all the tiny shells of sea creatures that died a hundred million years ago."

"Does that mean my Mother Rock was a crustacean?" I'd asked, holding her closer.

She'd smiled at me, cupping her palm along my cheek. "It means the harder the shell, the sweeter the insides."

I had finally called Jackie a few hours after the unsuccessful search of Estella Cruz's apartment. She had begged me to come and stay with her tonight at her mother's house. When I told her I couldn't, that I would be staying in our own home, she heard not only the steel-tipped defiance in my voice but also the pain and desperation. My lame excuses of not wanting to keep her up all night with my anxious tossing and turning were met with a lengthy silence, and then a resigned acceptance. What I didn't say, but what I suspected she understood, was that I was hoping Evangeline, or one of her minions, would try to break into the house again. I wanted a chance to end it early by discharging every round from my SIG Sauer into the invader's face.

I pick up my pace once more, trying and not succeeding to banish the fear that this time I've pushed Jackie to her limit.

A troubling mantra takes its place. *Two more days, two more days, two more days...*It's Tuesday night. Thursday is the deadline that El Cuchillo has given me to find Evangeline.

Once I hit the trail circling the lake, there are very few other runners or cyclists. Those on the trail give me a wide berth—as though sensing the emotional storm emanating from me like a tsunami.

The evening is warm, but it may rain later, and clouds are already dimming the advancing twilight. I press on, trying to make my mind, at least for a brief while, a vast, blank wasteland. But despite all my best efforts, I see in every form that walks or runs or lurches around the lake startling facsimiles of those who would stalk me, and worse. Ahead of me is a woman rapidly pushing a runner's baby carriage, eager to leave the lakefront before it gets too dark. The baby's face is upturned, rapturous, open mouth catching the wind. I pass an older woman, one of the homeless who camp out in the open-air pavilions, her long, wispy hair tied back with a bandanna into a wild gray mane.

"Whatever it is," she shouts at me, "you can't outrun it."

In an eerie echo I see my mother's face, her own hair gone gray within a year of her cancer diagnosis. I can remember sitting by her hospital bed, holding her hand—grown bony and insubstantial. And yet, some essential part of her had grown more resilient, even as the disease ravaged her body. The only people she would allow into her hospital room were me and Uncle Benny. My father was not allowed.

She had looked at me with concern, as though I were the one who was desperately ill. Following the suicide of my brother, I'd begun running six miles a day. Following my mother's diagnosis, seven or eight. I was gaunt, knotted with worry, a high-tension wire that could spark into flames at any moment.

"Betty, you punishing yourself will not change anything," she had said. "Promise me you'll look after yourself, and your uncle Benny. Promise me."

I had promised without revealing that I had overheard her extracting the same promise from Uncle Benny too.

The last words she spoke to me were in Polish. *Wole walczyć trzy, niż raz rodzic.*

I'd rather do battle three times than give birth once...

Once I return to the house, I wander the silent rooms, checking the locks on windows and doors, every room except the nursery. I place the palm of my hand over the closed door as though feeling for directional vibrations, but I don't go in. Before I crawl into bed, I look at my naked body in the full-length mirror, examining the damage of justice served, and justice delayed: the large tattoo of Saint Michael covering, but not quite obscuring, the long scar over my Achilles tendon, the still-red wound where El Cuchillo's skinning knife punctured the hollow at the base of my throat, the scars on the back of both hands from the fire. And I would rather face all of those things again than have to feel just one time the pain of losing the child in my care.

I have every intention of staying alert, but I soon fall into a twilight state—not completely asleep and yet not fully awake—my gun by my side.

In the curious way of dreams, blackness gives way to light, immediate and revelatory. I'm standing under the magnificent vaulted ceiling of Saint Stanislaus Catholic Church in Greenpoint, Brooklyn. The church where my mother's funeral service was held. To the right of the altar is a larger-than-life statue of Saint Michael standing upon a rocky ledge, his wings spread, holding a sword aloft, one sandaled foot firmly fixed over the head of the Evil Serpent. And standing with his back to me, observing the statue, is Uncle Benny wearing his full-dress uniform, the uniform he wore to pay his final respects to his brother's wife.

"You know, if you had been born a boy, your mother was going to name you Michael." He says it over his shoulder without turning around. He senses it's me standing behind him in the nave. "I think she knew that he would forever be your guardian angel."

"You loved her, didn't you?" I ask.

He nods. "Always have. Always will. But I think you knew that."

I take a few steps toward him. He points to something on the plinth below Saint Michael and motions me closer. Four ones—"1111"—are chiseled into the granite.

"Do you know why this number is important?" he asks. He looks at me briefly and smiles, and I'm made breathless once more with pride and admiration, just as I was as a child. "Your grandmother would have said it was the time when your guardian angel was opening up a celestial portal. Your father would have insisted it had something to do with medieval Polish history."

I'm standing next to him, inhaling the comforting scent of his Old Spice cologne. "What happened in Poland in 1111?"

He turns to me and laughs. "Not a goddam thing, as far as I know."

As he looks at me, his face turns grave and he leans closer, his breath in my face. "What does a religious leader always look for?"

"A congregation," I say.

"And where will she house that congregation?"

"In a church."

He looks once more at the statue of Saint Michael. "And upon what rock will she build this church?"

I remember full well the Roy matriarch telling me of her fevered visions of Saint Michael, and of her belief that he had chosen her to dominate the earth with her redheaded followers.

"The Archangel," I whisper.

He holds me in the warmth of his gaze. "And what happened at eleven eleven o'clock?"

"I don't know."

"It's the time you were born." He puts his finger against my forehead and pushes. "Time for the awakening, Betty."

As soon as my eyes open to the murky shadows in my bedroom, I know, even before looking at the digital clock, that the time is 11:11 p.m. I rub the middle of my forehead where Uncle Benny's finger pressed into my flesh. And I smile, certain that I'll sleep the rest of the night undisturbed.

I now know where to start looking for Evangeline Roy.

34

Dallas Police Department, North Central Division
Wednesday, September 24, 2014

Arriving early at the station, I'm surprised to see Seth already at his desk. He looks like he didn't sleep at all last night. I stride past him on my way to my office and gesture for him to follow me.

Sitting at my desk, I start a search of all the churches in the Dallas area named Saint Michael's. Or any that make reference to the Archangel.

Seth is lingering in the doorway, and I beckon him in. "I know where to start looking for Evangeline Roy," I say, tapping at the keyboard. "I had a spark of inspiration last night, and now—"

I look up at my partner, who's still standing in front of my desk. He looks haggard, almost ill.

"Are you not feeling well?" I ask.

He turns and closes the door before sitting in one of the visitor's chairs. He stares down at his hands and then looks up at me. "Riz," he says, his voice ragged. "Something's happened."

I'd stand but my legs wouldn't hold me. His eyes are red and swollen. Whatever it is, it's bad. I grab the edge of the desk.

"Is it...is there news about Elizabeth?"

He shakes his head and clears his throat. "It's Kevin."

I sit back in my chair. "Kevin? Our Kevin?"

"He's gone."

My partner's not making any sense. "Gone? What do you mean? Gone where?"

"Riz, he's dead. He was shot."

Now I do stand up, my mouth open and panting. *He's dead. He was shot.* The nonsensical sounds have coalesced around a terrible clarity. A crippling pain inside my ribs begins to swell, and I mash a hand against my sternum to keep it from cracking open.

"No." My head spasms back and forth. "No. No. *No!*"

Seth stands as well, his hands held palms upward, like a supplicant beseeching pity, or understanding.

"It happened last night," he says.

"Evangeline."

"No." He takes a breath. "It was the kid he was mentoring. The kid tried to rob a convenience store, and a bunch of patrol cars showed up. He called Kevin, saying he'd give himself up if Kevin was there to make sure he wasn't shot."

He grabs my arm, abruptly, as though to steady me, and I sink back down into my chair.

Moving his chair closer to mine, he sits so we're knee to knee. "I spoke to the cops on the scene. They said that Kevin talked to the kid for some time, and it looked like he was giving himself up. Kevin reached to take the gun away, and the gun discharged." He runs a hand over his mouth.

"The kid shot him? Why?" I wail. Kevin Ryan, the

baby-faced detective who'd decided he could make a difference...the man who was finally going to be a father. Snuffed out by a messed-up teenager?

"I don't know," Seth says. "He's being interviewed this morning."

"Oh my God," I whisper. "Where's Craddock? Who's with Kevin's wife?"

"Craddock is with Karen now. He was with Kevin when it happened and rode in the ambulance to the hospital. Kevin died en route."

There's a knock at the door. The outside world is waiting to intrude.

I look at Seth, panicked.

"I'll take care of it." He turns and edges out the door, quickly closing it.

There is a murmur of voices—Philbo's broad, flat vowels over Seth's languid drawl—and then the voices retreat. The hand at my chest has gone numb, and I lower it slowly to my lap, nesting it on top of the other. My two hands cupping nothing but air. Nothing but empty space.

Less than twenty-four hours ago, Kevin had been listening unhappily to my decision to station him in the surveillance van for his own protection. *Call me superstitious,* I had told him. I had truly believed that I could keep him safe. That I could somehow keep the seemingly random, destructive chaos of the world at bay and prevent a decent man from dying. Clenching my fingers into fists, I want to overturn the desk, to hurl a chair through a plate-glass window, to howl at the four walls enclosing me until my vocal cords are shredded and useless. But instead, I put my head on the desk and fill my empty hands with bitter, angry tears.

★ ★ ★

At some point my phones begin to ring: Jackie, James Earle, Wayne. I can't begin to summon the strength to explain the enormity of what's happened, and I let all the calls go to voice mail. But I know that I will have to wrestle my grief into a tightly bound box and bury it deep inside me. There will be a time to grieve, but that time is not now. The day the Towers came down, I remember Uncle Benny telling me, *Betty, you can't help the dead....Save your strength for the survivors.* I have to go on faith that there will be survivors after Evangeline is captured or destroyed.

When Peg Bartles calls, I drag my shirtsleeve across my face, take a deep breath, and answer.

"What's wrong with you? You sound terrible," Peg says.

I tell her about Ryan, not even trying to hide my anguish.

"Jesus, I'm so sorry. What can we do to help?"

"As of today, I'm going to stop looking for Mary Grace," I say. "I've got to find Evangeline Roy by midnight tomorrow or more people may be hurt. My contract with you ends soon, so for now I need you and Rocky to change tactics. Can you do that for me?"

"Just try and stop us."

I then tell her what I want her, and her partner, to do.

There are only four of us in the incident room this time. Seth has already told Philbo and Esparza about Kevin's death, and about Craddock's absence. The faces of the three men are sober, downcast. Even Philbo has lost all traces of his usual cynical swagger.

"There are two people who should be in this room today—"
My voice gives out, and it takes me a moment to recover. I
cannot let myself break down again. Digging my nails into my
palms, I press on. "The chief, along with Lieutenant Bradford,
is also with Karen Ryan this morning and will advise us when
Ryan's funeral will take place.

"Right now, the best way to honor Kevin Ryan is to
do what we do best. So we're going to get back to work.
Evangeline Roy is a cult leader. And what every cult leader
needs is some kind of physical base of operations to house
her followers and use as a respectable cover for their drug
dealing. Evangeline is cunning, but she's also batshit crazy.
She believes, down to the soles of her orthopedic shoes, that
she has a special relationship with the Archangel Michael."

I begin handing out copies of a list of targeted churches
in the Dallas–Fort Worth area. "There are nine active
churches named Saint Michael's, another four that have been
abandoned or closed but still have existing structures, two
more churches with the word 'Archangel' in the name, and,
finally, one church named Sword of the Spirit and another
one named Men of the Sword Tabernacle. The sword is a part
of the Roy family emblem.

"I've indicated who will be visiting which church today.
We're going to start east and north of Dallas proper and work
our way west."

Philbo looks at me questioningly. "Several of these are
marked with the initials B&B."

"Bartles and Bentner. Private Investigators. We're short on
numbers, so I've enlisted them to help canvass."

"Where's the DEA in all of this?" Esparza asks.

"Fred Dunlap is focusing on arresting the Honduran gang

members in Five Points, as well as the men Detectives Dutton and Esparza followed after Junior's drop, hoping it will point them to Flaco. They're also doing forensics on the SUV we recovered from Estella Cruz's garage. I want us to check out all seventeen of these churches within twenty-four hours. With three teams, we'll have five or six churches per team, spread out over a lot of miles. We need to get started right away.

"One last thing. Apart from Flaco and his dealers, I have no idea how much manpower Evangeline has. She's a psychopath and dangerous. Do not try and engage her alone. Once we pinpoint her position, we'll have a SWAT team come in and do the heavy lifting. Any questions?"

There are none, and the four of us leave together for the garage. Every cop at every desk in the entire station house is silent at our passing.

The first church on my list is Saint Michael the Archangel in McKinney, north of Dallas. The drive will take close to forty-five minutes, and for most of that drive Seth and I don't speak. My partner looks at me from time to time, but he knows me well enough not to make small talk.

This particular Saint Michael's is a contemporary Spanish-style edifice with a bright, airy interior, a world away from the elaborate icon-heavy church of my youth. I've picked this church to visit first because of the large number of Honduran and El Salvadoran congregants. The only person who knows more than a guerrilla fighter about the politics and societal struggles of a country in crisis is the local priest. Father Simeon, a short, round Hispanic man with a large smile, greets us in his office. His smile fades somewhat when we show him our badges. He motions for us to sit in two well-worn visitors' chairs.

"What can I do for you?" he asks.

On my cell phone I pull up the still photo of Evangeline taken from my home surveillance camera. "Have you ever seen this woman?"

Simeon puts on his glasses and scrutinizes the image. "No. She doesn't look familiar to me."

"Has anyone approached you, looking to rent any of the surplus buildings that this parish may own?"

He shakes his head and beams. "We have a very full congregation. Latino mainly, but we also allocate alternate times for our Korean parishioners. We are well provided for by the diocese and so have no need to rent out space. May I ask what this is about?"

"The woman in the photo is named Evangeline Roy," I say. "She's been building up drug operations in Honduras and is looking to expand her distribution here in Texas."

Simeon cocks his head, confused. "What does this have to do with Saint Michael's Church?"

"She believes she has a special connection with the Archangel. That he speaks to her, directly. As her own spiritual beacon. It's possible she may be looking to set up shop behind the respectable facade of a church."

Now Simeon looks shocked. "And yet she distributes drugs?"

"She's crazy, and very dangerous, Father," Seth says. He hands Simeon the list of churches that we'll be visiting.

"Do you suspect any of my parishioners?" Simeon asks, studying the names.

"We're only interested in finding this woman," I say. "Unless you feel someone in your flock can provide some useful information."

Simeon gives me a disappointed frown. "Because all Hondurans, or Guatemalans, or Salvadorans are connected to drug dealing."

"No, Father, that's not it at all. The truth is, we're flying blind here. I'm grasping at straws. As my partner stated, she's dangerous, and people are going to die if we don't find her."

Simeon regards me thoughtfully while pinching his lower lip. "Wait here. I'll make a few calls."

He bustles from the room, taking the list with him, leaving Seth and me to stare at the sparse objects on display. Opposite the desk, there is a large painting of a sad-eyed Madonna holding the infant Jesus, who is gazing up at her with an equally tragic expression. The painting has taken on the cracked, green-tinged patina of age, turning the tender flesh of both mother and child to a morbid hue. Disturbed by the image of the doomed infant, I look away, and my throat tightens.

Nearby is a bookshelf filled with dual-language canonical books, a Spanish-language catechism, and half a dozen books on psychology. There are even several well-thumbed paperback novels. I pick up one titled *Havana Red* and show Seth the lurid cover.

"Looks like our good Father is a bit of a radical," he says.

In that moment, Simeon walks back into his office and gestures to the book in my hand. "Leonardo Padura is a genius. He writes about displacement, hunger, racial and economic injustice. Addiction," he adds, pointing a finger for emphasis, and sits down in his chair behind the desk. He places the list of churches in front of me.

"I called Saint Michael's in Garland, and also Saint Michael's in Grand Prairie, without any luck. They are part of the greater diocese in Dallas, and I know their priests in residence. They've not heard of your Evangeline Roy, nor have they recently rented out their property to any new congregations. The Saint Michael's in Richmond Hills is Anglican, so I can't be of much help there.

"However, there are sixty-nine parishes within the Dallas diocese, so I called the bishop's office. His secretary told me that there was a Catholic orphanage, now long closed, not far from the arboretum, also named Saint Michael's. It's being used exclusively as a storage facility for church records, including those of properties which are rented to outside groups. I can give you the name, number, and address of the secretary there."

He writes out the information, and Seth and I stand to go. "Thank you, Father," I say, shaking his hand, giving one last look at the painting. The Madonna holds her baby in her left arm, cradling him close to her heart, her expression clearly saying that her son cannot be saved.

Simeon's eyes have strayed to the two Saint Michael medallions around my neck. "You're a Catholic?"

I let go of his hand. "Ish," I say. "I like some of the message—"

"Just not the messengers," he finishes for me, smiling sadly.

Simeon walks us to the front entrance, but he taps me on the arm. When I turn toward him, he says, "'I will remain on Spartacus's side, never on the side of the Caesars.' Do you know who said that? Our friend Leonardo Padura." Simeon gives me a searching look. "He is also not fond of the Catholic Church. But he's a true social warrior. Do you know why I went the extra distance to help you, Sergeant Rhyzyk?"

When I shake my head, he says, "Because even those who carry the sword need an army clearing the road ahead. We've lost too many children in this city to drugs. I wish you luck, Detective. The hardest job on this earth is protecting the innocent."

35

Saint Michael's Orphanage
Wednesday, September 24, 2014

The arboretum is one of the city's jewels: a lake-facing public garden with sixty-plus acres of seasonal flowers, pavilions, outdoor sculptures, and, in the summer months, live music after sunset for enthusiastic, if sweaty, Dallasites looking for some good, clean, recycled fun.

The former Catholic orphanage is a few miles east and south of the gardens, but a world away from its pristine, well-resourced amenities and the expensive real estate of Lakewood. The houses are small and packed tightly together. The apartment buildings are poorly maintained, their tenants struggling paycheck to paycheck. This Saint Michael's is a two-story lumbering, redbrick building built in the middle of the last century. And yet its blandness, its lack of embellishments, its very utilitarianism seem to transmit the message that nothing decorative should be wasted on the unwanted and neglected children that were at one time housed within.

"Abandon hope, all ye who enter here," Seth mutters.

The parking lot is cracked and overgrown with weeds, and a chain-link fence, cluttered with errant bits of trash and newspaper, surrounds most of the orphanage lot. There are only a few cars parked nearby, one of them most likely belonging to the secretary who keeps track of the church records.

I feel a jolt of anger, looking at the old orphanage and its decaying grounds. I'm already anticipating the usual frustrating, obstreperous bureaucracy of the Catholic Church, and their holy trinity of denial, deflection, and denigration.

Seth and I get out of the car and walk up a few steps to the front door. I ring the visitors' bell and a woman's tinny voice comes through the intercom.

"Yes?" she says.

"Detectives Rhyzyk and Dutton from the Dallas Police Department," I say. "We're here to talk to a Ms. Reardon."

"May I ask what this is about?" The voice sounds mildly irritated.

Seth's exhalation also sounds irritated.

"Once we're inside we can tell you why we're here," I say.

"Can you please stand back a few steps and show your badges to the camera above the door," the voice orders.

We step back and hold our badges aloft. A buzzer sounds, and the safety lock is released, causing the door to open inward a few inches. We push our way into a dark hall, pausing to let our eyes adjust to the murky light. The wide hallway stretches in a straight line for maybe sixty yards to the back of the building; an uncarpeted stairway to the second floor rises steeply to our left. Muted fluorescent lighting reflects dully off worn linoleum tiles that were new thirty years ago. There are doorways on either side of the hall spaced at even intervals. They're all closed, but two-thirds of the way toward the rear of the building, a woman walks out of a room and stands motionless. The space is too ill lit to see many singular features other than an indistinct outline of a roundish, older woman wearing a formless dress and glasses.

For the beat of a few seconds, the thought that it's Evangeline Roy roots me in place, and my right hand instinctively goes to my gun. But as soon as the thought forms, it's dispelled. The woman does not have red hair, and she's younger than the cult leader.

Seth looks sharply at me, and I call out, "Ms. Reardon?"

"We can talk in my office," she says.

She disappears back into the room, and we walk toward the rear of the building, our shoes squeaking loudly on the worn tiles. By the time we reach the office door, which has been left open, the woman has seated herself behind an impressively large oak desk. She looks at us expectantly.

"Ms. Reardon?" I ask.

She gestures to a couple of wooden high-backed chairs that appear to have been pilfered from the orphanage chapel. "It's Miss, and yes, I'm she."

Agnes Reardon looks to be in her mid-forties, and, typical of some women who've devoted their entire lives to a religious order, she seems to have existed wholly on a diet of starch, communion wine, and guilt, topped off with a generous helping of shame. Her pinched lips look barely able to part for even the thinnest communion wafer.

"We were referred to you by Father Simeon at Saint Michael's in McKinney," I say.

One of Reardon's eyebrows lifts slightly. "Oh?"

"We're looking for a woman, Evangeline Roy, who we believe may be trying to rent, or purchase, property from one of the local churches named Saint Michael's."

She stares at us, mute, her hands on her lap.

Seth leans forward impatiently in his chair. "Have you been approached by Evangeline Roy? Or ever heard of the name?"

Her brow bunches delicately, as though considering the question. "I'm in charge of the diocese's historical records, but I'm afraid I don't have knowledge of more current, day-to-day affairs. Have you tried the diocese of Dallas?"

"They recommended we talk to you," I say. I slide my phone with the photo of the Roy matriarch across the desk. Reardon glances at it and then slides it back to me.

"I'm sorry, but she's unknown to me," she says. "Is that all?"

Something about her brusqueness sets my teeth on edge. "I was told that you also keep track of church-owned properties in the Dallas area that are rented to outside parties."

She folds her hands on top of her desk. "That's true, but I'm afraid I couldn't give you any information without the express permission of the bishop."

Her fingers play along the flat edge of an old-fashioned letter opener made of heavy, ornate brass and looking substantial enough to whittle oak. My eyes stray to the desk nameplate engraved with the name MRS. ELEANOR FLYNN.

"Who's Mrs. Flynn?" I ask.

"My predecessor," Reardon answers.

"When did you start working here?" Seth asks.

"I've only just recently started working for the diocese." Her mouth stretches into what may be a smile.

"What happened to Mrs. Flynn?" I ask.

"She became ill and retired. I haven't had time to change the nameplate."

"Perhaps there's someone else here we can talk to," Seth says.

She swivels her head toward him. "I'm afraid not. I work alone."

I notice that her fingers are now loosely wrapped around the hilt of the letter opener. The gaze behind the eyeglasses is reminiscent of my sixth-grade teacher, Sister Mary Ignatius. The old nun had sported the same look: suspicious, watchful, and amused in the way of all bullies by the discomfiture of defenseless things. The one time Sister Mary tried to apply "the rod"—a wooden yardstick that had been nicknamed The Screamer—to the back of my legs, I'd wrestled it from her and broken it over her sizable arms.

That memory, fueled by the fury and the pain of the past few days, is growing in my head like an irradiated mushroom inside a reactor.

"Why don't we just call the bishop," I say. "Right now, and ask him for permission to see the rental-property records."

My tone has erased some of the smugness from her demeanor. "That's not the usual protocol—"

"Miss Reardon," I say, leaning forward in my chair. "This is a police investigation. We can do this the easy way, with your cooperation. Or I can leave and get a search warrant. I can also contact the media, who would just love to recycle old horror stories of why this institution no longer houses children."

"Saint Michael's Orphanage was not like that."

"And I can assure you that it most probably was. Do you

want to embarrass the diocese, and the bishop? Look at my face and tell me I won't do it."

Reardon studies me, unblinking, for the count of ten. "What is it you want to know?"

"I want to know who in the last month has rented, or has inquired about renting, church property, specifically those properties affiliated with churches named Saint Michael's."

She sighs but stands and picks up a large journal from a cabinet nearby. Placing it on the desk, she turns to a page and then swivels the journal so I can read it.

Pointing to the most recently dated entries, she says, "We've only had two rentals in the last month, neither of them related to any Saint Michael's in the Dallas diocese. And, as you can see, your person of interest is not named."

She takes her seat again. "Anything else?"

"What about inquiries?" Seth asks.

"I would have no idea about those. I only record actual renters." She rustles through some papers on the desk. "Now if you'll excuse me, I have a lot of work to do."

The unmistakable sound of something being dragged across the second floor interrupts her. Her eyes don't stray toward the ceiling, but her posture has grown rigid.

"Who else is here in the building?" I ask.

There are more sliding noises and a bump, like something heavy has fallen over.

Seth stands. "I thought you said you were the only one here."

"It must be the cleaning crew," she says.

She's lying, and she knows that I know she's lying. "Seth," I say.

My partner, already headed toward the hallway, says, "On it."

Reardon and I lock eyes. She's grown notably paler, and her grip on the letter opener has whitened her knuckles.

She stands abruptly. "I have to go."

"Sit down," I order.

"No, I need to—"

Rising quickly, I stop her before she's taken two steps toward the door. "Sit down!"

She lowers herself back into her chair. We glare at each other, listening intently while the moments unspool. But it's silent. Unnervingly so. Reardon looks increasingly agitated, breathing in rapid pulses.

"I'll ask you again," I say. "Do you have knowledge of Evangeline Roy?"

If possible, her mouth constricts even further, but she doesn't answer. Concerned, I move backward toward the open office door, keeping my eyes on the woman behind the desk.

Stepping into the hallway, I yell, "Seth?"

There's no answer, and I pull my phone out to call for backup. Seth's been gone too long, and it's too quiet. A movement out of the corner of my eye brings my gaze back to Reardon. She's slumped facedown, motionless over the desk.

Oh my God. She's had a stroke or a heart attack.

Rushing to her side, I bend down to check her pulse. Her head pops up like a cork out of a bottle, and her arm swings in a vicious arc toward my chest. Moving defensively, I feel a sharp pain in my right shoulder. The brass letter opener is partially embedded in my deltoid muscle.

With surprising strength, she pushes against me. But I push

back with my left forearm. Before I can flinch, she's buried her teeth in my skin, drawing blood. Like a rabid terrier, she keeps her jaws clenched even when I haul her to her feet. Grabbing a hank of her hair, I pull backward as hard as I can, and with a yowl she finally releases my arm. During several minutes of struggling, we crash onto the desk, careen into walls, knock over boxes, and finally fall to the floor. I sit on top of her, trying to wrestle her with one arm while I reach for the cuffs, but she bucks and twists, biting, scratching, spitting, and kicking. I finally get her on her stomach, twist one arm behind her back, and slip one cuff on her wrist, then yank her closer to the desk so I can lock the other cuff to the leg of the massive desk.

On my ass, I scoot away from her as fast as I can, my breathing raspy and hitched. Reardon pulls hard at the desk, but it won't budge. She's not going anywhere. She stares hatefully at me, spittle foaming at the corners of her mouth. At some point during the struggle the letter opener has fallen free of my shoulder.

I've got blood streaming from the painful wounds in both arms, as well as from several scratches. My shirt is torn and streaked with red. One of my phones has been smashed in the struggle, and the other one is missing, kicked under a piece of furniture, or covered by a mountain of scattered files. I haul myself up to standing and pull my SIG Sauer out of its holster, wincing from the pain.

"You would have made one hell of a nun," I wheeze, and stumble out into the hallway.

We created so much noise that I can't believe someone else hasn't come to investigate. But I hear nothing coming from the second floor. I can call for backup from the landline in the office, but the gap in time, waiting to get through to emergency services, may prove fatal to my partner.

"Seth?" I call up the stairway.

I pause to listen again before walking slowly toward the top of the stairs. There is a balustrade along the second-floor landing, and as soon as my line of sight clears the floor, I look in both directions. To the left, at the far end of the hallway, is a door marked EXIT.

"Dallas Police. Make yourself known so no one gets hurt."

There's no movement, and it's very quiet. I have to slow my breathing against the growing certainty that something really bad has happened.

"Seth?"

Across from the stairway is a large room with the metal frames of single beds scattered haphazardly, as though blown about by a strong wind: the main sleeping area. There are also dozens of bankers' boxes stacked in rows—no doubt church records long ago packed away and forgotten.

Crouching defensively, I dash across the hall toward the large bedroom and do a rapid 180-degree sweep from the doorway. There's no one hiding inside.

Hugging the wall, I walk softly toward the back of the building, wondering if the rear exit is locked or barred. There's another large room to my left. It looks to be a play area or classroom, and it's also filled with storage boxes. A careful check behind the tallest stack reveals nothing but dust bunnies and broken chalk.

Next to the playroom is a door with the word BATHROOM in chipped black paint. It's closed but the doorknob turns easily. Standing to one side, I shove the door open and hit the floor, only to find a bank of toilet stalls and, opposite those, shower stalls, all without doors or curtains. All empty.

The blood from the wound on my shoulder, mixed with my sweat, has dripped down to my right palm, making the grip on my weapon tentative. But I'm nearing the end of the hallway, and there are only two doors left, one to the left and one to the right.

Two possibilities remain to find my partner, and whoever else was up here. The fact that no one has responded—that Seth hasn't called out or signaled—has set fire to my sense of dread. Moving closer to the door on the left, I place my ear against the wood and hear a muffled sound. I close my eyes for an instant, my back to the wall, then reach down, twist the knob, and fling the door open.

Inside, on the floor, is Seth. He's bound, hands behind his back, and gagged with a rag. As I approach, he raises his head, eyes wide, and shakes it back and forth violently. A sound behind me makes me turn. A man is striding, almost running, toward me from the opposite room, his gun pointed. He's in the middle of the hallway already, and I know he's going to shoot me.

An explosive bang and bright light echo from the exit end of the hall. The man falters and turns instinctively toward the sound. Hidden from view a gun discharges, the force of the bullet knocking the man back several feet. He crashes to the floor, moaning and writhing in pain, bleeding from his side heavily. There are approaching footsteps. I feel the jolt of surprise, followed by a flood of relief. It's Philbo, gun drawn and pointed at the wounded man.

Without taking his eyes off him, he asks me, "You okay?"

"How'd you know we were here?" I say, kneeling to pull the rag from Seth's mouth.

"Dutton called us. We were ten minutes away. Told us where you were. Esparza's out front with four patrol officers."

Seth takes a few desperate breaths. "I called him the minute I left Reardon's office."

Philbo's gun is still pointed at the man's head. There's a cold deadness to his expression, similar to the look he wore that night we interrogated Junior. Philbo taps the fallen gun closer to the prone man with the tip of his shoe. "The front door was locked, so Esparza called for backup while I circled the building and came up the fire escape."

I use the knife in my pocket—El Cuchillo's knife—to sever the zip ties binding Seth's wrists and help him to his feet.

"You're lucky the exit door was open." Philbo taps the gun even closer to the man. "Go on," he tells him. "Reach for it."

"What're you doing?" Seth asks, massaging his wrists.

Philbo prods the man's hip with his shoe, making him scream. "I'm giving this piece of shit the excuse I need to shoot him and save the taxpayers a lot of time and grief."

"Detective Philbo!" I yell, and wait for him to meet my gaze. He's still in an adrenaline-fueled fury, retreated to the place where violence holds rational thought at bay. Seth tenses as though preparing for action.

"He was going to murder a cop," Philbo says.

I take two steps forward. "Holster your weapon. Now!"

Without looking at me, Philbo finally complies, and this time kicks the gun away from the man, who looks to have lapsed into unconsciousness. Seth calls Esparza and tells him he's coming to let them into the building.

Half an hour later Seth and I are sitting in Reardon's office, an EMT tending to my wounds.

"You really need to go to the hospital for stitches," she tells me. "And you're going to need antibiotics and a tetanus shot."

"And probably a rabies shot as well," Seth adds, grimacing along with me as my injuries are cleaned and bandaged. He has found my missing phone and places it gently in my lap.

I thank the med tech, promising I'll follow up with my doctor. I have no intention of going to the hospital. I'm counting hours now and have no time to waste.

Fred Dunlap's DEA team had arrived within fifteen minutes. The gunman was still alive and was transported to the hospital by ambulance, a patrolman along for the ride. It took only a few minutes of searching for DEA to find a cache of about twenty kilos of heroin, worth over six hundred thousand dollars. Wholesale. It'd been in the last room on the right, hidden in the same bankers' boxes in the play area.

Seth had gotten the honor of wrestling the uncooperative Agnes Reardon into a patrol car. He was still stinging from having a gun slammed into his head and from being tied up and gagged, so he was none too gentle. He reported that there were two men upstairs until one panicked at my voice and ran out the back exit. They'd most likely been moving the drugs into the back of the building via the second-floor exit. That's why the exit was unlocked when Philbo barreled his way in.

Seth and I follow Philbo and Esparza out of the building.

"You think the wounded perp was Honduran?" I ask Esparza.

"When DEA ID'ed him, he had a common Honduran surname," he answers. "So, yeah, I'd say there's a possibility we've made another dent in Flaco's operation. Good haul today, Sergeant."

He smiles and starts to walk toward his car with his partner. I think of Billy Sands's admonition about an unstable cop: *It's not a question of if they'd explode but a matter of when.* I call Philbo back and pull him aside.

"You already give your statement to Homicide?" I ask.

He sucks on his teeth impatiently. "Yep."

"Then you know the drill," I say. "You're on admin leave—"

"It was a righteous shoot," Philbo says defensively.

"And you're to turn your weapon in to Lieutenant Bradford immediately."

He looks at me, his jaw clenched. "Sure thing, Sergeant." He leans in closer. "Just don't ever forget I saved your life today."

Philbo saunters to his partner's car. Seth watches him with hooded eyes, chin lowered, arms tightly crossed.

"We've got a problem with that one," he says, meeting my gaze. "You don't do something about Squid, and it's going to get somebody killed."

Again, I remember Uncle Benny's reminder that the one who's saved a life is forever bound to the one who's been saved. Until today, that had been an elevating thought. But Philbo's little aside sounded more like a threat than a comforting reminder. And my partner is right: Philbo's the most dangerous kind of cop. The troubled kind who keeps his footing only by balancing every perceived slight against every favor dished out. Eventually one will outweigh the other, and the resulting fall is often fatal. If not for the cop, then for the poor bastard who happens to be standing in the way.

36

UT Southwestern Medical Center
Wednesday, September 24, 2014

We're a few miles from the station when my personal cell phone rings with Jackie's number. I sigh and answer.

"I need to see you right away," she says breathlessly.

Her voice is quivery with emotion.

"What's wrong? You don't sound good."

"I'm in the emergency room at UT Southwestern—"

"*What!* What happened? Are you all right?"

"I'll tell you when you get here. Just hurry, please."

She disconnects, and I sit for a moment, stupefied, wondering how much more bad news I can take. I tell Seth that if we're not at the hospital in fifteen minutes, I'm going to throw him from the car and drive myself.

I race into the emergency waiting room, fully panicked, Seth following close behind.

"I'm here to see Dr. Jackie Nesbitt," I tell the woman behind the admitting desk. "She called me from the emergency room."

"Are you Detective Rhyzyk?"

"Yes, is she okay? Can I see her?"

The woman nervously directs Seth to stay in the waiting room, and a male attendant takes me back to the treatment rooms. He seems to be moving at a glacial pace.

"What happened to Dr. Nesbitt?" I ask, my paranoia growing by the second.

Instead of answering me, he points to a curtained bay next to the nurses' station. Taking a deep breath, I try to ratchet down my darkest thoughts of mortal injury or bodily destruction, my wife's unmoving form bandaged, bags of plasma hanging from metal rods. I pull the curtain back. And see Jackie sitting upright in a chair, fully dressed and wearing her doctor's coat.

I collapse to my knees, taking both of her hands in mine. "Jackie, what happened? Why are you here?"

She turns her beautiful face to me, and says, "I'm here for you, Betty. Now take your clothes off so the doctor can treat you."

My wounds have been cleaned again, the gash in my shoulder closed with staples, and everything rebandaged. I've been handed a prescription for oral antibiotics, poked with a tetanus shot, and supplied with tubes of antibacterial cream for the scratches. I've been given a stern lecture by the resident ER doc for disregarding my potentially serious injuries. She also tells me I can't leave until I've had a cranial X-ray to see if I sustained a concussion when Flaco bashed me in the head with his gun.

"Seth called me," Jackie says. "He said you'd refused to

seek adequate treatment, so I took matters into my own hands."

"That was a dirty trick," I tell her.

"It worked, didn't it?"

I'm feeling peevish and foolish in equal measures. "Can I get something for the pain?"

"Not from me, you won't." We stare at each other for a moment. And I want nothing more than to let her take me home and hold me for the next forty-eight hours.

"Have you made any progress in finding Mary Grace or Elizabeth?" she asks.

I can't meet her gaze anymore, so I stare at the bulky bandage on my forearm. "No. We're getting closer to finding Evangeline and one of her main dealers. But—" I can't finish the thought.

"Seth told me about Kevin Ryan. I can't even imagine what Karen is going through."

I nod and take a steadying breath. "I think you need to go away for a few days. You and your mom."

"Go away? Why?"

Evangeline's poisoned voice in my ear. *"Have you ever drowned puppies…?"* El Cuchillo's voice telling me I'm not moving fast enough to find her. "Because it's going to get bad."

Jackie makes a strangled noise, and she looks at me the way you'd look at a psychotic patient. "'*Going* to get bad.' Is that what you just said? Do you know what the last twenty-four hours has been like for me?"

"Jackie, I—"

"No! Just shut up. Shut up and *listen*."

A medical technician has poked his head through the

curtain, but, seeing the ferocious look on Jackie's face, he quickly retreats, muttering, "I'll be back in a few."

Jackie stands, confronting me. "You don't get to do this. Dole out little bits of the story, and mostly by text, thinking that what I don't know won't hurt me. It's bad enough that I have to hear about what's going on from your partner, but that you didn't think to call me when you were injured…It's already on the news that someone was shot and killed at that church."

"Orphanage," I say.

She brings both fists up. "Oh God, I just want to punch you right now. When are you going to stop underestimating me?" When I don't answer, she sighs and sits back in the chair, running both hands through her hair.

"Do you remember that time in Brooklyn when Mom came to visit for a few weeks?"

I nodded that I did remember the occasion. I was away for a police training seminar. It was the first time her mom had been to New York, and her first afternoon there, Jackie took her to the corner market to get vegetables for dinner. They were inside shopping when a woman, clearly delusional and talking to herself, came in and started yelling at the man behind the counter. Jackie told her mom to just ignore the woman. That it happened all the time. Mentally ill but harmless people wandering the streets at all hours.

What Jackie didn't notice until it was almost too late was that the woman had a knife. When the owner came out from behind the counter to chase her away, the woman pulled the knife and slashed him across the arms. Jackie's mom screamed, and the woman started moving toward her. Without thinking,

Jackie attacked her with the only thing she had to hand. A folded umbrella.

I smile at the memory. We had laughed about it after the fact. My gentle "First, do no harm" wife viciously wielding an umbrella as a sword. But now, in hindsight, it strikes a more somber note.

Jackie shakes her head as though perplexed by the memory. "I didn't think about it as it was happening. I just did what I had to do to protect my loved one. There was no question in my mind that if it came down to it, I would tackle that woman before I let her harm my mother."

She stands again, facing me. "Do you think I don't know that you make those kinds of decisions on a daily basis? And do you think I don't know that you'll throw everything you have into getting Elizabeth back?" She makes me meet her gaze. "What aren't you telling me?"

If I open my mouth now, every poisonous, nightmarish thing I've heard from Evangeline Roy about drowning Elizabeth will come vomiting out, and there will forever be a chasm—a toxic, unnavigable expanse—between Jackie and me. It will be an image that neither Jackie nor I will ever be able to forget. I can only shake my head and pray that she doesn't ask that question again.

Placing her hand on my shoulder, she says, "Do what you have to do, no matter what. And then come home to me. I'll be waiting."

She parts the curtain and leaves me alone to deal with the remaining tests, the paperwork for release, and the ticking clock.

★ ★ ★

An hour later, I walk into the ER waiting room, a bottle of pain pills in hand, and I'm surprised to find Craddock there instead of Seth. His eyes are red-rimmed and puffy, his tie hanging loose around his neck, and he's wearing the same wrinkled suit from yesterday.

"What are you doing here?" I ask. "Where's Seth?"

He stands, the sorrow radiating from every pore. "I sent him back to the station. I need to tell you something."

He leads me to his car, and I sit in the front passenger seat. When he gets behind the wheel I ask, "What's wrong?"

Craddock faces me, his jaw set, his breathing labored. "After Kevin was shot—" His voice breaks and he swallows a few times, fighting to gain control of his emotions. "Before I left in the ambulance with Kevin, I asked to talk to the kid who shot him. He'd been handcuffed and put in the back of a patrol car. I wanted to kill the little bastard, to tear him apart with my own hands."

His face is flushed and mottled, and he undoes the top button of his shirt with shaking fingers as though it's strangling him. "He was sitting in the back of the car, sobbing, saying, 'I'm sorry, I'm sorry,' over and over again. I got in his face and asked him, 'Why'd you do it? Why?'"

Craddock turns to look through the windshield, as though he can't bear to meet my gaze. "The kid kept saying, 'He made me do it. He made me.' When I asked him who he was talking about, he couldn't answer, he was crying so hard."

He takes a deep, steadying breath. "I got a call from Homicide just thirty minutes ago. They really leaned hard on the kid today, and he finally told them that a Sinaloa cartel boss, an enforcer, had told him that if he didn't get rid of Kevin, they'd kill his family. His younger brother had already gone missing, and they said they'd start the job with him. Piece by piece."

I know where this is going, and I don't want to know. My shock and disbelief make me feel uncoupled from the pull of gravity, and I clutch the dashboard to keep from floating away.

Craddock's face is a mask of agony. "The kid also said he was to give you a message."

He reaches for my hand, his grip turning my knuckles white. "The message was 'Miss your deadline and more will follow.'"

It wasn't enough that El Cuchillo had Kevin Ryan murdered, but he'd had him assassinated by someone Ryan had tried to help, someone he trusted. It was masterful, really. A precision cut. The soft mortar of my unrelenting pain was hardening into something closer to white-hot rage.

Craddock has been quiet, watching me, waiting for me to come back to the here and now. "There's something you need to listen to," he says.

He pulls out his cell phone and plays back a recorded message. The familiar sound of Kevin Ryan's voice fills the space around us.

"Hey, partner, you know the guy in Estella Cruz's apartment we busted the other day? First blush he didn't have a record. But I did a deeper dive. Figured if he was in Cruz's bed, maybe he was somehow also involved in Flaco's business. Turns out the guy's father owns a warehouse in the Trinity Grove area. I'll text the address. We should follow up on this tomorrow."

Craddock pulls up Ryan's text thread. "He left that message around seven o'clock last night. A few hours before he went to the scene of the robbery."

He shows me the text. It's an address on West Main Street.

"I pulled it up on the map," Craddock says. "It's behind the old Argos cement plant, not far from the river. It's large, it's isolated, perfect for moving product in and out."

He waits for me to take it all in.

"Betty, first things first," Craddock says, his voice now sure and steady.

"We take the Red Queen off the board. Then we can settle the score with the Knife."

Once more, I hear Benny's voice in my head urging, *Betty, you can't help the dead....Save your strength for the survivors.*

"Take me there now," I tell him.

Less than half an hour later, Craddock is driving across the Trinity River on the Margaret Hunt Hill Bridge. No sooner than I finish calling Lieutenant Bradford and fill him in on Ryan's message, my phone rings with an unfamiliar Dallas number. I answer it and hear Alan Turner's heated voice in my ear.

"I just want you to know that you'll be served court papers tomorrow. I'm suing you for criminal neglect of a child while in your custody. And if my granddaughter is found, assuming she's still alive, I will not only get custody, but I will use every media outlet at my disposal to ruin—"

I end the call midsentence. Craddock starts to ask me what the call was about, but I hold up a cautioning hand. "Tom, don't. Just don't."

West Main Street is a short stretch of road running parallel to the old train tracks just south of the cement factory in Trinity Grove. We drive past trendy restaurants and warehouses being torn down to make room for sleek new apartments, which will have killer views of the river and the city skyline to the east. But less than half a mile away are stunted, sagging bungalows, some of them built before the Second World War, to accommodate the factory workers. Many are still occupied by third-generation families, who bemoan the increasing land taxes that are the inevitable result of gentrification.

Our targeted address is not easily accessed, as most of the north-south connecting streets have been blocked off, keeping the less desirable elements from polluting the newer, burgeoning neighborhood. We make several turns onto dead ends before we find a through street. Passing decaying warehouses and trash from the few remaining derelict shacks that were emptied upon tenant eviction, as well as thickly overgrown lots, we find the building we're looking for near the end of the street. Surrounded by a high chain-link fence with a locked gate, the warehouse is not new, but it looks in decent order, and there are several company vans and an SUV parked close to the loading docks.

Craddock does a drive-by and then turns around and pulls off into an old driveway bordered by trees, shielding us from view. He retrieves a pair of binoculars from the glove compartment, and we get out, carefully approaching to get a better view. He parts some low-lying branches and stares through the binoculars for a few minutes. Then he hands them to me.

"I don't see any activity, but that doesn't mean there's no one inside," he says.

The lot around the warehouse is quiet, but the SUV is clean, like it's been recently washed. Scattered around the property are piles of metal scrap and what look to be old rail ties. Two large metal barrels are filled with assorted paper trash and dried brush cut and cleared some time ago.

"Let's run the plates on the vehicles and see what comes up," I say.

We watch for several minutes, writing down license plate numbers and brushing away swarms of mosquitoes, then return to the car.

In five minutes we have information from dispatch. Two of the vans are commercial vehicles registered to the parent company of the warehouse. The third, unmarked van and the SUV are out-of-state rentals from a national rental company.

Craddock scratches his chin thoughtfully. "We can call the rental company, but they're under no obligation to give us the ID of the drivers without paper telling them they have to."

"True," I say. "But drop Fred Dunlap's name and number, and the fact that we have an ongoing federal narcotics investigation, and they might."

Craddock calls the dedicated number for law enforcement and is put on hold. Four times. Twenty more minutes crawl by, and still we wait to talk to a person who can give us the information we need. The music in the background is irritating in its bland cheerfulness.

A sense of urgency is building in my head, my impatience waxing and waning like the intermittent pain in my wounded shoulder. There are people in that warehouse, of that I'm sure. But there's no way we can search inside without a warrant. And if we were to ask them to voluntarily let us search, it might tip off the very people we're looking for.

If someone would just exit the building...if we could just see who's inside.

I can't wait any longer.

"Tom," I say, "you got any flares?"

"Yes."

I open my door and step out. "Pop the trunk, will you?"

He looks at me questioningly, but he complies.

"As soon as I give you the signal," I say, "call the fire department."

Before he can ask any questions, I close the door and move to the back of the car to gather up a couple of flares. Walking the short distance to the warehouse gate, I pause and wait to see if anyone is watching. There are a few cameras mounted above the loading doors, but they seem to be pointed downward to close-capture trucks or transport vans coming into or leaving the warehouse. The few windows in the front of the building have been painted over with opaque white paint.

Shoving the flares into my pants pockets, I climb the fence with a great deal of difficulty and drop over into the parking area. My shirtsleeve, stained with blood to begin with, glistens red at the shoulder, indicating that I've already torn loose some staples. Crouching down, I wait to see if anyone comes charging out of the exits, but everything remains still. I approach the trash barrels cautiously, pulling the first flare out of my pocket. It's new and only has to be struck once to ignite. I drop it into the nearest container. Igniting the second flare, I drop this one into the next barrel. I've barely turned away when the contents of both barrels catch fire with an explosive rush, and a series of muffled popping noises accompany me while I climb over the fence again. The smoke boiling up from the twin fires is thick and copious.

As I approach Craddock's car, I signal to him to make the

call. By the time I'm settled in the passenger seat again, he's already contacted the fire department.

"Fire Station Forty-five is less than two miles away," he says. "They'll be here in five minutes."

Grabbing the binoculars, I ask, "Care to watch the show?"

We take our position at the tree cover again, and in four and a half minutes, two large fire trucks, lights and sirens blaring, roar their way eastward on West Main. The lead truck stops, and one of the firefighters leaps down and removes the lock on the gate with a bolt cutter. He then swings the gate open, allowing both trucks to enter the parking lot. Almost immediately, four men come running out of the warehouse, shouting questions in Spanish.

Examining them through the binoculars, I decide that the men don't look familiar. But one of the loading bay doors slides open, and a pair of men remain inside, watching the firefighters turning their hoses on the burning barrels. The taller of the two—thin, and with the number $X8$ tattooed on his neck—looks very familiar.

I hand the binoculars to Craddock.

Craddock exhales air through his teeth and murmurs, "My partner was a smart fuckin' cop."

37

The House
Wednesday, September 24, 2014

I pull into the driveway and turn off the engine. There are no more patrol officers watching the rear of the house, and no plainclothes detective in front. Lieutenant Bradford had removed our protection after ordering me to spend the next few nights elsewhere. His parting words were "You're an idiot if you don't." I've told Jackie that I'll be spending the night with her, but like a black hole with a strong centripetal force, the house has pulled me back. Just for a little while. Just on the off chance that Evangeline shows up and I can preemptively put an end to this nightmare.

Aching from my numerous wounds, my right shoulder still leaking blood, I chew and then swallow a couple of pain pills the ER doctor had given me, finally allowing myself to give in to the need for relief. I close my eyes, resting my head against the steering wheel, dirty, bloodied, and exhausted, waiting for the first rush of narcotic warmth to steal its way through my body. It won't take long; I haven't eaten anything since this morning.

The last few hours of the day have been hard to get through.

After spotting Flaco at the warehouse, Craddock and I both took photos of all the men visible. We then drove back to the station to make our reports, begin the warrant process, and get status updates on the targeted churches from the rest of the team. So far, no one had turned up any leads on finding Evangeline.

Seth took one look at me and dragged me into my office and handed me one of the clean T-shirts from his desk. He gave me a wad of paper towels to shove up under the right sleeve to serve as a bandage and poured a good measure of Jameson into a coffee cup, then made sure I downed all of it.

In the late afternoon I called the team together in the briefing room, where we were joined by Fred Dunlap and two of his DEA agents to discuss strategy, as well as three members of the Dallas SWAT team to devise the tactical means to breach the compound.

By early evening we had still not obtained the floor plan of the warehouse, so we could only devise a tentative strategy for executing the arrests, which would begin at ten a.m. tomorrow. We were pretty sure any deliveries, or possible drug production, would be going on in shifts, but we had to pick a coordinated time, not too early and not too late. In all, we counted six men in the photographs we had taken, but we had no idea if anyone had stayed in the building while the fire department did its work. I could only hope that Flaco would be there for the sweep. Our biggest concern was the heightened vigilance of the warehouse crew following the fires. Any diligent examination of the containers would probably show the remnants of the flares, and it wasn't likely that Flaco would believe they were the work of pranksters.

"Did you recognize the man standing next to Flaco?" Dunlap asked me, studying the photos.

The man was tall and looked fit and muscular. Something about his confidence and ramrod straight posture screamed ex-military. But the most notable thing was his shock of red hair. "I'm not sure," I answered. "But something tells me he's one of Evangeline's chosen few."

Now, in the car, I begin to experience the peculiar glow of the narco rush; the contrary sensations of my body uncoupling from the physics of quotidian existence. Both a heaviness, as though the gravitational field surrounding the car has increased, and a feeling that my limbs were becoming lighter, as though I were being filled with helium.

Unfolding myself from the driver's seat, I walk slowly to the front door, unlock it, and pour myself inside. The house is quiet and dark, but I do a cautious search of all the rooms before splashing some Jameson into a glass and collapsing onto the couch. I know I should take a shower and clean and tend to the stab wound in my shoulder, but I can't seem to summon the will to get up. The Jameson burns my throat in a pleasant way, adding to the heat of the drug.

Knowing that Jackie would scold me for consuming alcohol while on pain medication, I quickly finish the whiskey and then nudge the empty glass under the couch, as though I'm a guilty teenager hiding the fact that I've raided my parents' liquor cabinet. And then I remember through the growing fog that Jackie isn't here to scold me. She's at her mother's house, and I'm alone. I'll rest here for a few more moments while I gather my strength.

Then I'll get up...

The muffled buzz of my cell phone ringing rouses me, and I pull it from my pocket.

"Hello?" My voice sounds as though I'm speaking through a cotton mask.

There is a moment of silence, and then the crying begins. Not the cries of an adult, or even of an adolescent. They are the cries of a baby. Not the full-throated protestations of a healthy child, but the frail, puny wailing of a sickly infant. There's a weird echoey quality to the sound, and I realize almost immediately that it's a recording, not a real-time occurrence. And yet the sound is haunting, and it pierces me like a pencil jammed into my ear canal. I pull the phone away and check the number. It's unfamiliar but has a local area code, which could mean the call is coming from Evangeline or one of her people. It could also be one of El Cuchillo's henchmen, taunting me.

I disconnect, throwing the phone across the room. Crossing my arms over my face, I embrace the pain of the staples tugging at the torn and bruised skin. For the second time today, I weep. The jagged, visceral kind of weeping that I'd only ever experienced once before—at the death of Detective Sergeant Bernard Rhyzyk.

When I'm hollowed out, I lie on the couch, my breath hiccuping, my face soaked with tears and snot. I reach into my other pants pocket and remove the bottle of pain pills and claw out another two and crush them with my teeth, letting the bitterness coat the inside of my mouth, my throat. Capping the bottle again, I hold it to my chest as I would a talisman to ward off an evil miasma.

Soon, like a weight belt on a scuba diver's suit, the inevitable pull on my consciousness commences, and I begin the slide into some deeper, darker place. Not a place of dreaming so much as the altered state of opiated musings. Not asleep and yet not fully awake.

I'm in the Brooklyn church again, but there's no one there. No priest, no parishioners, and no Uncle Benny. There is the impression of complete disrepair, an air of slow and creeping decay, as though the chapel has been deserted for a thousand years. The walls and columns have cracked and buckled, soot coats the vaulted ceiling, covering the images of saints and angels, and thick bands of ivy and other vines hang from the wrought-iron chandeliers like an ancient forest. The floor is scattered with hymnals, the covers singed and curled by the heat of some fast-moving conflagration.

To the right of the altar—its cloth torn and filthy with mold—a large baptismal font sits, carved with fantastic beasts and flowering plants, the marble glowing as if lit from the inside. I know that the entire receptacle is thin, as delicate as bone china, because I can see something floating within the font. Something small, but solid.

Approaching the altar, my footsteps echo loudly in the ruined chapel. The light from inside the marble pulses gently, steadily. Like a beating heart. The font is tall, and as I approach the lip, I have to stand on tiptoe to see into the bowl. There is something floating inside. Something small and pale, bobbing gently in the water, a halo of delicate tendrils emerging from one rounded end, drifting on the surface, beckoning like the finest of seaweed.

It's not seaweed.

It's hair.

The fine, almost translucent hair of an infant...

★ ★ ★

My eyes snap open to a dark room—it's fully evening outside now. I'm on the couch in the living room. And someone is in the house with me.

A stealthy rustling is coming from another room. I should be disoriented, my thoughts in chaos. But my mind is clear, my vision hyperfocused, as though being force-fed oxygen by my thundering heart. I jackknife into a sitting position, my feet swinging onto the floor. There is a momentary rush of the drug throughout my body—I'm stupendously, calamitously high—and yet it's slowing my throbbing heartbeat, calming my breathing, even though the image of the lifeless object in the baptismal font has followed me into wakefulness. I am fully resolved now to eradicate whoever has breached my sanctuary.

My gun is on the coffee table where I left it. I reach for it and stand, my head swiveling to pinpoint the furtive noises. They're coming from the kitchen.

I glide quietly across the living room, my footfalls seeming to float above the carpet. Pausing with my back to the adjoining wall, I ready myself to face whoever is in the next room. Evangeline, Flaco, one of his enforcers?

From the sound of it, it's only one person. I swing around to stand in the doorway. I take aim, my arms extended, my finger ready to squeeze the trigger. In that moment, the intruder switches the light on.

Oh sweet Jesus, it's Jackie.

I freeze, holding my breath, my gun still at the ready, while the walls appear to bow outward with the enormous realization that I've almost shot my life partner. She stares at me, wide-eyed and motionless, taking in my rigidly aggressive posture, my hair matted with sweat and blood, my pupils pinned and fixed.

I lower the gun and sink to the floor.

Jackie takes a breath and whispers, her lips barely moving, "Seth told me you would come here first. I brought you some food—"

The loofah on my shoulder blades feels indescribably good. Jackie has drawn me a warm bath and she sits on the side of the tub, gently scrubbing life back into my limbs while I soak. She has cleaned and sutured the places on my shoulder where the skin has pulled away from the staples.

"This is going to leave an ugly scar," she tells me.

I rest my head on my knees. "I guess I'll have to just get another tattoo. Something Celtic, like a Viking something or other…"

When she realizes that I'm drifting off again, she coaxes me out of the tub and wraps me in a large bath towel. Leading me into the bedroom, she dresses me and puts me in bed, where a warm cup of herbal tea waits on the bedside table.

"I don't suppose you'd agree to some Jameson?" I murmur.

She stands over me, her arms crossed. "No fucking way. You'll be high as a kite for the next twelve hours as it is."

I look up at her and reach for her hand. "Alan Turner said he was serving me with court papers tomorrow, suing me for child negligence. I'll be out in the field most of the morning, and if he can't find me, the server may track you down."

She covers me with the blanket. "He can try serving me, if he can find me."

"You shouldn't be here, Jackie. We shouldn't be here. It's not safe."

I realize that she's moved away and is sitting in the chair at the foot of the bed, a cup of coffee on the table beside her. "So far, the only person who's pointed a weapon at me is you."

She's turned on the reading light next to the chair and holds up her own gun, a Glock. "You get some sleep. I'll keep watch."

Bleary-eyed, I stare at Jackie seated upright, poised and vigilant, her dark hair haloed by lamplight. "Whatever happened to 'First, do no harm'?"

Jackie smiles without much mirth. "I'll try harsh language first."

I close my eyes, but, whereas I was nodding off only ten minutes earlier, my legs are now jerky and restless and my mind is one giant termite mound of possible scenarios. I sigh and twist under the sheet.

"It's the Oxy," Jackie says. "It may be a while before you can sleep."

"Talk to me, then. Tell me a story. I want to hear your voice."

She's quiet for a moment. "You know I used to go hunting with my dad the years we lived in Oregon, right?"

Jackie's mother, Anne, had moved to Oregon shortly after getting married, and Jackie had grown up trekking for days with her dad through the forests of the Great Northwest. She'd gotten her first hunting rifle at twelve, and she's as proficient with firearms as I am.

"One October I went with Dad to the Coast Range. It's a mountainous region in western Oregon. Old-growth forests, steep ridges, ferns the size of Volkswagens. It's beautiful, but in the late fall you get a lot of rain and fog and near-freezing temperatures at night. It can be really challenging for the camper who's not prepared. And even for an experienced hiker, the terrain can be treacherous.

"I'd been hunting with Dad dozens of times, but it was the first time I'd ever gone with him to the western ranges. We'd made camp in the trees and were out scouting for black-tailed deer. The visibility was terrible, and Dad slipped off an escarpment and fell thirty feet to a lower ledge. It knocked him out for close to an hour, and I had a terrible time getting him back to the campsite."

She leans her head back on the chair, but her eyes are still on me. "I was young, only fifteen, and didn't know the dangers for a person with a head injury. I treated his wounds as best I could, but he passed out in his sleeping bag, and I couldn't wake him up. That was the longest night of my life. I sat in the tent most of the night, trying to keep him warm, wondering if I'd have to leave him where he was to go get help."

She takes a sip of her coffee. "A few hours before dawn, I heard something moving through the campsite, overturning the cookstove, pulling down the food bags that we'd hung from tree branches. I thought at first it was a bear or a cougar. I picked up my rifle, ready to fire warning shots to scare whatever it was away. Or, if I had to, to shoot it dead if it tried coming into the tent.

"But then I heard a low monotone, talking. It was a man eating our food and sorting through our gear. I would hear his footsteps approaching the tent, but then he'd stumble away, muttering to himself, clearly drunk. It was quiet for a long time, and I thought he'd left the campsite. Until I realized that he was waiting, listening, just outside the zippered opening to the tent. I could hear him breathing, deciding whether to enter. I could actually smell the violence on him.

"For close to an hour, I sat next to my dad, my rifle pointed at the tent flap, knowing that, if the man tried to gain access, I'd have to shoot him. Shortly before dawn he walked away. I was able to rouse my dad and, later that day, we packed up and hiked back to our truck."

She takes another few sips from the coffee mug. "It was months before I told my dad what had happened. And how scared I was that I might have to use the rifle on the man. But that I would have done it to protect the both of us. I also told him that I had discovered two things about myself that night in the tent. The first was that I wanted to be a doctor so I'd know how to help treat the sick and the injured. And the second was that I knew in my heart of hearts that I could kill someone if they were going to harm my loved ones. So you see, I have more than umbrellas in my arsenal."

"Come hold me for a little while," I say.

She slides into the bed next to me, spooning me with her warm body. I tell her of my nightmare in the church. About what I'd seen in the baptismal font. The telling unburdens me, and my body relaxes against hers.

Her last words to me before I fall into sleep are "Betty, it's not your fault…"

38

Reyes Warehouse
Thursday, September 25, 2014

Thirteen hours left.

The staging area for the raid on the warehouse is about half a mile west of the targeted area; the lumbering SWAT Tactical Command Post van hidden from sight in a vacant lot of an old auto auction yard on the south side of West Main. Parked in the lot, as well, are two APCs, Armored Personnel Carriers, which will be conveying two SWAT assault teams of ten men each. Besides the two assault teams, two snipers will be posted on the back side of the warehouse, hiding in the brush in case any of the suspects break away from the building.

Seth and I stand toward the rear of the van—this first phase of the takedown is not our rodeo—along with Fred Dunlap and one of his agents. Craddock and Esparza wait outside with another two DEA agents. Philbo has been put on administrative leave pending investigation of the shooting at the orphanage. He's proven himself to be a smart cop, but I don't think I'm alone in feeling relieved that he's been sidelined before this engagement.

The senior corporal giving the briefing is the beefy SWAT commander who was present at the arrest of the dealer EZ, the guy who'd kidnapped the doctors and connected me to El Cuchillo. As soon as he lays eyes on me, I can sense his displeasure at my presence. But he gives me a nod of recognition.

An unmarked van has already executed several passes in front of the warehouse and made an unfortunate discovery. Since yesterday, Flaco, or someone working for him, has installed new security cameras over the front entrance and the windows. We're not yet sure how many exits there are in the rear. The snipers have already been deployed to their positions in order to give us information.

There is not enough room inside the van for all twenty of the SWAT officers, so the two team leaders take notes and duplicate any drawings their commander is making. They'll take them and brief their respective teams before the launch.

With colored markers the corporal has drawn a rectangular box on the large whiteboard, representing the warehouse, and filled in the known front entrance and the two side bays on the western side.

He adds features to the drawing as he speaks. "There is one entrance on the Alpha side of the building here, surmounted by a security camera. There are two barred windows, here and here, each with its own camera. The windows have been painted over, so we won't be able to get a visual on any activity taking place inside the building. Here, on the Beta side, we have two loading bays, also with cameras.

"Sniper team is being deployed now. As soon as they're in place, we'll know how many exits there are on the Charlie side and whether or not they are fitted with cameras. We can assume, though, that there'll be eyes there as well. There are no doors or windows on the Delta side of the building.

"We have no idea of the layout of the warehouse or how many suspects are inside. And we have to assume all suspects will be armed. If there are internal walls erected for offices, we could be set up for a fatal funnel, so we're going to deploy gas canisters first, to see if we can drive the suspects out of the building. We don't want to have to go in blind."

The corporal points to Fred Dunlap. "Once we've secured and cleared the building, DEA will be able to gain access and determine what drugs, if any, are inside."

One of the assault team leaders asks, "And if we can't flush the building with gas?"

"We'll move Team One in the APC to the Alpha position here," the corporal says, pointing to the front side of the drawing. "The men will exit the carrier and position themselves defensively along the front wall. Obscure the camera lenses first thing, break the glass on both windows, and deploy a flash-bang with more gas. You'll then breach the front door and enter. At the same time, Team Two will position itself on the Beta side. We need to get those bay doors open as quickly as possible after taking out the cameras so we can have a coordinated dual-direction assault. We'll assume that the bay doors are locked from the inside, so we'll deploy pull ropes to yank one of them off their tracks. I'll leave it up to the team leaders to assign individual positions to the men."

The corporal's radio crackles.

"This is Team Three." The snipers are reporting from their position.

"Go ahead, Team Three."

"One door on the Charlie side. Camera mounted overhead. No windows."

"Okay, Team Three." The corporal nods to the Team Two leader. "I'll be sending two men from the Beta side around to assist. About twenty minutes to engagement. Sit tight. Over."

The corporal carefully sets the markers aside. His jaw is flexing like a rottweiler chewing on a sow's ear. "One last thing: we need Roberto Flores, aka Flaco, alive if at all possible." He shoots me a glance. "But if it's a choice between you and this scumbag, smoke him."

He looks at the group. "Any questions? No? Ready your teams and wait for my signal."

The two SWAT team leaders clomp their way out of the van. Fred Dunlap, Seth, and I follow them out to the lot, now bustling with the preparations for a well-orchestrated assault. Craddock and Esparza stand well out of their way, talking quietly.

My partner pulls me aside, eyeing the teams as they gear up: massive men wearing massive Kevlar vests and helmets, protective eyewear, and knee pads. They carry assault rifles, ballistic shields, battering rams, and Halligan tools for prying open locked doors.

"If Flaco's in there, what do you think the odds are of him coming out of this alive?" he asks.

I shake my head. "It's out of our hands now. Dunlap wants Flaco taken off the board, whether he goes to prison or to the ME's Office. If he is killed, Evangeline may just have to pack up and head back to Honduras."

"Or it could piss her off even more."

"In which case, it may be me and Jackie moving to Portugal."

"You going back into the van?"

"I have a better idea."

The Reyes warehouse is the next-to-the-last building on West Main, which dead-ends at North Beckley. The building at the corner is a now-defunct fire extinguisher supply house. I drive Seth's car past our targeted warehouse, make the left onto Beckley, pull a U-turn, and park in front of the abandoned supply house, out of sight.

Seth looks at me puzzled. "What are we doing?"

"Getting a bird's-eye view of the action."

"What does that mean?"

"We're climbing onto the roof."

He gives me a look but follows me around to the back of the building. An ancient trailer is parked under a protective corrugated-iron awning. Both the trailer and the awning are coated in rust, covered with seasons of dried leaves. With Seth's help I hoist myself up to the top of the trailer and then onto the awning. It creaks loudly but doesn't collapse. From there, the lip of the roofline is only a foot higher than my head. Pushing off with my thighs, I pull myself up.

Seth manages to duplicate my movements, and soon we're standing with a clear view of the Reyes warehouse, the easternmost side of the building closest to us. The early intel was good. There doesn't seem to be a door or window on the Delta side of the building. We can't see the SWAT vehicles, still hidden from view.

Seth checks his watch. "Ten minutes till fireworks."

The drugs from last night are still clogging my system. The exertion, as well as pent-up adrenaline, has caused me to feel light-headed. Under my coat I feel some wetness seeping through the bandage on my shoulder. I may have pulled the staples loose. Again.

Seth looks at me, concern on his face. "You doing okay?"

"How long have you known me?"

"Couple of years."

I scowl. "Then you know the answer to that question."

My phone rings, and expecting the lieutenant, I check the number. It's a caller with the country code of Mexico. Fear and anger flow through every vein like an electrical current in the blood. My hands shake so badly, I almost drop the phone.

"Did you get my message?" the familiar male voice asks.

"You had a cop killed. Someone on my team. You didn't need to—"

"Sergeant Rhyzyk, you're wasting time. Get it done, or more will die."

The line goes dead. It's only midmorning, but the passage of time seems to have revved to warp speed. Seth puts a comforting hand on my arm, and I have to resist shaking it off.

We nervously watch for the SWAT team, our eyes glued to the street. The roar of powerful diesel engines breaks the silence, and seconds later, the two SWAT APCs break from the auction lot and swing right onto West Main.

Seth gives me a nudge. "Here we go."

Team One's APC increases its speed as it approaches the warehouse fence and crashes through the gate as easily as cutting through aluminum foil. Both APCs park broadside at the front of the building to offer maximum cover to the men exiting the vehicles and lining up behind its bulletproof bulk.

Two officers fire gas canisters expertly into the front windows, and within seconds gray vapor is seen swirling inside the building. After thirty seconds, two more canisters are fired through the broken glass.

One of the team leader's voices comes over the Loud-hailer. "This is Dallas Police SWAT. The building is surrounded. You need to exit now, hands up, and surrender yourselves to the officers."

Nothing happens for several minutes. "We have the building covered on all sides. Everyone inside needs to come out, hands raised," the team leader says, his voice a flat monotone, as though an impending raid is just like sorting through laundry.

After another five minutes, a signal is given, and the coordinated attack begins. Team One quickly positions itself along the Alpha wall. Team Two's APC pulls up to the Beta side of the building, and the officers inside scramble onto the loading platforms with bolt cutters and battering rams. All the men are wearing gas masks. As soon as both teams are in place, I hear the command given to breach the doors. A pull rope attached to APC Team Two yanks one of the bay doors off its track, and at the same time, several flash-bangs are deployed through the Alpha side windows. The front door is battered open, and with shouts of "Police! Police! Police!..." and "Get down! Get down! Get down!..." the officers pour into the warehouse from two sides.

The snipers at the rear of the building have crawled closer to the wall, their focus, and their rifles, pointed at the back door.

There are short bursts of automatic gunfire coming from inside the building. Smoke from the gas canisters boils out of the windows, and the muffled shouted commands and warnings continue.

"Shit just got real," Seth says, his voice tense.

Movement at the Delta side of the building, the side closest to us, draws my gaze. Something that was flush with the ground, disguised by loose soil, has hinged itself open. And someone is crawling up out of what must be a basement. It's a man who, as soon as he gains his feet, stumbles toward the fence and slips through a large gash in the chain links. The sharp edges catch at his coat, which he sheds like a snakeskin, and he begins to run toward the supply house where we're standing.

"Is that—" Seth asks.

"He's making for Beckley!"

With Seth close behind me, I vault from the roof onto the metal carport, then drop to the ground. We both run to the side of the building facing West Main, but we don't see Flaco.

"Riz," Seth yells. "He must have passed around us, through the brush."

I'm behind Seth when we round the corner to the front of the supply house and see Flaco running, feet flying, north on the sidewalk in the direction of Trinity Grove. He turns toward us and fires several shots. The shots go wild, and we hit the sidewalk, facedown. There's not a lot of traffic on Beckley, but the street is not empty.

"Skinny fucker's fast," Seth pants. "Good thing he's a bad shot."

Ahead is an overpass for the railroad tracks. Once he's past that, the land to our left slopes away to a leveled area upon which the power grid for the old cement factory stands. It's surrounded by a fence, but it will be easy for Flaco to climb it and hide in the warren of the abandoned buildings.

"Call Craddock. Tell him to grab Esparza and drive like hell over to Singleton and stake out the front of the factory."

Without waiting for my partner, I run after Flaco, who's gained a good hundred yards on me. Shadows stipple his form as he passes under the railroad track, and a few feet beyond the bridge, he throws himself down the embankment.

By the time I've made it to the other side of the overpass, he's already climbing the fence to the power grid. I manage to stay on my feet, skittering down the sloped earth, giving me forward momentum. He flips himself over the fence, dropping into a crouched position. He fires at me again. This time a malignant buzzing whips past my ear, and I drop to my belly. My gun is drawn, but I don't return fire. I need him alive.

"Flaco!" I yell. "Other officers are coming. You don't have to die today."

He raises his gun, but shots fired from behind me send him scrabbling away and into the power grid's dense forest of vertical relays. My partner has caught up with me.

"Craddock and Esparza are on their way. SWAT's still actively engaged inside the warehouse." Seth helps me to my feet, and we approach the fence cautiously.

"Look." Seth points.

Flaco has run diagonally across the grid and is climbing the fence on the far side, which will put him in the rear parking lot of the cement plant. We scramble up and over the fence as quickly as we can and then race for the far side. By the time we've managed to climb the other security barrier, and drop onto the empty lot, Flaco has disappeared into the buildings and silos.

The looming exhaust stacks of the plant cast long shadows between the buildings, creating multiple dark places to hide. We hear a repeated banging noise, like someone trying to break open a door.

"This way," Seth says, moving in the direction of the sound.

We ease our way around the silos and main processing plant, doing quick look-sees before advancing toward the front of the complex, the boxy, one-story office buildings where the plant manager and staff would have been housed. They are the buildings closest to Singleton, the main commercial avenue for Trinity Grove and the newly opened mall of patio restaurants and apartment buildings on the opposite side of the street.

One of the office doors has been forced open. I take one side of the door, Seth the other.

"Flaco!" I call. "Come out now! Headfirst or feetfirst, your choice."

It's quiet inside the office. The air smells dry and chalky, like the mouth of a desert cave.

"Flaco! Don't make us come in and get you."

We listen again for movement, but there's nothing.

"I really don't want to go in without backup," Seth says.

Craddock should already be parked on the avenue in front of the plant. "Stay here," I say, running from the shadows into the sunlit parking lot at the factory entrance. Scanning the two-way traffic on Singleton, I see no sign yet of Craddock's car. But what I do see is Flaco loping diagonally across the street. Toward the long bank of restaurants.

"Seth!" I yell to my partner, so forcefully that, for an instant, dark spots cloud my vision. "He's crossing the avenue!"

The moment I reach the curb, Craddock's car pulls up, and

I gesture frantically for him, and for Esparza, to follow me across to the mall. The traffic is light, but the few cars are approaching at high speeds. I navigate my way to the sidewalk on the north side and sprint to the front entrance, and toward a concrete stairway leading up to a lengthy elevated patio crowded with tables and chairs. Flaco is nowhere in sight.

I take the steps two at a time, pausing to let my eyes adjust to the darker ambient light under the restaurant awnings. The walkway to the right is filled with diners, none of whom look like my suspect. I snap my head to the left and see, toward the far end of the patio, Flaco walking calmly but briskly, his head down, trying not to attract any attention. He looks over his shoulder, sees me, and stops. Next to him is a large table with a dozen men, women, and children eating and drinking. I'm twenty feet away when he pulls his gun and yanks a seated woman to her feet. The woman has been nursing an infant at the table and she yelps in fright, almost dropping the baby.

The people at the woman's table sit in stunned silence, but the other diners erupt into chaos, screaming, knocking over chairs, running panicked for the exits. Behind Flaco, approaching carefully, are Craddock and Esparza. Seth is to my left, slowly easing his way forward.

Flaco presses his gun more firmly against the woman's temple. "Stop!" he orders, his eyes darting from me to Seth. "Back up!" he yells over his shoulder to Craddock.

The hostage begins to cry loudly, begging in Spanish to be released. Her eyes are wide in terror, one breast still exposed, making her appear all the more vulnerable. Another woman at her table reaches for the squalling infant, but Flaco kicks at her to move away.

I'm standing well within fatal shooting distance. I'm not

wearing a vest, and by the look on Flaco's face, I have no doubt that he'd love nothing more than to murder me. And yet he hasn't pointed the gun at me. Seth had said he was a lousy shot. But now I'm thinking that he missed on purpose. Maybe because Evangeline has made it very clear that, if that scenario plays out, she wants to be the one to make it happen.

"I'm walking with this woman to the parking lot," Flaco says, tightening his arm around the woman's throat and shuffling backward. "A car is coming to pick me up. I'll let her go then."

The hostage is looking at me, pleading with her eyes for me to help her. To save her baby.

"Let the woman go now," I say, "and you can take me instead. Look, I'm giving up my weapon."

I begin to hand Seth my gun, my focus shifting for an instant to my partner's alarmed face. There's a loud explosion of a single gunshot. An eruption of frightened yelling, people ducking to take cover, tables and chairs overturning. Flaco lies prone on the floor, the flailing woman and baby on top of him. Seth, Craddock, and Esparza are all crouched defensively, their weapons pointed at a single source—a large solitary man, still standing, his shooting arm outstretched, holding a small nine-millimeter handgun.

He looks around, blinking. "I got him. Goddammit, I got him." The man turns to my partner, grinning crazily. "Did you see that? I fucking got the bastard."

I run to check on the woman, while my three colleagues tackle and disarm the shooter, who's begun to protest loudly that he only did what we were too chickenshit to do. The woman's face and hair are covered in blood, but it's Flaco's blood, and she and the baby are quickly surrounded and shielded by her family.

Flaco is dead, blood leaking from a wound in his forehead. The woman's face was only inches from his. Any miscalculation on the shooter's part would have left the baby instantly motherless.

We call for emergency backup, which arrives quickly, along with three homicide detectives. I sit with the woman and her baby while they are examined by an EMT, and they're soon released. Witnesses are interviewed, curious onlookers dispersed. The parking lot is searched for any suspicious cars or trucks that could have been waiting for Flaco, but nothing of interest is found.

I stare at Flaco's lifeless body, thinking about the past few desperate weeks spent searching for Evangeline Roy. Fourteen days, in which time both Mary Grace and Elizabeth have gone missing. Connie's disappeared. Kevin Ryan is dead. Johnny B snuffed out. Finding Flaco was the closest thing I had to making contact with the Roy matriarch. Arresting him would have at least given me a possibility of information.

The shooter is still seated on the hard floor—legs outstretched below his enormous belly—handcuffed. He's been arrested, charged with endangering the public, interfering with a police operation, and possibly manslaughter.

He sees me striding toward him, and he flinches.

"I have a carry permit," he yells. "You should be thanking me for—"

I crouch down so he can see my expression up close. "You want us to thank you? For what, killing a potential witness on a federal case? Or almost killing two innocent bystanders?" I lean in so he can feel my outraged breath on his face. "*Thank you?* I'm going to make it my personal mission to slap as many felonies on you as will cover your big fat ass. You have no idea what you've—"

I feel my partner's cautioning hand on my shoulder, and I stand up. To a nearby patrolman I yell, "Put this tub of lard in your car before I stomp on his kneecaps."

Today was the last day on El Cuchillo's timetable that I had to find my redheaded nemesis. But my best hope in making that happen is now being bagged for transport to the ME's Office.

Craddock makes eye contact. "Just spoke with Fred Dunlap. The raid is over. He wants us back at the warehouse."

39

Dallas Police Department, North Central Division
Thursday, September 25, 2014

The tally for the warehouse raid: two SWAT officers injured, two warehouse suspects shot and killed, four more arrested, twenty kilos of raw heroin confiscated. Value of the drug before being stepped on, over a million and a half dollars.

It's a huge win for the DEA, and for DPD. Dunlap, upon hearing of Flaco's demise, had shrugged and said, "More joy for us."

When he saw the look on my face, he had added, "Of course, we'll do everything we can to help you find the Roy woman. But we've crippled her operation, taken out her number-one man. I think she's been rendered toothless. At least for now."

I wanted to tell him that, like a shark, Evangeline regrew teeth at an alarming rate. I had watched as the SWAT officers removed their gear—soberly and without the usual backslapping banter—packing up after a hard mission, and probably going home for a hot meal and a beer or two.

Relieved that they could forget, at least for a few hours, that they might have a target on their backs.

I get in Dunlap's face. "Listen, I'm still on a ticking clock. You know I've already lost one officer to El Cuchillo. I've only got a small window of time left before he goes after my family. *Do you get that?*"

He makes a conciliatory gesture. "Of course. We'll give you whatever support we can to help track down Evangeline Roy."

"What about the guys in the warehouse you arrested, and the two who didn't make it?" I ask. "Can you run their IDs and let me know as soon as possible?"

He grasps my arm reassuringly. "I'll make it a priority."

Returning to my office at the station, I close the door and make a call to Jackie.

"Do you think there will be a day that goes by when you'll *not* be on the news?" she asks.

She hears the distressed sound I make and changes her tone. "Am I going to be seeing you anytime soon?"

"Tomorrow," I tell her.

"You promise?" she asks.

"Yes."

"Betty, is everything going to be all right?"

I lie and assure her that it will be. It's three o'clock in the afternoon. Nine hours to midnight. I put my head down on the desk, my ears ringing with exhaustion, and probably the last chemical wave of narcotics being expelled from my system. I need to make my report to the lieutenant, but I'm just so fucking tired. Too tired to form cohesive sentences. Too tired to sleep. Too tired to be scared.

A knock at my door, and Peg Bartles comes in, followed by Rocky, carrying a takeout food bag. Rocky drops the bag on my desk, and they sit in the visitors' chairs, looking at me like two concerned aunties. I open the bag, and the aroma of a greasy burger and fries assaults my nose.

I groan with hunger. I've eaten nothing since yesterday. Grabbing the burger, I rip the waxed paper off and take a bite. "Oh God," I say to Rocky. "Will you marry me?"

"Sorry," she says, in all seriousness. "I'm off women this month."

"Today's our last day on the contract," Peg says. "We're still on the clock until midnight tonight, though." She pauses for a moment. "But, uh—"

She looks at Rocky.

I chew and swallow. Something's happened. "What?"

"We have some news for you," Rocky says. "But I don't know if you're going to thank us for it."

I carefully set the burger down and wipe the grease off my hands. "Okay."

"So, we thought we'd trawl some of the pavement citizens again last night. You know, thinking that maybe someone had caught a glimpse of Mary Grace recently. We've got a good relationship with a lot of the regular sex workers downtown."

"We slip them some money, feed them on occasion," Peg says. "They in turn keep an eye out for any runaways new on the scene."

Rocky nods. "Some of these regulars are pretty young themselves."

"Like sixteen, seventeen years young," Peg adds.

"None of them seemed to know where Mary Grace is. But on a whim I showed Connie's picture around. And we got a hit."

My stomach clenches. "Someone recognized Connie?"

Rocky leans forward in the chair, as though to prepare me. "Yep."

"Where is she?" I ask.

"We still don't know where she is," Peg says. "But we know now who she is."

"Connie's real name, at least her unmarried name, was Constance Renée Broussard," Rocky says.

It takes a moment for the pieces to fall into place. I'm looking at Rocky, and then the dime drops. The discussion with Turner about his former wife replays in my head. "Connie is Alan Turner's ex-wife."

"That's right," Peg says. "Before our little informant worked the streets, she was a happy high school student whose father worked for Turner. When she was fourteen, Turner seduced—"

"You mean raped," Rocky says.

"Turner raped the girl. Gave her drugs, fucked with her head so bad she dropped out of school and ended up giving twenty-dollar blow jobs to fund her heroin habit."

"She'd been inside Turner's home a few times," Rocky says. "She recognized a photo of Connie in Mary Grace's room."

Peg makes a disgusted noise. "Can you believe the scumbag had sex with her in his stepdaughter's bed?"

I throw up my hands, the band of tension across my forehead threatening to crush my skull. "Wait a minute. So you're telling me that Connie is not only Turner's ex but also Mary Grace's mother?"

"Looks like," Rocky says.

"That's why Mary Grace lied about Connie's references," I say. "But that still doesn't explain why Connie wouldn't tell us where her daughter is."

"Maybe she didn't know," Peg says, concern furrowing her brow.

"And why take the baby so long after Mary Grace disappeared?" I ask.

Rocky gives me a troubled look. "The girl we talked to says that the rumor in Turner's society circles is that Connie is a drug addict, and so desperate for money, she'd do just about anything to get it."

I think of Connie's neat little house, and the way she'd always put herself together. Certainly not the usual appearance of a drug addict. But then again, there were legions of high-functioning narco-heads living seemingly normal lives.

"So...what?" I say. "You're saying that Connie would be willing to sell her own granddaughter back to Turner?"

"Or maybe someone else," Rocky says. "Like Evangeline Roy."

I think of the glossy brochure in Connie's house. Rocky and Peg are sitting very still, looking at me. Waiting for me to make the connections. The few bites of the burger in my stomach have turned to a cold, congealed mass.

"Evangeline Roy." I repeat the name in a whisper.

Seth has appeared at my door. Behind him stands a short, portly man wearing a cowboy hat and boots. My partner gives me a look that I can't decipher. The man brushes his way past Seth and into the room. He's holding a piece of paper in one hand.

Peg snorts. "Hello, Joe. Still doing the devil's work, I see."

He nods to her briefly. "Elizabeth Rhyzyk?" he asks me.

"Yes."

The piece of paper is dropped onto my desk. "You've been served."

He turns, dipping the brim of his hat at Peg, and walks quickly for the door.

It's a court summons from Alan P. Turner for a custody hearing for Elizabeth one month from today. Seth gives Joe a hard shoulder bump as he exits the office and glares at him. Joe has no sooner walked away than Craddock enters the now-crowded room, closely followed by Esparza.

"Don't worry," I say. "You haven't missed the wake."

"We got a few names from the roundup today," he says. "All but one of the men are Honduran nationals. Two of them were in the system. The last one, the Anglo guy, also came back with a hit. A Martin Collie, although he insists that everyone call him Reverend."

Something about the name stirs a memory in the sludge that now serves as my brain. I look at Seth and see a mirrored reaction.

"Seth?" I say, prompting him. And then it comes to me. Johnny B talking about his reservation in Arizona, and the new crew of meth-making toughs. The man calling himself Reverend Martin, who'd greeted Evangeline Roy when she arrived, smiling and giving out candy to the children.

"He went AWOL from the army twelve years ago," Craddock says. "Worked as a mercenary and then in security for a while. And by 'security,' I mean pointing guns at the little people so wealthy crime bosses and tin-pot dictators could walk safely from their cars to their favorite restaurants. Then, a few years ago, a big blank space in his record."

"Until today," I say. "Where's he now?"

"Being interrogated at DEA headquarters."

I look at Seth. "I want to talk to him."

"All due respect," Esparza says, "I'm not sure he's going to talk to you. The guy seems hard as nails."

I think of Philbo, now on administrative leave. *We work with what we're handed,* he had said.

"Then I'll do all the talking."

Seth drives me down to the DEA field office, which is a compact, three-story white building fitted with large panels of green-tinted glass. It's surrounded by massive asphalt parking areas, not too far from the Gas Monkey Bar N' Grill, the place where I first met Wayne, who was Seth's CI at the time. It looks like any other industrial or medical complex on Technology Boulevard.

We're taken to Fred Dunlap's third-floor office. He's still got on the sweat-stained street clothes he was wearing at the raid. He does not look thrilled to see us.

"We've been trying to interrogate Martin Collie for the past two hours, but he hasn't said a word," Dunlap says.

"He hasn't asked for a lawyer?" Seth asks.

Dunlap shakes his head. "Nope. He's said very little. Mostly he just sits there, with a shit-eating grin on his face."

"Does he know about Flaco?" I ask.

"Not yet."

"Good. I want to be the one who tells him."

Dunlap's brows come down in concern. "Are you sure you want to go in there? He's part of a group that's been threatening you."

"That's why I need to see him. Besides, I won't be alone. Seth's going to be with me."

Dunlap squints and works his mouth as though considering a way to refuse my request. He finally says, "Okay, but keep it short. We have to get him processed into Lew Sterrett. We've already kept him here too long."

Seth and I stand for a few minutes, watching Collie on a surveillance monitor. He sits alone in the interrogation room with his arms crossed, chin belligerently thrust forward, his shoulders pulled back.

"Full of himself, isn't he," Seth says.

I mutter something in Polish.

Seth turns to me. "What's that?"

"Just an old proverb. Loosely translated, it means 'Pride goes before the fall.'"

"How do you want to play this?" Seth asks.

I lean in closer to the monitor, trying to glean any information I can through our suspect's body language. My partner doesn't have any inside track on Collie's history, like he used to gain cooperation from Tony Diego. And I can't, and won't, pull the "cooperating snitch" move that Philbo orchestrated with Junior. Collie's presenting himself as a tough guy, but he's not completely comfortable. A true tough guy, a bad-to-the-bone killer, would be cool, calm, and loose. Manspreading. Owning the space he inhabits. Collie's sitting like he's got a stick up his ass, afraid to relax.

"Paper tiger," I say.

My partner studies me for a moment. "What are you up to?"

"What's the surest way to get under an arrogant prick's thin skin?"

After a pause, Seth grins. "Get a woman to laugh at him?"

"Bingo."

Seth follows me into the interrogation room, which could have been found inside any law enforcement facility. Blank walls, soundproof ceiling tiles, a table and a few chairs, with two cameras mounted in opposing corners.

I sit in front of Collie with a file of papers borrowed from Dunlap, Seth sitting next to me. The file is merely a prop, which I settle on my lap out of his line of sight. I pretend to study it for a while and then look up at Collie. His face is streaked with dirt, clothes blackened with something that looks like motor oil.

"Good afternoon, Mr. Collie," I say, pleasantly. "It's been a long day for you."

His upper lip curls upward. "It's Reverend."

"Do you know who we are?" I ask.

Collie exhales air dismissively through his nose.

"Good, then we don't have to waste time with introductions." I look down at the file again. "You were sitting on quite a haul inside that warehouse. Twenty kilos of raw heroin. That's going to rack up some serious jail time for you, Mr. Collie."

"It's Reverend Collie," he says, with a bit more emphasis on his title.

"Yeah, whatever." I throw a disbelieving look at Seth, and my partner ducks his head and covers his mouth, as though trying to hide a smirk.

"Okay, *Reverend,* I was going to try and work out some kind of deal with you. You know, you tell us about Flaco and

Evangeline Roy's operations. Maybe shift some of the burden off you and onto some of the other players. But, uh, looks like you'll be the mule carrying the heaviest load."

I riffle through some papers. "Two of your compadres are dead—"

"Oops," Seth says, holding up three fingers.

"Oh, right," I say, tapping my forehead. "Two shot dead at the warehouse, and the guy at the orphanage."

Seth puts a hand on my arm. "Wait, it's four. Flaco getting his head drilled by an armed civilian, remember?"

Collie is looking from me to my partner, trying to decide if we're telling the truth. He'd been hustled quickly from the warehouse after the raid, put alone into an undercover DEA car, and brought immediately to the field office, given no access to the news or the Internet.

"Yeah, Flaco's dead," I say. "He's gone, the drugs that Junior put in the dumpster are history, your stash at the Reyes warehouse is gone, as well as the supply of heroin at the Catholic orphanage. That was a cute touch, by the way. Was that Evangeline's idea?"

"It has to have been Evangeline's idea." Seth gestures to Collie. "I mean, look at this guy. SWAT told me he'd crawled belly first under some machinery, trying to hide while his buddies were returning fire."

"Figures," I say, with a laugh. "The Reverend here has a history of running away from fights. Going AWOL after being deployed to Afghanistan, right?"

Seth crosses his arms over his chest, shaking his head. "Once a coward, always a coward. I wonder what fly-by-night mail-order racket ordained this fool."

We snort and giggle together for a moment.

Collie's breathing has accelerated, becoming shallower, and his face has reddened. "When Evangeline—"

As soon as I hear her name, I yawn, loudly. "That old hag's time is nearing an end." I lean closer to Collie. "Why don't you do yourself a favor and tell us where she is. Save us all a lot of time and trouble. And we'll put in a good word with the DA for a reduced sentence. We're going to find Evangeline— with your help or without it."

He leans in as well, his jaw twitching with tension. "But will it be in time to save who you've been looking for."

"You better hope that it is, jackwad. Or it won't just be jail time for drug offenses. It'll be for kidnapping and murder."

Seth sniffs at the air. "A child murder conviction in Texas. You smell something frying, Sergeant?"

Collie glares at my partner. "'Rejoice, O ye nations, with His people: for He will avenge the blood of his servants—'"

"Ah, Deuteronomy," Seth says. "How about this one, *Reverend*? 'Vengeance is *mine,* thus sayeth the Lord.'"

"'The righteous shall rejoice when He seeth the vengeance: He shall wash His feet in the blood of the wicked—'"

"Dude, just stop," Seth says, slapping the table. "I was raised Southern Baptist. You can quote Psalms all day long, and I'll match you verse for verse."

"Uh-oh," I say, pointing at Collie's contorting face. "Looks like this one's gonna stroke out before he's even processed into Lew Lew." I look at Seth. "You bored? I'm really bored."

"Yeah, me too," he says. "Evangeline's probably already on a plane heading for Honduras, anyway."

Collie makes a strangled noise. He looks at me, his eyes twin orbs of pure hatred. "She's closer than you think," he says, pointing a finger at me. "She will never leave Dallas while you're still breathing."

I give a disinterested sigh. "Yeah, well, you have ten seconds to tell me where Evangeline is, or we're walking out of here, and there'll be no more offers of a reduced sentence. DEA wants you buried and forgotten."

Collie waits for the count of nine, then says, "'When I sharpen my flashing sword, and my hand takes hold of judgment—'"

I stand abruptly, showing him my teeth in a wide grin and placing my two hands palms down on the table. "Good old Deuteronomy, yet again. I know it well, Mr. Collie. But I prefer the gospel of Saint Michael the Archangel, who said, 'I'm going to let the powers that be kick your ass to hell and back again, and then bury you in a deep, dark hole.'"

I turn and walk out of the room, Seth following. As soon as the door closes, a wave of dizziness overcomes me, and I have to lean against the wall. It took everything I had not to claw Collie's face off when he questioned whether or not I'd find Evangeline in time to save Elizabeth. I close my eyes against the thought that it's already too late. Seth leaves me and goes to scrounge a Coke from a break room somewhere, then makes me drink half of it before we leave the building.

We walk in silence to his car, and he waits for me to settle in my seat before turning to me. "Riz, we're going to find her."

I look out at the skyline and feel a crushing uncertainty. "I wouldn't even know where to start looking now."

"Well, one thing's pretty certain," Seth says, putting the car in drive. "That crazy bitch is still somewhere in Dallas."

40

Temple of the Archangel
Thursday, September 25, 2014

It's five thirty by the time Seth and I return to the station. Craddock and Esparza are still waiting for us, looking grimy and spent. I fill them in on our conversation with Collie and then send them home for the evening. Seth asks if I want to spend another night at his place, but I tell him that I'll be going to Jackie's mom's house.

"I owe it to Jackie to spend some time with her," I say. "I have no idea what tomorrow will bring."

I perch on his desk as he gathers his things. He strips off his dirty T-shirt and puts on a clean one. "Date night with Patty?" I ask teasingly.

He ducks his chin, his face pinched with some unspoken emotion. "Not tonight. Just don't want to scare away the farm animals."

"Seth," I say, placing a hand on his arm. "Thank you."

"Just doing what a partner does."

"No. You've..." My voice trails away, beaten down by

exhaustion, fear, and anger. Seth shifts uncomfortably, waiting for me to pull it together. "Just thank you."

He nods, squeezes my shoulder, and walks away.

I'm filling out the last of the incident reports in my office when my private phone rings, making me jump. I now have roughly six hours left to find Evangeline. We've crippled her operations, but the woman herself has eluded us.

The familiar voice of Peg Bartles crackles in my ear. "Hey, it's me."

"Please tell me you have some news," I beg.

"I think we may have a possible lead on Evangeline."

"Where are you?"

"A church in Oak Cliff. It's not called Saint Michael's, but it's got a big-ass statue of him behind the building."

"I'm leaving now."

The location Peg has given me is north of Jefferson, the main thoroughfare in eastern Oak Cliff, crowded with *mercados*, bridal shops, and other small family-owned stores—some with cheerful signs that read POR TODOS SUS FIESTAS! The area, settled right after the Civil War, had historically been a vibrant community of freed slaves. The only remnant of that time now is a cemetery, lovingly cared for by the descendants of those buried beneath the gravestones.

The lowering sun flares painfully in my eyes as I drive west, looking for the small street where the church is located. Finding the street sign, I make the turn and drive past a few small warehouses and a field that's been roughly

transformed into a baseball diamond. The address brings me
to an abandoned building with a pitted steeple crowned by a
leaning cross, and graffiti-filled boards over the windows. Tall
grass and weeds growing in riotous tufts on both sides give
way to untamed trees and bushes at the back. A weathered
sign in front of the building reads WELCOME TO THE CHURCH
OF THE NAZARENE.

Peg Bartles's van is parked out front, but the vehicle is
empty. I climb out of my car.

"Peg? Rocky?" I call. When I get no answer, I try the front
door. It's solid wood, and it's locked.

Some of the grass has been trampled, and I follow the trail.
"Peg, are you here?"

"I'm around back," Peg yells.

Peg is standing in the tangled mass of what must have been
the church garden, an overgrown thicket of vines and dead
ferns. In the middle, stained with bird droppings, is the classic
figure of the Archangel. Not as finely detailed as the one in my
Brooklyn church, nor as big. But just as determined, his foot
firmly anchoring a writhing serpent, although the statue's now
almost entirely covered with weeds. The head of the snake is
raised to peek menacingly out at the viewer—its shimmering
eyes made of glass—giving the impression that the serpent is
more alive, more present, than the protecting angel.

"How'd you find this place?" I ask.

"Rocky and I talked to some street contacts today, hard-
core junkies, and they told us about it. Evidently, before it
was the Church of the Nazarene, it was called the Temple of
the Archangel. It's been abandoned for a long time, and the
druggies used it as a place to grab a fix in peace. Until, that is,

they were chased out by a group of people who took over the church. People with crazy eyes."

I realize I haven't seen Peg's partner. "Where's Rocky?"

The PI points to a dormer window flush with the roofline. "The lock on the back door was too muscular, so she climbed in through the attic."

"How'd she get up there?"

"As I said before, Rocky's part monkey," Peg says, smiling. "Not a lot of body weight to pull."

I shake my head. "I think that's called breaking and entering."

Peg shrugs. "Not if you don't get caught. Look, we banged on the doors, and nobody answered." She points to a stained-glass window—one with several broken leaded panes—that hadn't been boarded over. "No one's home, and there's no apparent security system."

She turns to face me. "Evangeline and her people are not going to fight fair. Why should we?"

There's a rattling at the back door, and it opens. Rocky steps out, brushing the dust off her clothes. "Piece of cake," she says.

Peg and I follow Rocky into the chapel. The pews are made of heavy wood and must be bolted to the floor; otherwise they would have been upended or pilfered long ago. Scattered about are leftover paper bags from fast-food places, and some old, discarded drug paraphernalia. There's a layer of dust covering every surface, and the silence is absolute.

It's nearing sunset, and from the one window not boarded over, colored light spills across the altar, scalding everything with a crimson glow. The image is of the Virgin cradling the infant Jesus, angels hovering overhead. Her expression is one of contentment, as is her son's. But behind her stands Saint Anne, staring out at me, brooding, intense. As though, in this version of events, she's been given the bad news ahead of her daughter and grandson.

Rocky heads to the back of the chapel to a set of closed double doors. She rattles and pulls on the handles, but they don't budge. She kneels and takes out her lockpick gear and goes to work.

"Where'd you learn all this?" I ask. "You opened Connie's back door in under ten seconds."

"One of my clients' kids. Eleven years old and could pick any lock like Houdini."

"I'd like to hear that story sometime."

She gives me a quick glance and grins. "You buy the booze, and I'll talk."

"That was some feat, climbing up to the window," I tell her.

"Eh, it wasn't so hard," she says, her brow furrowed in concentration. "I had a drainpipe to hold on to. Hard is scaling an apartment balcony three stories up, easing open a sliding glass door, rousing a teenager who's been pumped full of downers, and sneaking her past her pimp in the middle of the night."

"Did you get her out safely?"

Rocky sighs and looks up at me again. "Yeah, we got her back to her folks. Three weeks later, she'd run away again. Dead of an overdose within six months." She gives up on the lock, packs the gear away, and stands. "We rescue the kids. We don't save them."

For an instant I see raw emotion breaking through her practiced detachment. She looks every bit the damaged teenager she pretends to be. But then she scowls and turns away. "I think the door must be bolted from the other side."

"There's probably a foyer between the chapel and the front door," Peg says. "Maybe it was bolted before the owners exited and locked the front."

"What now?" Rocky asks.

I realize I've been holding my breath, willing Rocky to find some way to open the door. The crushing realization that I'm going to miss El Cuchillo's deadline—that my family or more of my colleagues may be paying for my failure—causes my knees to buckle, and I have to sit for a moment on one of the pews.

"I'll talk to a judge tonight," I say. "See if I can get a search warrant and a team here first thing tomorrow morning."

I manage to stand, and we walk out of the chapel and into the church garden just as the red ball of the sun disappears beneath the horizon.

"You gonna be okay tonight?" Peg asks me. "You can always bunk with us."

It shouldn't be surprising that Peg and Rocky share a living space too. But I have a hard time imagining them keeping house together.

"Thanks," I say, "but I'm with Jackie tonight."

"Lucky you," Rocky calls over her shoulder as she follows Peg back toward the street. Night is fast approaching. I pull out my phone and wave it around, trying to get a stronger connection so I can touch base with Jackie before hitting the road. After a few minutes I give up. I snap a few pictures of the garden and the back door for the team, and turn to leave. But a movement behind the glass startles me: a fast-moving figure inside. I approach the window and peer through one of the broken panels. A girl wearing an army surplus coat, her hair covered by a knitted cap, is running down the aisle between the pews. She turns her head slightly to look over her shoulder, revealing for an instant the curve of one pale cheek.

"Mary Grace!" I yell.

She races through the chapel doors, now miraculously open, slamming them shut behind her. I race back inside and run down the center aisle. I yank at the double doors, expecting them to be barred again, but they part easily, and I step into the foyer. I pause to let my eyes adjust to the darkened space. There are boxed windows near the ceiling and through them the sky has turned leaden.

At one end of the foyer is a stairway that descends into total darkness. I activate the flashlight function on my phone and make sure no one is standing there, waiting for me in the shadows.

"Mary Grace," I call out. "It's Betty Rhyzyk. Please don't be afraid."

I strain to listen for any movement but hear only silence. Walking closer to the top of the stairs, I try to steady my breathing, to relax my throat muscles so I can speak. "Please talk to me."

There's a slight rustling noise from below, and the whispery sound of someone crying.

Casting the beam of light to the bottom of the stairwell, I see what appears to be a dark curtain drawn closed, obscuring the space beyond. The curtain ripples as though touched by a subterranean wind. Or someone moving rapidly away.

I draw my gun and step quietly down. Taking a few slow inhalations, I yank the curtain aside and do a sweep of the space: a poorly lit basement with a few tables and chairs scattered about, closed doors leading perhaps to offices or classrooms, and, standing at the far end against the wall, her hands covering her face, is the girl. She turns away, as though ashamed, or afraid.

I want to run to her, to hug her tightly, to carry her if necessary, out of this dark place and back to safety. To make her tell me if she knows where Elizabeth is.

"Mary Grace," I say quietly, my heart thundering in my chest. Glancing over my shoulder to make sure we're alone, I holster my gun and move slowly toward her. "Where have you been? We've been searching for you for weeks."

She covers her face with both hands, her head bent, weeping loudly now.

"Are you okay?" I reach out to touch her shoulder.

She wheels around to face me, her eyes dry, her mouth upturned in a challenging smile. She pulls the cap off her head, revealing a long tumble of red hair. It's one of the twins from the courthouse.

I snatch my hand back, and in that moment I'm tackled from behind. Several bodies wrestle me to the ground. My hair pulled viciously. The gun wrenched from my hand. Fingernails raked across my neck. A sharp, stinging pain in my thigh. The familiar warmth of a paralyzing narcotic, and a slow immersion into unconsciousness. But not before my fist has connected with something fleshy and alterable.

My eyes open to the hazy glare of overhead fluorescent lights. My mouth is dry, the muscles in my neck cramping at the unnatural angle of my head sagging against one shoulder. I try to move my hand to ease the spasms but can't. I'm tied, arms and legs, to a high-backed wooden chair. An elaborate antique that a bishop would be proud to own. I groan involuntarily as a wave of nausea overtakes me. Panting, I clench my teeth and wait for the sensation to pass.

A motion to my left catches my eye. Gathered in a tight little cluster a few feet away are the redheaded twins and Donna Parcell, holding a cloth beneath her bloodied, and recently broken, nose.

"Untie me," I croak, "and I'll realign that for you."

Even speaking those few words make me dizzy, and for a moment I think I'll pass out again. Wincing, I turn my head. Evangeline Roy stands to my right. There is no more facade of piety or human empathy, no further attempts at social niceties left in her demeanor, or in her expression. She is all staring eyes and grinding teeth. Skin stretched tight over a skull, rotting from the inside with hatred for me.

"Where's Mary Grace?" I demand.

Evangeline moves closer, peering into my face. "You thought you'd found her, didn't you? So blind with hope. I didn't expect you to get here so soon, but I'm very glad you did."

"This place is going to be swarming with DPD."

Her lips curl back from her teeth, and she shakes her head. "If you really believed I was here, you would have come with backup. But you had no idea. That was very poor planning on your part. But then, you've made some bad missteps the past few weeks."

"Not as bad as you."

She takes a breath and loses the smile. "That's true, Elizabeth. You've cost me dearly."

She pulls a small chair closer and sits down. She crosses

her feet neatly at the ankles, smooths the wrinkles out of her skirt, and folds her hands together. She leans in, and her eyes come up to meet mine. They burn with the angry intensity of an acetylene torch, and I hear Johnny B's voice in my head telling me, *"I'll never not see that old bitch, man."*

"You've taken everything from me," she says. "Resources, manpower, money, connections. Things I've spent years planning and putting into effect. But I'd give it all up a million times over to have my boys back."

"Your 'boys,'" I whisper, swallowing the bile at the back of my throat. "You mean the murdering, drug-running, would-be rapists?"

Evangeline jerks to her feet as though pulled up by a trip wire. Another wave of dizziness threatens to eject what little I have in my stomach onto my lap.

"'An eye for an eye, and a—'" she intones.

"Oh, Jesus," I moan, "stop with the sanctimonious bullshit. You're finished. You're done. You've got a lot of things to answer for, but so far, killing a cop isn't one of them. At least not with your own hands."

"A thing that can be easily corrected." She motions to the twins. "You can bring it out now."

The twins disappear into one of the rooms, closing the door behind them.

"I've dreamed about this moment more times than you can imagine. Not just about ending you. But the part that comes before."

The door opens again, and the two young women struggle to wheel out a dolly, weighted down with an aluminum cask. When they right the dolly in front of me, liquid in the cask sloshes loudly. Evangeline places one hand on top of it.

"Do you know what's inside?" she whispers. "Can you guess?"

The memory of my dream—the one of the baptismal font and the tiny object floating in the water—opens up channels of fear I'd never known existed.

"Have you ever drowned puppies...?"

I desperately want to lash out, laugh cynically to show I don't buy her crazy ranting or somehow puncture what little of her self-control remains, but all the spit has dried up inside my mouth. I can't drag my eyes away from her fingers, stroking the top of the cask. Something else besides nausea, a mindless panic, begins clutching at the pit of my stomach.

"It happened very quickly, you'll be happy to hear," she says, her fingers restless and groping over the smooth metal. "There was no real struggle. Just a few bubbles, floating gently to the surface."

I meet her gaze, taking in the whole of her face. The glazed eyes, the crepey, discolored lids housing them, the mouth puckered with vertical lines so deep and so dark that they could be mistaken for trauma sutures.

"The fulfillment of my vengeance is in leaving you here for the next hour, to contemplate what's in front of you. Imagining both the *how* of it and the *why* of it as well."

She pats the top of the cask. "It happened just this morning. So you see, if you'd only been a little bit quicker in finding me, you might have saved her—"

Without conscious thought, I've begun to thrash violently against the ropes anchoring me to the chair. Evangeline is still talking, talking, talking at me, the words vomiting from her mouth. A river of sewage, of noxious effluvia. Enough to poison every ocean in the world.

My mouth opens, and I scream at her. Threats, curses, entreaties, desperate pleas, incoherent babbling.

But it's not enough to drown out her final words to me.

She turns and walks away, followed by her three acolytes. I hear footsteps climbing up to the anteroom, and then the lights are turned out in the basement. All except the ones illuminating the cask. I clench my jaws to stop my teeth from chattering; I'm shaking uncontrollably. A sour sweat runs down my face. My outburst has increased the dizziness and droning in my ears.

I try looking everywhere but at what's in front of me. Squeezing my eyes shut makes it worse. Because then I'm imagining what's inside the cask. I want to believe that her insanity would only go so far. That torturing me with uncertainty might be enough to meet her twisted demand for satisfaction. But she's killed without remorse in the past. And I took from her the only things that had tethered her to any semblance of human tenderness: her two sons, Tommy and Curtis Roy.

The ropes securing me to the chair are coarse and thick, and they've been tied expertly. Despite the sweat slicking my arms, the bonds are so tight that my limbs have begun to go numb, any movement quickly rubbing the skin raw.

The flesh turns pink, then the deep red of a chemical burn, and still I keep struggling to free my arms. The pain is almost unbearable, but necessary. Not only for what it moves me toward, which is my possible freedom. But away from the awareness of what's in front of me. Away from remembering Evangeline's parting words.

"This is all your doing, Elizabeth."

When the final layer of skin breaks, and the ropes are

slimed with blood, I envision the people that I will spend my whole life—if I have any life left after tonight—hunting down and killing. To erase the pain, the anger. The guilt. Connie, for taking Elizabeth. The redheaded twins. Donna Parcell. And, most of all, Evangeline.

The agony grows until I am panting like a maimed dog. An animal-like keening begins, which fills the entire dark basement with watery echoes before I realize that it's me making the sounds. Distressed noises of hopelessness. A continuing mantra of excruciating despair.

I'msorryI'msorryI'msorryI'msorry...

When I can't struggle anymore, I give in to acceptance, to the certainty that Evangeline Roy is insane enough, and evil enough, to have drowned an infant in order to cause me pain.

I let my head drop and release myself to the promise of renewed unconsciousness. But the physical agony, and the awareness of Elizabeth's likely terror in her last few moments, have pinned me to an ever-expanding present, a horror of the continuing *now*.

When Uncle Benny lay dying, I was able to offer him words of comfort. As well as for my mother in her last days. To sit with her and hold her hand. To listen to her labored breathing, her frequent lapses into Polish. Wiping her brow and singing to her. The same lullaby that she had sung to my brother and me when we were little.

Oj lulaj, lulaj, Siwe, oczka stulaj....

Go to sleep, go to sleep, close your blue eyes...

I'm still tunelessly mouthing the words—as an offering of remorse, a prayer for forgiveness—when Evangeline walks quietly into the circle of light to stand in front of me, like an actor taking her mark on a stage. In her clasped hands she holds a gun.

"My only regret, Elizabeth, is that I couldn't make you sit here all night. But even though we've shut off your phone, someone may soon come looking for you."

"There'll be nowhere you can go after this where you can hide."

"The mountains of Honduras are formidable," she says, moving around to the back of my chair. "Even for those who've grown up there."

Her breath puffs against my ear when she says, "Fog, torrential rainstorms, deep, plunging chasms. Why, it's almost biblical."

Reflexively, I tense forward, as though a few more inches will make any difference when she pulls the trigger.

Evangeline presses the barrel of the gun against the base of my skull. "I came here only to fulfill a promise I made to my sons."

Like drowning ants holding on to a speck of balsa wood, my thoughts coalesce around my uncle Benny, shining in his dress uniform, his eyes luminous, still full of compassion for his fellow man. His lips are moving. He's talking to me, but I can't hear what he's saying. I close my eyes, straining to amplify the sounds, willing him to speak to me in a way that I can hear him. So that I can take his last words with me into the darkness. In my mind's eye he's holding his hand out to me, smiling winningly, telling me in a now-thundering voice what he thinks of the red witch standing behind me.

"*Tchorz!*"

"Who said that?" Evangeline asks, her voice alarmed. I hear her take a few shuffling steps backward.

"Coward," I yell, repeating what Benny has just trumpeted in Polish.

"Whose voice was that?" she demands.

A feeling dangerously close to hysterical glee is bubbling up from the deepest part of my gut. I bark out a laugh. "Coward! You can't even face me when you put a bullet in my head."

The laughter is now boiling up, unstoppable, like dry ice out of a cauldron. "Coward, coward, coward, coward…"

It's going to happen soon, I think. The last of the Rhyzyk clan, going out, not with a whimper but with a belly full of unhinged, raging laughter. Somewhere, Benny is laughing with me.

"Coward, coward, coward…" I scream, untethered now from my fear. From my unbearable sorrow.

There are scuffling noises behind me, as though Evangeline has lost her footing. There's even a tiny yelp. And then silence.

I struggle against the ropes. "Go on, do it, already!"

Dragging footsteps are circling back around me—twin figures, one in front of the other, moving through the shadows to stand facing me. Flashes of reflective light pull my gaze down to the floor. A pair of boots with highly polished silver tips. The leather decorated in fanciful designs. I know what the markings are. Tattoos etched into the skin of a once-living man.

The tall figure of El Cuchillo stands before me, one hand grasping Evangeline's impossibly red hair tightly in his fingers, the other holding his long skinning knife against her throat. Evangeline's mouth opens and closes soundlessly. She is much shorter than El Cuchillo, and his face, angular and shadowy, towers over her like that of an Old Testament prophet. The appropriateness of the image pulls my mouth into a savage grin. Even if he turns his knife on me, I will have been a witness to the end of Evangeline Roy. Nothing else matters now but her death. For the first time, the hatred in Evangeline's eyes has turned to terror.

"This pleases you," El Cuchillo says. It is not a question.

I look at him, unable to speak, unable to nod, but he reads the answer through my clenched fists and quickening breath.

"In this moment, you and I are very close," he murmurs, his voice low and intimate. "We will have shared something no one else can have."

Evangeline makes a noise at the back of her throat, and the man with the knife tightens his hold on her scalp.

"You will never, never forget this," he whispers. "And it will change you."

They both look at me, two sets of eyes unblinking, frozen momentarily, as though in a tableau of inevitability. And both sets of eyes remain open and unblinking even when the blade is passed smoothly, almost gently, across the folds of her wrinkled skin, the white exposed subdermis and neck gristle rapidly filling with blood, cascading down the front of Evangeline's sweater and onto the floor. Evangeline continues to stare at me, even after the light of recognition has drained from her sight.

El Cuchillo slowly lowers Evangeline's body to the floor, his gaze impassive and calm. He sheathes his knife and squats down so that we are eye to eye. The predatory face, the deeply hollowed, pock-marked cheeks, the hair as black and coarse as a horse's mane. He glances briefly at the scar between my collarbones. The one that was made by the tip of his blade.

"Well done, Betty," he says, his voice barely above a whisper. "I've tracked your phone, followed your every movement. To this place. To this time. And now I know who you are. I *see* you. You and I both lean into fear. But it's not our courage that makes you and me alike. It's our shared *vengeance* that drives us toward the flames."

His slackened jaw, the lowered eyelids, the deep and steady breathing, hold an afterglow like that of a spent suitor. He could have killed Evangeline at any time. But he waited. The anticipation of killing her in front of me building and building. Savoring the suffering of me, and my family, like a prelude to the main event.

I thrash against the ropes, panicked and sickened, but with a growing understanding of who, and what, is speaking. "I'm nothing like you."

"The look on your face when I killed her tells a very different story," he says. He sighs and pulls his lips into a parody of a smile, monstrous in its tenderness. "You met your deadline, Detective. But only just. It's approaching midnight."

His features are made even sharper now by the chemicals firing through my every cell. As though he's been punched out of another time and another reality and superimposed onto this one. Or perhaps it's I who have been snatched back from another reality; one where I've glimpsed the back side of the cosmic machine and the gears that move us inexorably toward its grinding teeth.

And then it comes to me. I know what time it is. I tell him with a certainty that belies my own terror. "It's eleven eleven."

He twists his wrist to check the time on his expensive watch. He blinks once, returning his gaze to me. "*Exactamente.*" He regards me as he would a newly discovered species of insect. *"El tiempo de las brujas. O los angeles."*

"Yes," I say, feeling as though I've been stripped bare as certainly as if I'd been flayed skin from bone with a sharp blade.

I am both the witch and the angel, and I am the one who devours her children and I am the one who rescues them.

"Better to do battle three times than to give birth once," my mother had said.

At the thought of my mother, my vision goes blurry with tears. "You had Kevin Ryan killed."

"The cost of war." He shrugs and moves with great precision to pluck a strand of hair from my eyes. "To torture a dog makes the meat sweeter."

I flinch and glance briefly at Evangeline's corpse, and the skin at the back of my neck tightens. "Planning on a new pair of boots?"

He sees through my bravado into the depths of my fear. "They would be of poor quality."

I take another shuddering breath. "You know this can't end here. I won't let it."

El Cuchillo nods. "I would expect nothing less."

My knuckles gripping the armrests have turned white. "What now?"

He stands again, in one fluid movement, pulling his knife from its sheath. The blade is gummed with fresh blood. He pauses for a moment, and I tense for the final thrust. But, instead, he cuts the ropes binding one arm and places in my lap my phone and the pocketknife Evangeline had earlier taken from me. The small knife that he had left for me before the fire at Delano's Gym. I look up at his deeply lined face.

He says, "I believe, Detective, that death will find me soon."

I think of our last confrontation months ago, in the well-appointed barn of an assassinated cartel banker, standing near my predecessor, Sergeant Marshall Maclin. El Cuchillo looking into my eyes, telling me that death, for him, will come in the form of a woman.

Then I hear the echo of Uncle Benny's voice in my ear again. We're sitting in Donovan's bar in Brooklyn after pulling Mrs. Janovicz off the ledge. He's telling me, *"You instinctively knew to touch on the one thing that was at the core of who she was. Remember that. That's the best way to work your way out of a bad situation."*

I know now what El Cuchillo needs from me.

I look at his face. "It's me, isn't it? I'm *La Pelona*."

He eases the knife back into its sheath, and a great sense of relief washes over his face. "We will see."

El Cuchillo then turns and walks away, his boot heels striking on the basement floor, and I'm left alone with the stiffening shell of a different monster.

Time advances and stalls. Becomes an erratic wasteland of black holes and searing stop-action images. Voices come and go. Coming closer and then receding.

"Get EMT down here, now....One female body in the basement, and three females in the chapel, throats all slit ear to ear....She's in shock...."

The feel of my partner's arms lifting me from the chair, raising my head to pour water into my mouth.

Lieutenant Bradford giving orders. The hushed tones of urgent action.

My own quavering voice saying, "El Cuchillo killed Evangeline...the cask...check the cask..."

And, finally, Craddock's exhausted, concerned face bending over my stretcher as I'm wheeled to the ambulance, holding my hand, smoothing the hair from my face.

"Betty, the cask. There's nothing in it but water—"

41

The House
Friday, September 26, 2014

My eyes open to the white expanse of the bedroom ceiling. I've been conscious for a while but unwilling to move from my cocoon of safety. The bed is still warm from Jackie's body, and I can hear her in the kitchen, making coffee, easing dishes from the cupboard, her slippers shuffling quietly over the floor. The sounds of peaceful life, within the protective bubble of brick walls, locked doors, and tempered glass.

I bring my arms up to my face. Both forearms are bandaged heavily with gauze, the exposed nerves throbbing even through the fog of morphine that I was given at the hospital. It was strongly recommended that I stay for the night, but I was released into the care of Dr. Nesbitt when I threatened to stumble out of the emergency room wearing only a sheet if necessary. The drive home is a blank space, as is my being stripped and put to bed. My only clear memory is of clinging to Jackie, slicked with sweat, sobbing and heaving with a pain exponentially greater than the shredded flesh on my body.

El Cuchillo's venomous voice in my head. *"You will never, never forget this...and it will change you...To torture a dog makes the meat sweeter..."*

She'd held on to me fiercely, her fingers dug into my back, as though I'd sprout wings like a succubus and be flung away with the storm.

The cask had been empty...

I sit up so abruptly that the room pitches and weaves and I flop back onto the mattress, blinking and panting.

The possibilities threaten to move me toward panic again. The cruel *what if*s.

I think of the adage used by homicide detectives that the absence of a body is not equal to no crime. The dark algebra of an investigation. The positive numbers—a murder weapon (plus one), DNA (plus two), fingerprints (plus three), a blood trail (plus four)—moving the equation painstakingly to its final, proven solution, which is ideally a body found. Case closed.

There'd been no body inside the cask. There is hope...

Uncle Benny would have counseled me to keep the faith.

I jackknife into a fetal position, my hands over my mouth. The sound of Evangeline crying out, "Who said that?" He'd called her a coward. And she'd heard him! She'd heard Benny's voice as though he'd been standing next to me.

Jackie knocks gently at the bedroom door, her face tight with worry. "Are you okay?"

I nod. "Yes, I'm fine. I think I'll get up for a bit."

She gives me a tentative smile and returns to the kitchen.

When the dizziness passes, I ease myself out of bed, put on a robe, and walk slowly to the kitchen. Confronted by the rich aroma of food, I'm suddenly ravenously hungry.

Jackie's made eggs and toast and coffee, and she sits me down at the table. The omelet is dense and rich, slathered with lots of butter, and she's added an extravagant amount of cream in my coffee, which I usually drink black. She stands behind me, tilts my head back, and kisses me on my forehead.

Her hair tickles my face, and in a delirium of sensory overload, I say, "Get naked with me."

A knock at the front door, and she kisses me on the mouth. "Mmmm, you taste like butter."

She smiles and walks out of the kitchen, her coffee cup in her hand.

Footsteps down the hall, the front door opening.

There's a sharp cry and the sound of something smashing and scattering across the tiles.

Thrusting myself from the table, I fumble against the chair before gaining the balance and momentum I need to launch myself down the hallway. Jackie is staggering backward as though impacted by a blow to the chest. Grabbing her shoulders, I push her aside, knocking her against the wall. I shield her with my body, ready to tear the screen door from its hinges.

A woman stands on the porch. She's backing away, alarmed, her arms raised defensively. I know the woman, her face etched into my every waking moment for days now. Constance Renée Broussard. Connie.

I yell and force the screen door outward. She scuttles to one side, mouthing something unintelligible. She gestures toward the street. To another figure. Another woman, much younger. Her face shining with expectation and hope. And in her arms, she holds a baby.

* * *

Connie and Mary Grace and Elizabeth, sitting in her mother's lap, perch together tensely on the sofa and peer at me expectantly. But, also, guardedly. They had feared that my reaction was going to be emotionally fraught. They just hadn't envisioned the magnitude of it. Jackie sits in a chair, staring at them as though they'll disappear again if she blinks.

Within the first few moments of walking into the house, both Connie and Mary Grace had stumbled through an explanation of the why, the how, and the when, trying to pierce through my frenetic pacing, swearing, indignant weeping, and hurling myself out of the living room only to retrace my steps and stand before them with trembling rage, with sorrow, with crippling relief.

When I'd worn myself out, I went into the kitchen. Pulled a tumbler and the bottle of Jameson out of the cabinet. Poured a few fingers' worth of the whiskey and downed it in one swallow. Grabbing the glass and the bottle, I return to the living room, sit in the hard-backed chair, and say to Mary Grace, "Do you have any idea what you've put us through?"

She hangs her head for a moment, but when she raises it again, her gaze is steady and defiant. "Connie and I felt we had no choice. You don't know my stepfather the way we do. What lengths he'll go to, to get what he wants. Our only safe option was to disappear."

Alan P. Turner, wealthy commercial real-estate developer, creep, Mary Grace's stepfather. And father of her child.

"But why didn't you contact us?" Jackie asks. "To let us know you were safe."

"Didn't you get my note?" Mary Grace says. "Connie left

it in Elizabeth's crib before she took the baby with her. It explained that we'd be in hiding for a few weeks and not to worry about us."

I start to refute her claim, and then I remember the image of Evangeline captured on the security footage after she'd broken into our house. She'd lifted a piece of paper from the crib and pocketed it.

"We never got to see the note," I say. "Evangeline took it."

Connie places a comforting hand on Mary Grace's arm. "We knew Alan would hire a private detective to look for us. And we knew he'd be watching this house. He might have even been listening in on our phone conversations. It wouldn't have been past him to try and kidnap Mary Grace, or Elizabeth. We couldn't take any chances. We are so, so sorry."

"Where have you been staying all this time?" Jackie asks. "Betty says that you haven't been at your house for weeks."

Mary Grace interlaces her fingers with Connie's. "We've been staying at a motel just outside Dallas."

I throw an accusing look at Connie. "You had one of Evangeline Roy's missionary brochures in your house."

"It was mine, the one Evangeline gave me months ago," Mary Grace says. "I showed it to you before the baby was born, remember?"

"So you never had contact with Evangeline?"

Both Connie and Mary Grace shake their heads in unison. Evangeline knew from the note left in the crib that Mary Grace and the baby were safe. But she played on my ignorance to prolong my agony. She never had the baby to begin with, but I would have gone to my death believing that Evangeline had drowned her.

I bury my face in my hands for a few moments. "But why come out of hiding now? What's changed?"

Mary Grace bundles Elizabeth to her mother and comes to kneel in front of me. "When I became pregnant, everything changed. You and Jackie rescued me. But what I wanted, what I needed, was for my mother to be with me too. I went looking for her, and we made peace with each other. It was me who brought Connie into this house, knowing that she'd help you out as well as me. Jackie was so busy at the hospital. And you—"

She places a hand on my leg. "You were so caught up with everything in your work. I started to feel guilty that we were becoming a burden to you."

Something painful catches in my throat. I trade a shame-filled look with Jackie.

The hand on my leg squeezes tighter. "We felt safe with you, until we didn't. And we thought that our presence here was putting you both in danger as well. We couldn't do that to the two people who'd saved our lives."

Connie hugs the baby tightly. "Working for you, and looking after Elizabeth, was my chance to redeem myself. To make up for all the mistakes I'd made as a mother."

"But today everything's different. Everything." Mary Grace smiles like the little girl who was captured in the photo that Peg Bartles had shown me. The girl with the freckles and sun-streaked hair.

"Wish me a happy birthday," she says. "I'm eighteen today. I'm free. My stepfather can never control me again. And he'll never get Elizabeth."

She stands and retrieves Elizabeth from Connie. She settles the baby on my lap, taking the whiskey glass from my hand.

The baby is heavier, fuller in the comfortable roundness of a healthy, well-cared-for infant. Elizabeth's head swivels from her mother's face to mine. Her own face is solemn, her eyes unwavering and unafraid. She sticks a finger in her mouth, and I can see the beginnings of a bottom set of teeth emerging from her gums. Teeth that will serve her well in an eat-or-be-eaten world.

Her brows come down, but she doesn't cry.

She doesn't cry.

And that's a good start.

42

Fuel City Car Wash and Taco Stand
Saturday, October 11, 2014

I sit under the covered patio to the side of the taco stand, watching the one remaining longhorn in the nearby pen rolling in the mud, and waiting for Seth to bring back our lunch. The air is cold and damp, rain pummeling the metal roof, but it feels good after the discomfort of wearing my dress uniform for hours during a ceremony we'd all been dreading.

The funeral and End of Watch call for Kevin Ryan had been heartfelt and unbearably sad. I've only been to two such ceremonies for officers in Dallas killed in the line of duty, and I hope this one is my last. It was attended by hundreds of officers in full dress uniform, many of them fighting back tears in honor of such a young and talented detective. He'd died for the noblest of causes, regardless of who orchestrated his death. He was proffering aid to a troubled young person in the hope of saving lives.

I served as one of the pallbearers, and sat next to his pregnant widow, Karen, as she was presented a flag and offered condolences from the chief and the mayor. It rained like hell, as was appropriate, and the air was filled with the sound of bagpipes, which would have made Kevin very happy.

As is done in all End of Watch ceremonies, a dispatcher called out the fallen officer's badge number three times. After each signal request, there was a moment of silence. When there was no final response from our own officer, the dispatcher retired the number, saying, *"Last Call for Detective Kevin Matthew Ryan, Badge number four-five-three, you are clear to go ten forty-two. May you rest in peace..."*

Karen had reached for my hand and gripped it tightly for most of the call, but she kept her composure in a way that confounded, and humbled, me. If it had been Jackie who was being buried today, I would have been howling at the heavens and tearing my skin off my bones like some raving shaman. Karen turned to me at one point and whispered, "Thank you for looking after him. He was so proud of making Detective. He told me he never wanted to be anything else."

How many hours since Kevin's death had I thought of the last substantive conversations I'd had with him? About his decision to stay with the force. And his delight in being a father. And how, ultimately, I had tried but failed to protect him. Those few words whispered to me were a supreme act of kindness that I know I will never forget.

At one point, Craddock, who was seated on the other side of Karen, caught my eye and signaled for me to look at Philbo standing with the line of officers opposite the casket. He met my gaze briefly and then looked away. Within a few days of the Reyes warehouse bust, Danny Philbo had requested a transfer out of Narcotics and into Homicide. My guess is, because of his vast experience in Chicago (and because his cowboy tactics have been circulating among the more cautious, methodical detectives in the Murder Squad), he'll end up either in Vice or with Manny Ortega in Gangland. I've already given Manny the heads-up to watch his back if Philbo joins the department. Manny, in typical fashion, responded, "*No problemo, Sargento.* And, just so you know, I made sure he found out about his nickname."

Craddock, currently without a partner, says he'll be very happy to work with "Jetta Joe" Esparza going forward.

There's a break in the rain falling on Fuel City, and I think of my early morning meeting with my CI Wayne. He'd parked on the curb in front of my house just after dawn in James Earle's beloved Crown Vic, the sun still showing through low-drifting clouds.

"How do you like my new wheels?" he'd asked, smiling proudly.

"James Earle gave you his car?" I'd asked.

"Nah, I bought it, man. Full Blue Book price."

"What's James going to do for transportation?" I'd tried imagining Jackie's great-uncle driving anything smaller than a Sherman tank.

"He said it was time to make some changes. Between you and me, I think Connie put that bug in his ear. You know, get a car that he could actually park without using a forklift." He'd pointed to the trunk of the car and explained he was taking Johnny B's ashes back to his people in Arizona.

"It just seemed wrong to let him go to some potter's field hole in the ground. I felt like it was partly my fault. Him being killed and all, just trying to get by, you know?"

I'd tried explaining to him that it wasn't his fault. But how many people had tried to assure me over the past few weeks that I hadn't been to blame for Mary Grace's and Elizabeth's disappearance? Butterfly strips trying to stanch the bleeding from a gaping wound.

"I've never seen the West," he'd said, looking like an excited kid about to go on a walkabout. "Hell, I've never been outside of Texas. Thought maybe I'd go on to California. Get my feet wet in the Pacific Ocean."

He handed me a piece of paper with his phone number on it. "I talked to Mary Grace last night." He grinned at me, but it was brief, and sad. "I told her...I told her, you know, that I was glad she was back." His back straightened visibly. "She told me she was proud of me."

"I am too, Wayne."

We then hugged awkwardly to avoid meeting each other's eyes, and I watched him drive away.

The jab of renewed sadness prompts me to call Jackie just to tell her I love her. She tells me that she's finished her shift at the hospital and is on her way to babysit Elizabeth for a few hours. Mary Grace is going to meet with Keri McCall, the family court lawyer, who will be representing her in court against her stepfather, who, against all decency and common sense, has filed again for custody of Elizabeth. He has a snowball's chance in hell of winning, as she's also filed criminal rape charges against him.

When I ask about Connie's whereabouts, Jackie actually giggles.

"She's on a date," she says, giving a dramatic pause. "With James Earle, driving his new car."

By the time Seth returns, with a tray overloaded with a dozen tacos, I'm grinning from ear to ear.

"This is quite a change," he says. "When I left ten minutes ago, you were looking like a dress shirt without the starch."

"Yeah, Kevin's funeral really took it out of me," I say, grabbing a taco. "But, while you were gone, I talked to Jackie. She's on her way to spend time with Elizabeth, Mary Grace is going to be kicking Alan Turner's ass in court, and James Earle and Connie are giving it a go. So, despite all the sadness of today, life is still pretty damn good."

Seth nods his agreement and eats half his taco in one bite.

"Speaking of giving it a go," I say. "What's up with you and Patty?"

My partner takes a long time chewing and swallowing his food.

"Uh-oh. You and Patty break up?"

He mumbles something and reaches for another taco. "Kind of."

"You have a fight?"

"Not exactly."

I pull the tray out of his reach. "Come on. Spill it."

He sighs, puts down his food, and looks at me. "Me and Rocky are—"

I ask him to repeat that, and he does. My eyes must be bulging out of my head, because Seth is squirming uncomfortably, but his jaw is set defensively. "You and Rocky Bentner are what? Taking up ax throwing? Skydiving naked? Taking a bondage show on the road?"

Laughter begins to bubble up, but I quickly stifle it. Sliding the tray back within his arm's reach, I say, "You know what, partner? Good for you. Life is for the living. Just make sure you're caught up on all your shots."

We eat in silence as the sun comes out, clearing the rain and the fog away, revealing the skyline of Dallas, solidly compact, reflecting light in a hundred colors, built to last for many decades. But a month ago, it was September 11. Two towers that had been meant to last for generations had come down in a few terror-filled hours. Nothing lasts forever, and nothing is certain, except the continuation of life and the inevitability of death.

As to what comes afterward...

Seth is studying my face. Since being rescued at the church, I catch him watching me often, checking for any signs of cracks.

"What?" I ask.

"Anytime you want to talk about—" He doesn't finish the sentence. My expression tells him that I'm not ready yet. And being the steadfast partner and friend that he is, he lets it go.

"You're a good sergeant," he tells me.

But I'm not so sure. I've still got one foot in the trenches. I haven't yet decided what I'm going to do about El Cuchillo. The part of me that's climbing on the ladder wants to let it go, to let it be someone else's problem. The part of me with mud on her boots wants to find him and finish the job.

Uncle Benny's cautionary voice blooms in my head: "*Kto pod kim dołki kopie, ten sam w nie wpada.*"

He who digs pits for others will fall in them himself.

I set down my food and look at Seth. "Remember I said to you once that I'd tell you about my uncle Benny? I think today might be a good day…"

Acknowledgments

M any thanks to Mulholland Books for all their support and encouragement in the development of the Detective Betty Rhyzyk series. The keen and sensitive editorial guidance from the superb Josh Kendall and Helen O'Hare ensured that Betty was consistently her best (and baddest) self. Bringing a novel to publication takes a team, and I'm very appreciative for all the support from the Mulholland/Little, Brown family: Michael Pietsch, Bruce Nichols, Terry Adams, Pamela Brown, Martha Bucci, Sabrina Callahan, Pat Jalbert-Levine, Sareena Kamath, Julianna Lee, Alyssa Persons, and Pamela Marshall.

Gratitude also goes to Brant Hickman, Plano Police Department (ret.), for his fascinating and sometimes hilarious tales from his thirty-plus years in law enforcement; to Keri McCall for lending her name to a character in the book; to Keri and her husband, Shannon McCall, for their continued support of Literary Instruction for Texas; and to Deana Konefal for helping with the Polish translations.

Finally, I want to thank my agent, Danny Baror, for his enthusiasm for and commitment to bringing *The Pledge* into the world.

About the Author

KATHLEEN KENT is a *New York Times* bestselling author and a two-time Edgar Award Nominee. She is the author of three award-winning historical novels, *The Heretic's Daughter*, *The Traitor's Wife*, and *The Outcasts*. In March 2020 she was inducted into the Texas Institute of Letters for her contribution to Texas literature. She lives in Dallas.

www.kathleenkent.com